IMAGE COMICS PRESENTS

TO ALL MY COLLABORATORS AND
IMAGE COMICS.
-FJB

FOR BRAM, H.G., SEAN, AND GEORGE.
-CTM

"THE DEMON AND THE DREAMSTONE"
ILLUSTRATED AND WRITTEN BY
S.M. VIDAURRI

"BOATS AGAINST THE CURRENT"
ILLUSTRATED BY JAMIE JONES
COLORED BY KELLY FITZPATRICK

BOOK PRODUCTION BY ADDISON DUKE

FIVE GHOSTS CREATED BY
BARBIERE & MOONEYHAM

IMAGE COMICS, INC.
Robert Kirkman – Chief Operating Officer
Erik Larsen – Chief Financial Officer
Todd McFarlane – President
Marc Silvestri – Chief Executive Officer
Jim Valentino – Vice-President

Eric Stephenson – Publisher
Corey Murphy – Director of Sales
Jeremy Sullivan – Director of Digital Sales
Kat Salazar – Director of PR & Marketing
Emily Miller – Director of Operations
Branwyn Bigglestone – Senior Accounts Manager
Sarah Mello – Accounts Manager
Drew Gill – Art Director
Jonathan Chan – Production Manager
Meredith Wallace – Print Manager
Randy Okamura – Marketing Production Designer
David Brothers – Branding Manager
Ally Power – Content Manager
Addison Duke – Production Artist
Vincent Kukua – Production Artist
Sasha Head – Production Artist
Tricia Ramos – Production Artist
Emilio Bautista – Sales Assistant
Chloe Ramos-Peterson – Administrative Assistant
IMAGECOMICS.COM

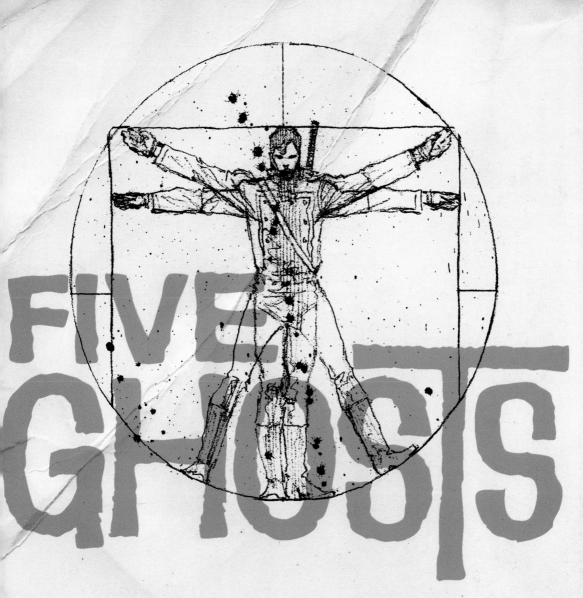

FIVE GHOSTS

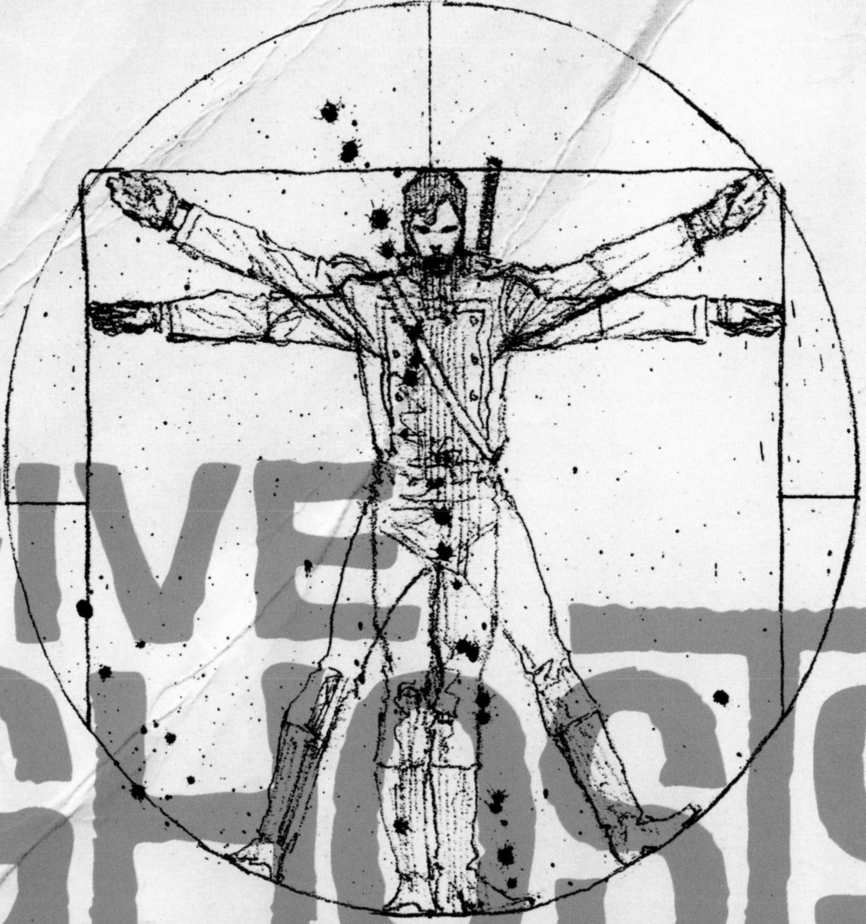

WRITTEN BY **FRANK J. BARBIERE**
ART BY **CHRIS MOONEYHAM**
COLORS BY **LAUREN AFFE**
LOGO AND GRAPHIC DESIGN BY **DYLAN TODD**

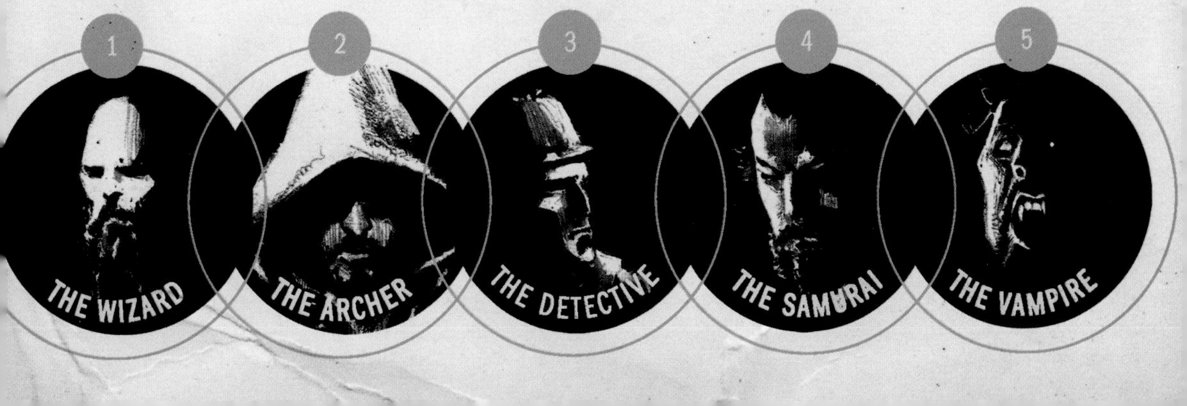
1
THE WIZARD
2
THE ARCHER
3
THE DETECTIVE
4
THE SAMURAI
5
THE VAMPIRE

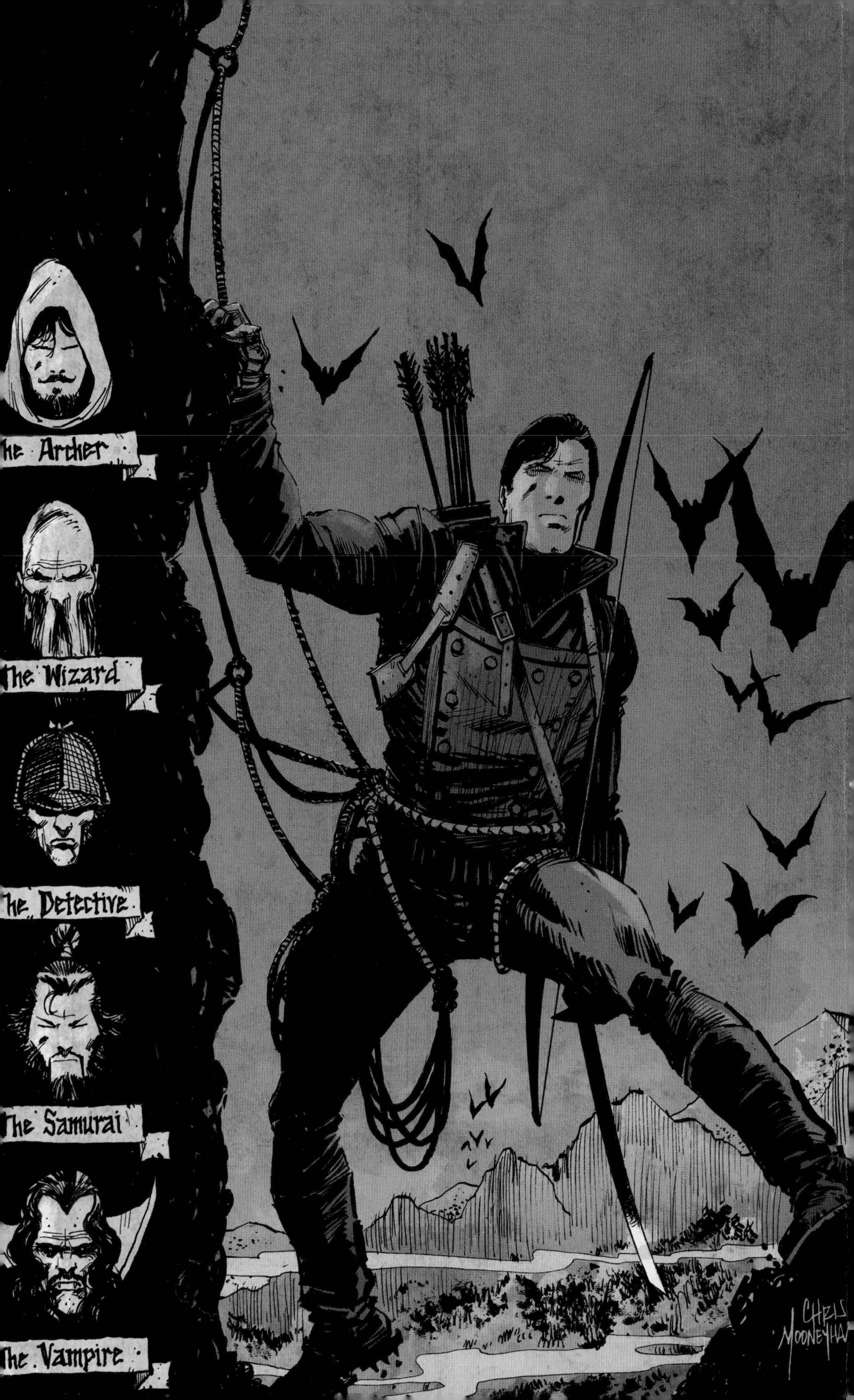

he Archer
The Wizard
he Detective
The Samurai
he Vampire
CHRIS MOONEYHA

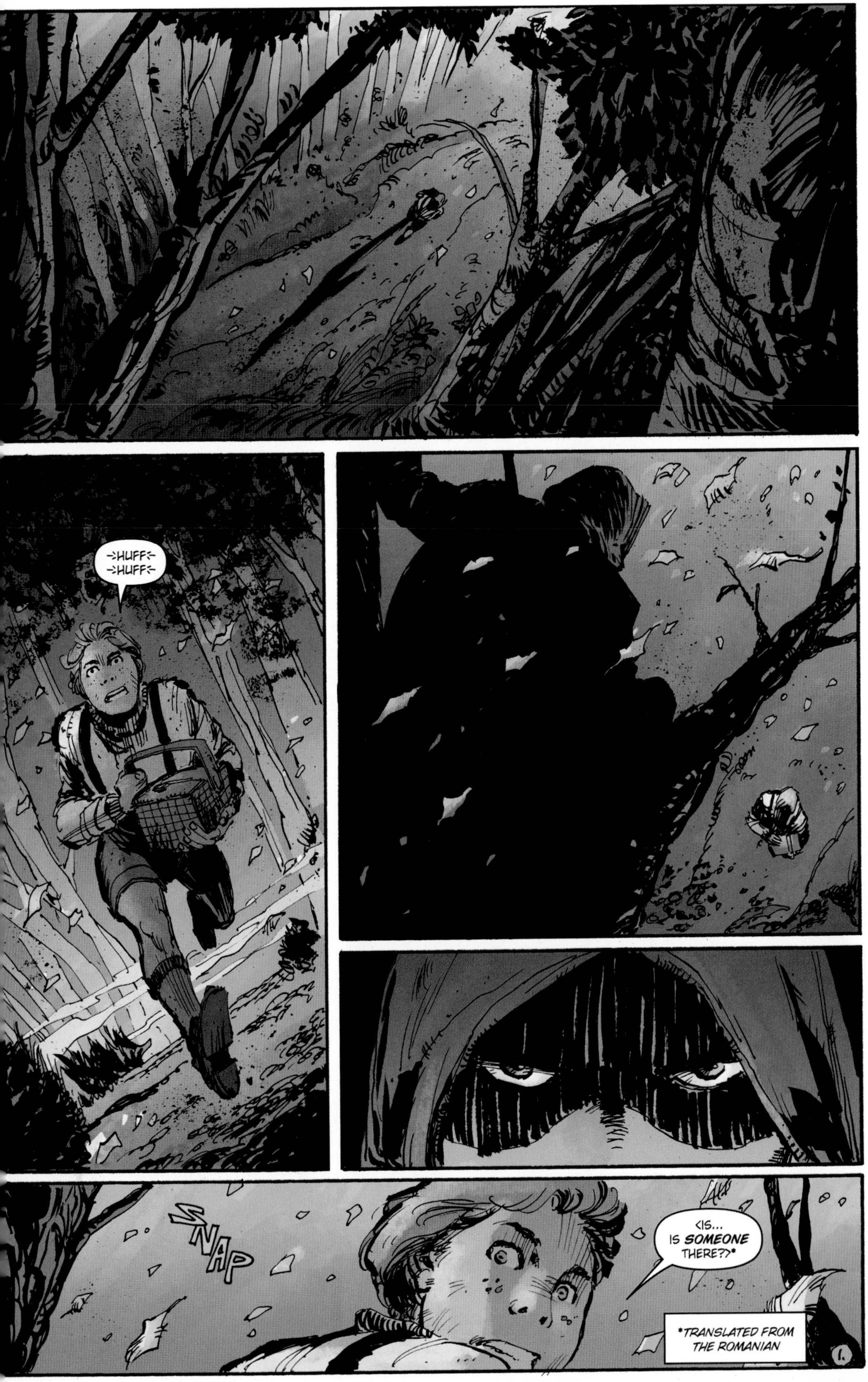
=HUFF= =HUFF=
SNAP
<IS... IS SOMEONE THERE?>*
*TRANSLATED FROM THE ROMANIAN

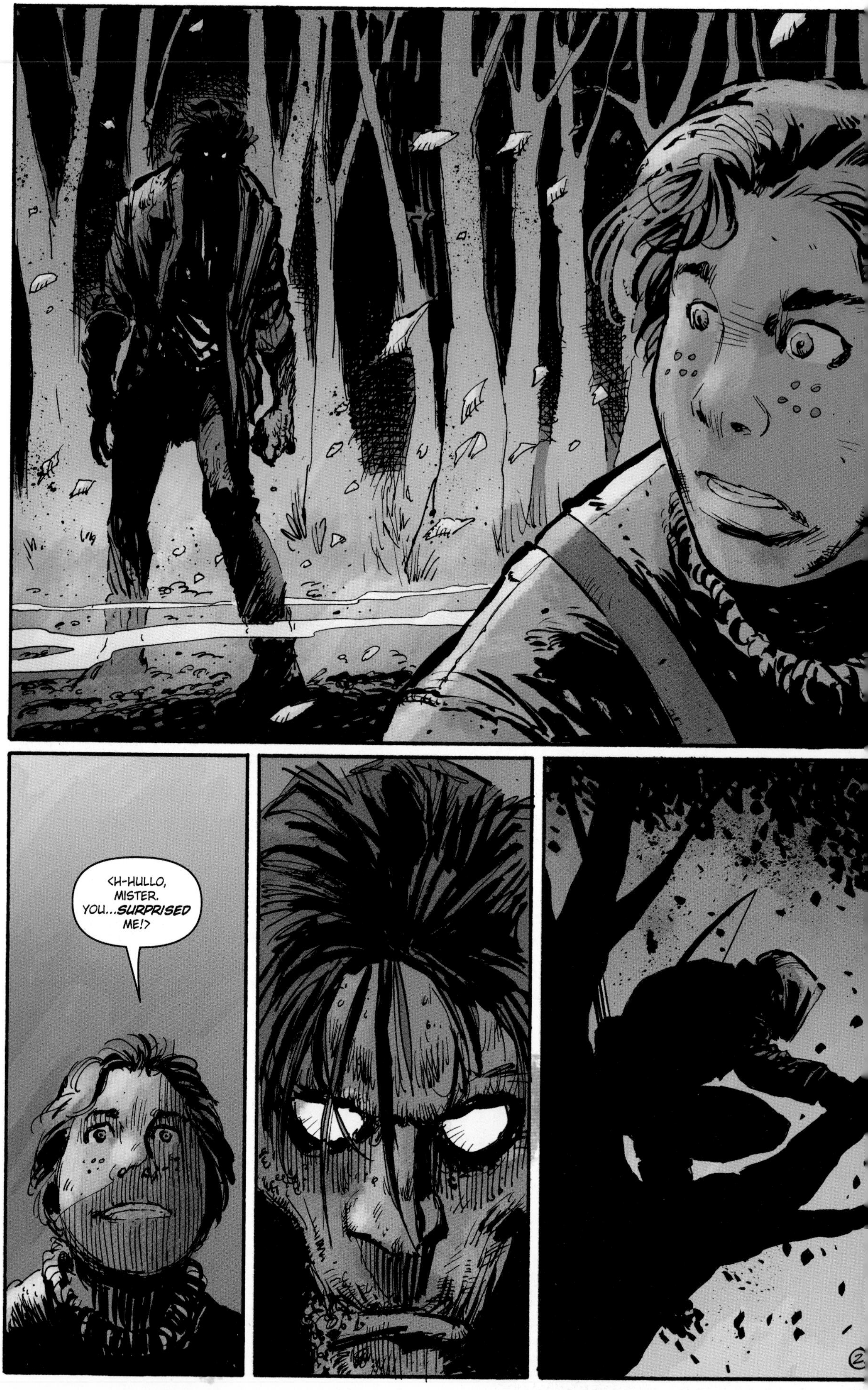
<H-HULLO, MISTER. YOU...SURPRISED ME!>

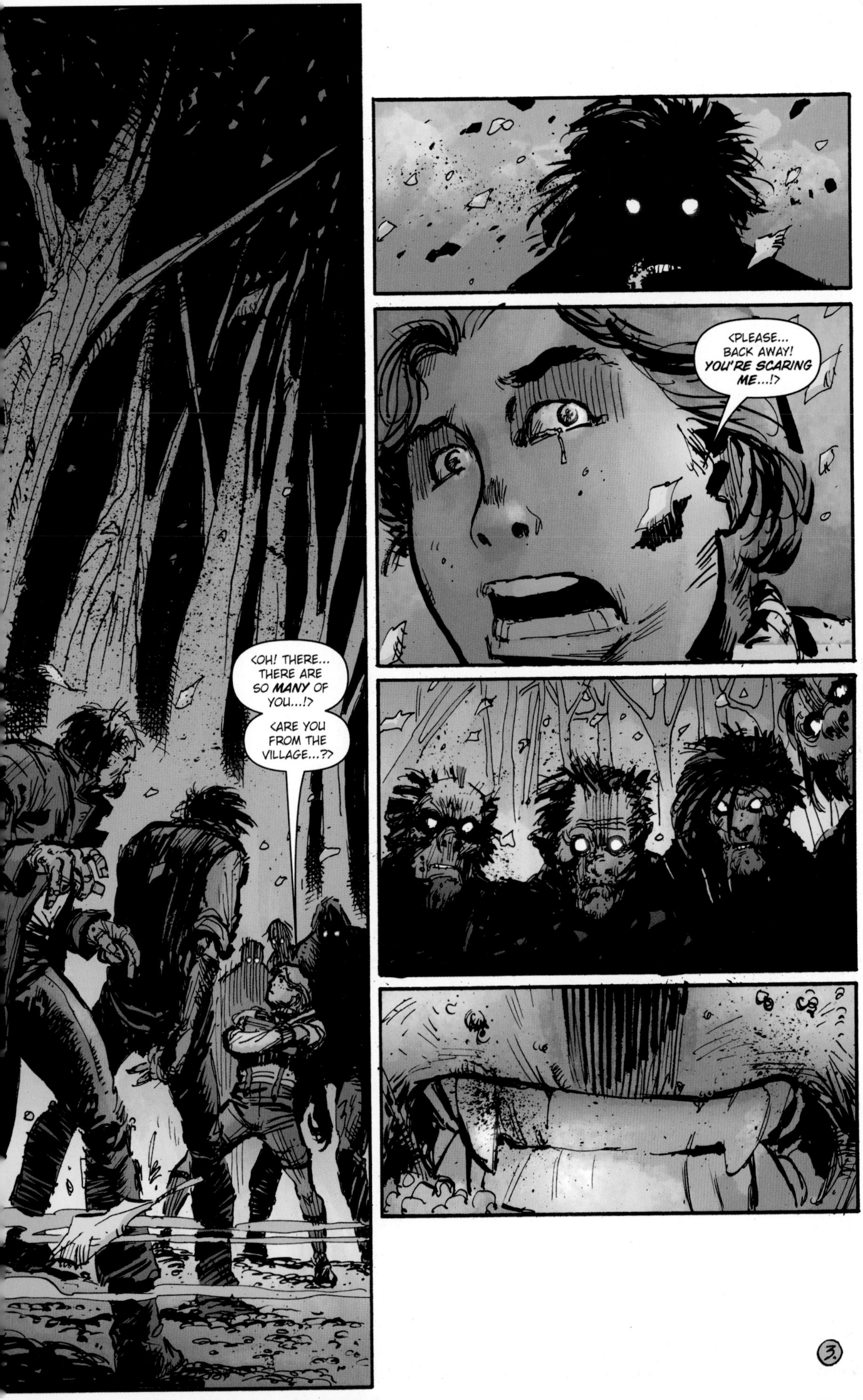

<PLEASE... BACK AWAY! YOU'RE SCARING ME...!>
<OH! THERE... THERE ARE SO MANY OF YOU...!>
<ARE YOU FROM THE VILLAGE...?>

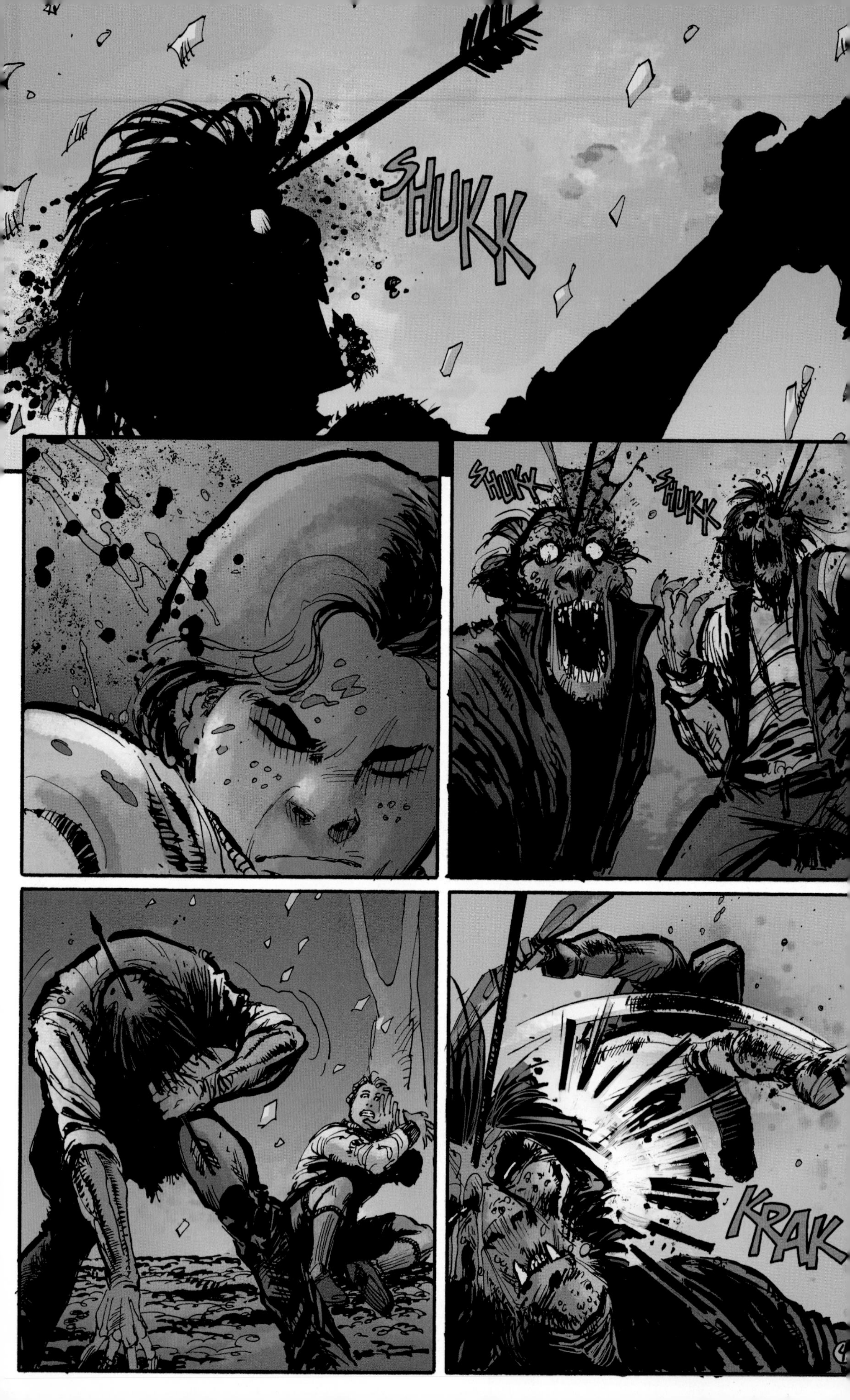
SHUKK
SHUKK
SHUKK
KRAK

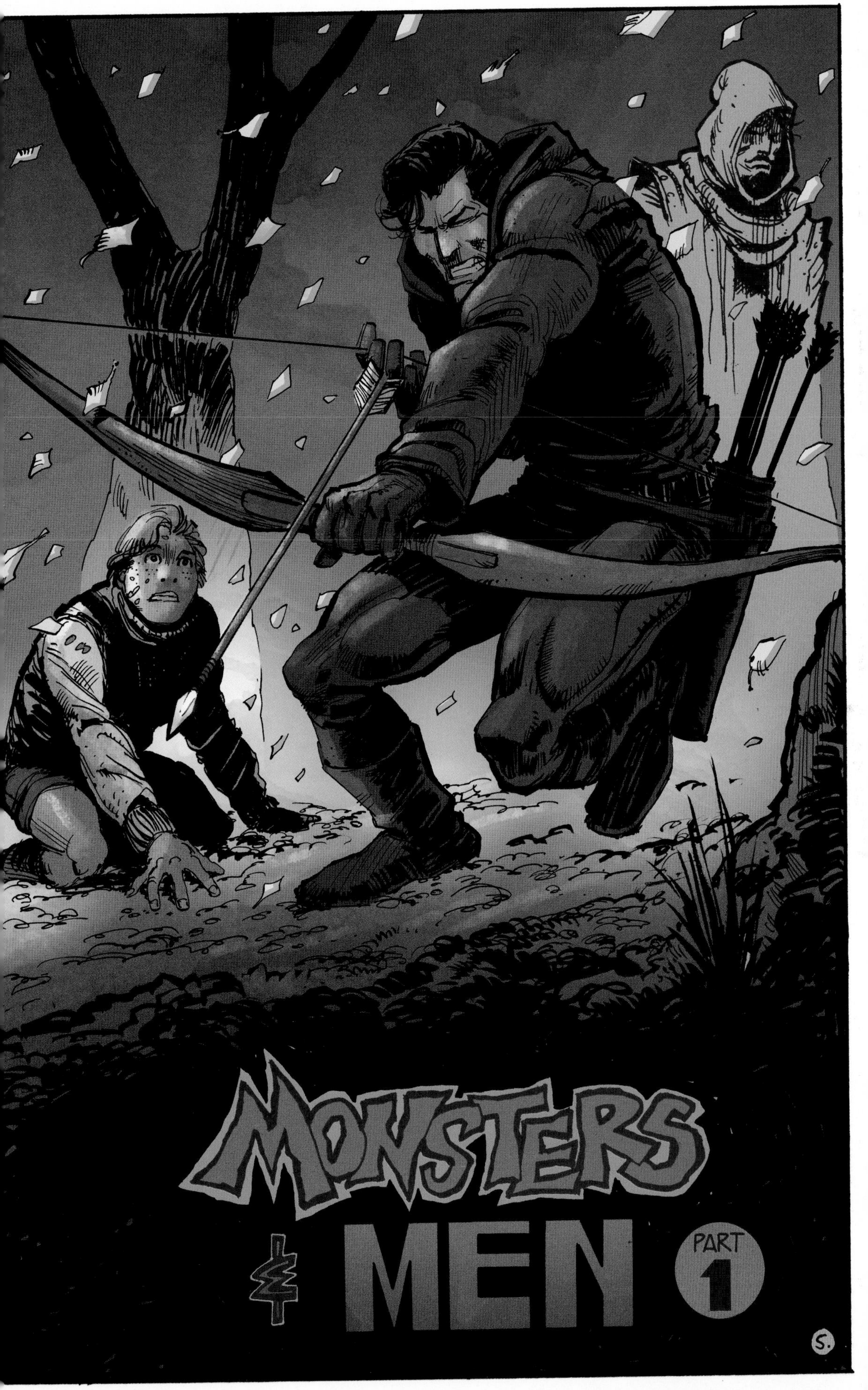
MONSTERS
& MEN
PART 1
5.

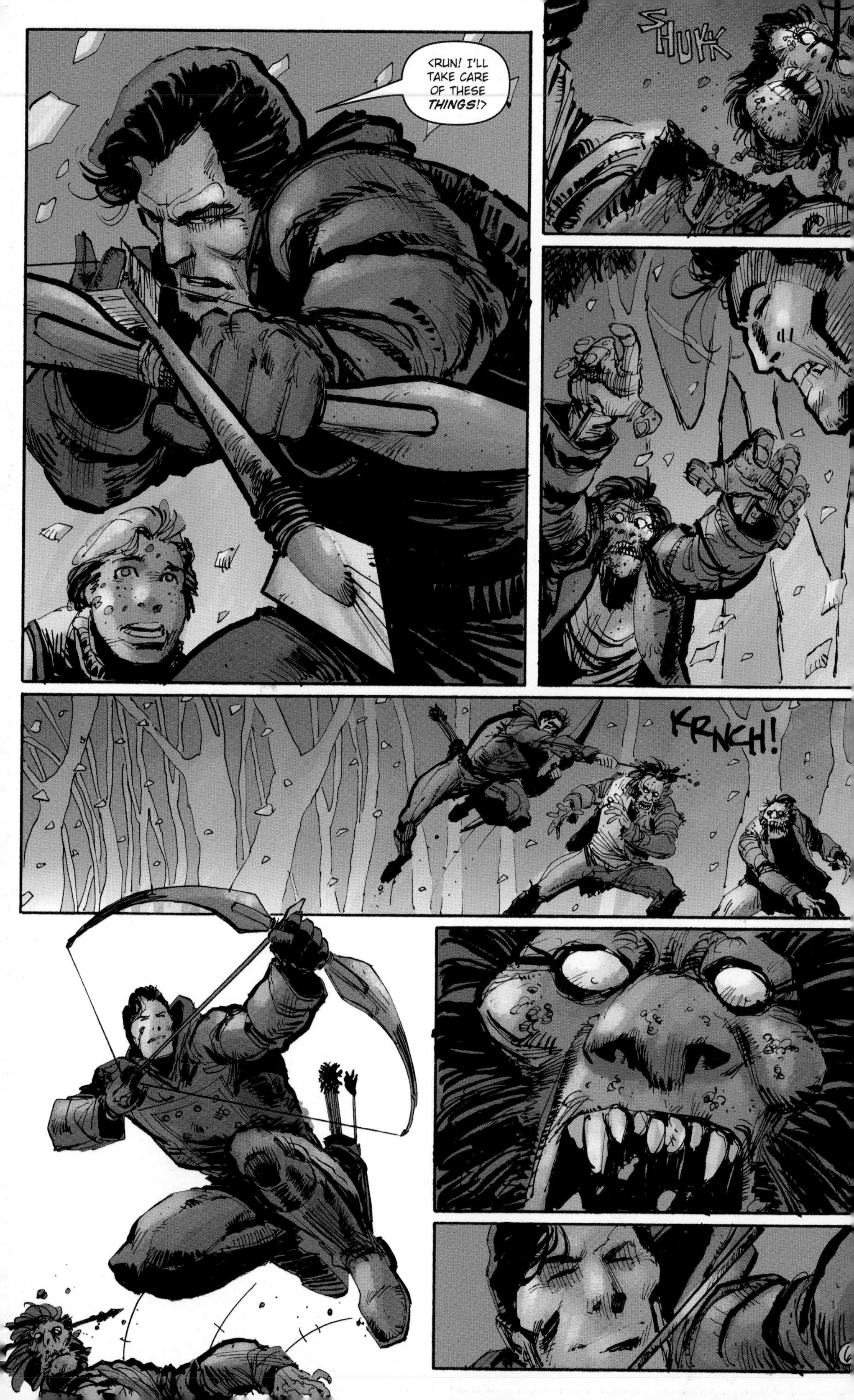

<RUN! I'LL TAKE CARE OF THESE THINGS!>
SHUKK
KRNCH!

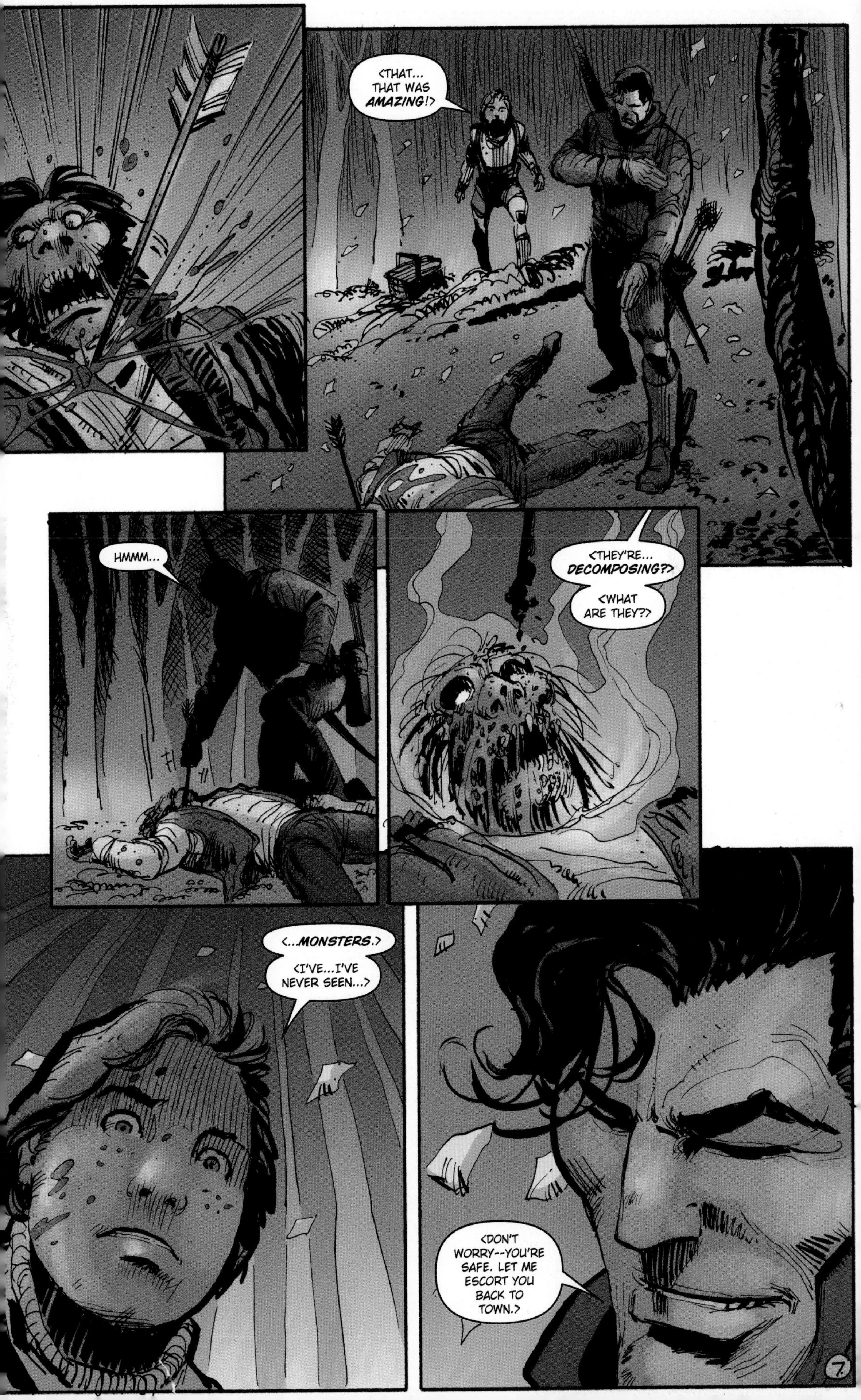
<THAT... THAT WAS **AMAZING**!>
HMMM...
<THEY'RE... **DECOMPOSING**?>
<WHAT ARE THEY?>
<...**MONSTERS**.>
<I'VE...I'VE NEVER SEEN...>
<DON'T WORRY--YOU'RE SAFE. LET ME ESCORT YOU BACK TO TOWN.>
7.

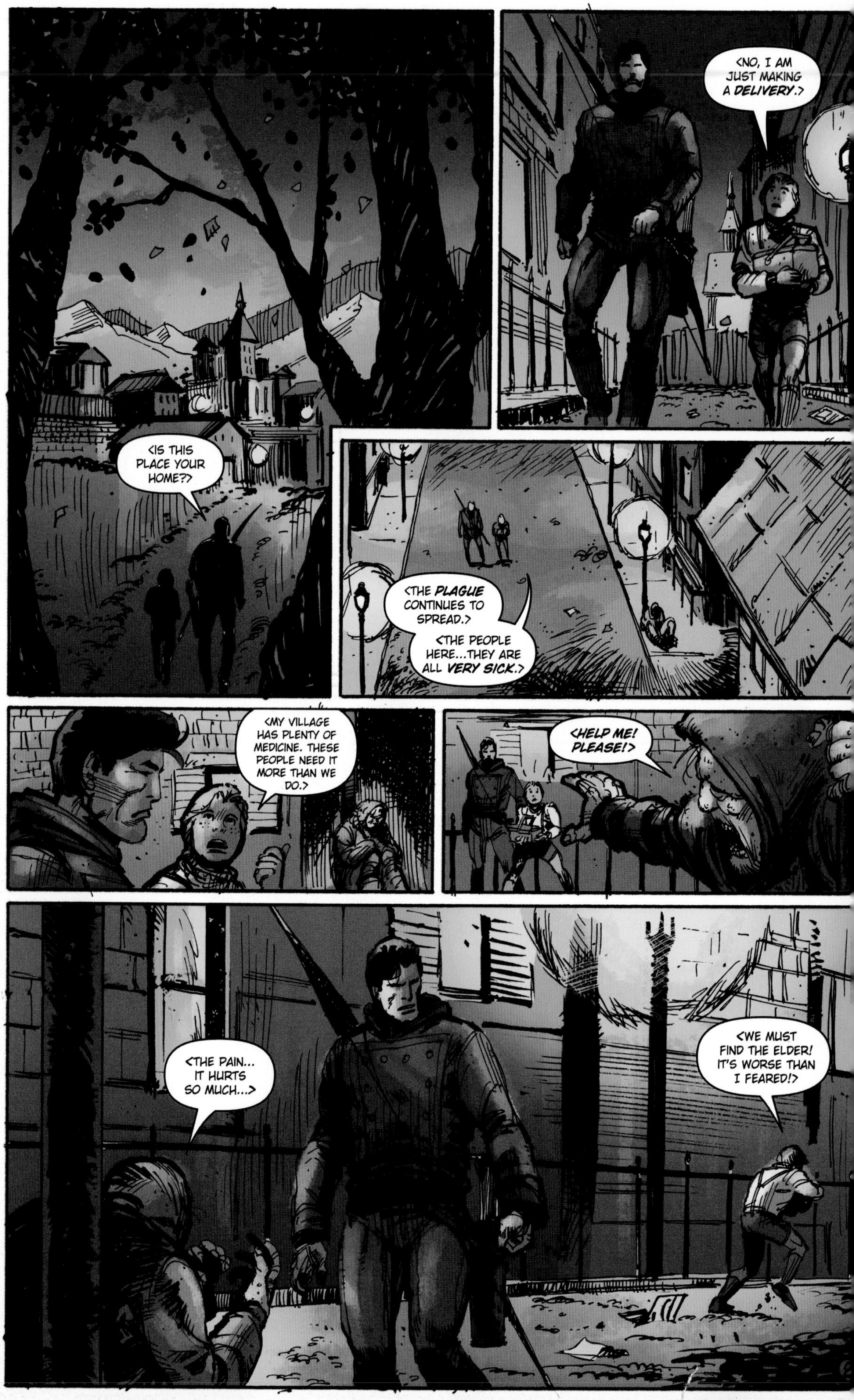

<IS THIS PLACE YOUR HOME?>
<NO, I AM JUST MAKING A DELIVERY.>
<THE PLAGUE CONTINUES TO SPREAD.>
<THE PEOPLE HERE...THEY ARE ALL VERY SICK.>
<MY VILLAGE HAS PLENTY OF MEDICINE. THESE PEOPLE NEED IT MORE THAN WE DO.>
<HELP ME! PLEASE!>
<THE PAIN... IT HURTS SO MUCH...>
<WE MUST FIND THE ELDER! IT'S WORSE THAN I FEARED!>

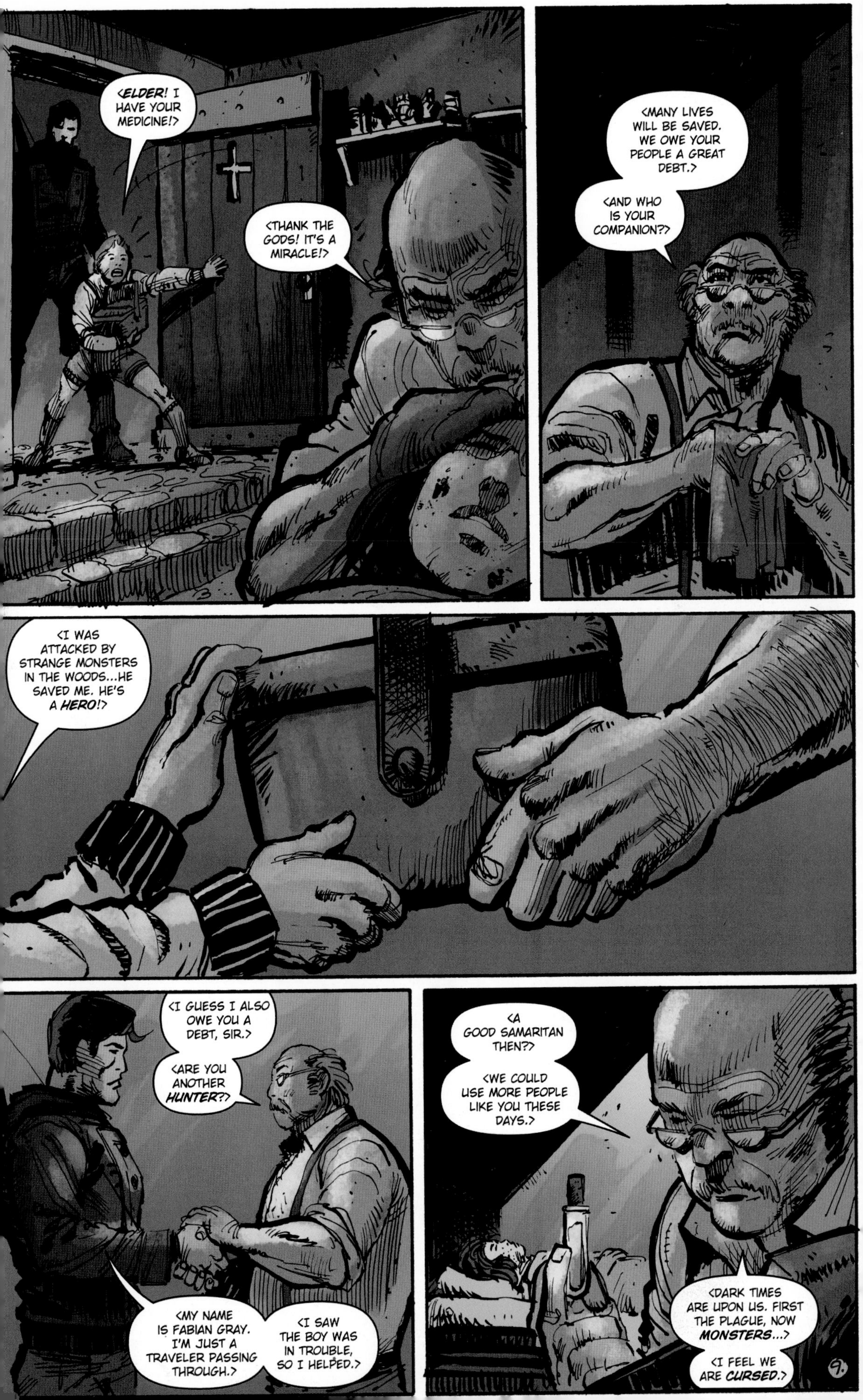
<ELDER! I HAVE YOUR MEDICINE!>
<THANK THE GODS! IT'S A MIRACLE!>
<MANY LIVES WILL BE SAVED. WE OWE YOUR PEOPLE A GREAT DEBT.>
<AND WHO IS YOUR COMPANION?>
<I WAS ATTACKED BY STRANGE MONSTERS IN THE WOODS...HE SAVED ME. HE'S A HERO!>
<I GUESS I ALSO OWE YOU A DEBT, SIR.>
<ARE YOU ANOTHER HUNTER?>
<MY NAME IS FABIAN GRAY. I'M JUST A TRAVELER PASSING THROUGH.>
<I SAW THE BOY WAS IN TROUBLE, SO I HELPED.>
<A GOOD SAMARITAN THEN?>
<WE COULD USE MORE PEOPLE LIKE YOU THESE DAYS.>
<DARK TIMES ARE UPON US. FIRST THE PLAGUE, NOW MONSTERS...>
<I FEEL WE ARE CURSED.>

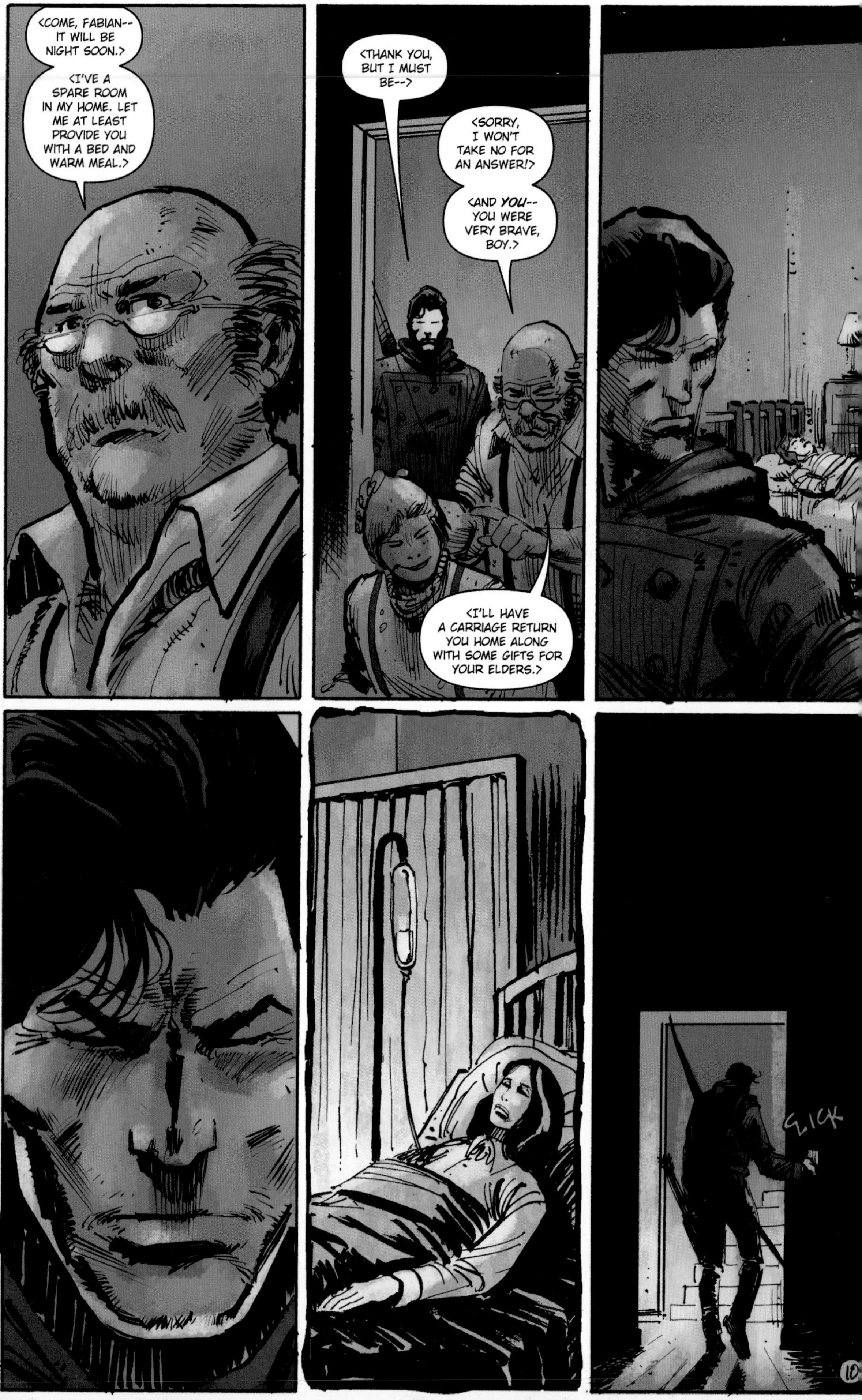
<COME, FABIAN-- IT WILL BE NIGHT SOON.>
<I'VE A SPARE ROOM IN MY HOME. LET ME AT LEAST PROVIDE YOU WITH A BED AND WARM MEAL.>
<THANK YOU, BUT I MUST BE-->
<SORRY, I WON'T TAKE NO FOR AN ANSWER!>
<AND *YOU*-- YOU WERE VERY BRAVE, BOY.>
<I'LL HAVE A CARRIAGE RETURN YOU HOME ALONG WITH SOME GIFTS FOR YOUR ELDERS.>
CLICK

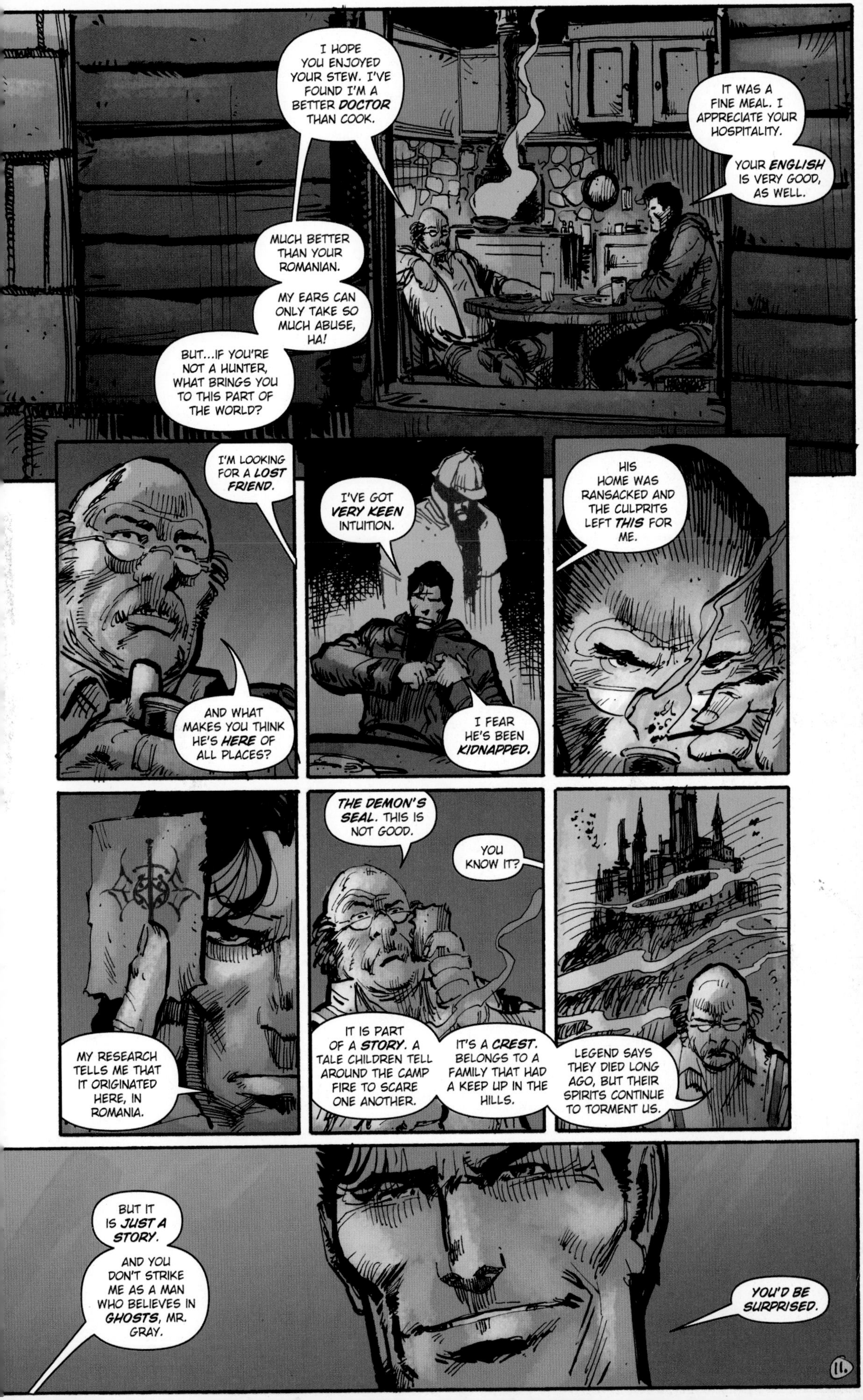
I HOPE YOU ENJOYED YOUR STEW. I'VE FOUND I'M A BETTER DOCTOR THAN COOK.
MUCH BETTER THAN YOUR ROMANIAN.
MY EARS CAN ONLY TAKE SO MUCH ABUSE, HA!
IT WAS A FINE MEAL. I APPRECIATE YOUR HOSPITALITY.
YOUR ENGLISH IS VERY GOOD, AS WELL.
BUT...IF YOU'RE NOT A HUNTER, WHAT BRINGS YOU TO THIS PART OF THE WORLD?
I'M LOOKING FOR A LOST FRIEND.
AND WHAT MAKES YOU THINK HE'S HERE OF ALL PLACES?
I'VE GOT VERY KEEN INTUITION.
I FEAR HE'S BEEN KIDNAPPED.
HIS HOME WAS RANSACKED AND THE CULPRITS LEFT THIS FOR ME.
MY RESEARCH TELLS ME THAT IT ORIGINATED HERE, IN ROMANIA.
THE DEMON'S SEAL. THIS IS NOT GOOD.
YOU KNOW IT?
IT IS PART OF A STORY. A TALE CHILDREN TELL AROUND THE CAMP FIRE TO SCARE ONE ANOTHER.
IT'S A CREST. BELONGS TO A FAMILY THAT HAD A KEEP UP IN THE HILLS.
LEGEND SAYS THEY DIED LONG AGO, BUT THEIR SPIRITS CONTINUE TO TORMENT US.
BUT IT IS JUST A STORY.
AND YOU DON'T STRIKE ME AS A MAN WHO BELIEVES IN GHOSTS, MR. GRAY.
YOU'D BE SURPRISED.
11.

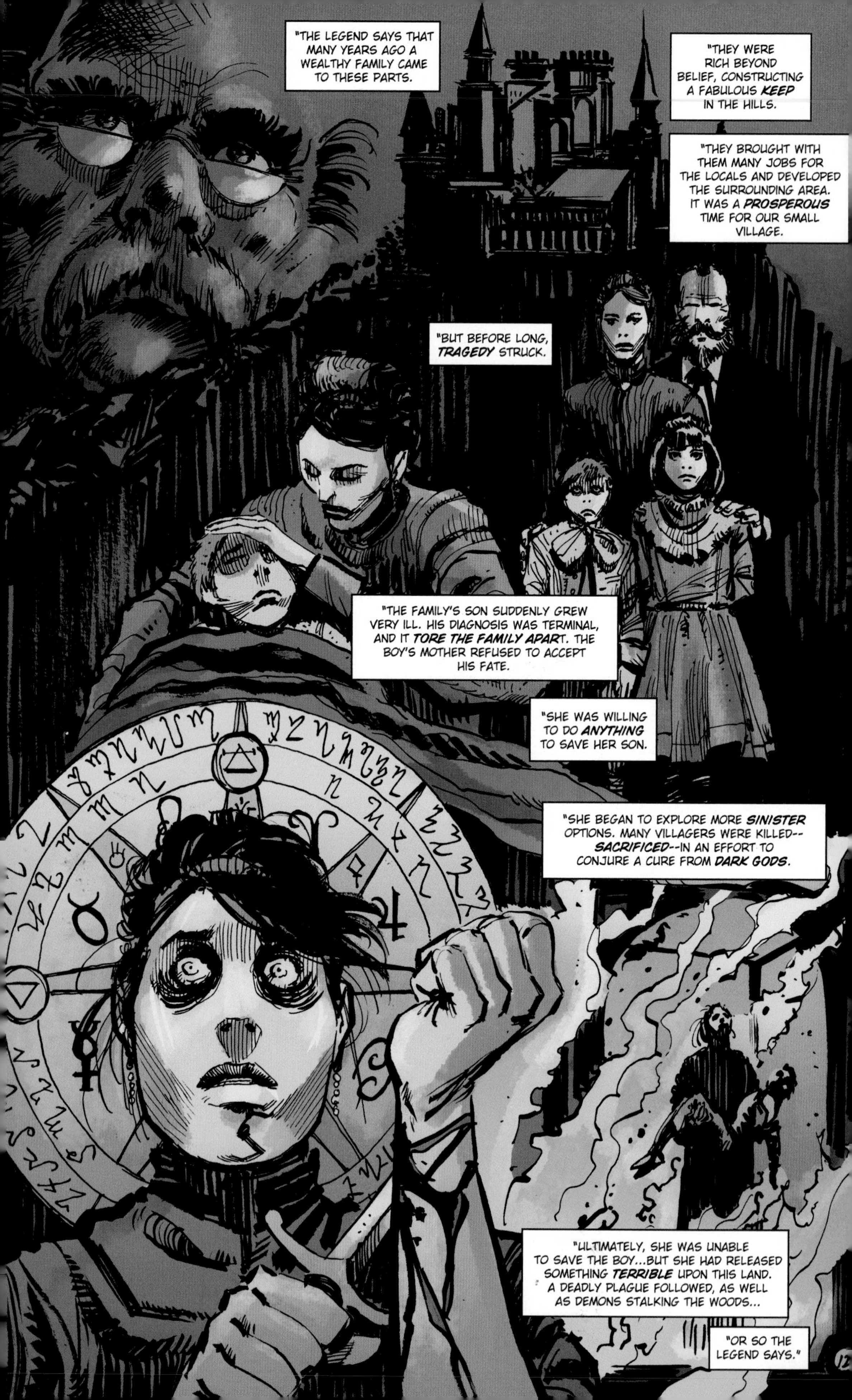
"THE LEGEND SAYS THAT MANY YEARS AGO A WEALTHY FAMILY CAME TO THESE PARTS.
"THEY WERE RICH BEYOND BELIEF, CONSTRUCTING A FABULOUS KEEP IN THE HILLS.
"THEY BROUGHT WITH THEM MANY JOBS FOR THE LOCALS AND DEVELOPED THE SURROUNDING AREA. IT WAS A PROSPEROUS TIME FOR OUR SMALL VILLAGE.
"BUT BEFORE LONG, TRAGEDY STRUCK.
"THE FAMILY'S SON SUDDENLY GREW VERY ILL. HIS DIAGNOSIS WAS TERMINAL, AND IT TORE THE FAMILY APART. THE BOY'S MOTHER REFUSED TO ACCEPT HIS FATE.
"SHE WAS WILLING TO DO ANYTHING TO SAVE HER SON.
"SHE BEGAN TO EXPLORE MORE SINISTER OPTIONS. MANY VILLAGERS WERE KILLED--SACRIFICED--IN AN EFFORT TO CONJURE A CURE FROM DARK GODS.
"ULTIMATELY, SHE WAS UNABLE TO SAVE THE BOY...BUT SHE HAD RELEASED SOMETHING TERRIBLE UPON THIS LAND. A DEADLY PLAGUE FOLLOWED, AS WELL AS DEMONS STALKING THE WOODS...
"OR SO THE LEGEND SAYS."

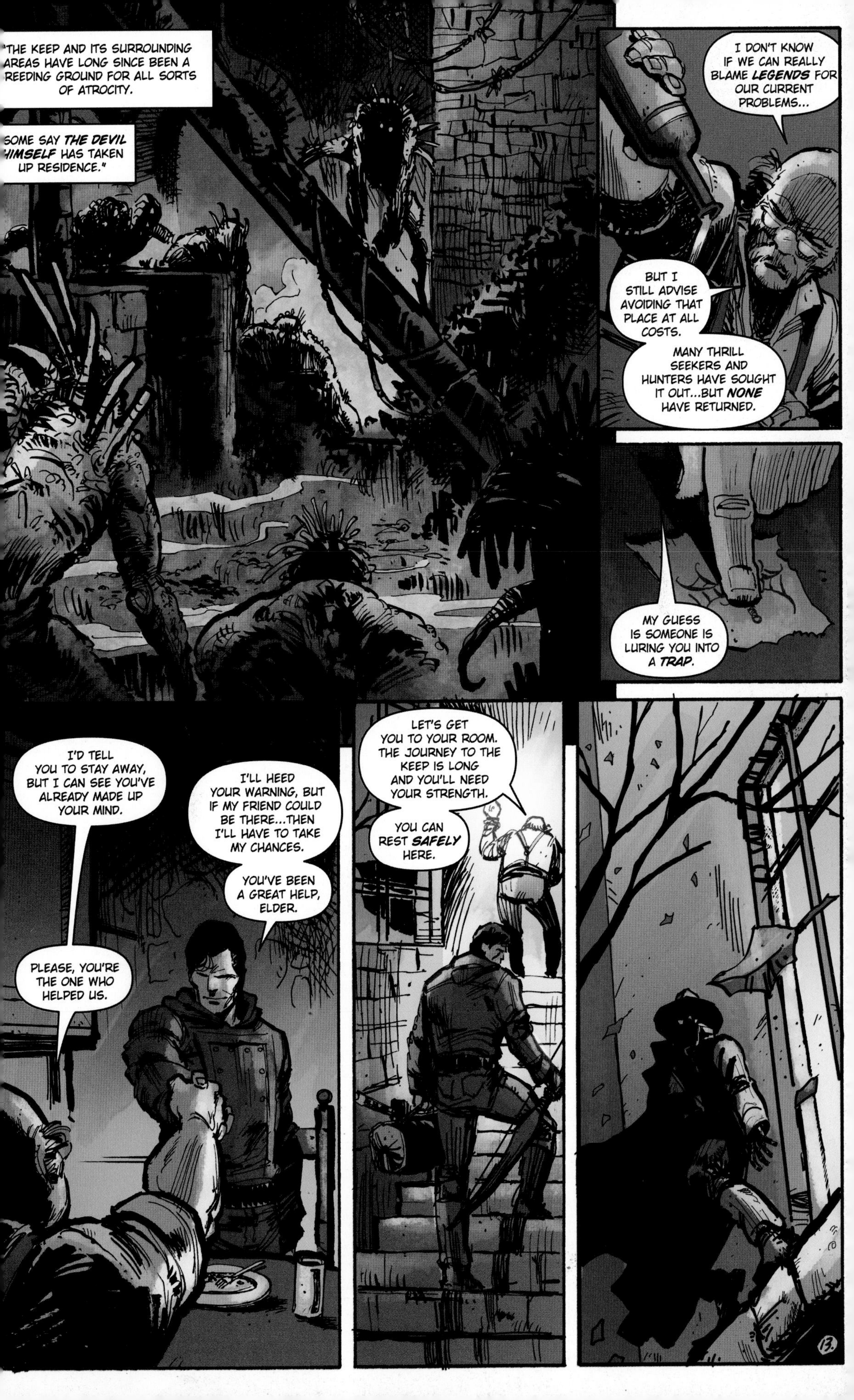

"THE KEEP AND ITS SURROUNDING AREAS HAVE LONG SINCE BEEN A BREEDING GROUND FOR ALL SORTS OF ATROCITY.
SOME SAY THE DEVIL HIMSELF HAS TAKEN UP RESIDENCE."
I DON'T KNOW IF WE CAN REALLY BLAME LEGENDS FOR OUR CURRENT PROBLEMS...
BUT I STILL ADVISE AVOIDING THAT PLACE AT ALL COSTS.
MANY THRILL SEEKERS AND HUNTERS HAVE SOUGHT IT OUT...BUT NONE HAVE RETURNED.
MY GUESS IS SOMEONE IS LURING YOU INTO A TRAP.
I'D TELL YOU TO STAY AWAY, BUT I CAN SEE YOU'VE ALREADY MADE UP YOUR MIND.
I'LL HEED YOUR WARNING, BUT IF MY FRIEND COULD BE THERE...THEN I'LL HAVE TO TAKE MY CHANCES.
YOU'VE BEEN A GREAT HELP, ELDER.
PLEASE, YOU'RE THE ONE WHO HELPED US.
LET'S GET YOU TO YOUR ROOM. THE JOURNEY TO THE KEEP IS LONG AND YOU'LL NEED YOUR STRENGTH.
YOU CAN REST SAFELY HERE.
13.

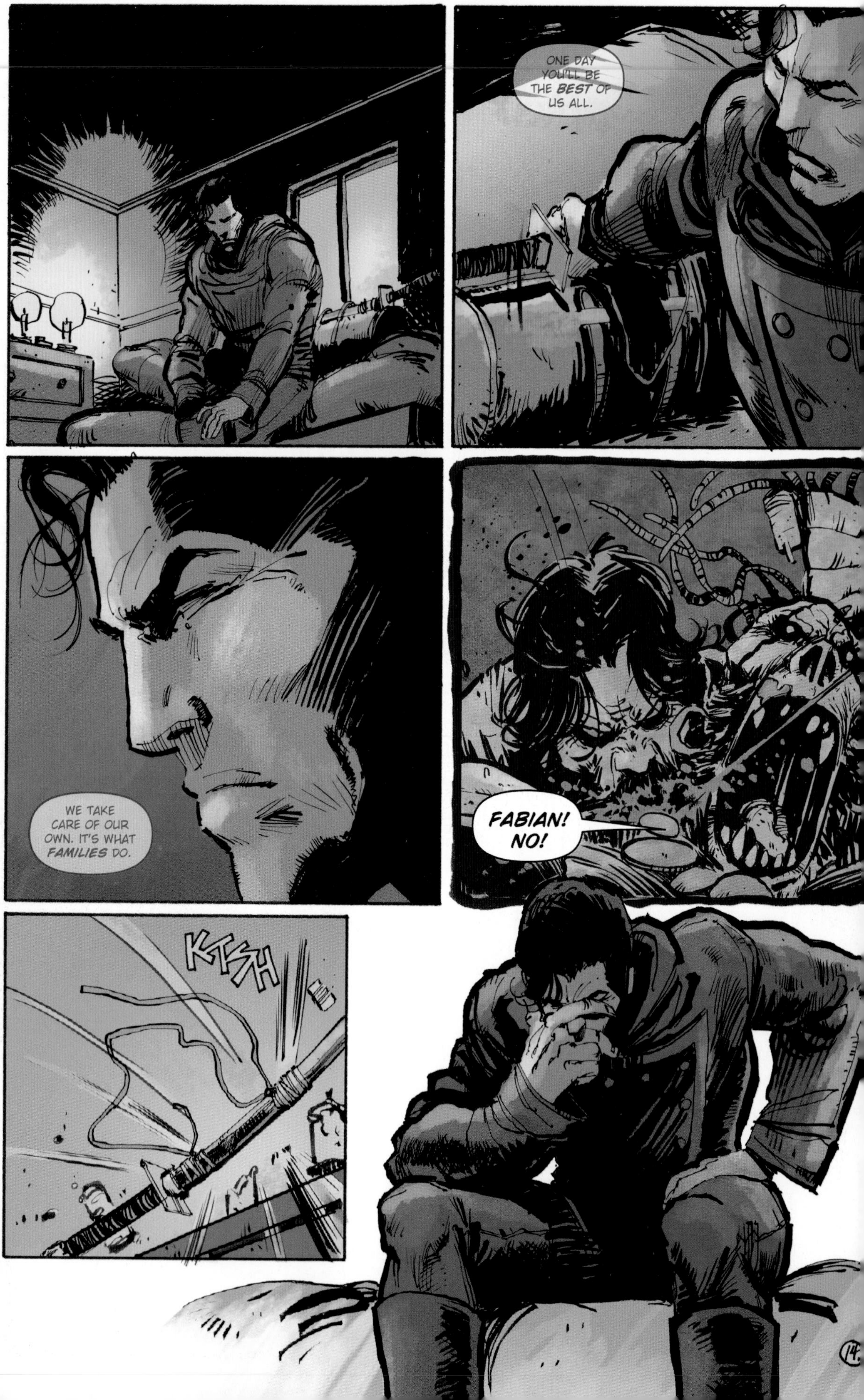
ONE DAY YOU'LL BE THE BEST OF US ALL.
WE TAKE CARE OF OUR OWN. IT'S WHAT FAMILIES DO.
FABIAN! NO!
KTSH
14.

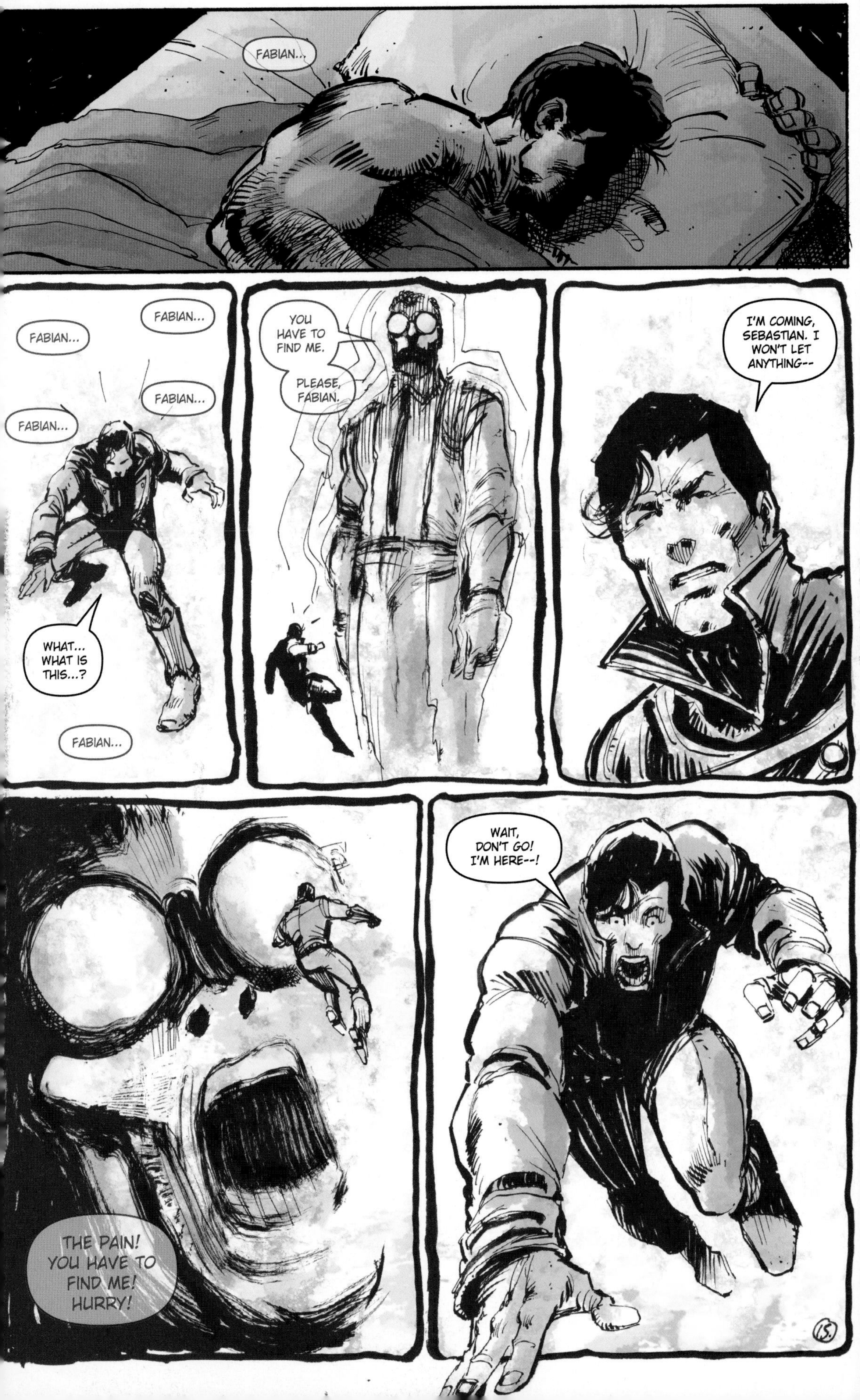

FABIAN...
FABIAN...
FABIAN...
FABIAN...
FABIAN...
WHAT... WHAT IS THIS...?
FABIAN...
YOU HAVE TO FIND ME.
PLEASE, FABIAN.
I'M COMING, SEBASTIAN. I WON'T LET ANYTHING--
THE PAIN! YOU HAVE TO FIND ME! HURRY!
WAIT, DON'T GO! I'M HERE--!

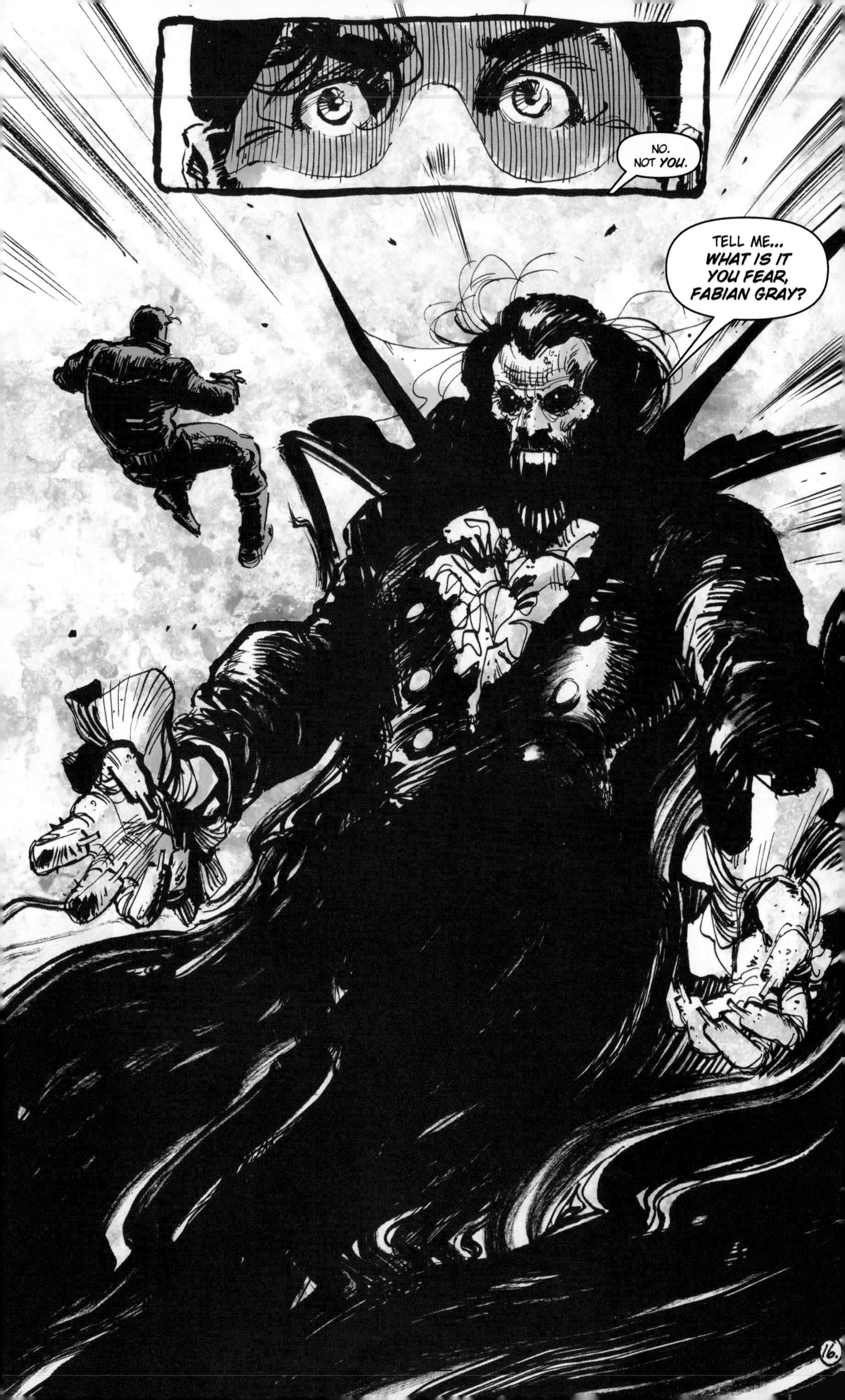
NO. NOT YOU.
TELL ME... WHAT IS IT YOU FEAR, FABIAN GRAY?
16.

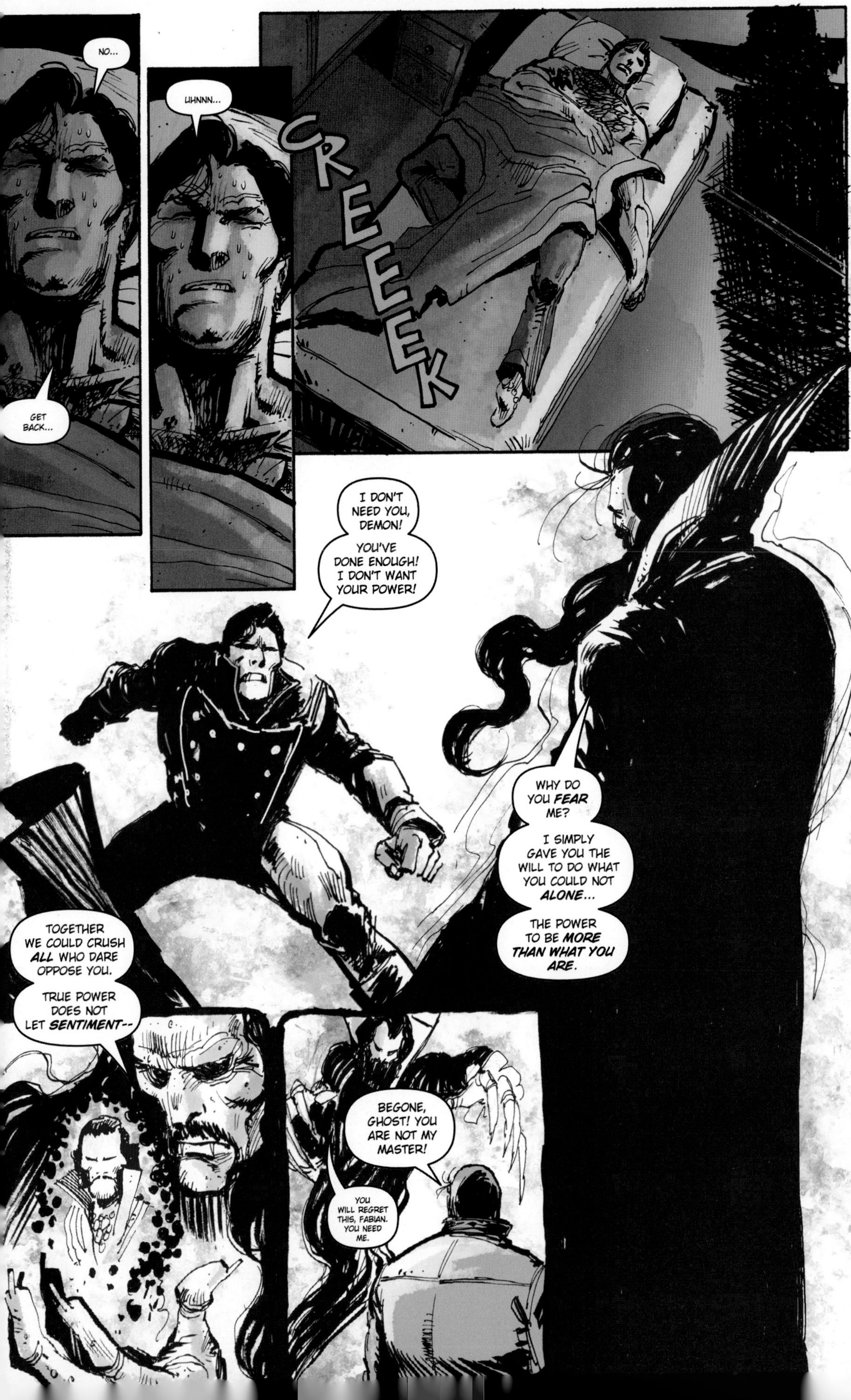
NO...
GET BACK...
UHNNN...
CREEEK
I DON'T NEED YOU, DEMON!
YOU'VE DONE ENOUGH! I DON'T WANT YOUR POWER!
WHY DO YOU FEAR ME?
I SIMPLY GAVE YOU THE WILL TO DO WHAT YOU COULD NOT ALONE...
THE POWER TO BE MORE THAN WHAT YOU ARE.
TOGETHER WE COULD CRUSH ALL WHO DARE OPPOSE YOU.
TRUE POWER DOES NOT LET SENTIMENT--
BEGONE, GHOST! YOU ARE NOT MY MASTER!
YOU WILL REGRET THIS, FABIAN. YOU NEED ME.

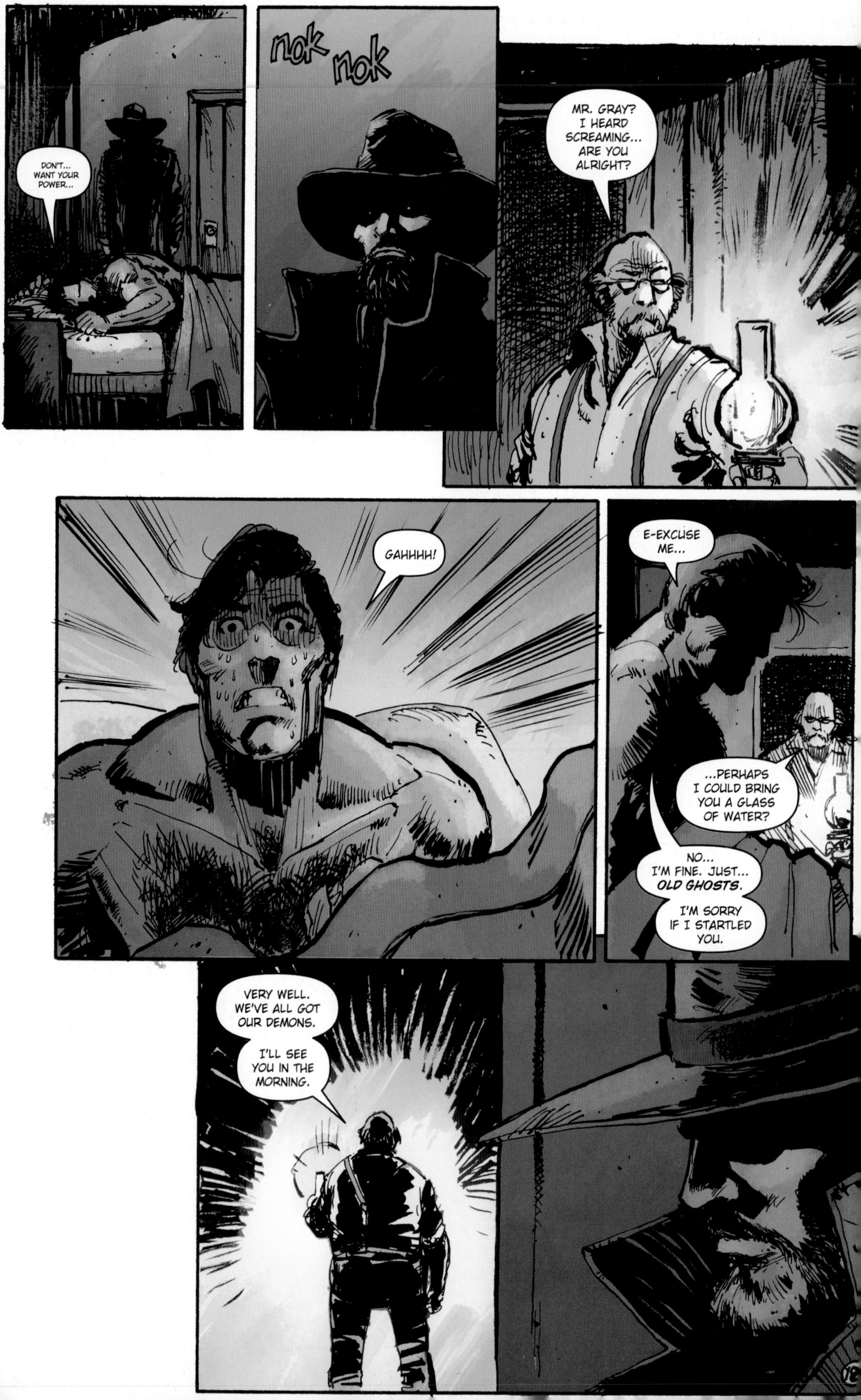
DON'T... WANT YOUR POWER...
nok nok
MR. GRAY? I HEARD SCREAMING... ARE YOU ALRIGHT?
GAHHHH!
E-EXCUSE ME...
...PERHAPS I COULD BRING YOU A GLASS OF WATER?
NO... I'M FINE. JUST... OLD GHOSTS.
I'M SORRY IF I STARTLED YOU.
VERY WELL. WE'VE ALL GOT OUR DEMONS.
I'LL SEE YOU IN THE MORNING.

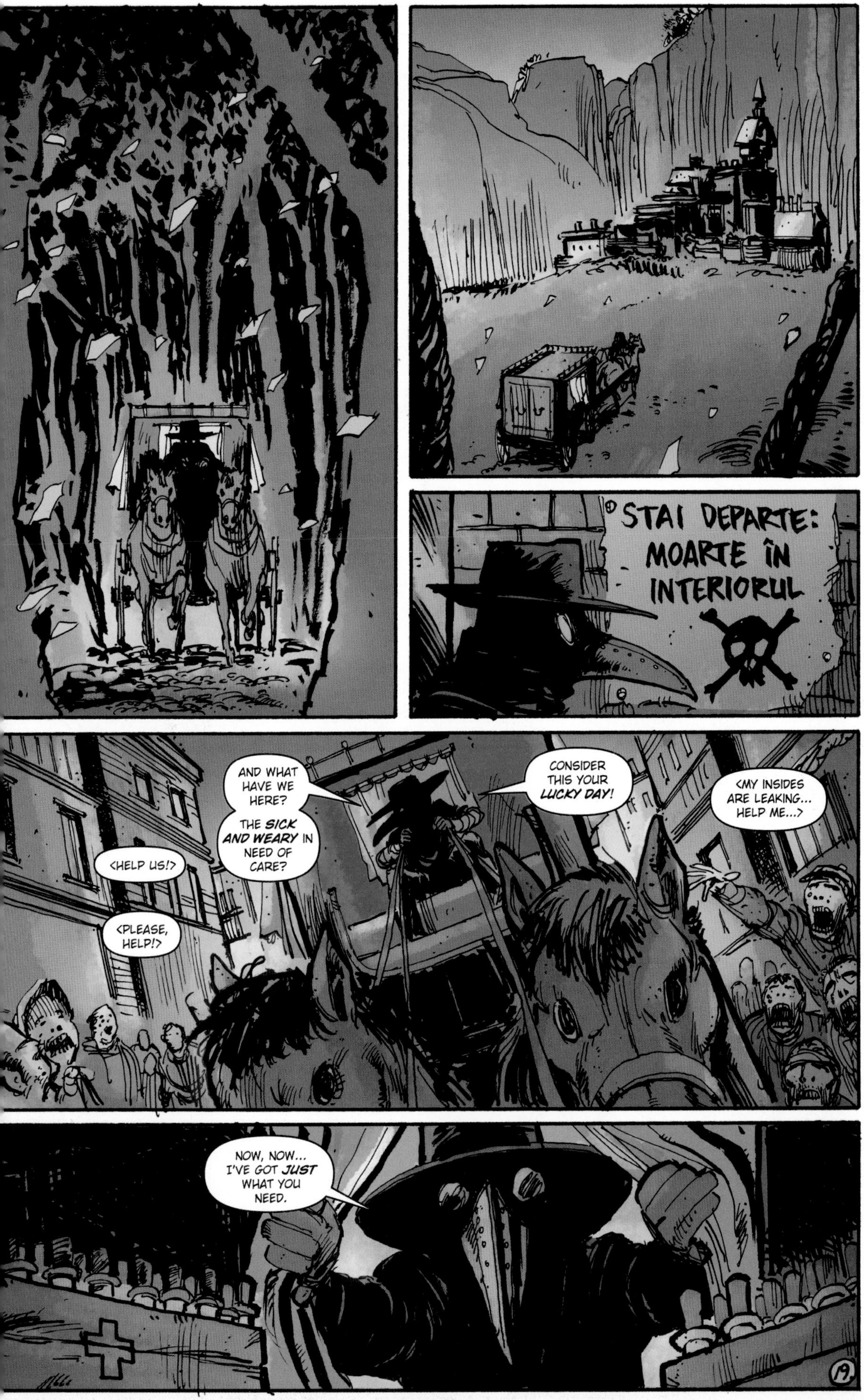
STAI DEPARTE: MOARTE ÎN INTERIORUL
AND WHAT HAVE WE HERE?
THE SICK AND WEARY IN NEED OF CARE?
CONSIDER THIS YOUR LUCKY DAY!
<HELP US!>
<PLEASE, HELP!>
<MY INSIDES ARE LEAKING... HELP ME...>
NOW, NOW... I'VE GOT JUST WHAT YOU NEED.
19

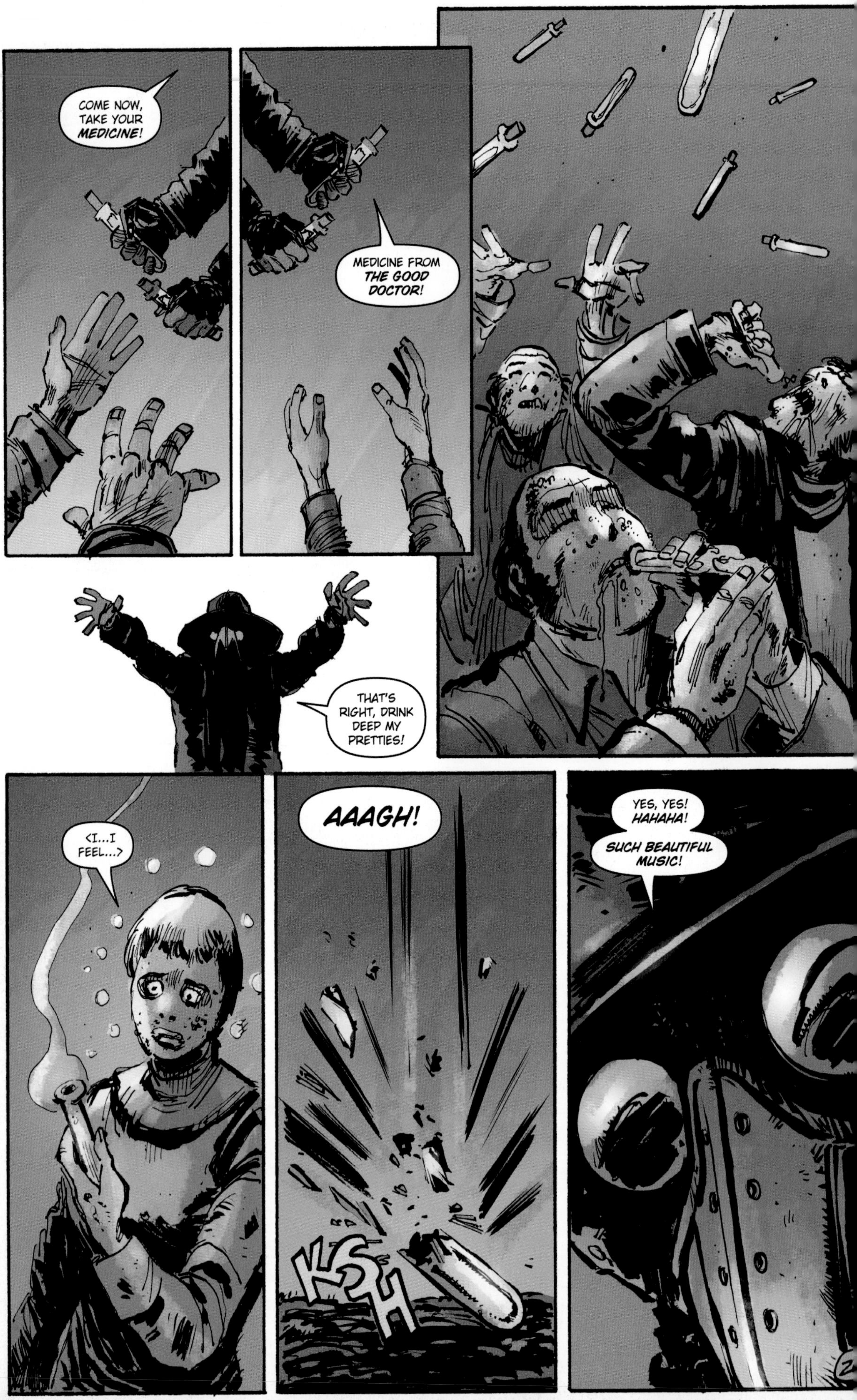
COME NOW, TAKE YOUR MEDICINE!
MEDICINE FROM THE GOOD DOCTOR!
THAT'S RIGHT, DRINK DEEP MY PRETTIES!
<I...I FEEL...>
AAAGH!
KSH
YES, YES! HAHAHA!
SUCH BEAUTIFUL MUSIC!

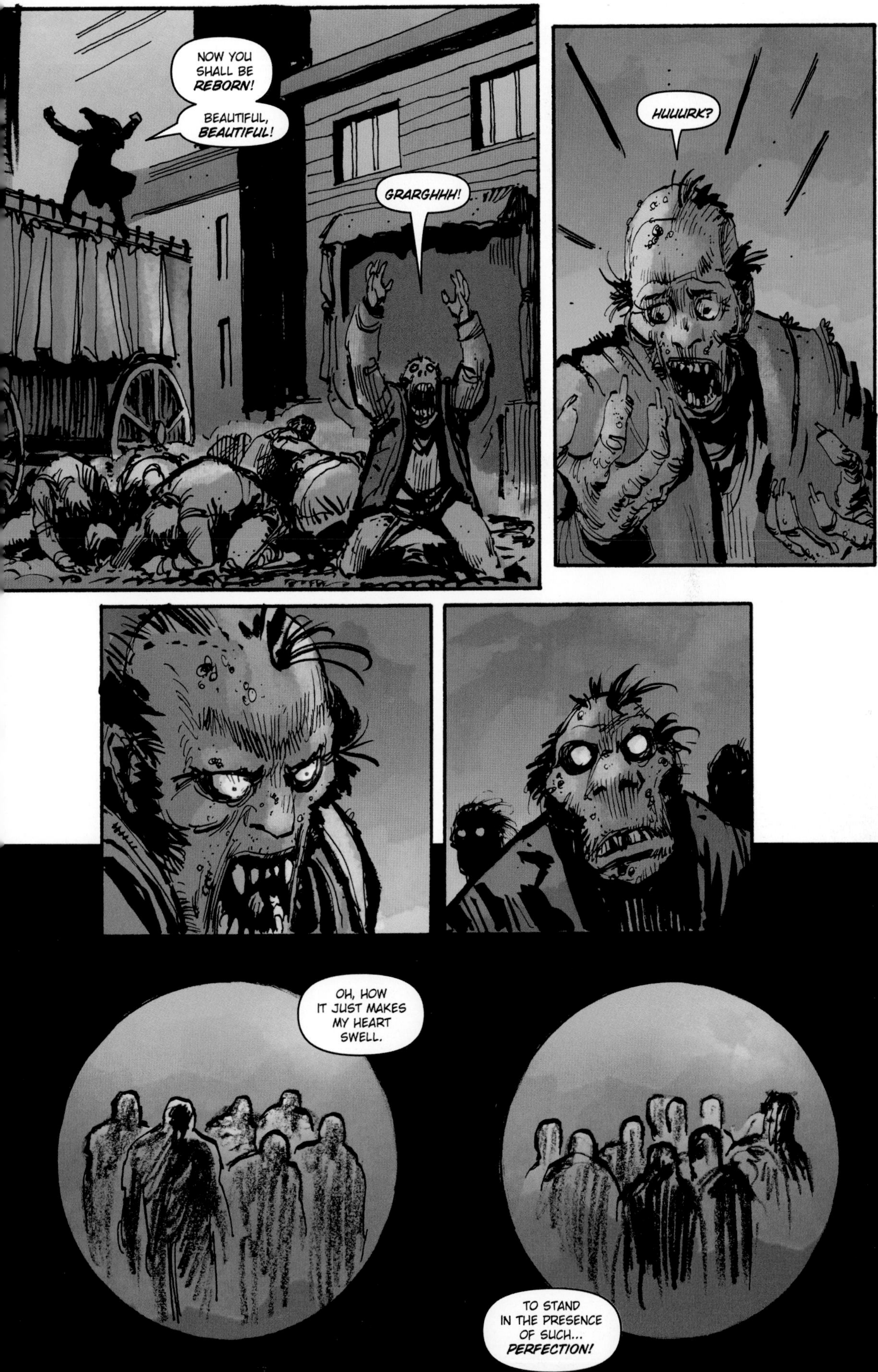
NOW YOU SHALL BE REBORN!
BEAUTIFUL, BEAUTIFUL!
GRARGHHH!
HUUURK?
OH, HOW IT JUST MAKES MY HEART SWELL.
TO STAND IN THE PRESENCE OF SUCH... PERFECTION!

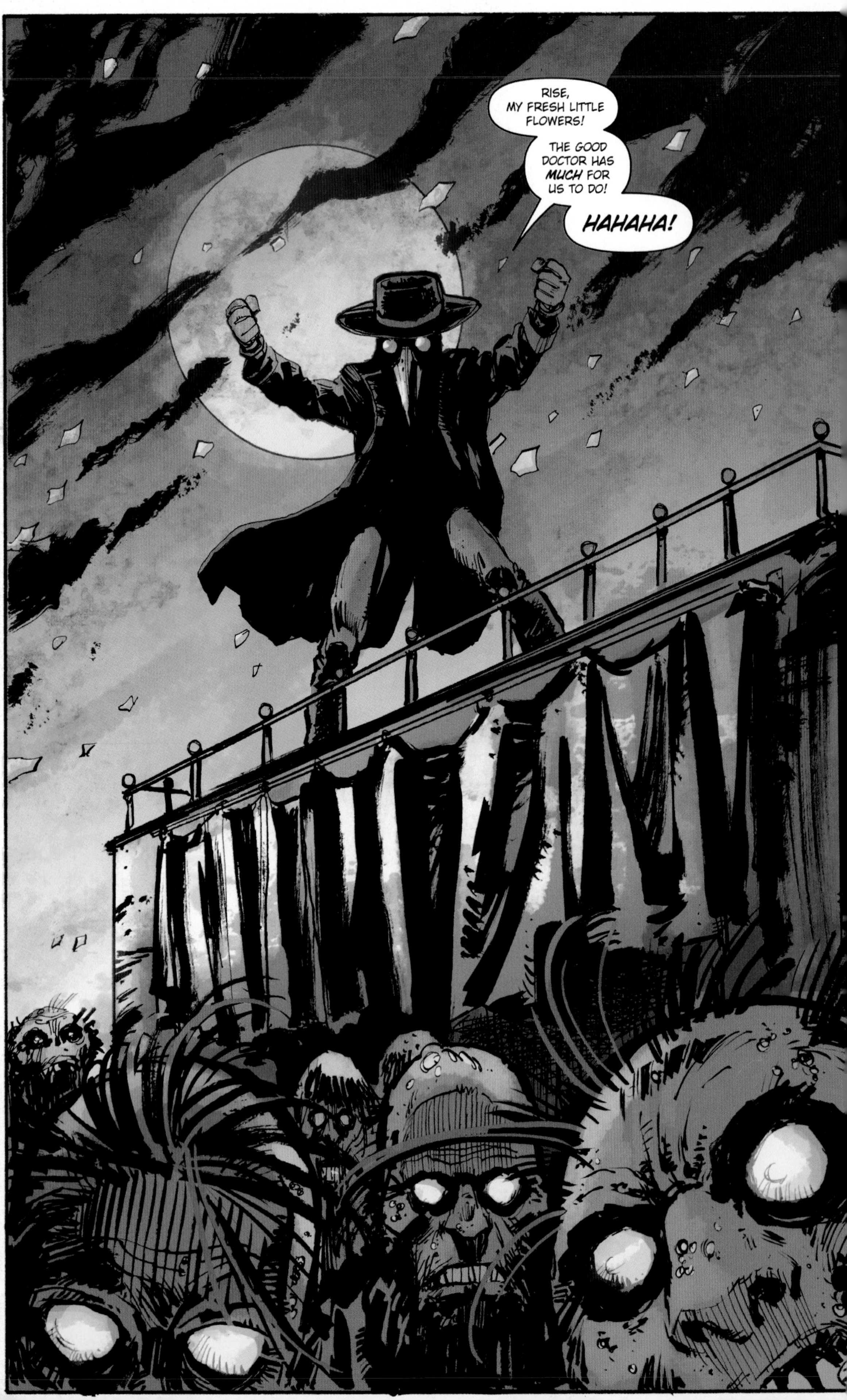
RISE, MY FRESH LITTLE FLOWERS!
THE GOOD DOCTOR HAS *MUCH* FOR US TO DO!
HAHAHA!

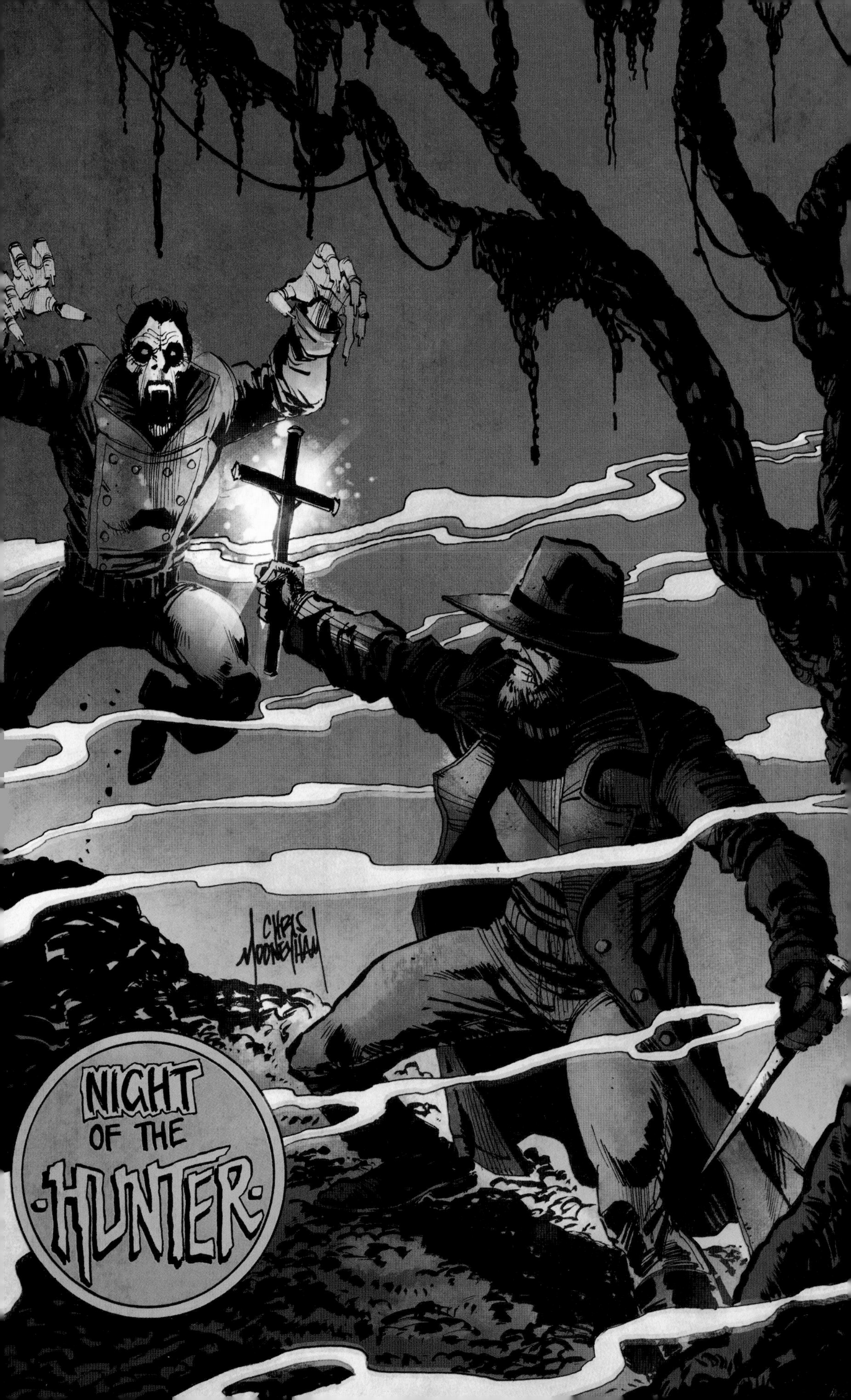
NIGHT OF THE HUNTER
CHRIS MOONEYHAM

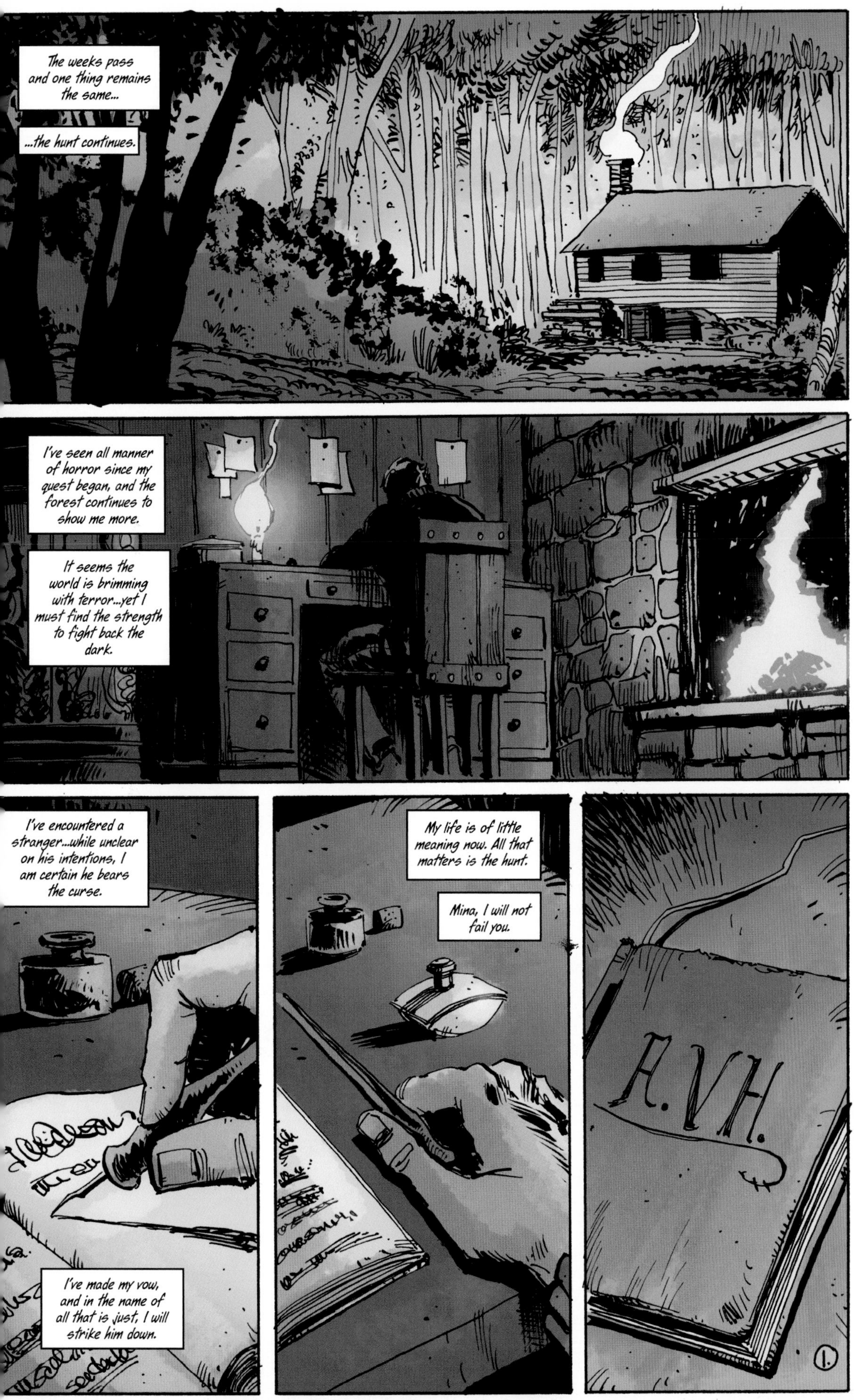
The weeks pass and one thing remains the same...
...the hunt continues.
I've seen all manner of horror since my quest began, and the forest continues to show me more.
It seems the world is brimming with terror...yet I must find the strength to fight back the dark.
I've encountered a stranger...while unclear on his intentions, I am certain he bears the curse.
I've made my vow, and in the name of all that is just, I will strike him down.
My life is of little meaning now. All that matters is the hunt.
Mina, I will not fail you.
A.V.H.

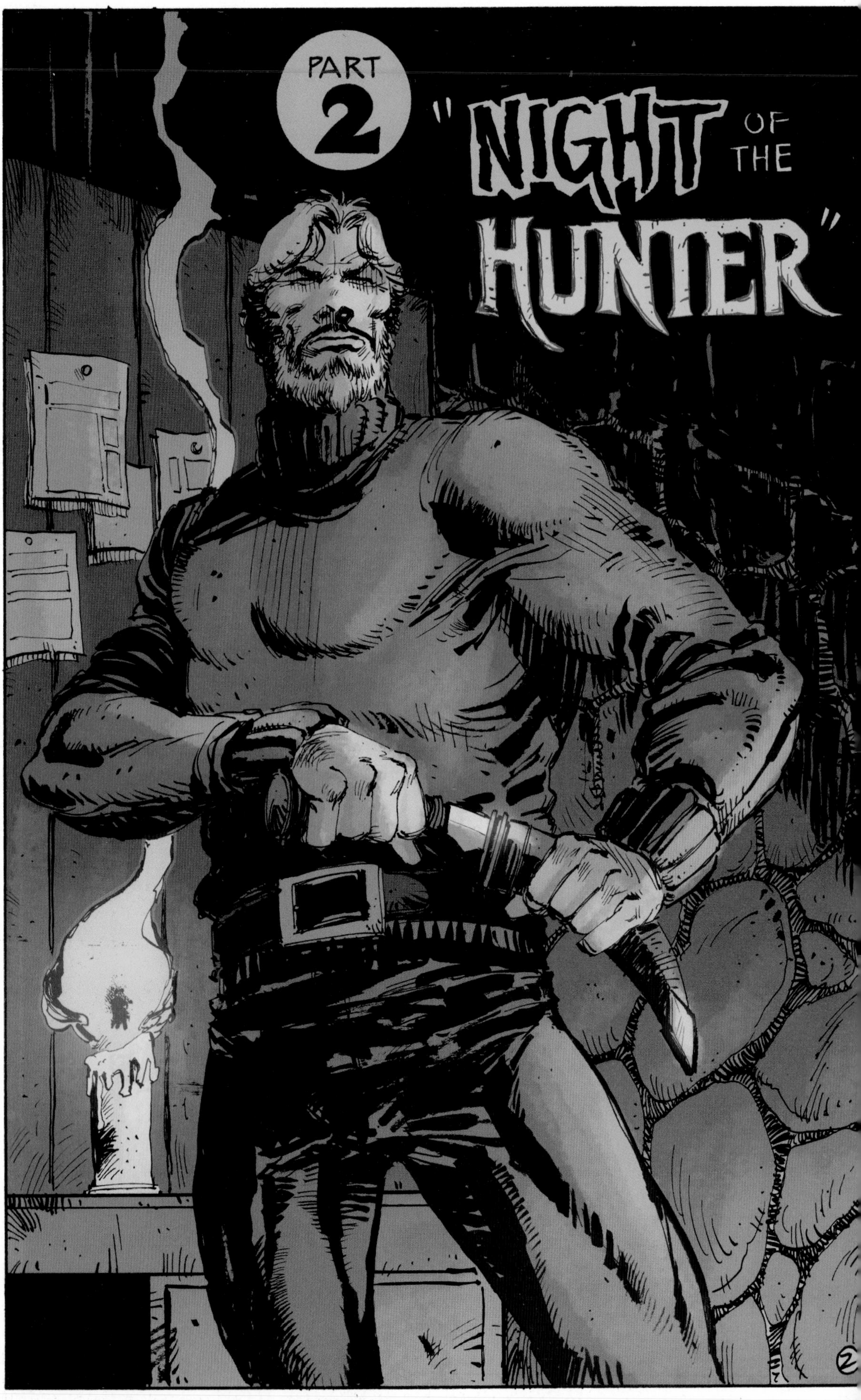
PART
2
"NIGHT OF THE HUNTER"
2

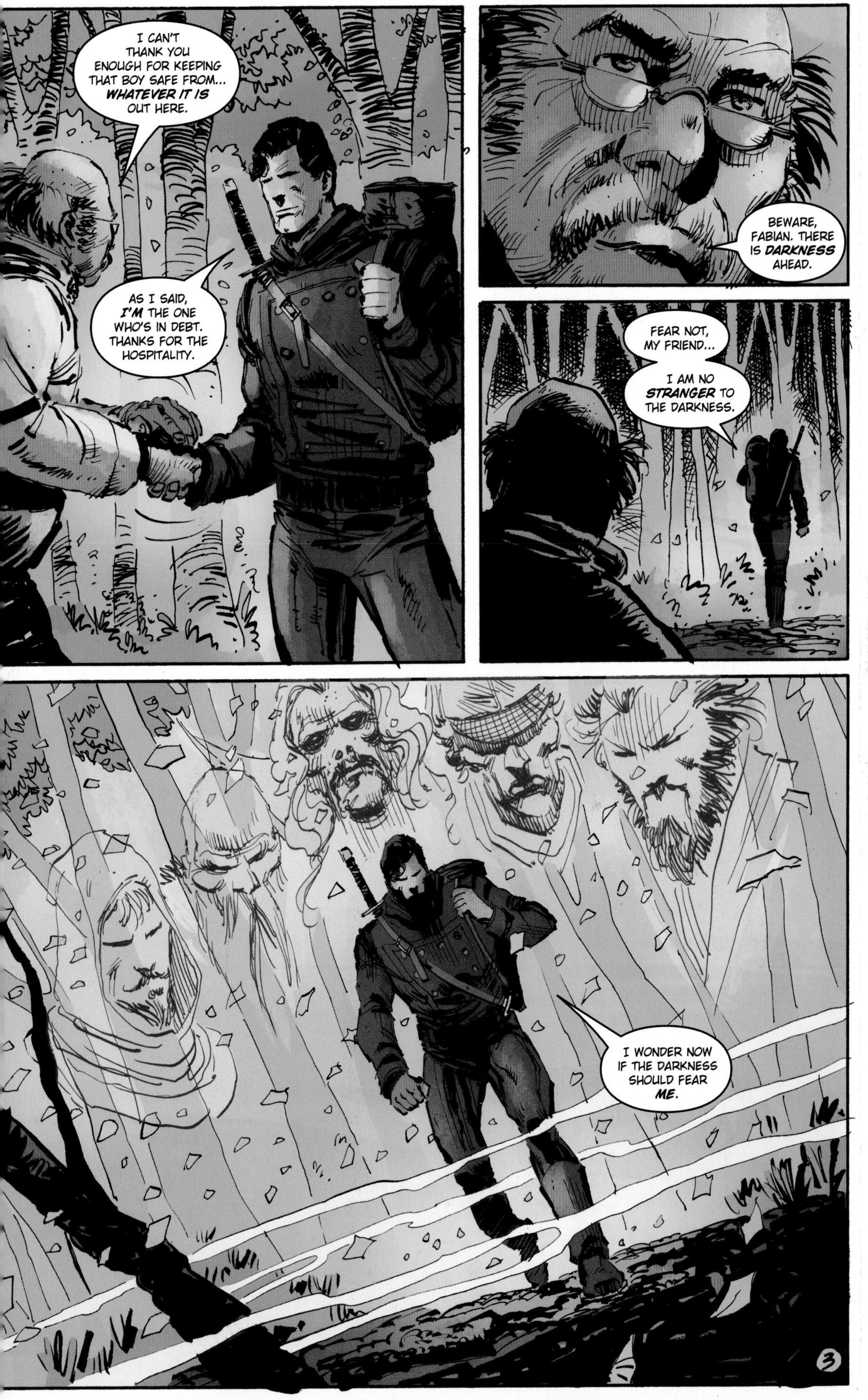
I CAN'T THANK YOU ENOUGH FOR KEEPING THAT BOY SAFE FROM... **WHATEVER IT IS** OUT HERE.
AS I SAID, ***I'M*** THE ONE WHO'S IN DEBT. THANKS FOR THE HOSPITALITY.
BEWARE, FABIAN. THERE IS ***DARKNESS*** AHEAD.
FEAR NOT, MY FRIEND...
I AM NO ***STRANGER*** TO THE DARKNESS.
I WONDER NOW IF THE DARKNESS SHOULD FEAR ***ME***.

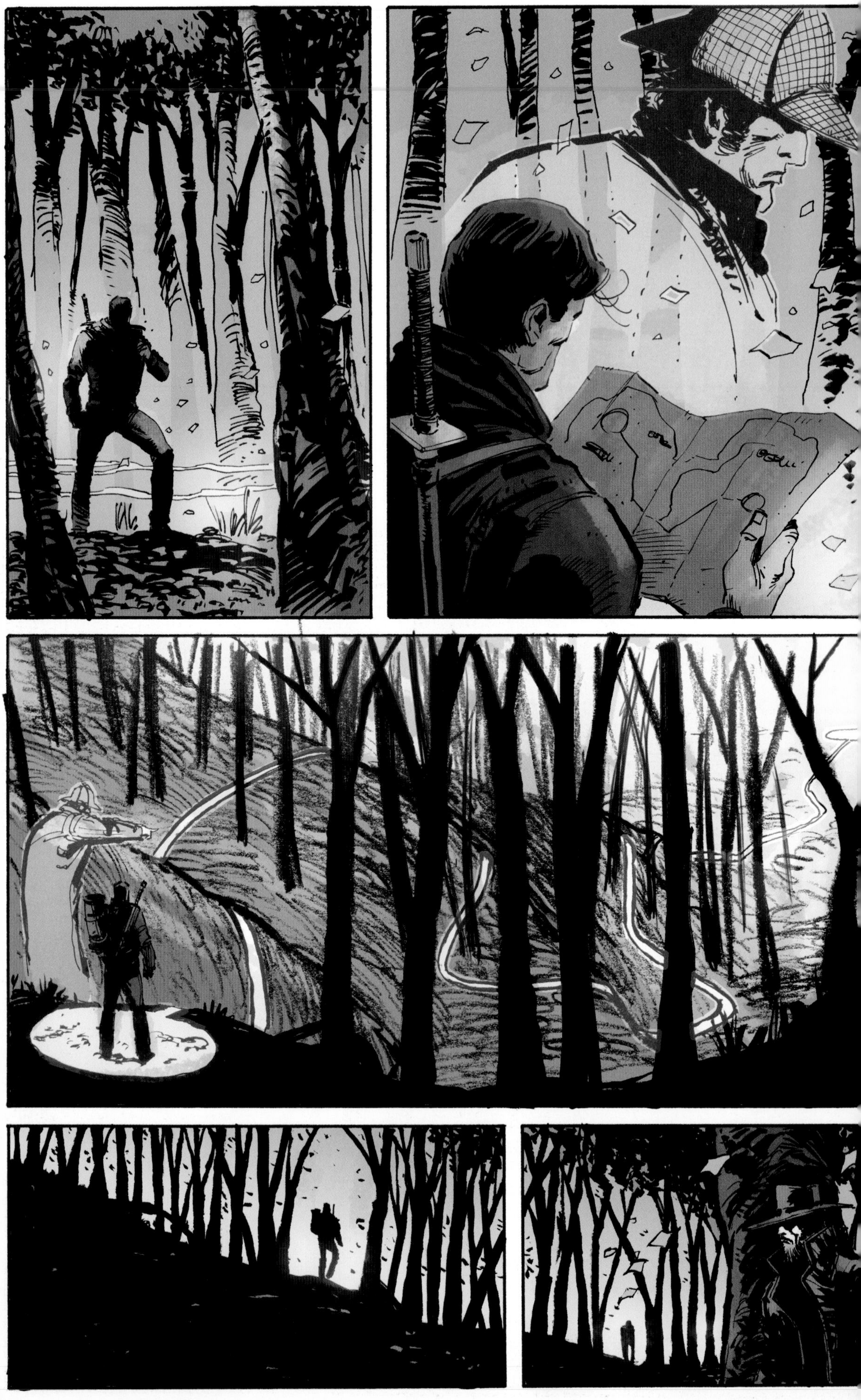

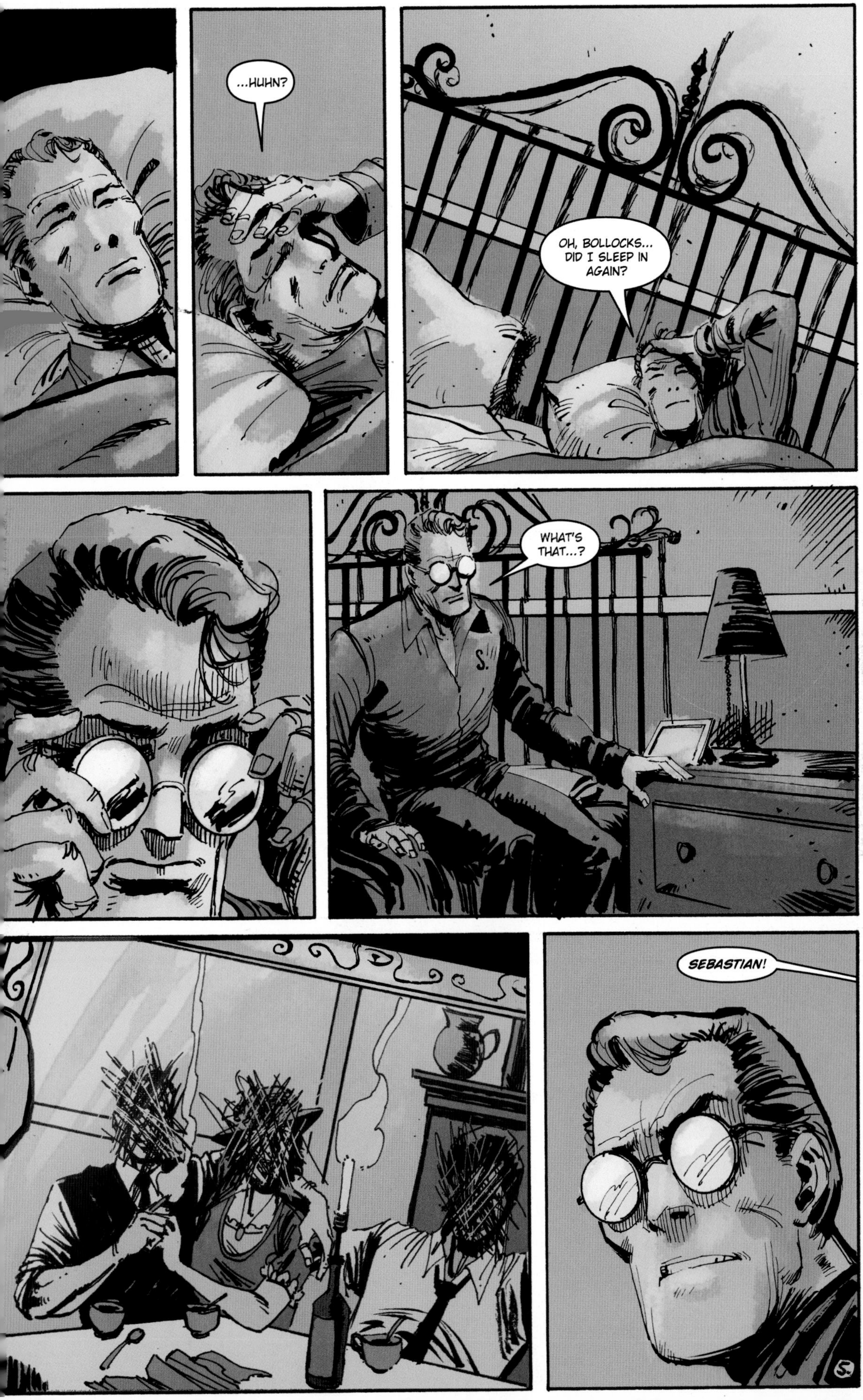
...HUHN?
OH, BOLLOCKS... DID I SLEEP IN AGAIN?
WHAT'S THAT...?
SEBASTIAN!
5.

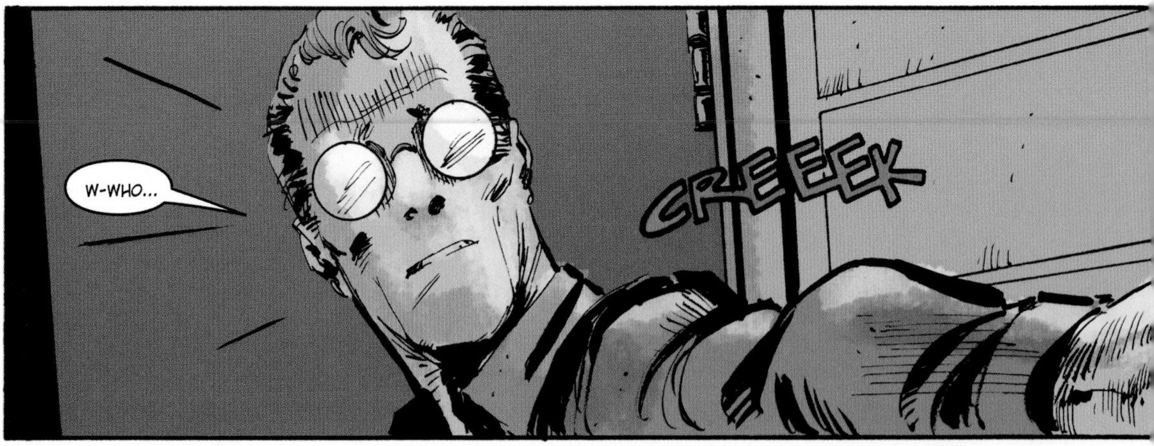
W-WHO...
CREEEK

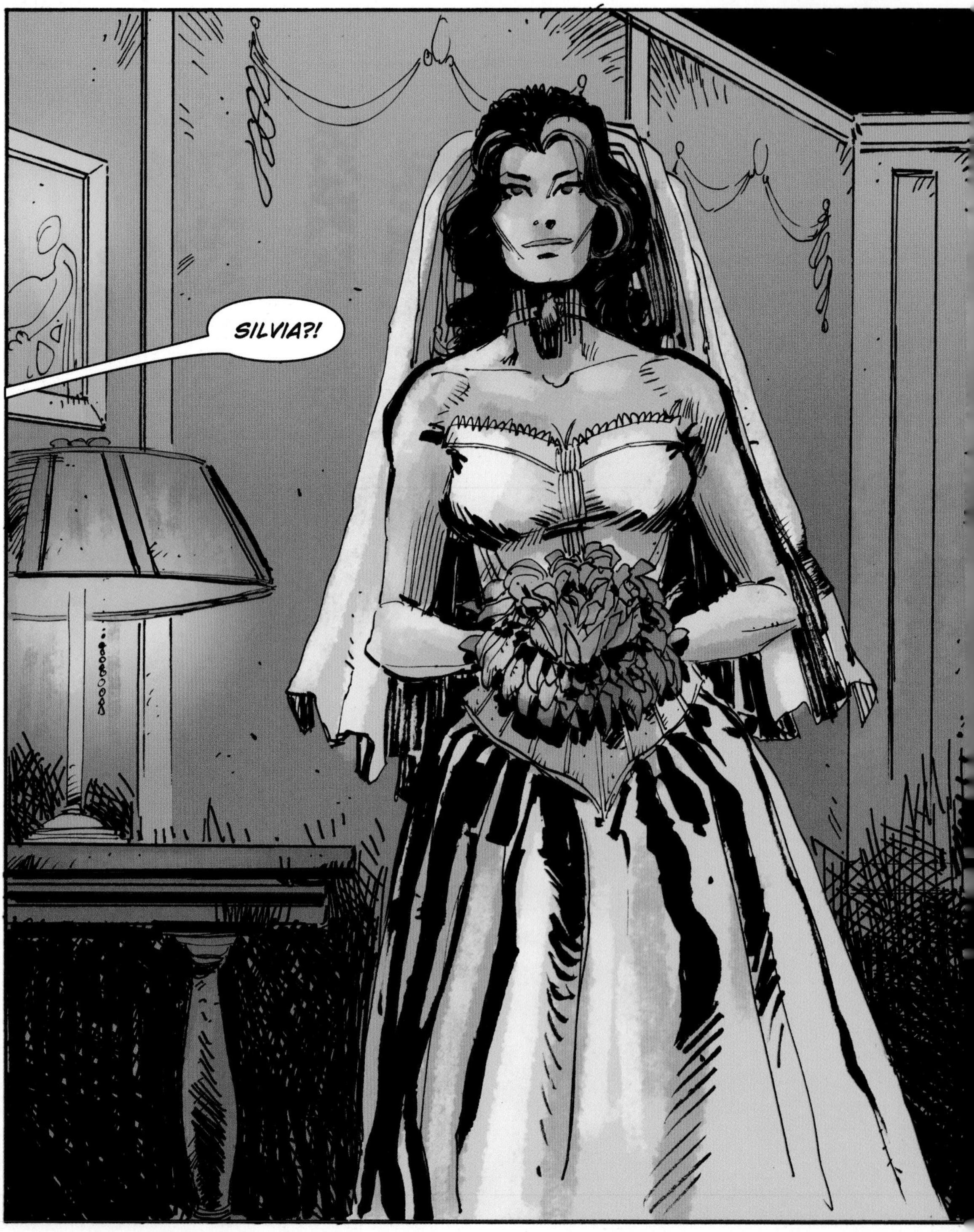
SILVIA?!

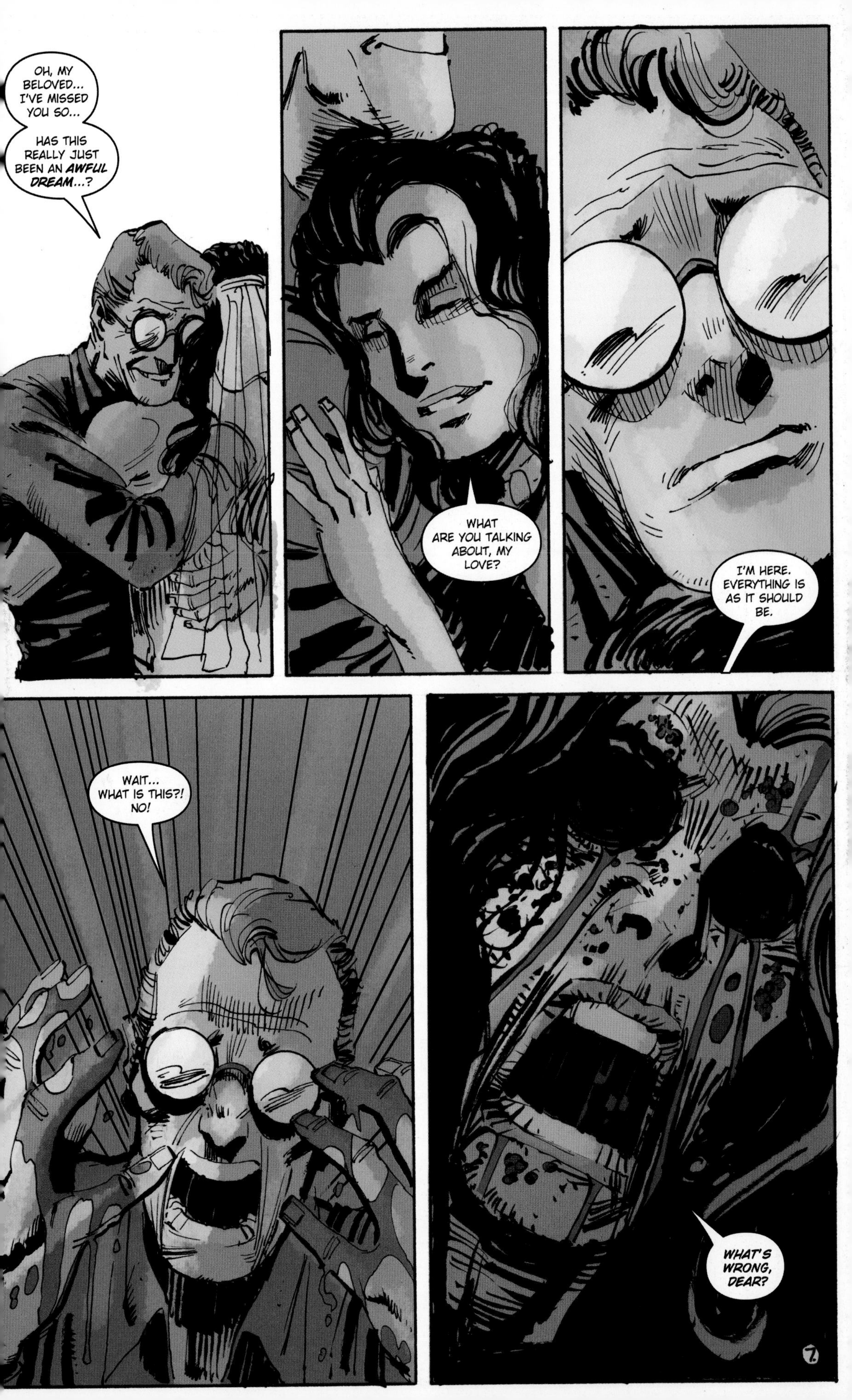
OH, MY BELOVED... I'VE MISSED YOU SO...
HAS THIS REALLY JUST BEEN AN *AWFUL DREAM*...?
WHAT ARE YOU TALKING ABOUT, MY LOVE?
I'M HERE. EVERYTHING IS AS IT SHOULD BE.
WAIT... WHAT IS THIS?! NO!
WHAT'S WRONG, DEAR?
7.

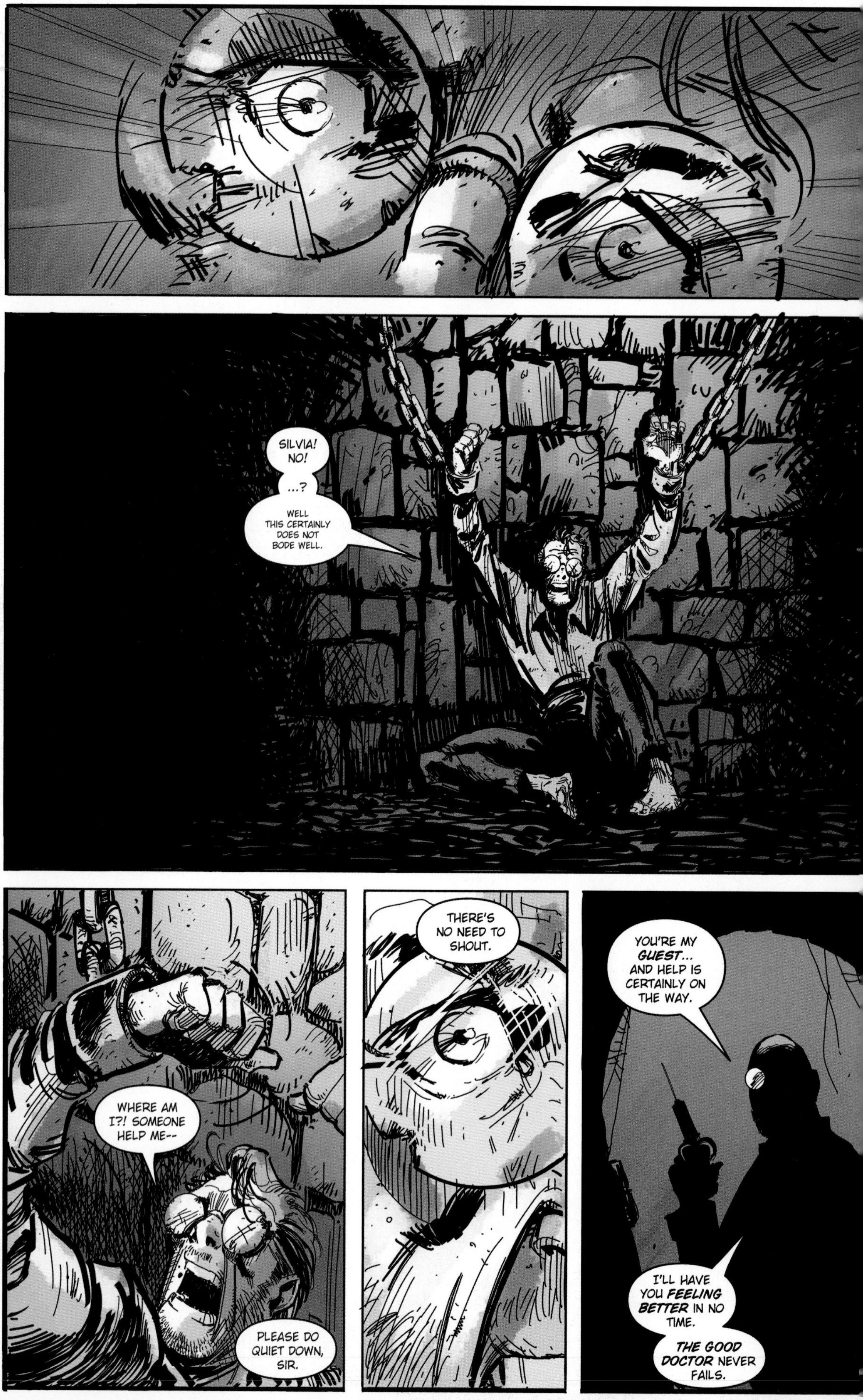
SILVIA! NO!
...?
WELL THIS CERTAINLY DOES NOT BODE WELL.
WHERE AM I?! SOMEONE HELP ME--
PLEASE DO QUIET DOWN, SIR.
THERE'S NO NEED TO SHOUT.
YOU'RE MY GUEST... AND HELP IS CERTAINLY ON THE WAY.
I'LL HAVE YOU FEELING BETTER IN NO TIME.
THE GOOD DOCTOR NEVER FAILS.

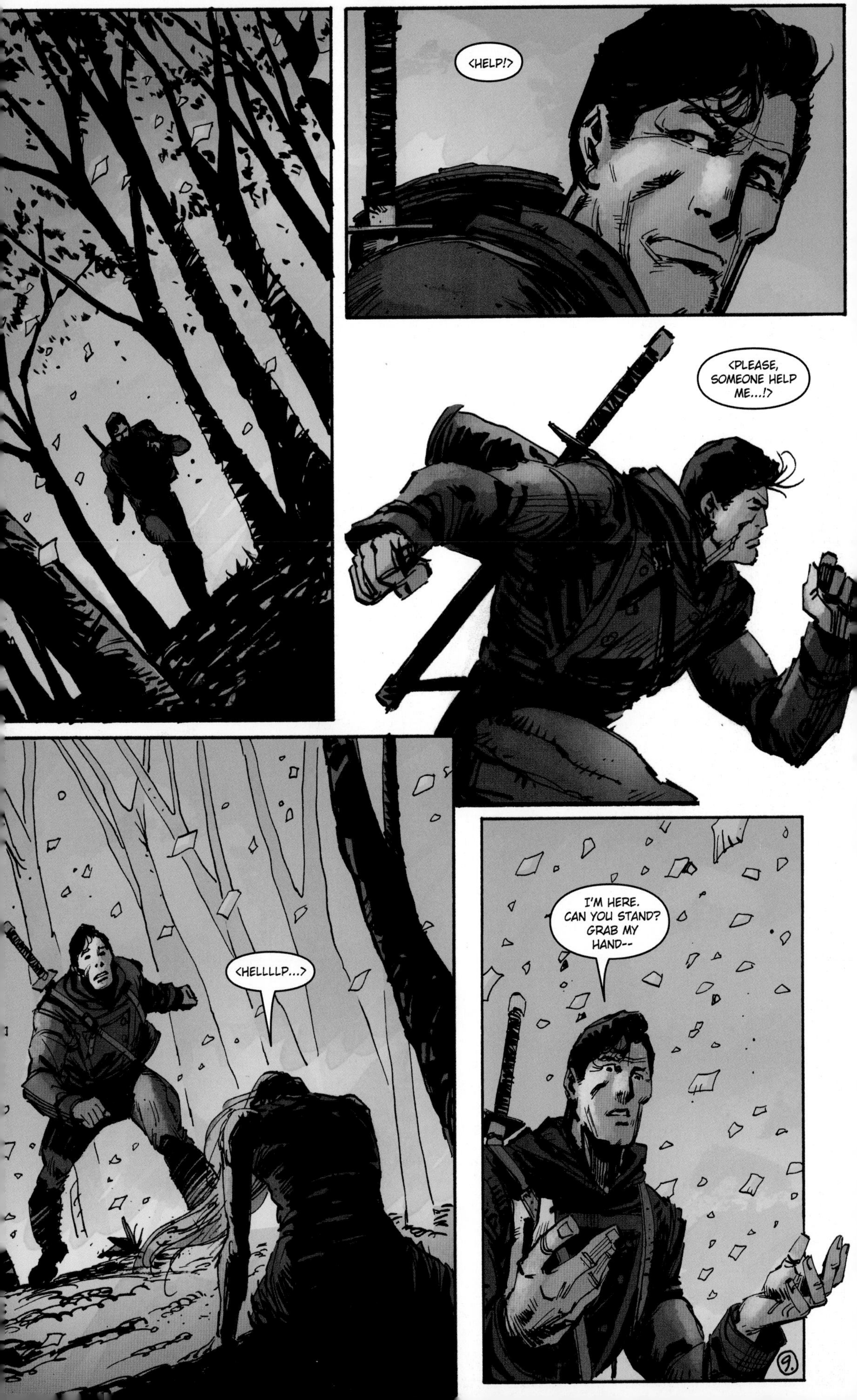
<HELP!>
<PLEASE, SOMEONE HELP ME...!>
<HELLLLP...>
I'M HERE. CAN YOU STAND? GRAB MY HAND--
9.

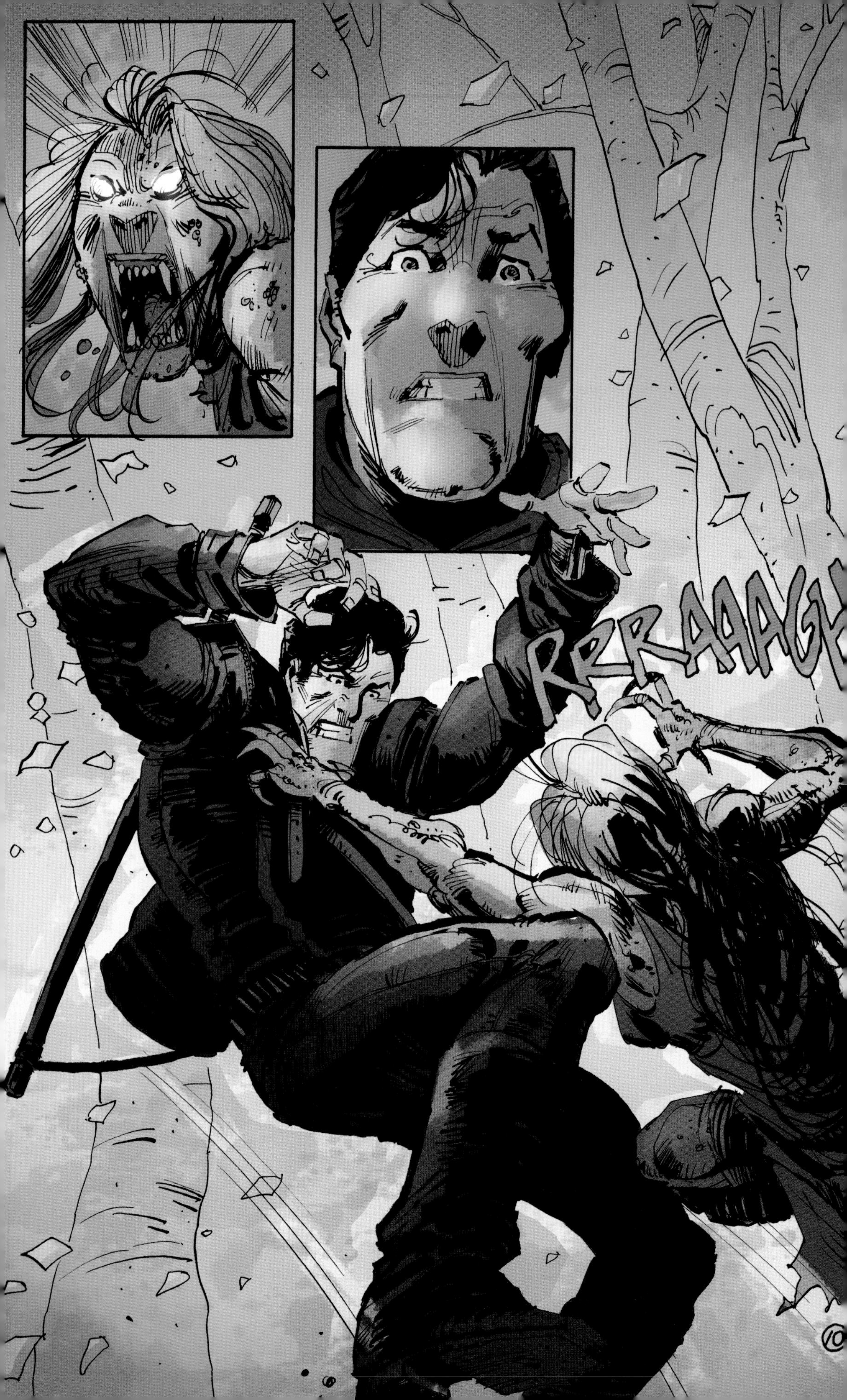
RRRAAAGH

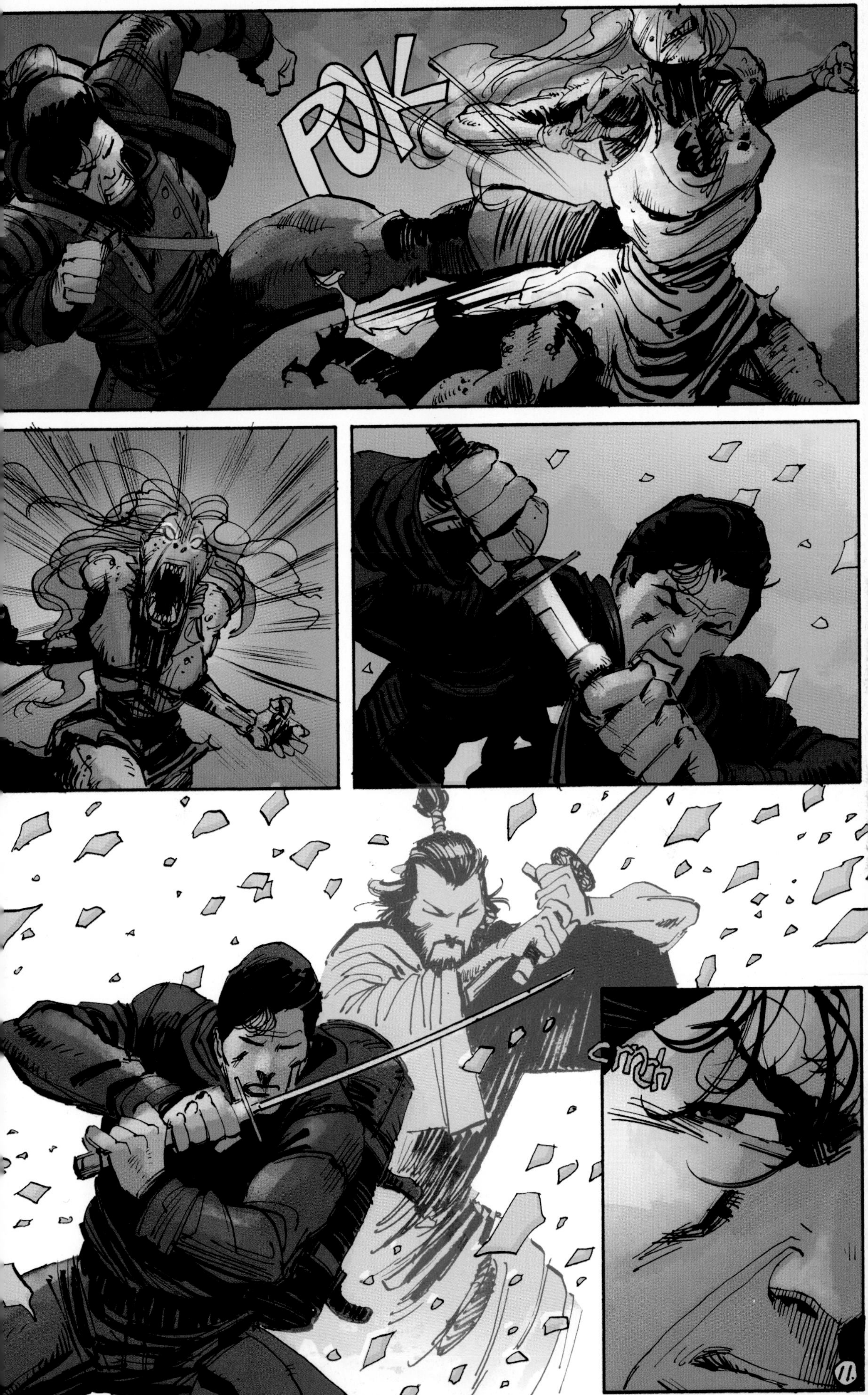
POK
Crnch

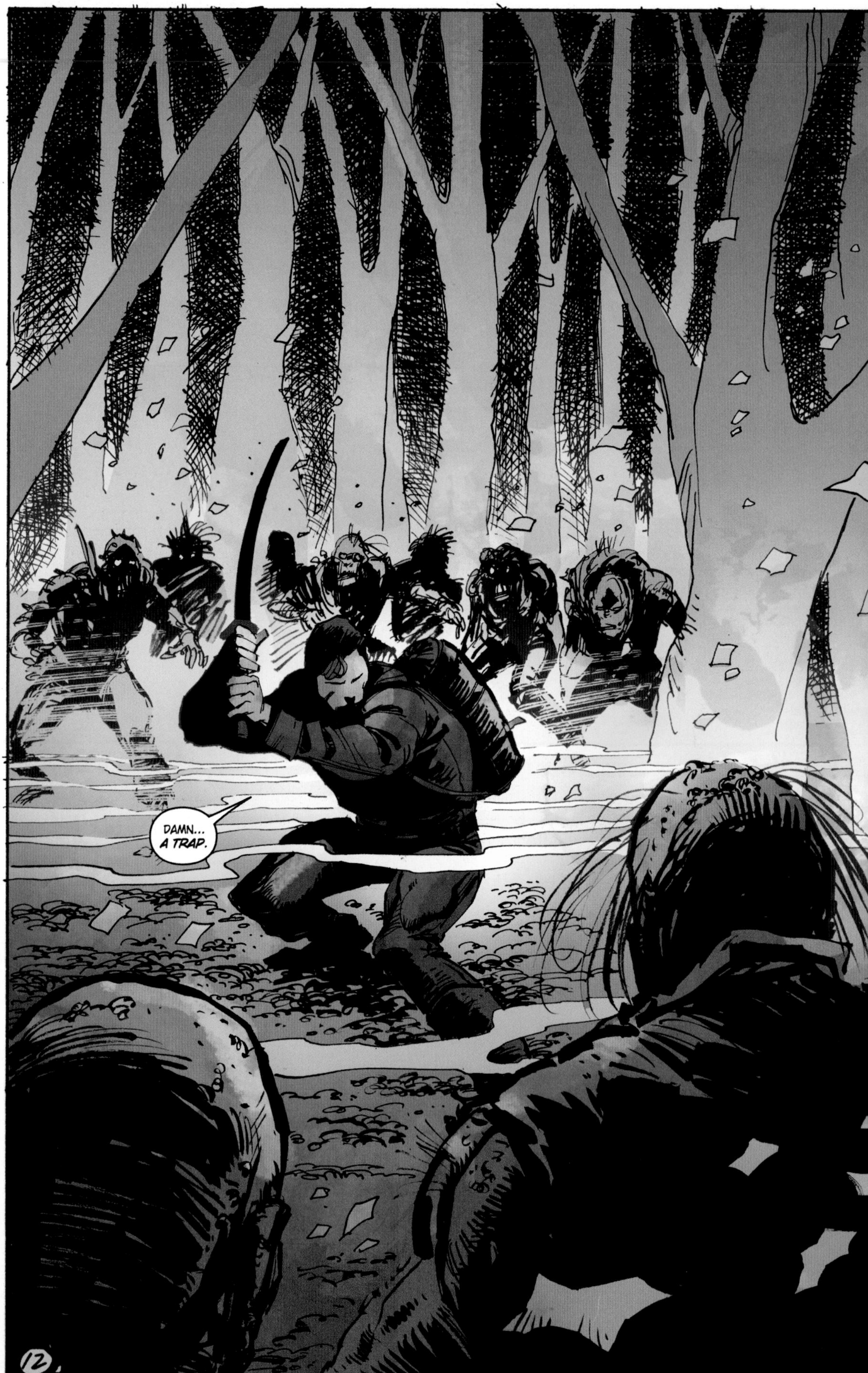
DAMN... A TRAP.

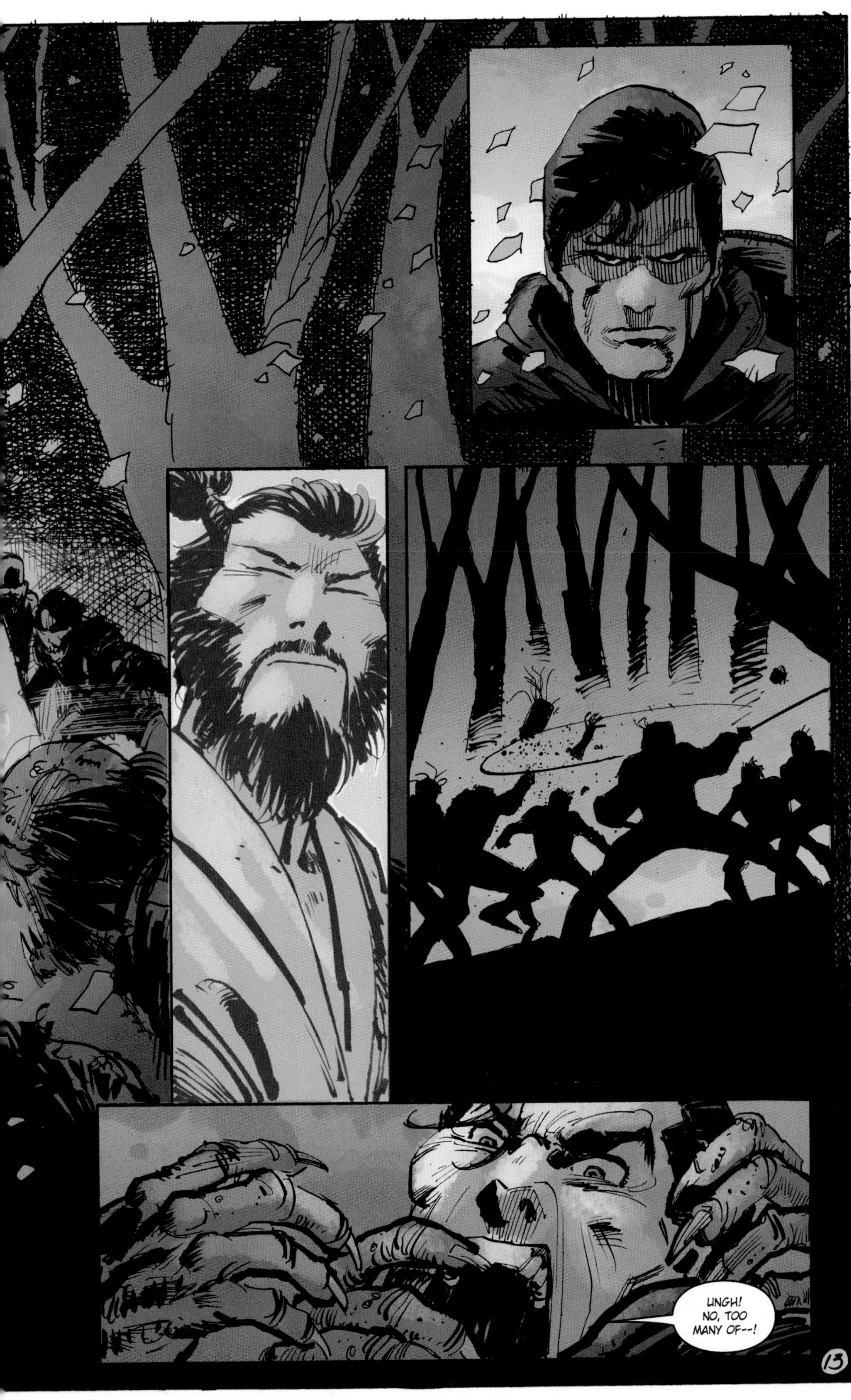
UNGH!
NO, TOO
MANY OF--!

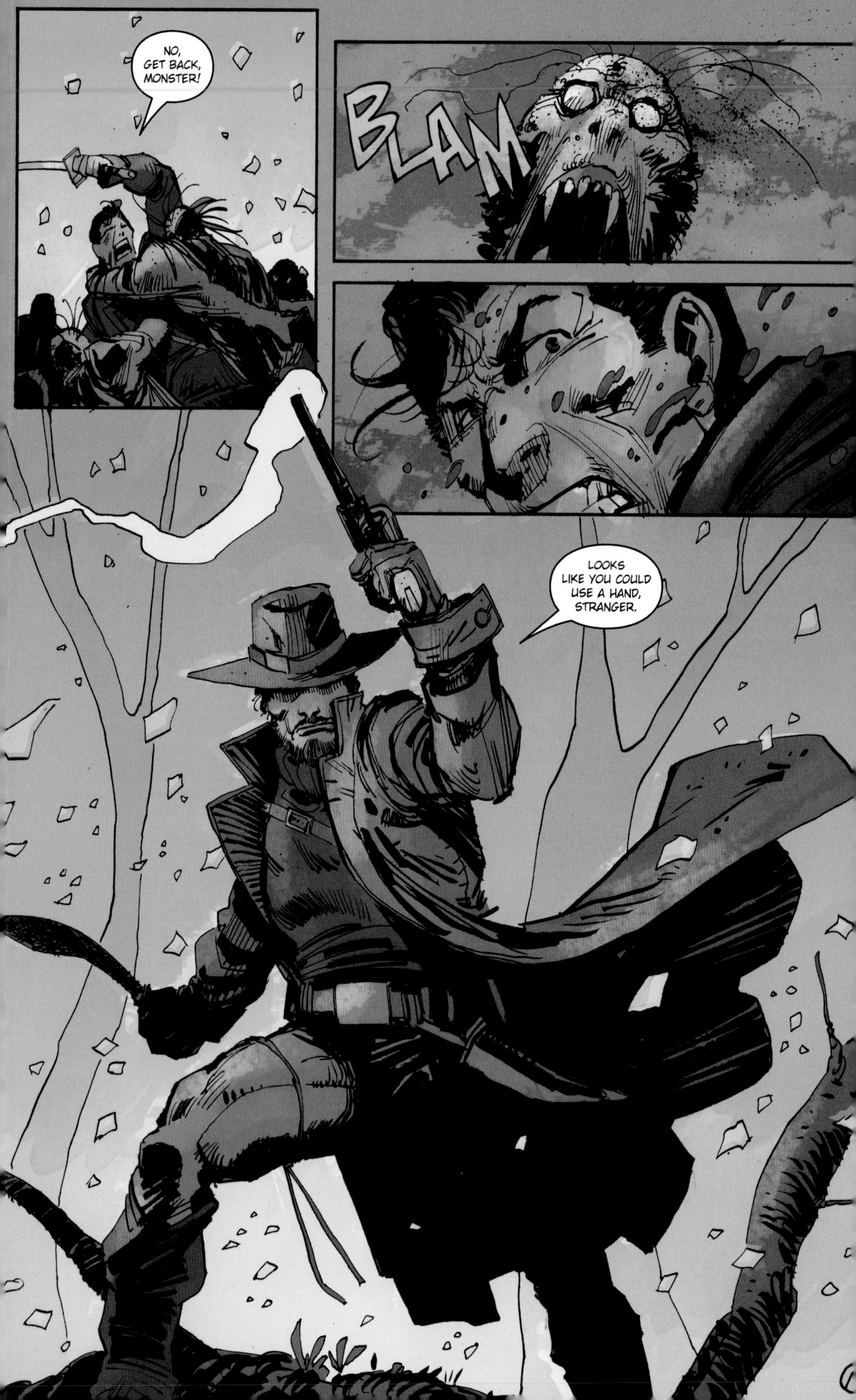
NO, GET BACK, MONSTER!
BLAM
LOOKS LIKE YOU COULD USE A HAND, STRANGER.

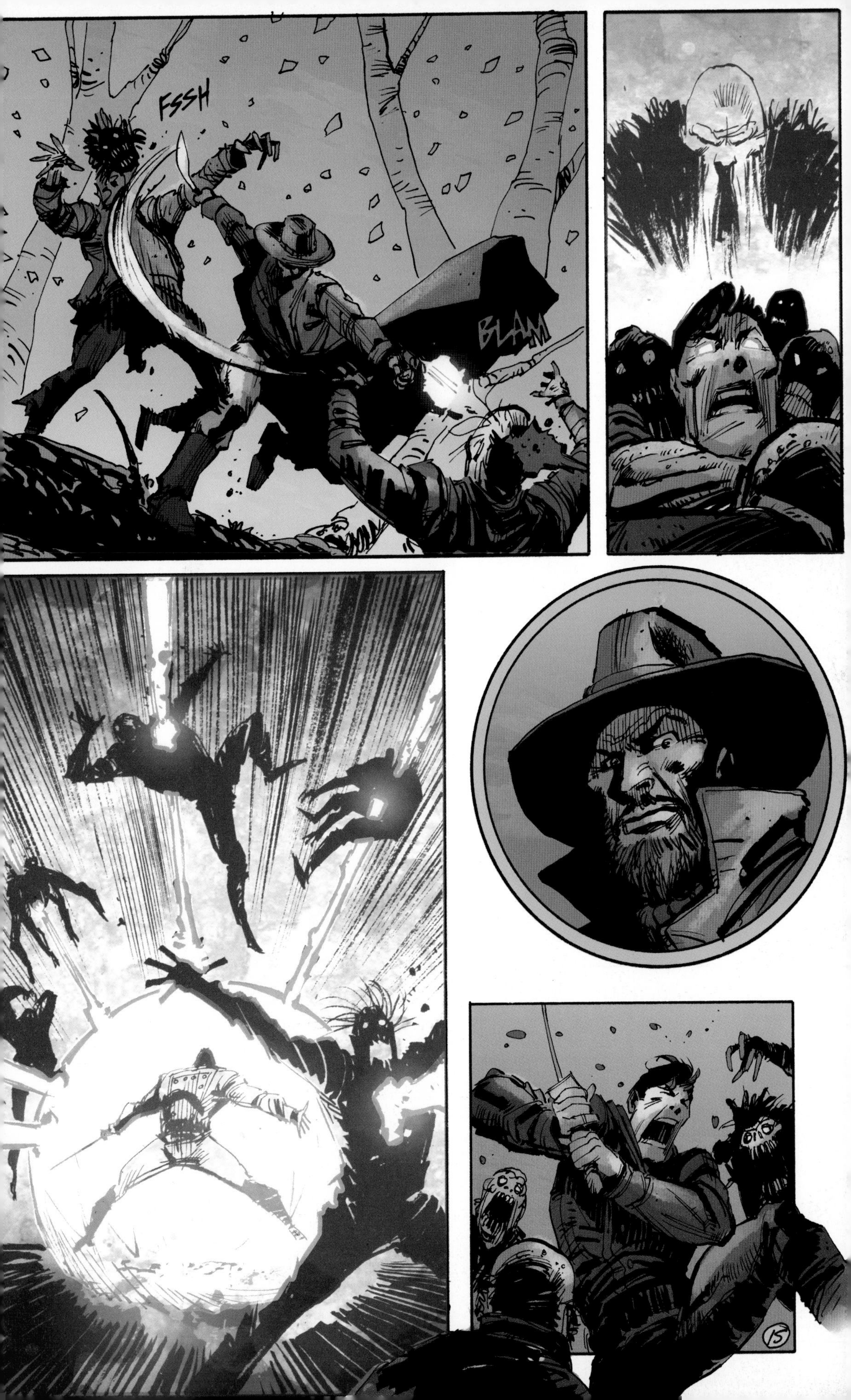
FSSH
BLAM

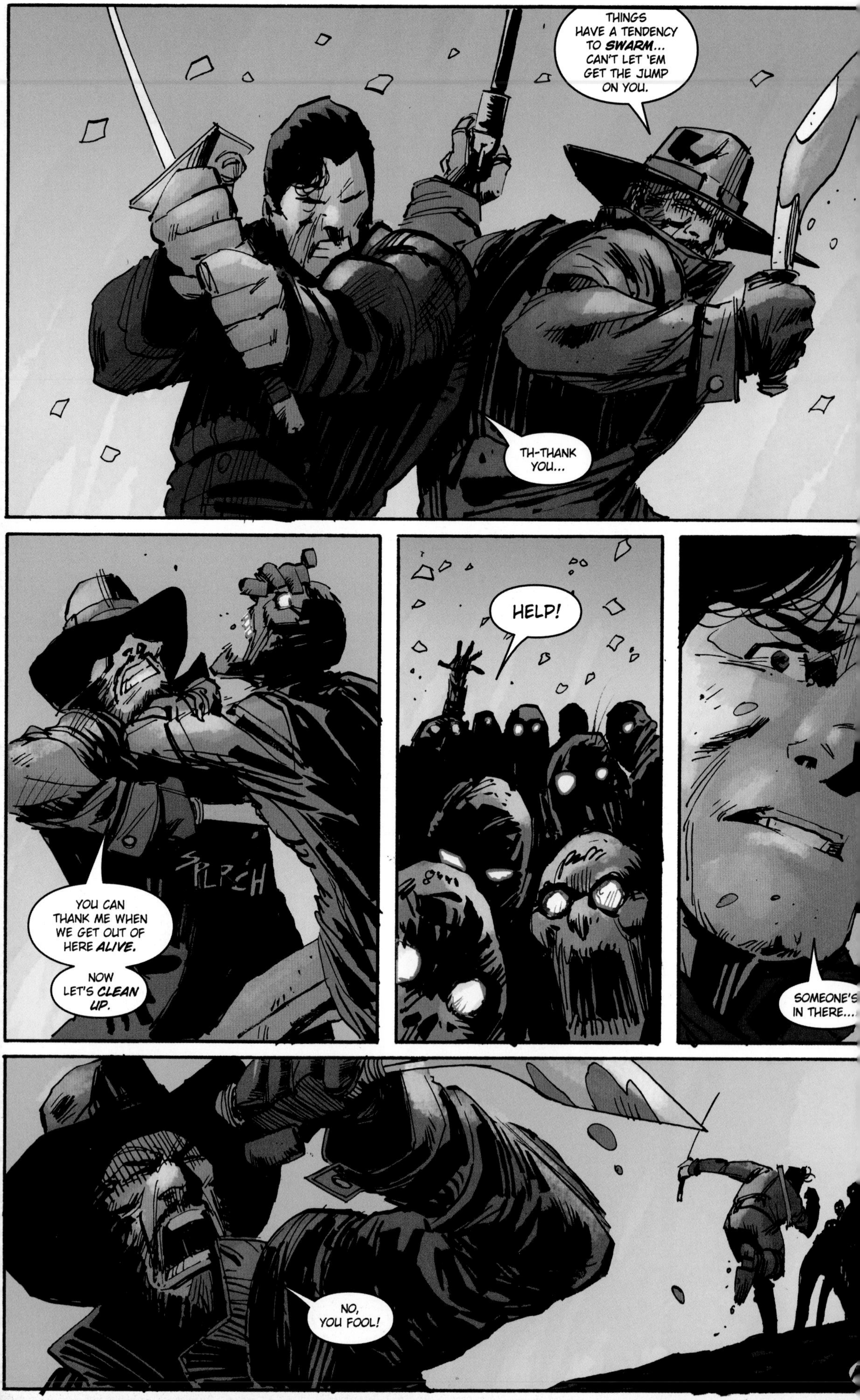
THINGS HAVE A TENDENCY TO SWARM... CAN'T LET 'EM GET THE JUMP ON YOU.
TH-THANK YOU...
SPLRCH
YOU CAN THANK ME WHEN WE GET OUT OF HERE ALIVE.
NOW LET'S CLEAN UP.
HELP!
SOMEONE'S IN THERE...
NO, YOU FOOL!

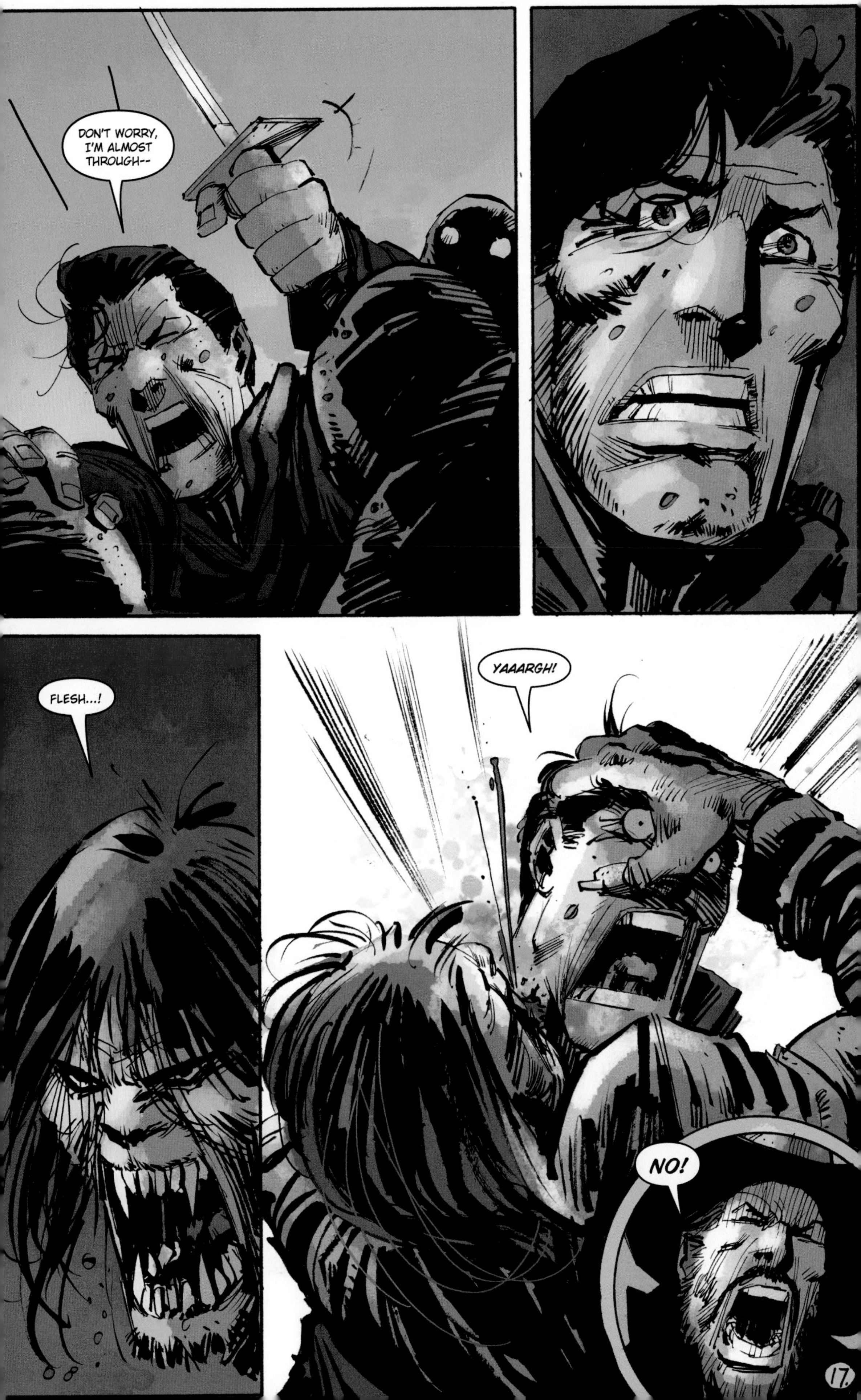
DON'T WORRY, I'M ALMOST THROUGH--
FLESH...!
YAAARGH!
NO!

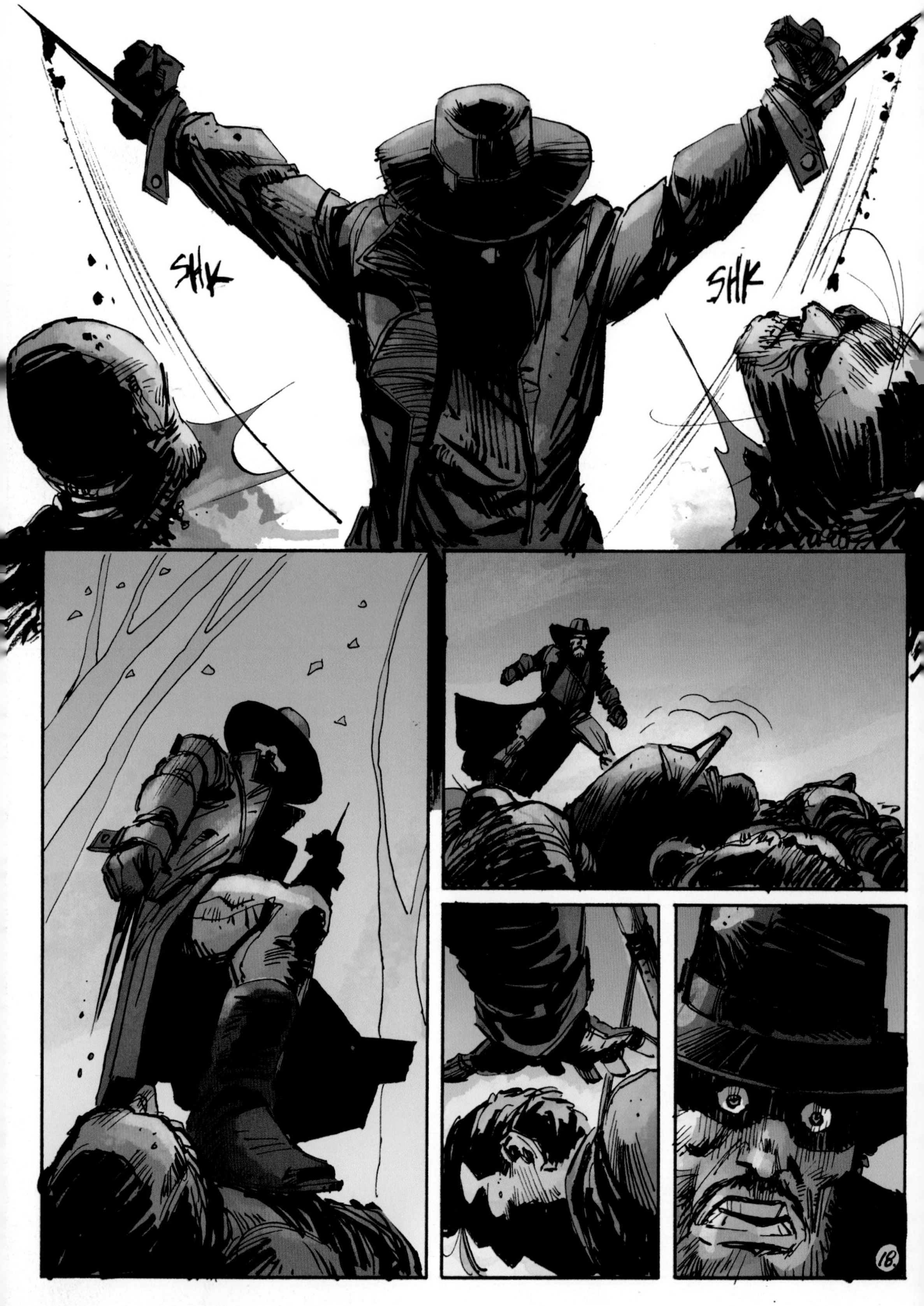
SHK
SHK

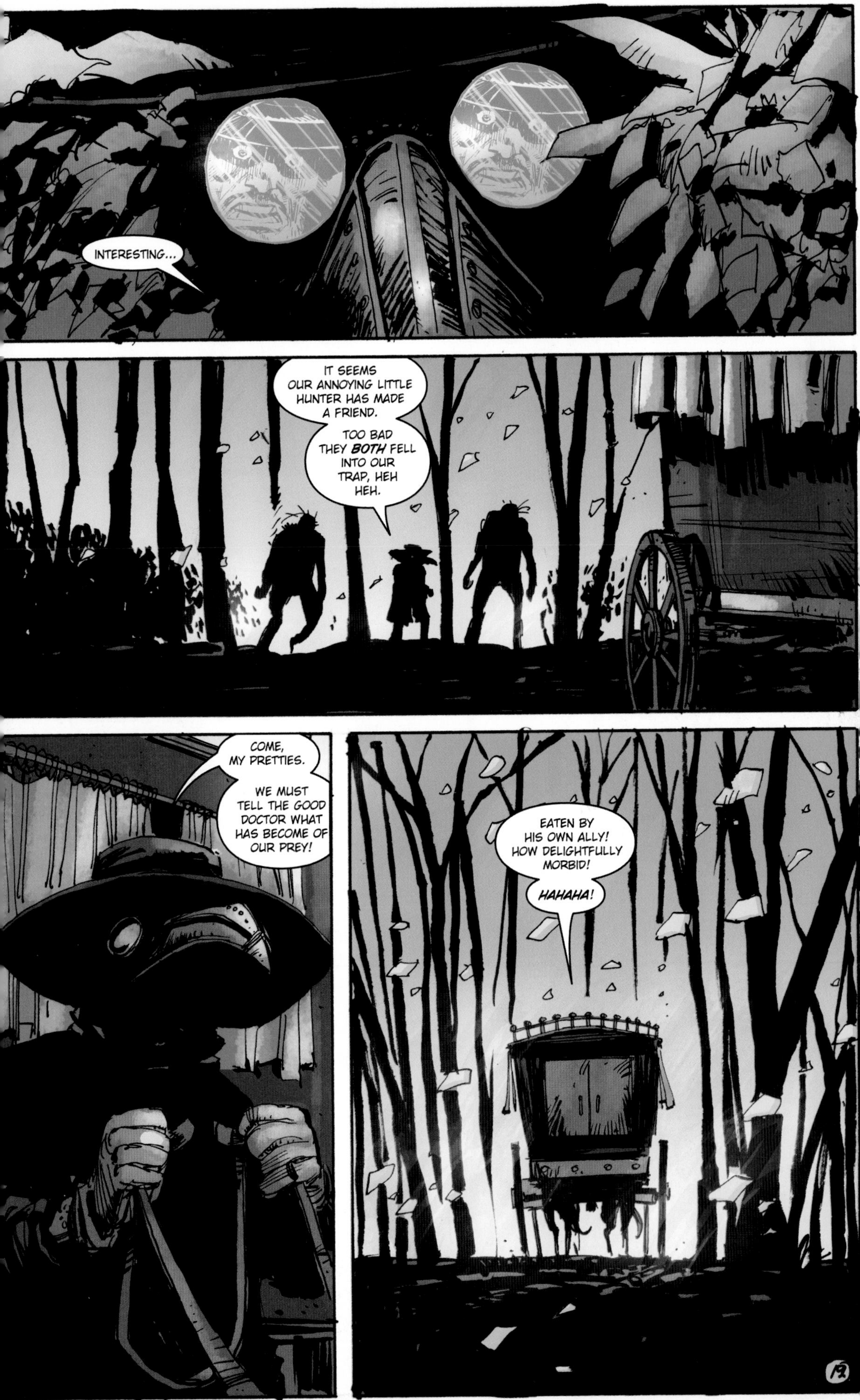
INTERESTING...
IT SEEMS OUR ANNOYING LITTLE HUNTER HAS MADE A FRIEND.
TOO BAD THEY BOTH FELL INTO OUR TRAP, HEH HEH.
COME, MY PRETTIES.
WE MUST TELL THE GOOD DOCTOR WHAT HAS BECOME OF OUR PREY!
EATEN BY HIS OWN ALLY! HOW DELIGHTFULLY MORBID!
HAHAHA!

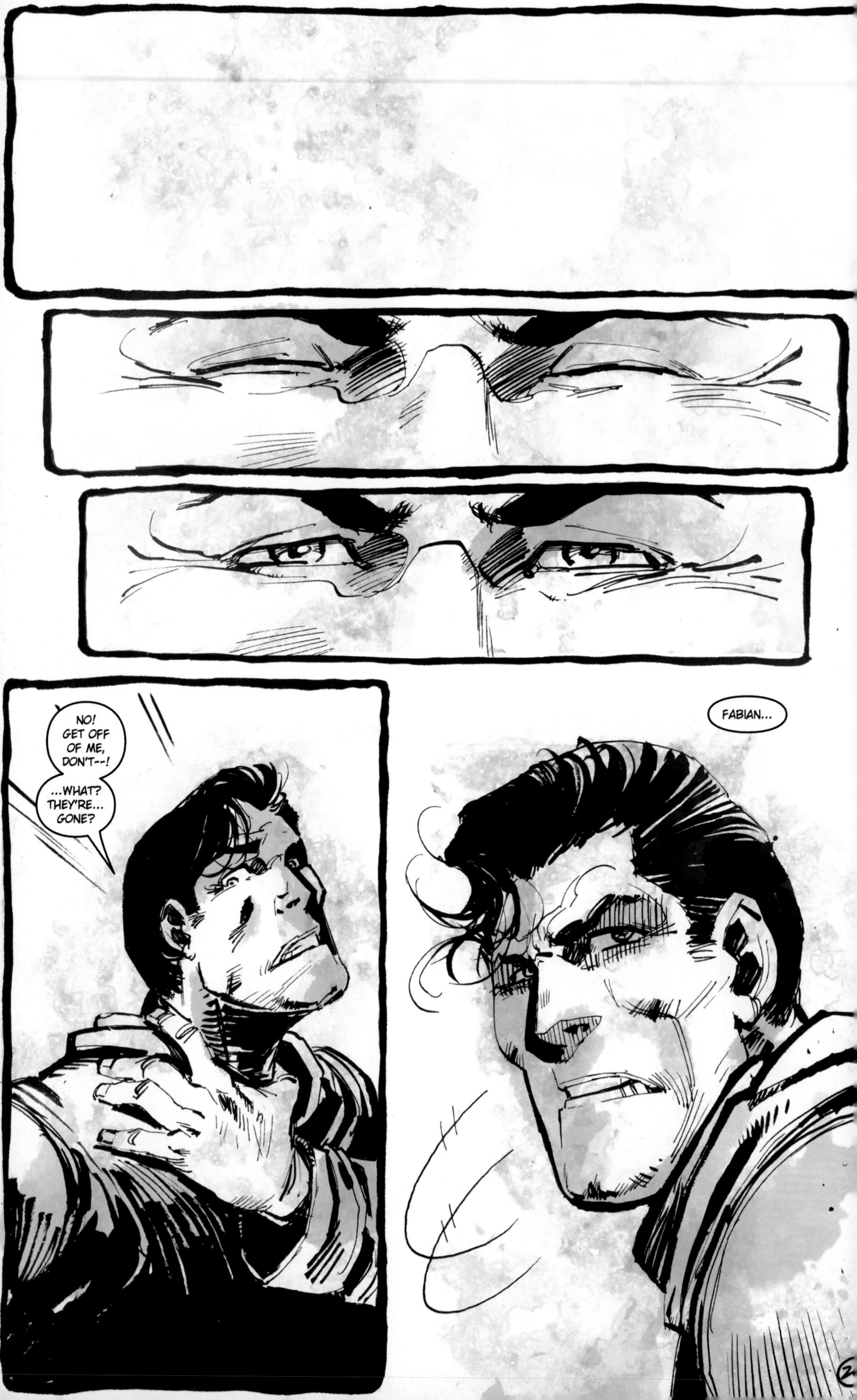
NO! GET OFF OF ME, DON'T--!
...WHAT? THEY'RE... GONE?
FABIAN...

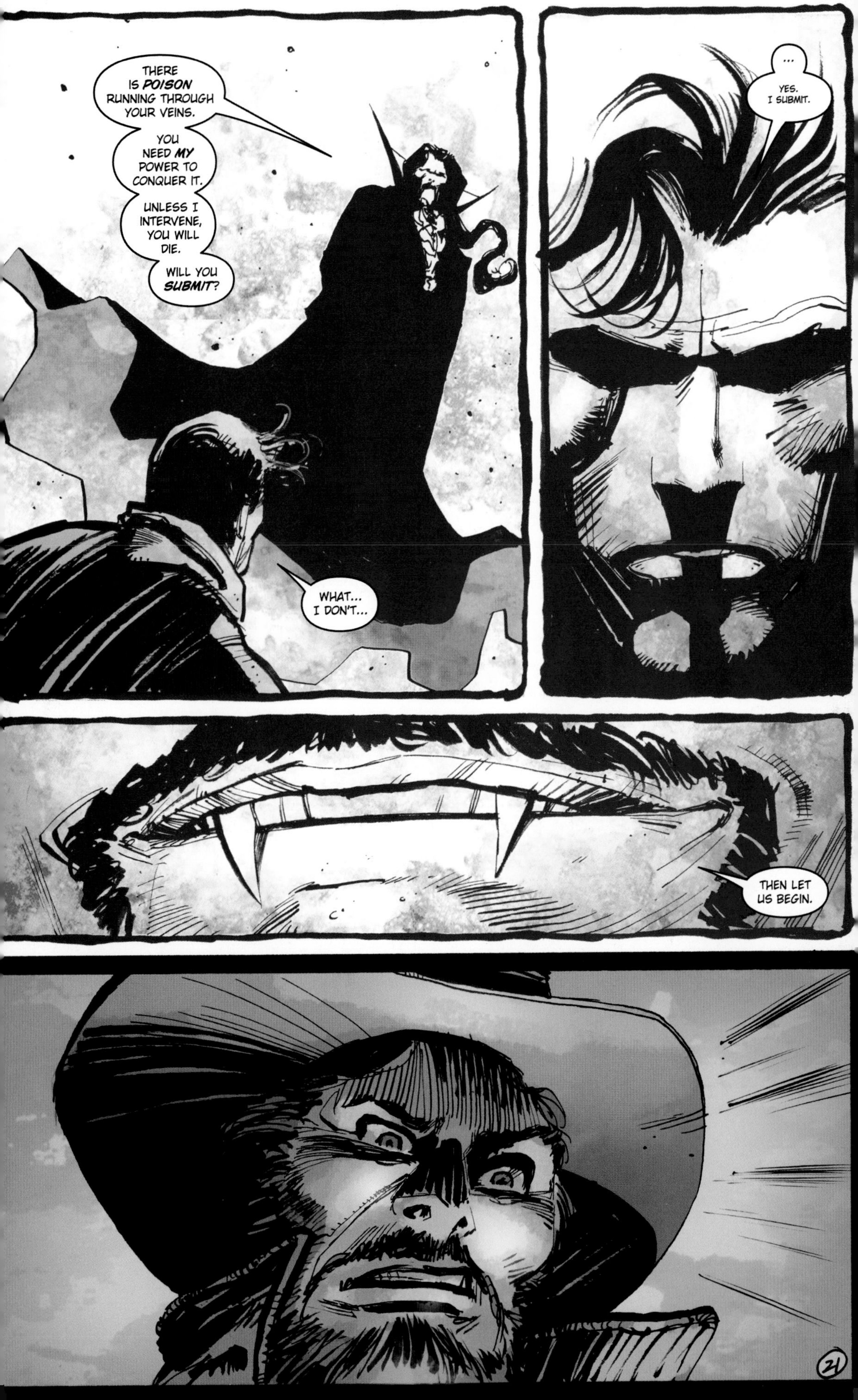
THERE IS POISON RUNNING THROUGH YOUR VEINS.
YOU NEED MY POWER TO CONQUER IT.
UNLESS I INTERVENE, YOU WILL DIE.
WILL YOU SUBMIT?
WHAT... I DON'T...
...
YES. I SUBMIT.
THEN LET US BEGIN.
21

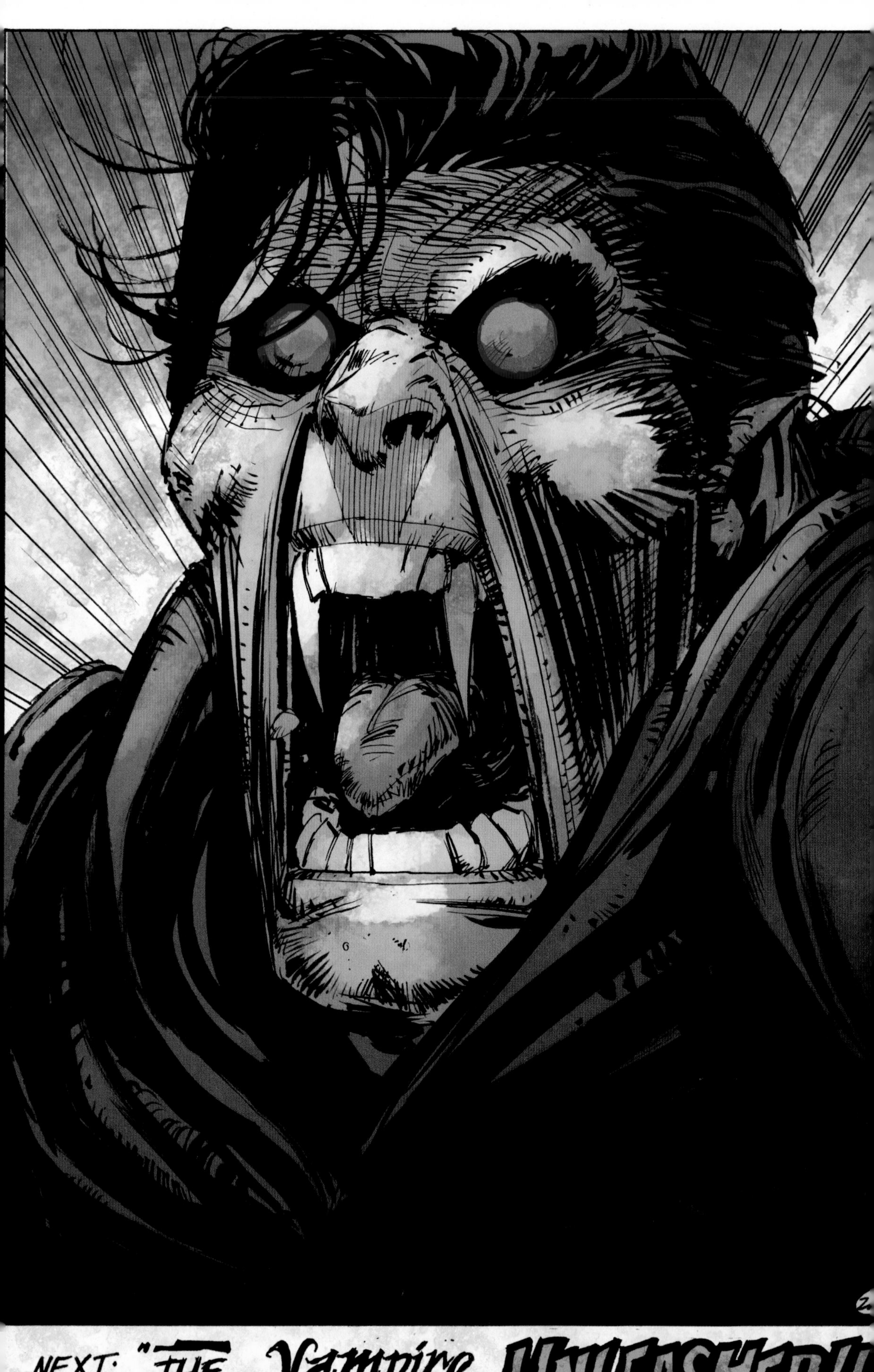

NEXT: "THE Vampire UNLEASHED!!

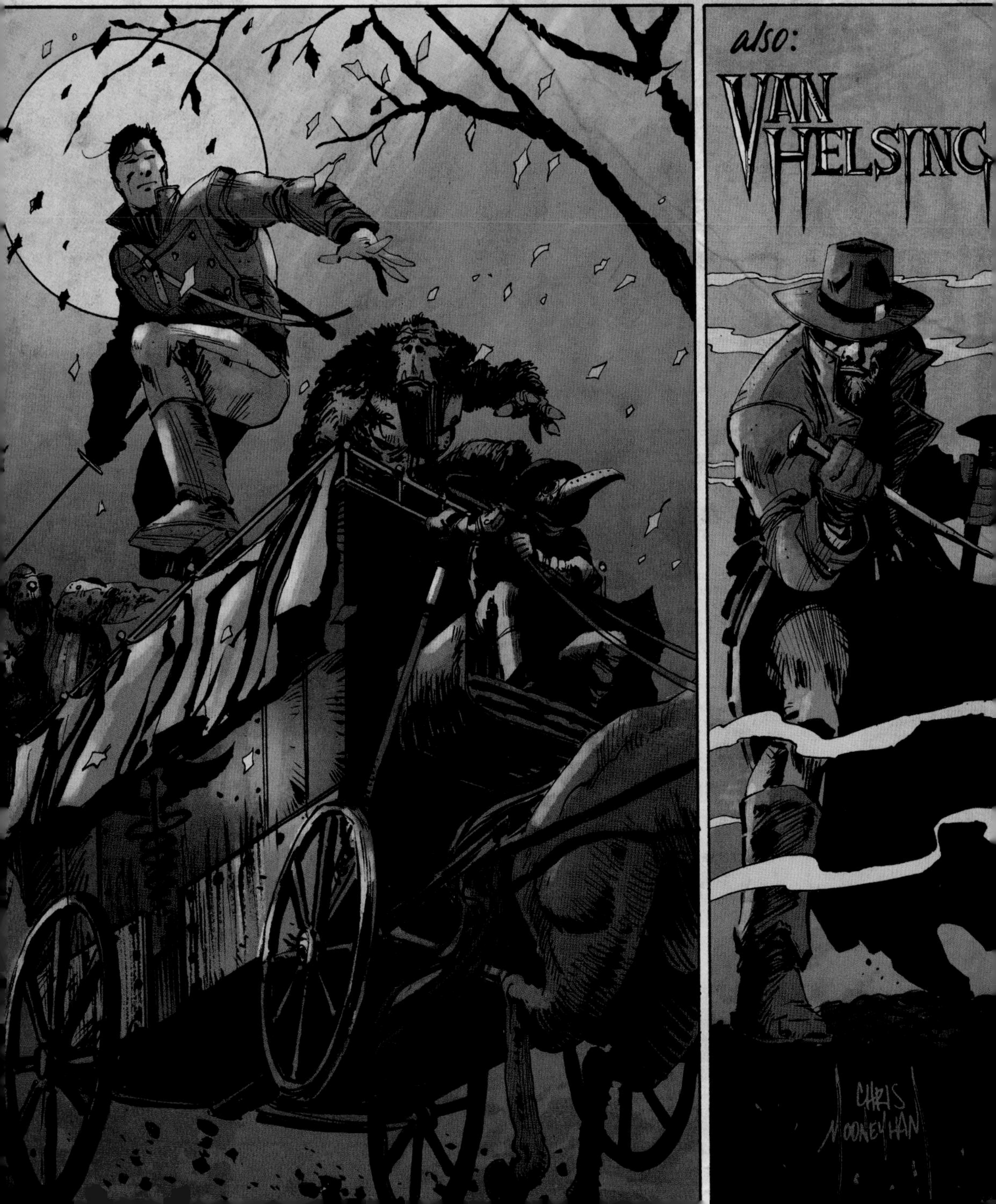
also:
VAN HELSING
CHRIS MOONEYHAN

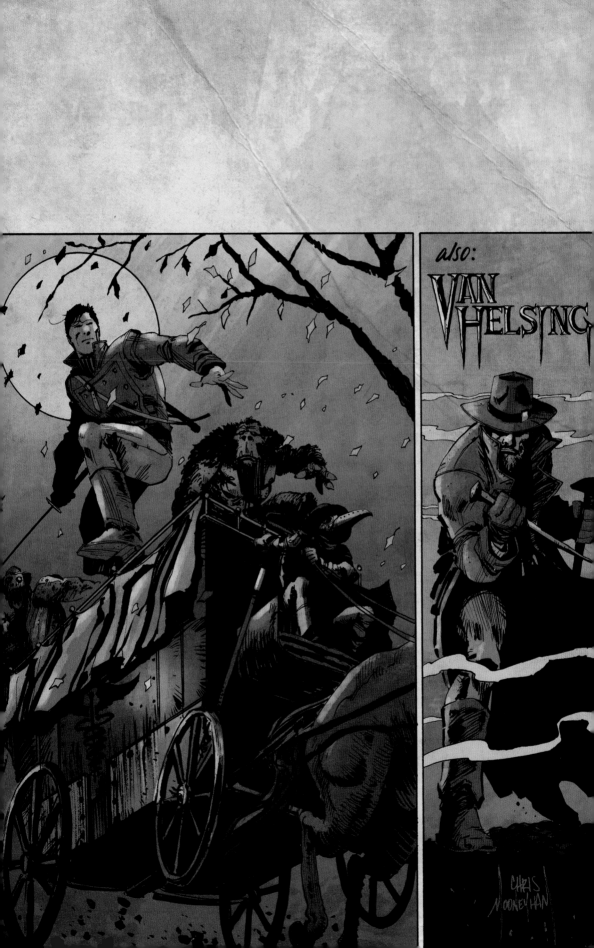

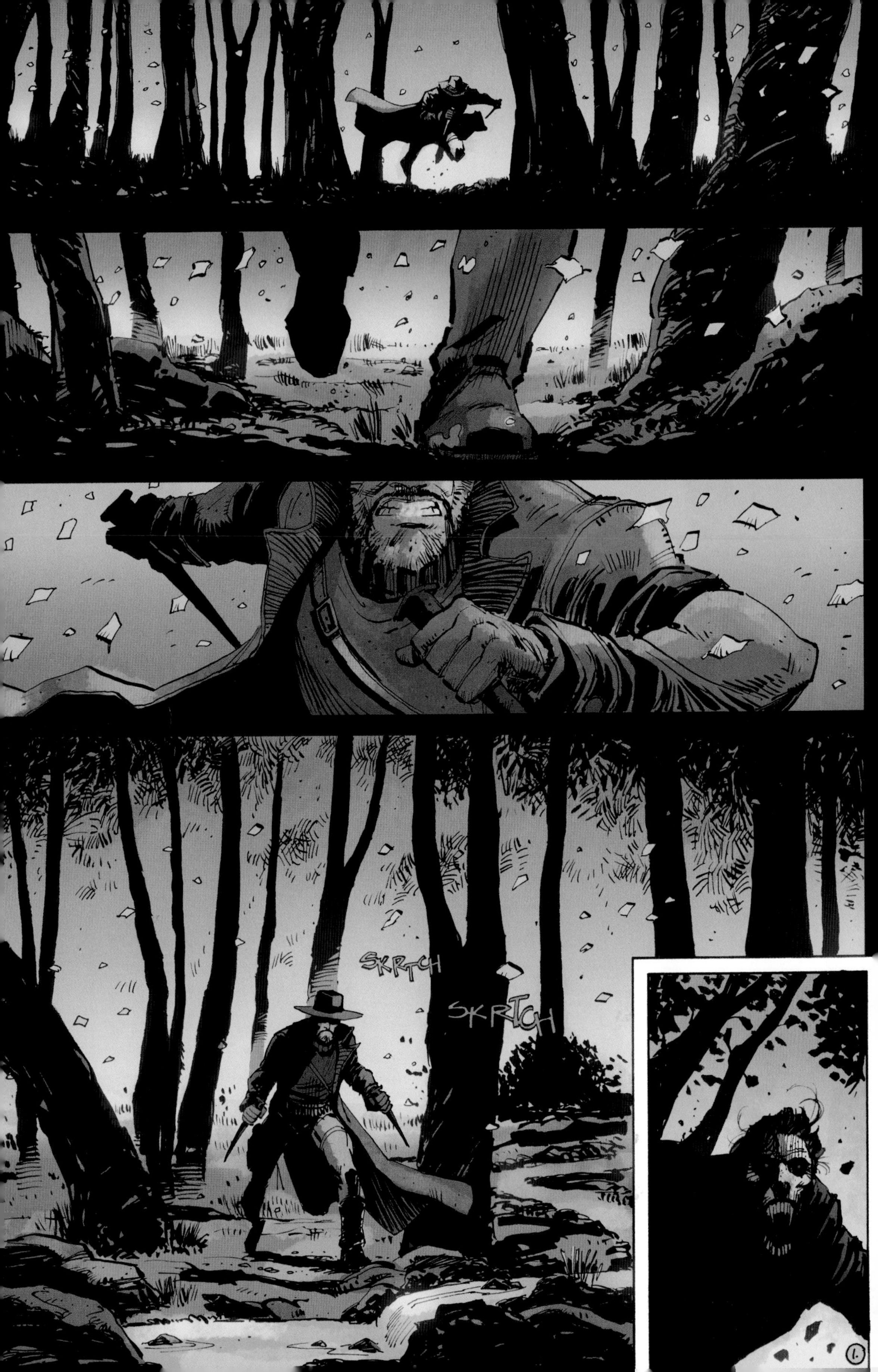
SKRTCH
SKRTCH
1.

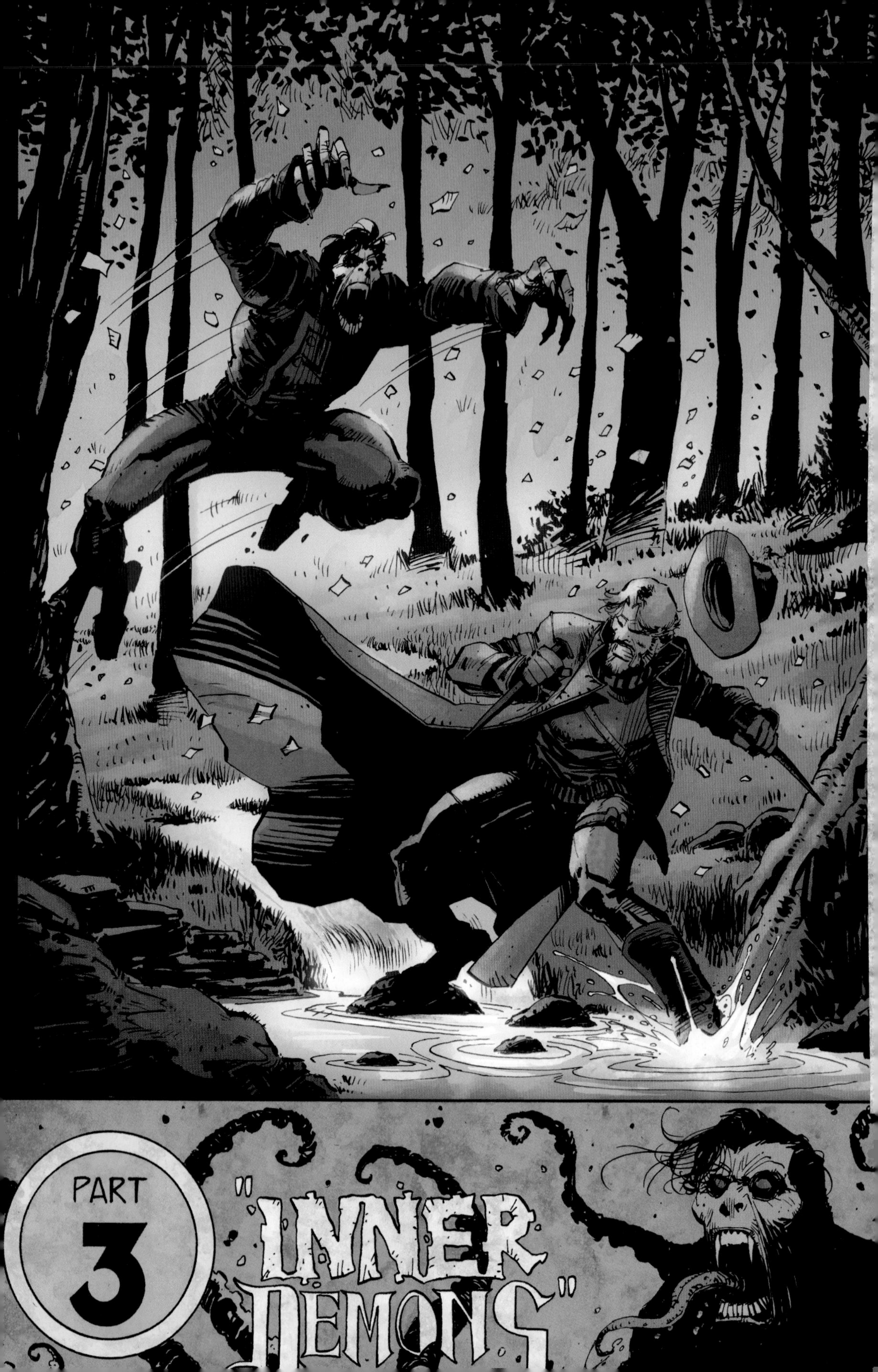
PART
3
"INNER
DEMONS"

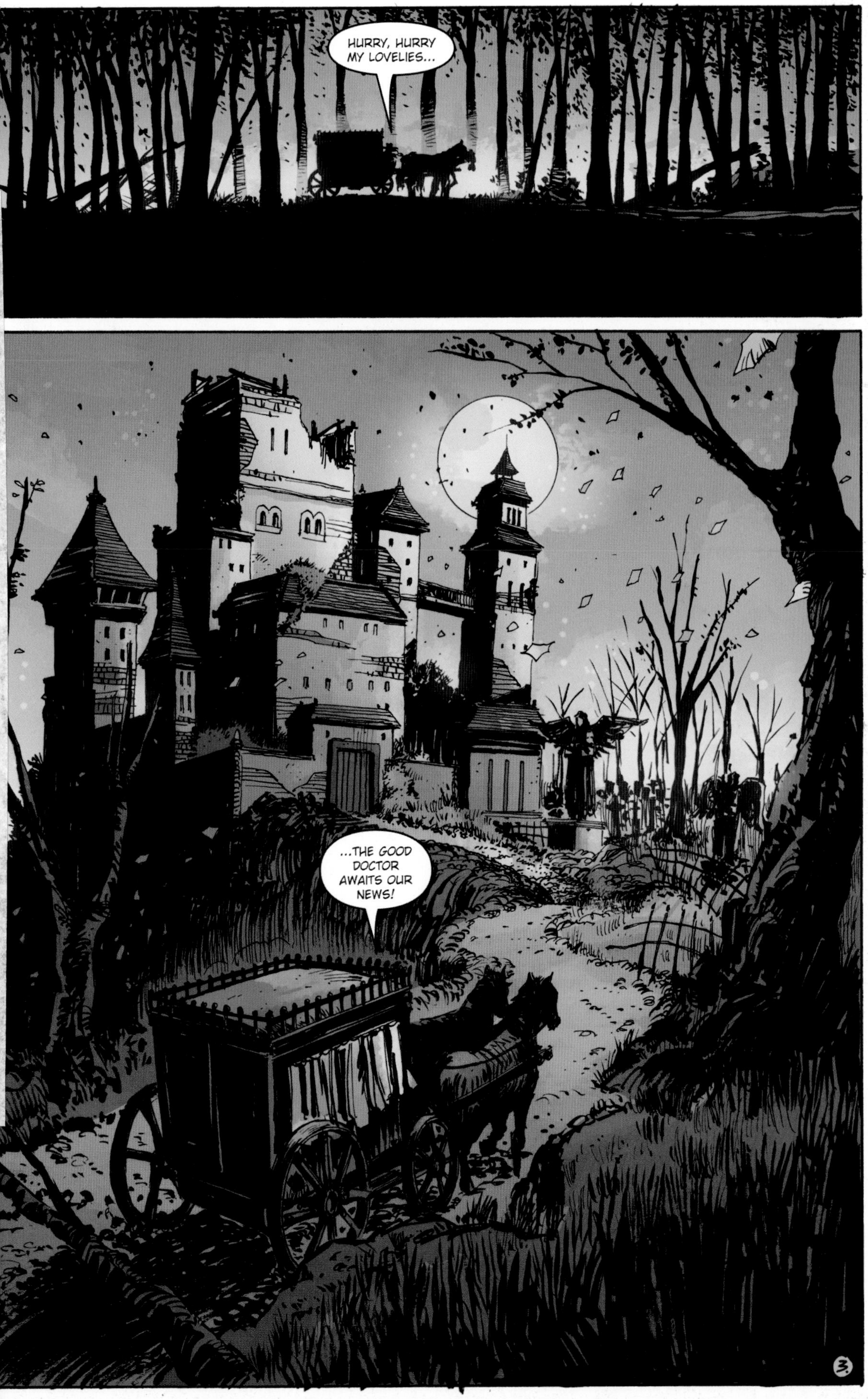
HURRY, HURRY MY LOVELIES...
...THE GOOD DOCTOR AWAITS OUR NEWS!

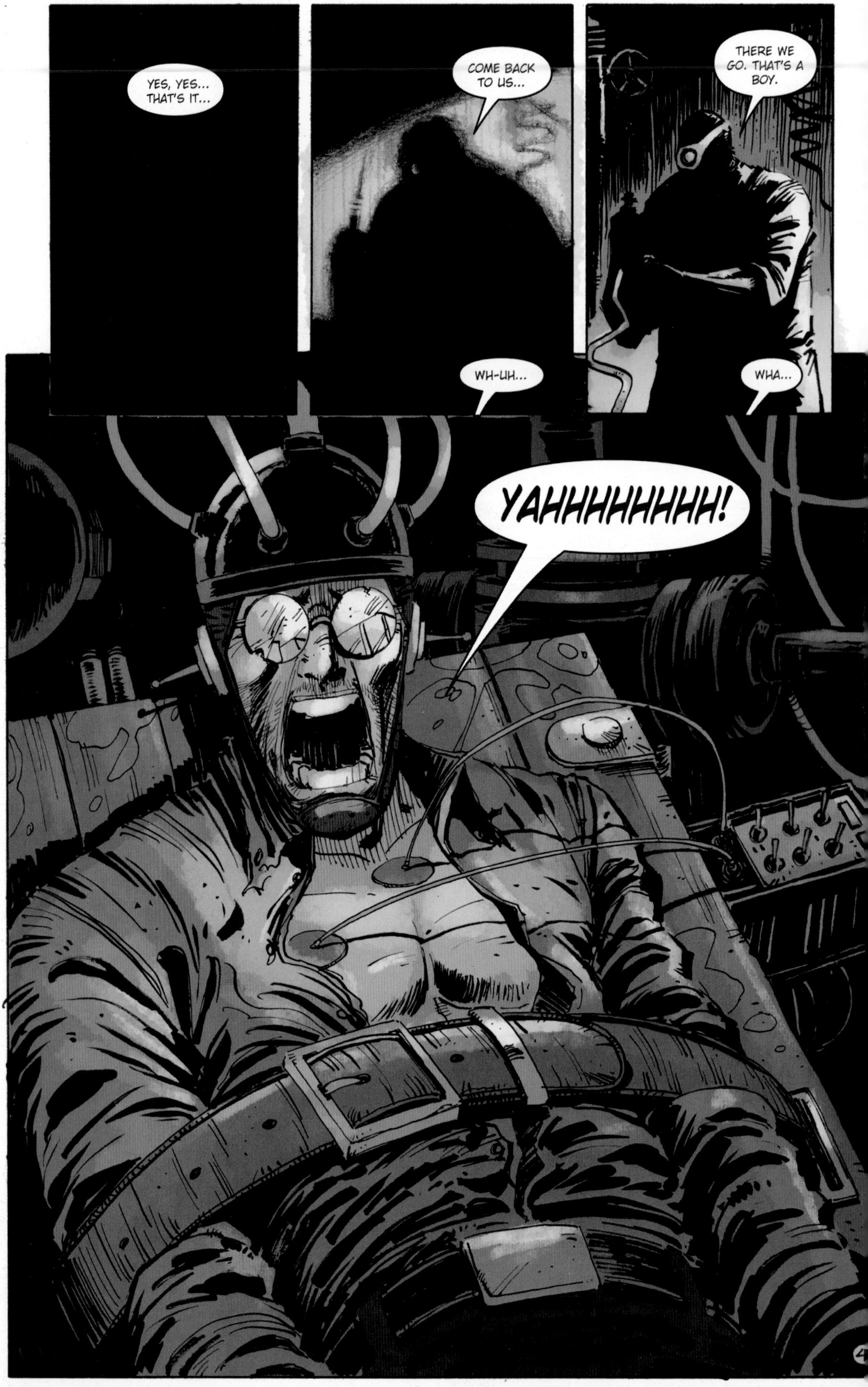
YES, YES... THAT'S IT...
COME BACK TO US...
WH-UH...
THERE WE GO. THAT'S A BOY.
WHA...
YAHHHHHHHH!

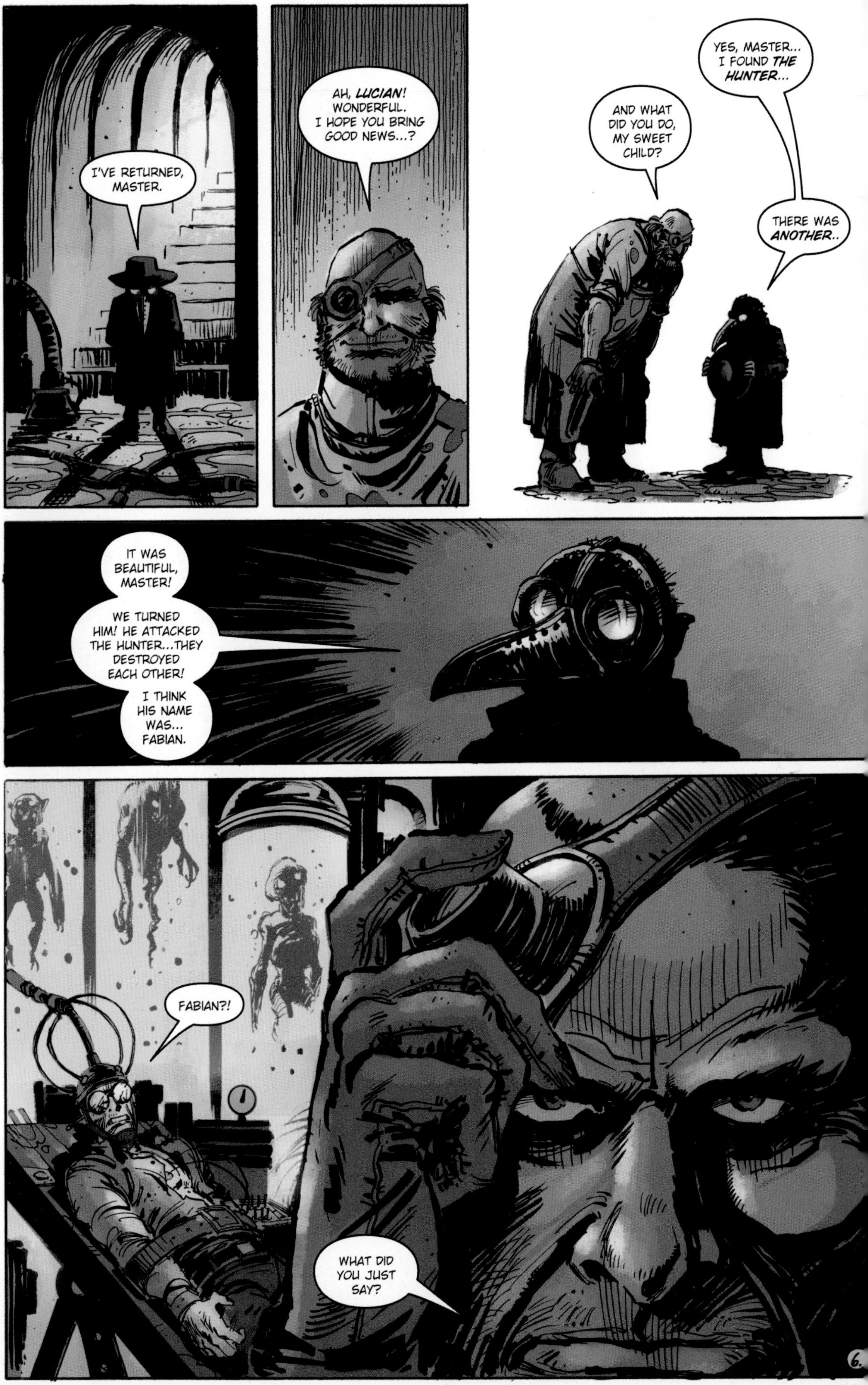
I'VE RETURNED, MASTER.
AH, *LUCIAN*! WONDERFUL. I HOPE YOU BRING GOOD NEWS...?
YES, MASTER... I FOUND *THE HUNTER*...
AND WHAT DID YOU DO, MY SWEET CHILD?
THERE WAS *ANOTHER*..
IT WAS BEAUTIFUL, MASTER!
WE TURNED HIM! HE ATTACKED THE HUNTER...THEY DESTROYED EACH OTHER!
I THINK HIS NAME WAS... FABIAN.
FABIAN?!
WHAT DID YOU JUST SAY?

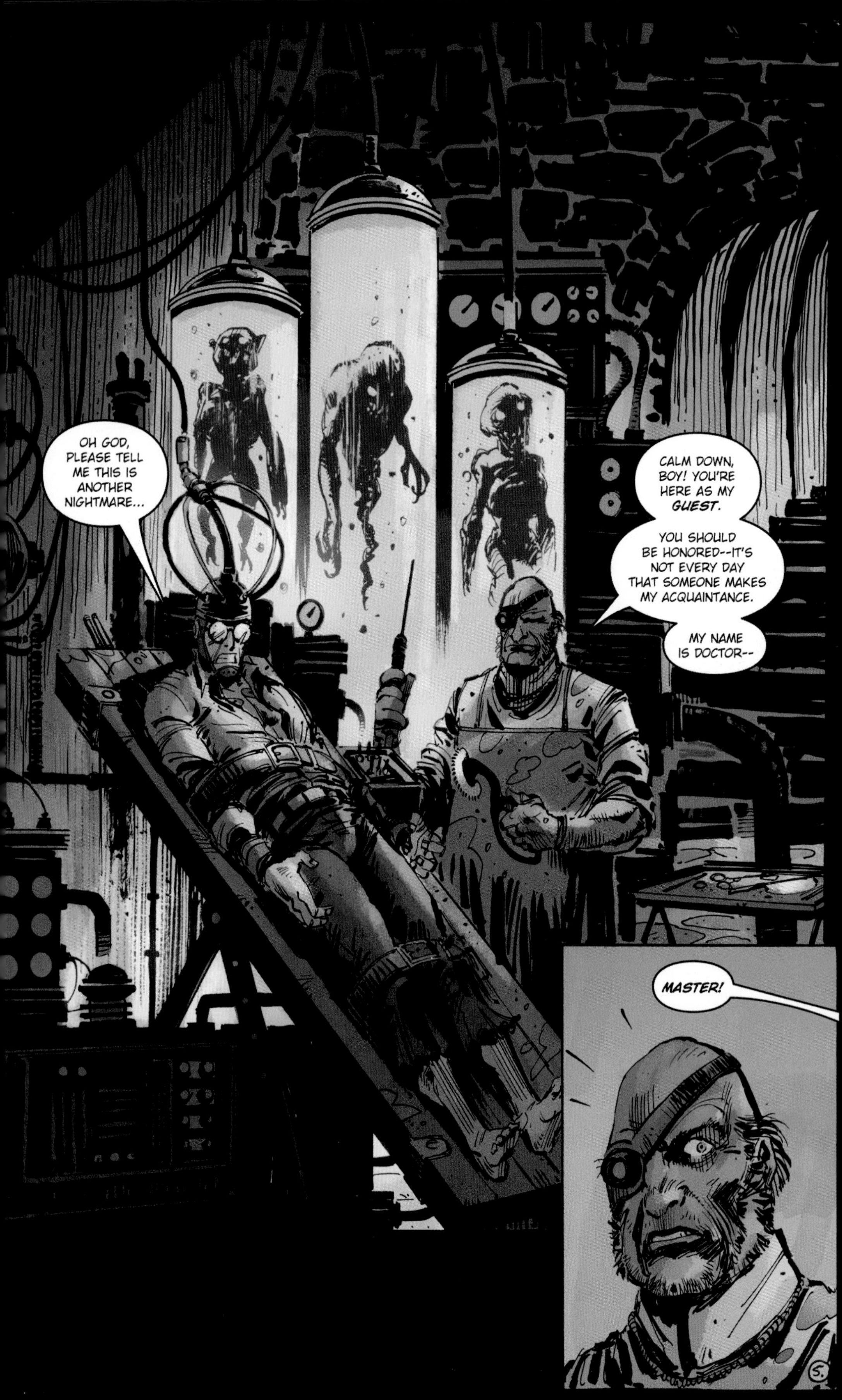
OH GOD, PLEASE TELL ME THIS IS ANOTHER NIGHTMARE...
CALM DOWN, BOY! YOU'RE HERE AS MY GUEST.
YOU SHOULD BE HONORED--IT'S NOT EVERY DAY THAT SOMEONE MAKES MY ACQUAINTANCE.
MY NAME IS DOCTOR--
MASTER!

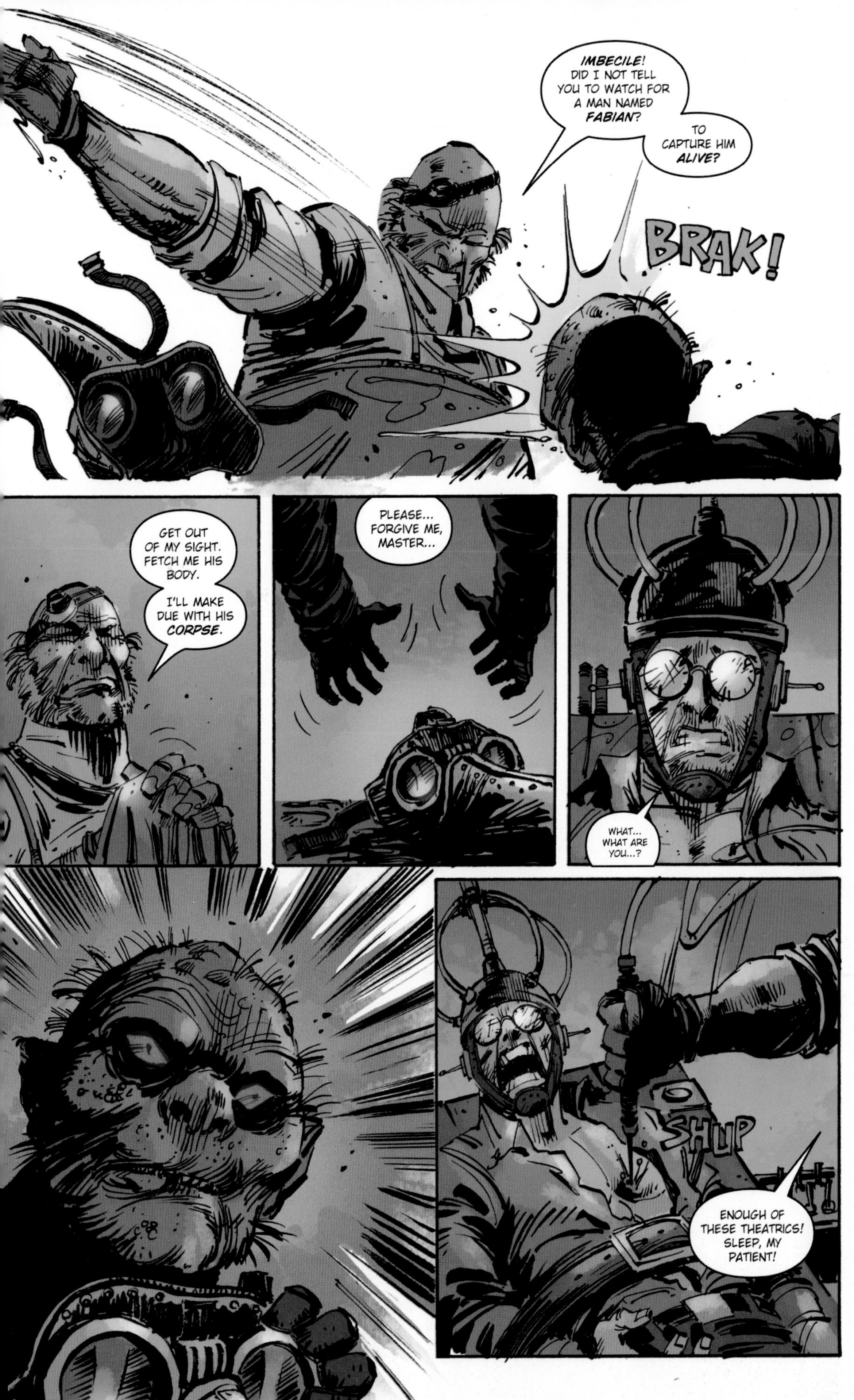
IMBECILE! DID I NOT TELL YOU TO WATCH FOR A MAN NAMED FABIAN?
TO CAPTURE HIM ALIVE?
BRAK!
GET OUT OF MY SIGHT. FETCH ME HIS BODY.
I'LL MAKE DUE WITH HIS CORPSE.
PLEASE... FORGIVE ME, MASTER...
WHAT... WHAT ARE YOU...?
SHUP
ENOUGH OF THESE THEATRICS! SLEEP, MY PATIENT!

KRA

THUD

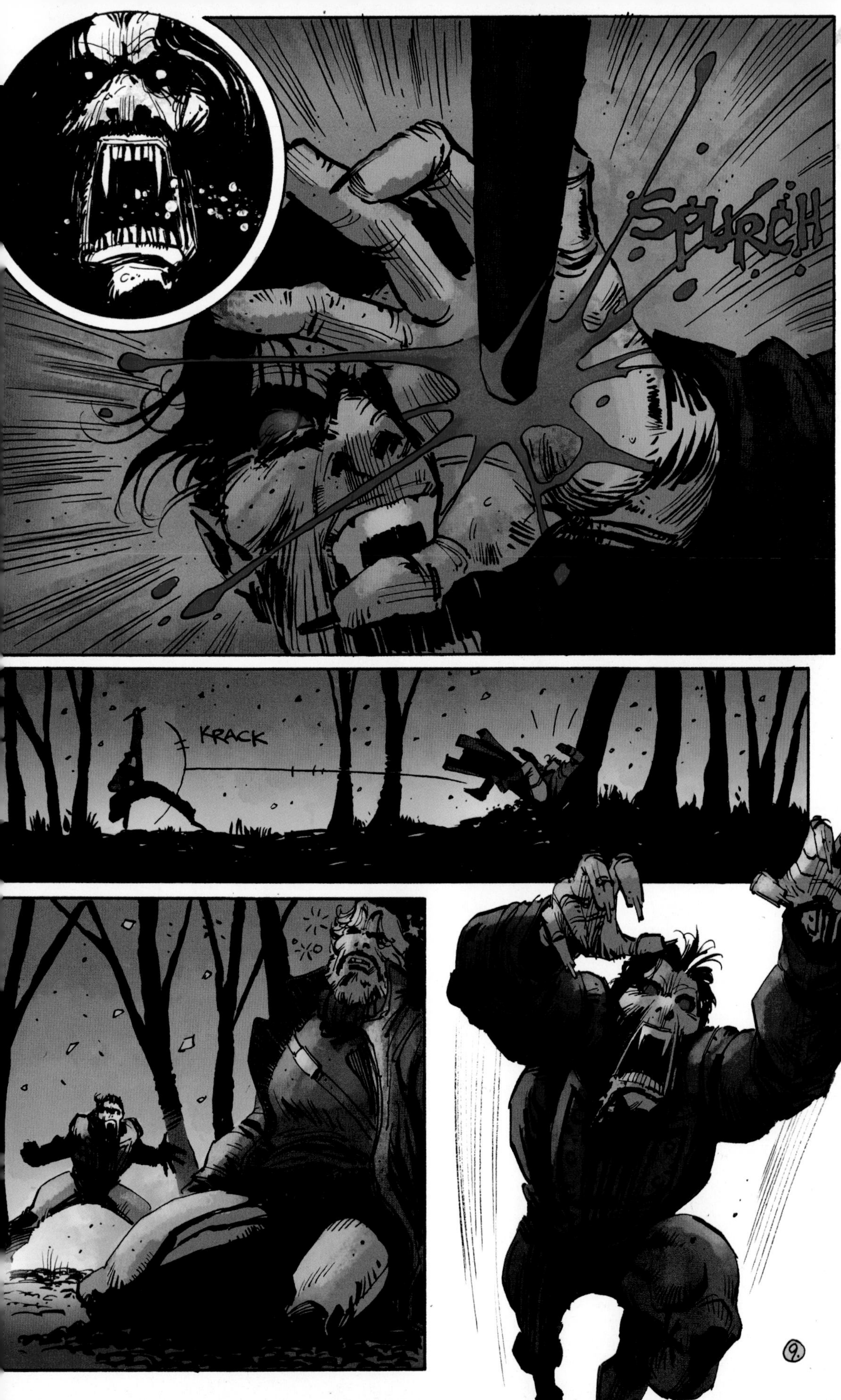
SPLURCH
KRACK

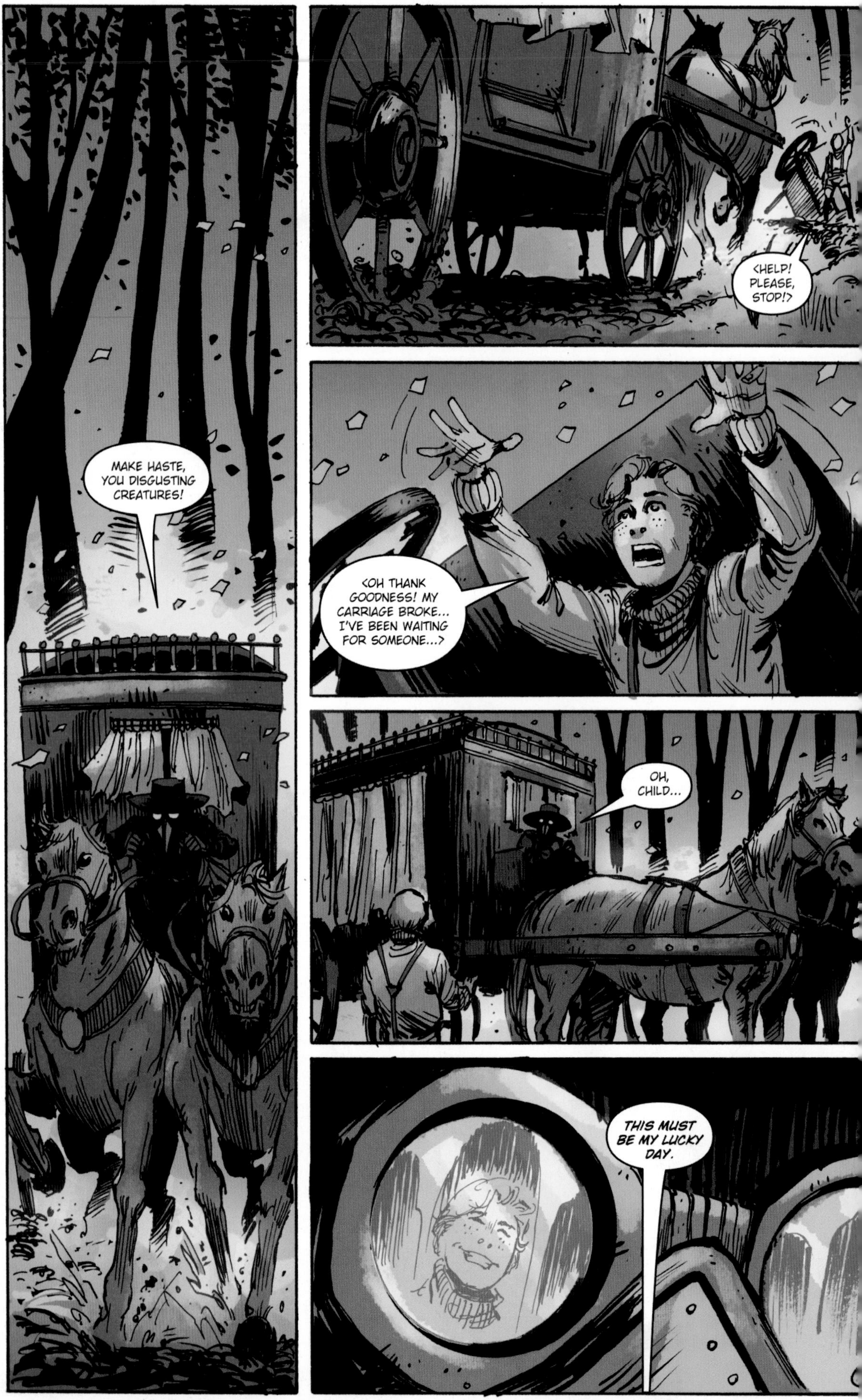
MAKE HASTE, YOU DISGUSTING CREATURES!
<HELP! PLEASE, STOP!>
<OH THANK GOODNESS! MY CARRIAGE BROKE... I'VE BEEN WAITING FOR SOMEONE...>
OH, CHILD...
THIS MUST BE MY LUCKY DAY.

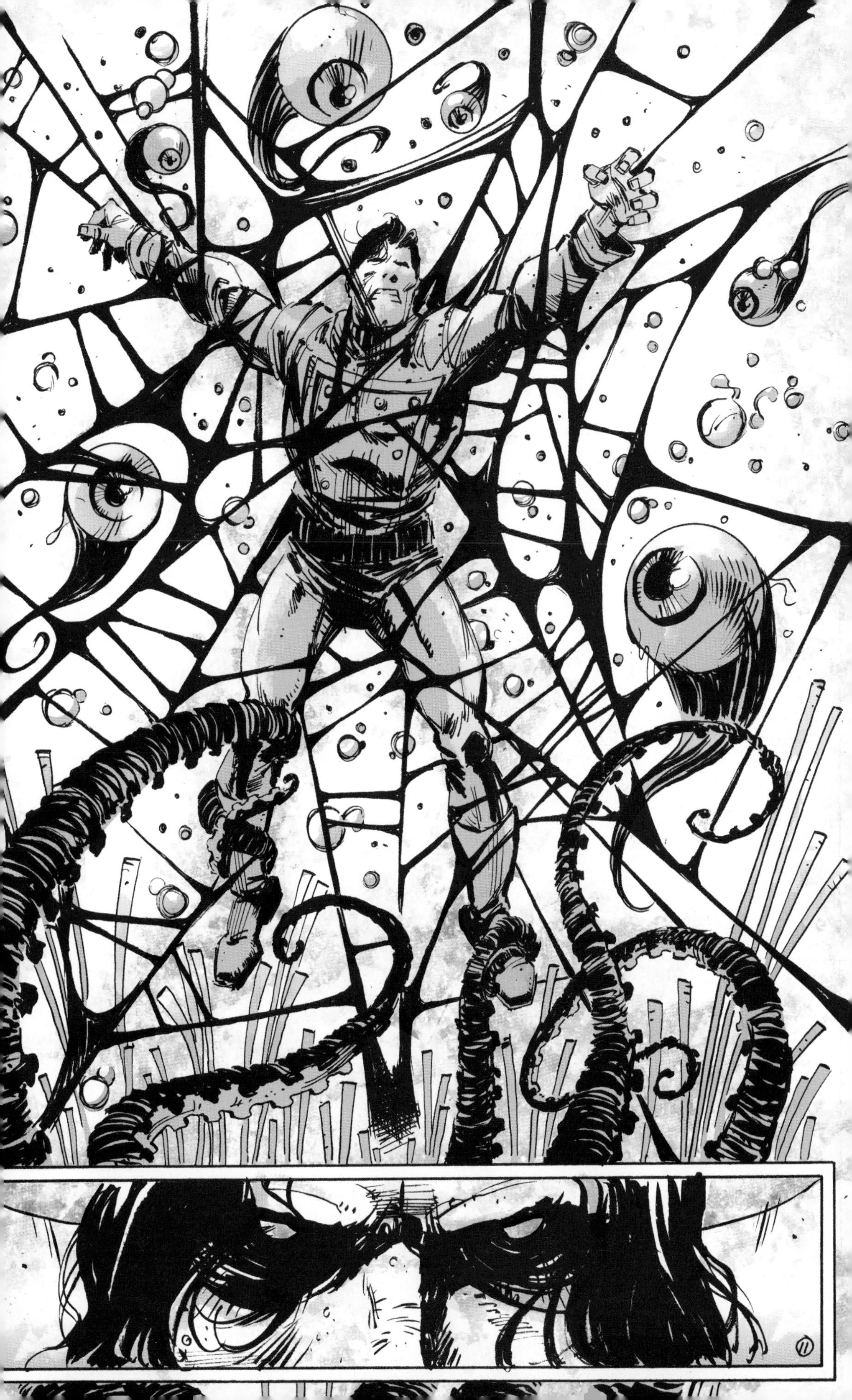

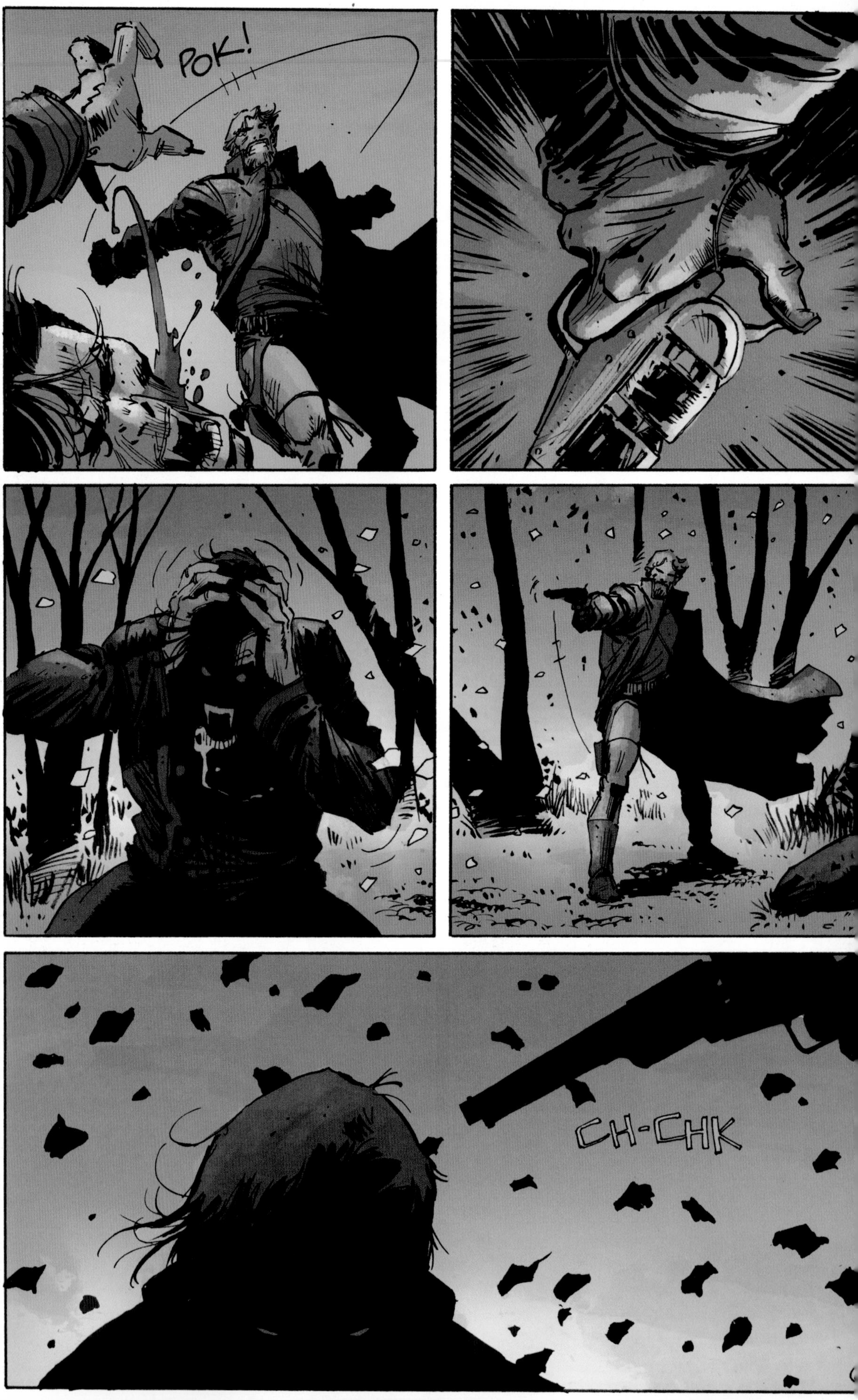
POK!
CH-CHK

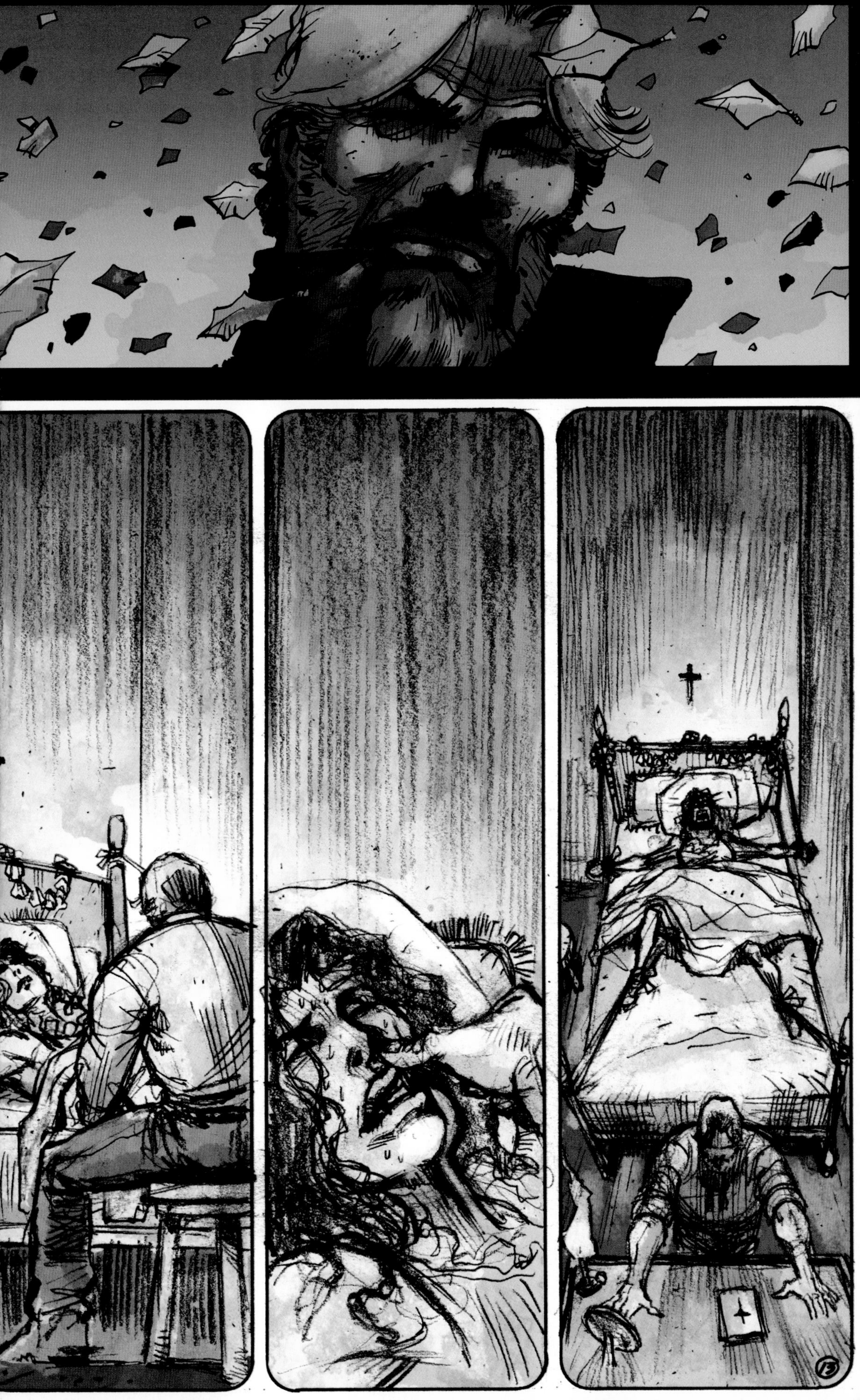

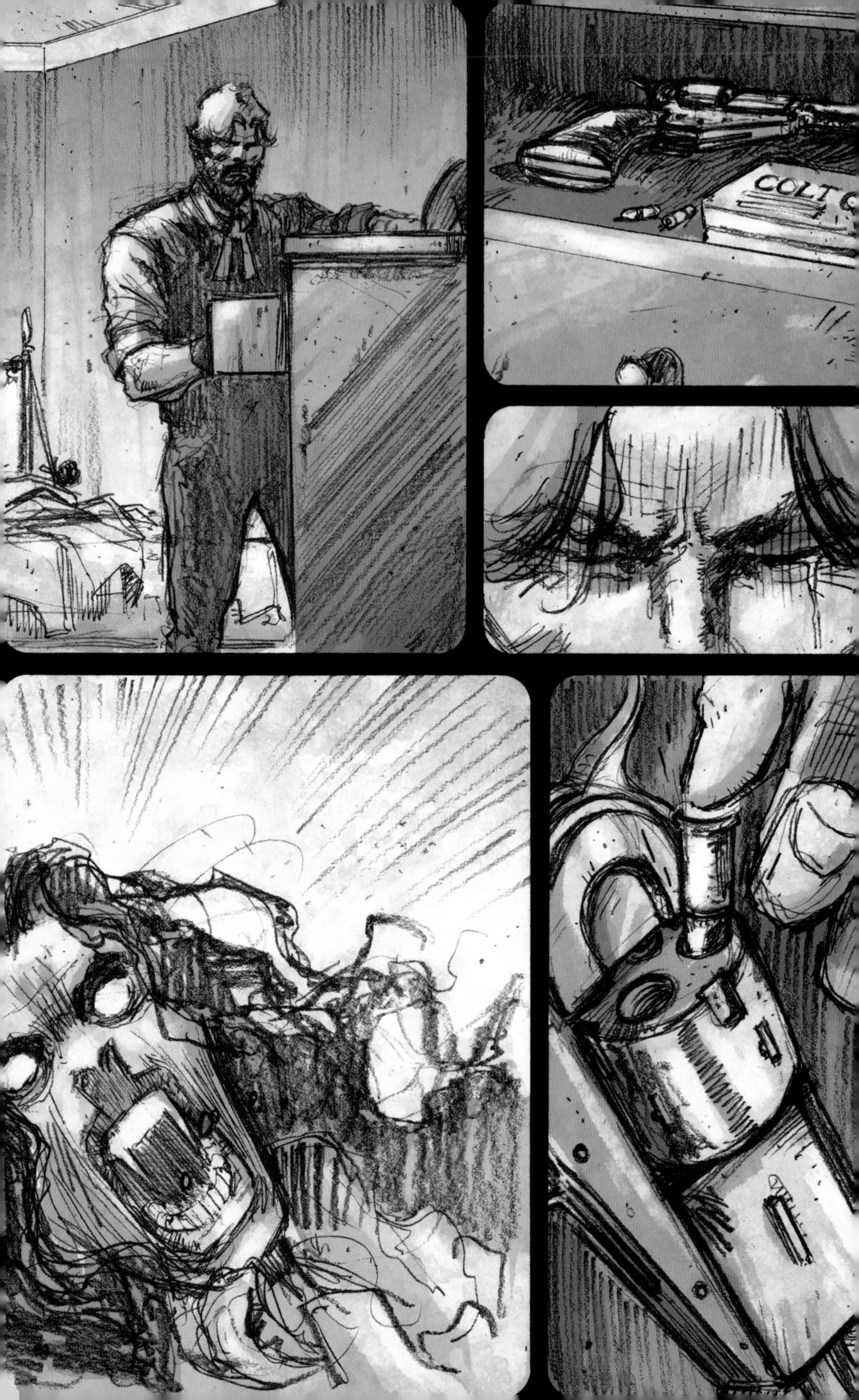
COLT

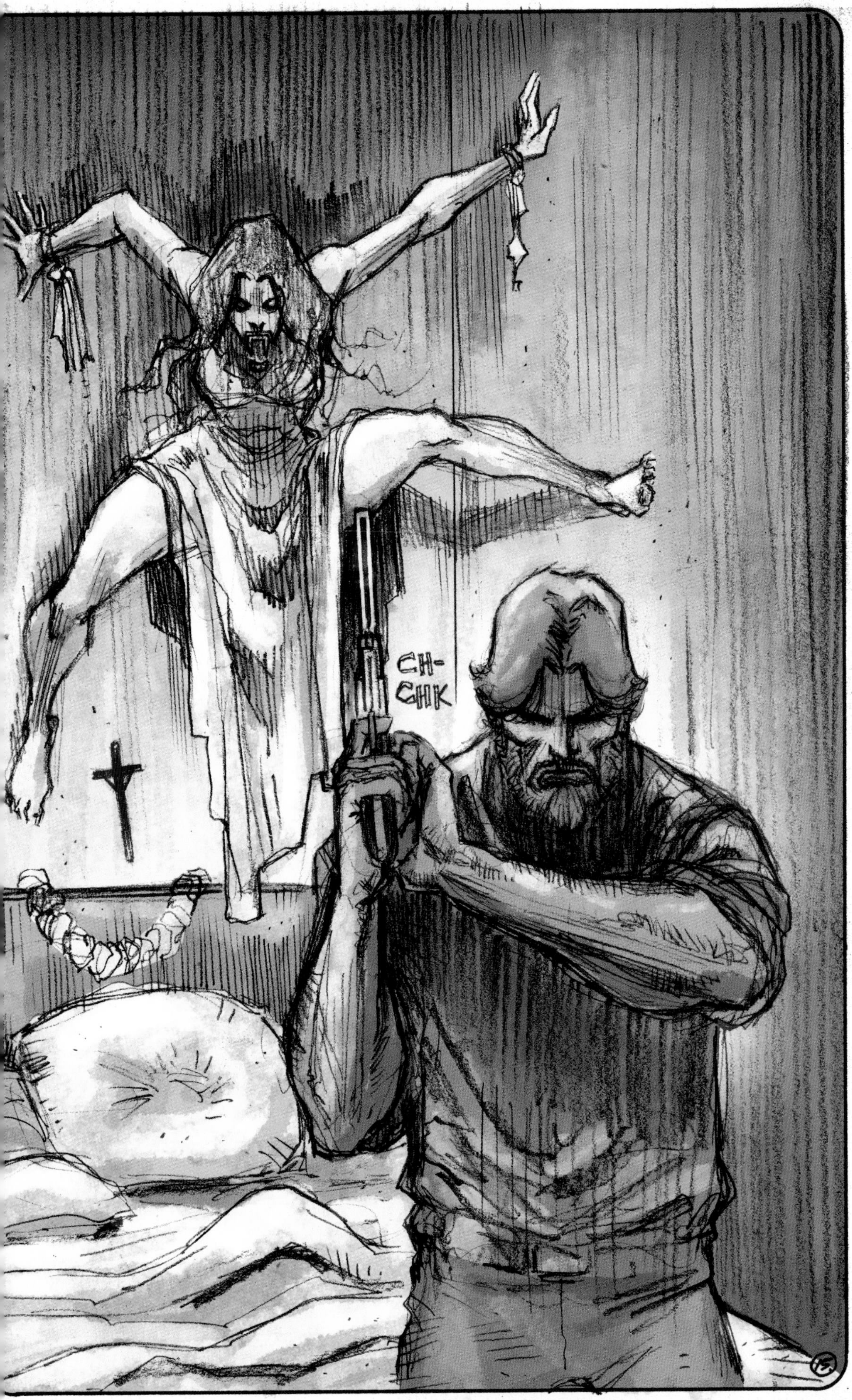
CH-
CHK

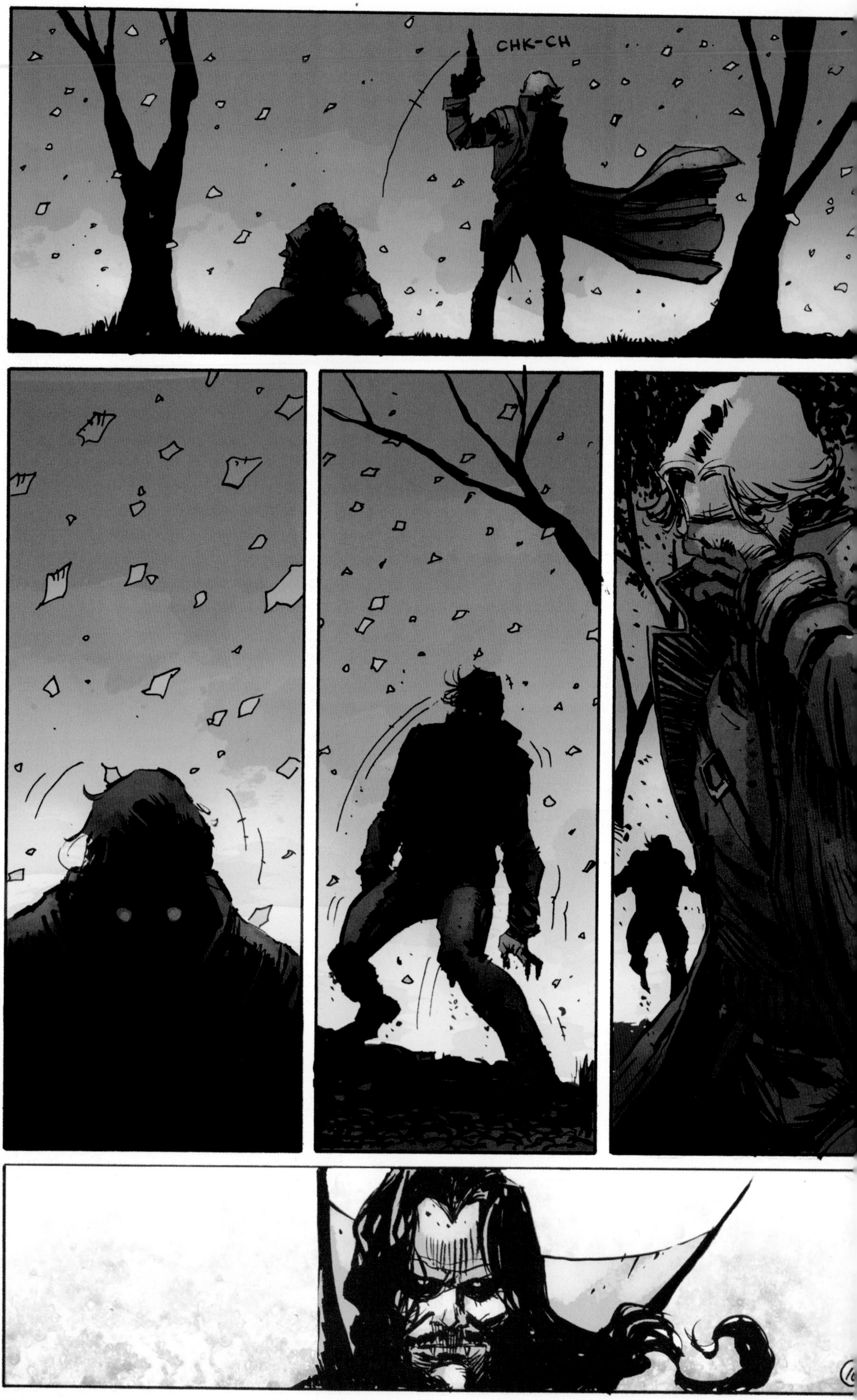
CHK-CH

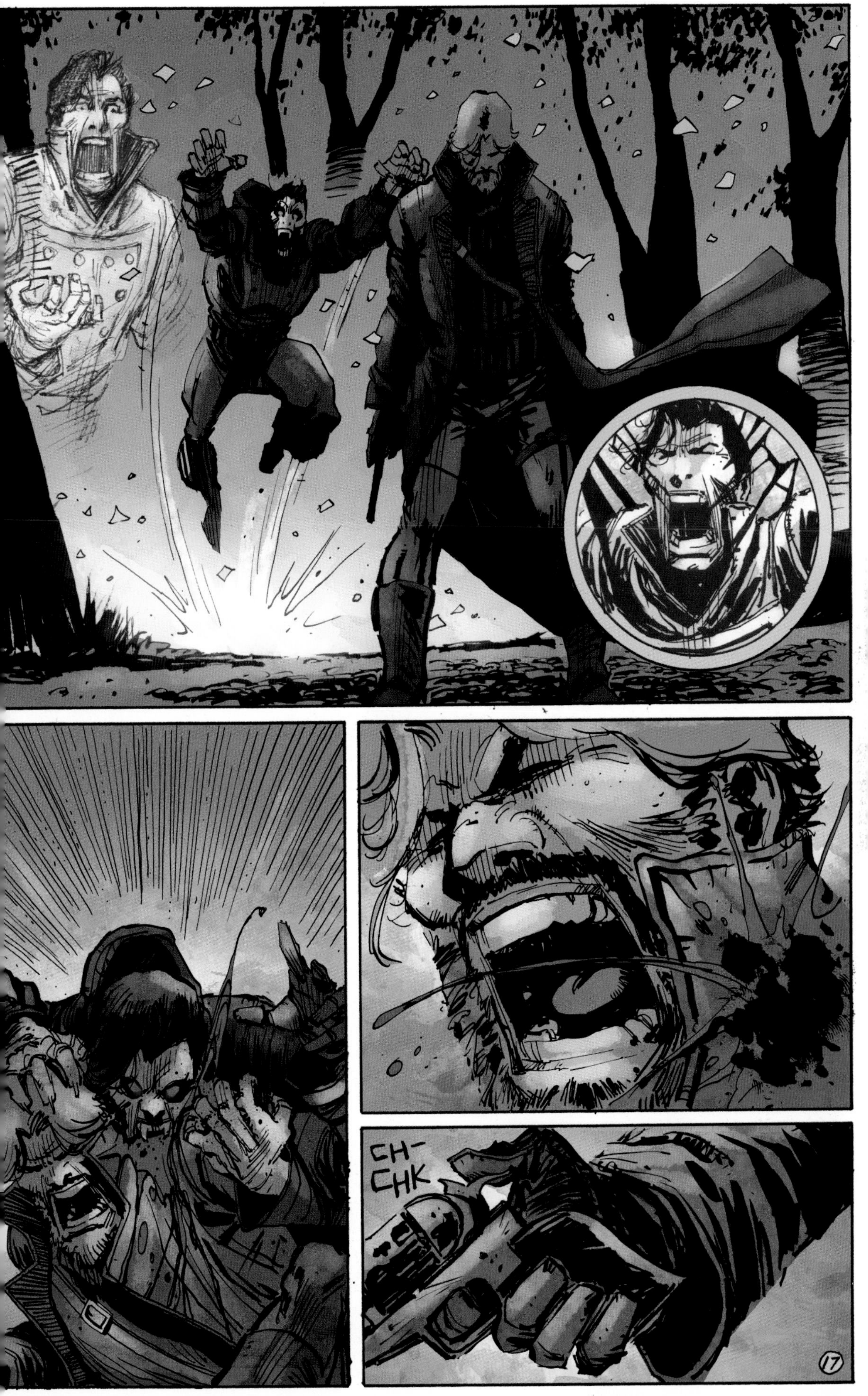
CH-
CHK

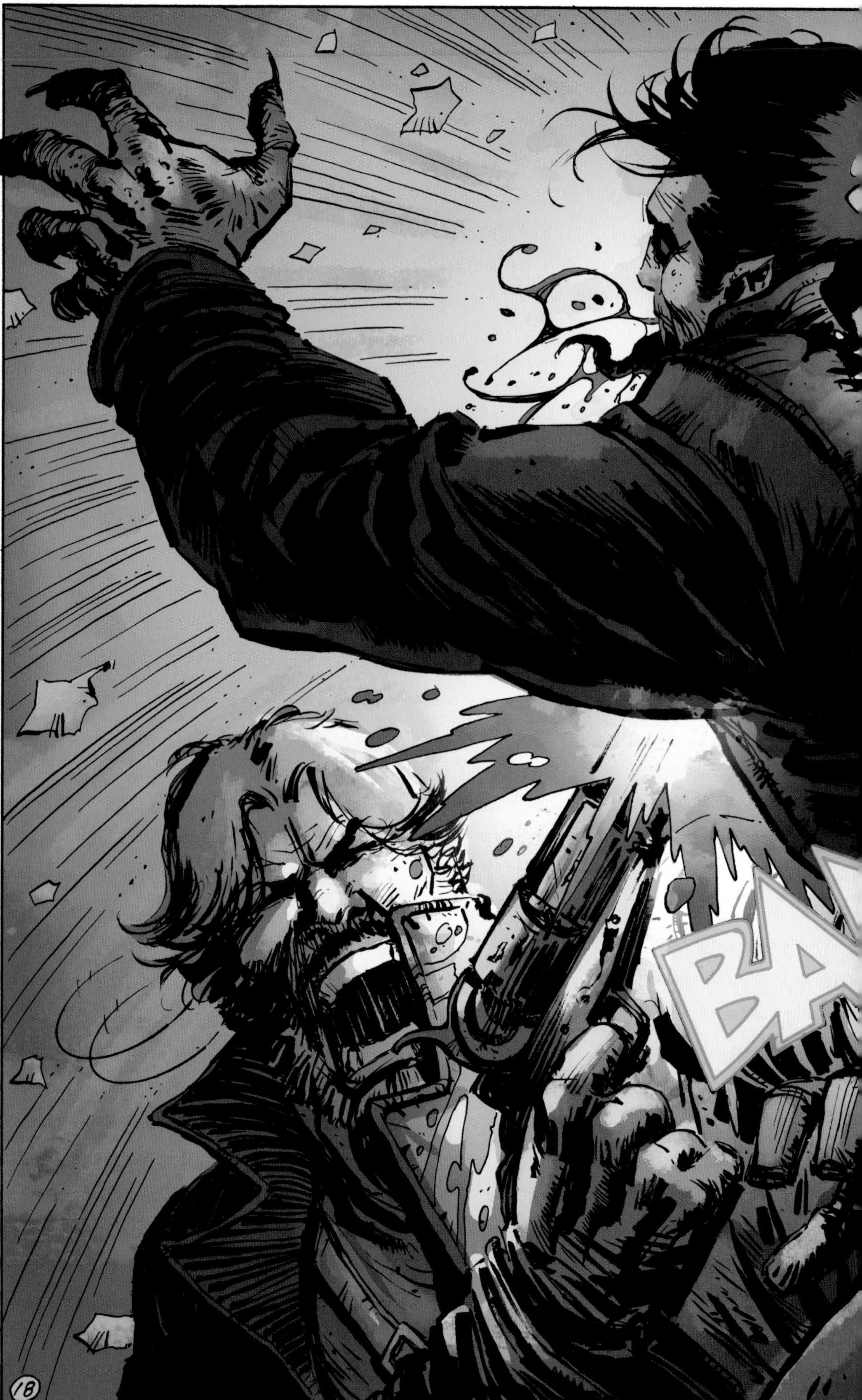

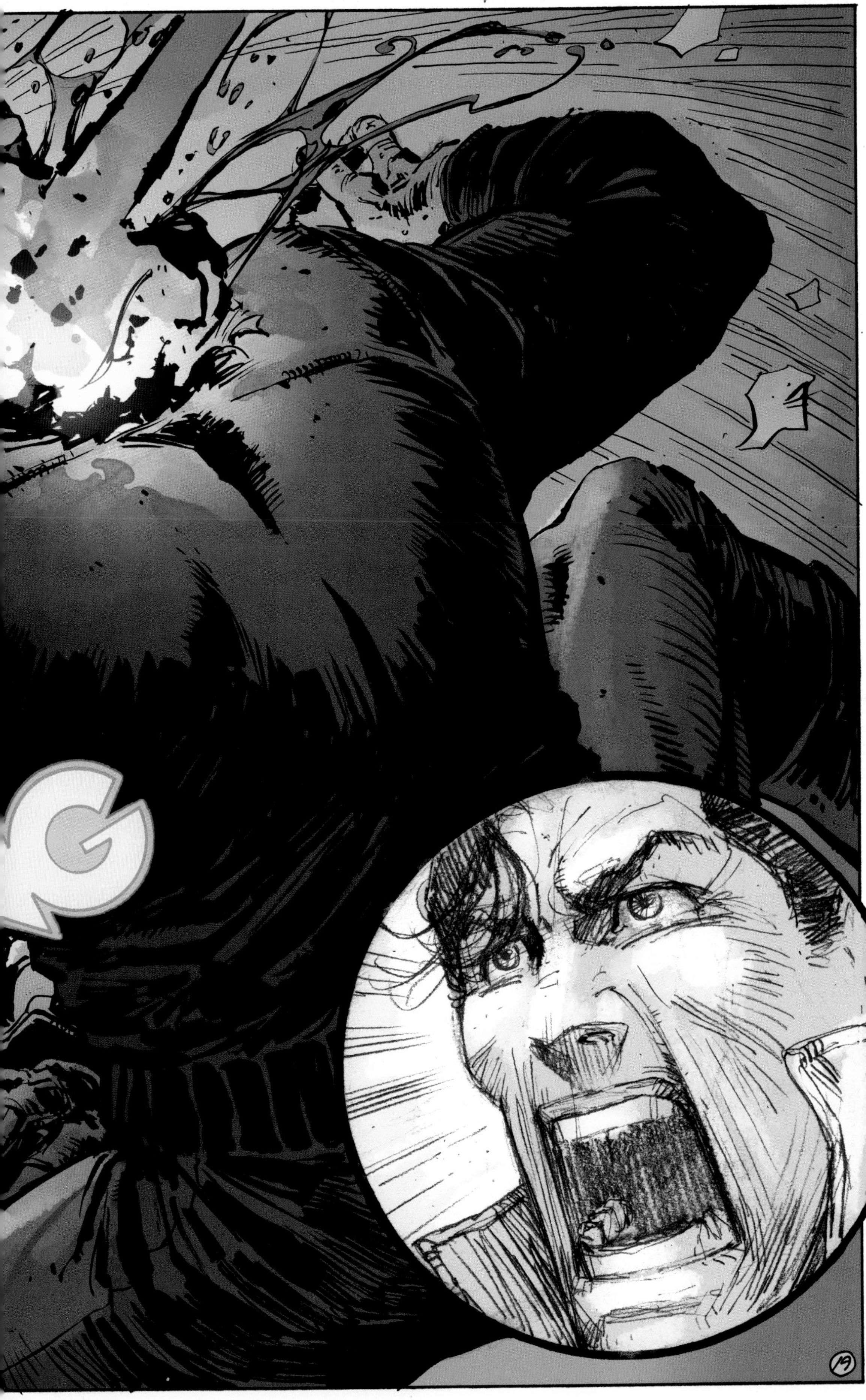

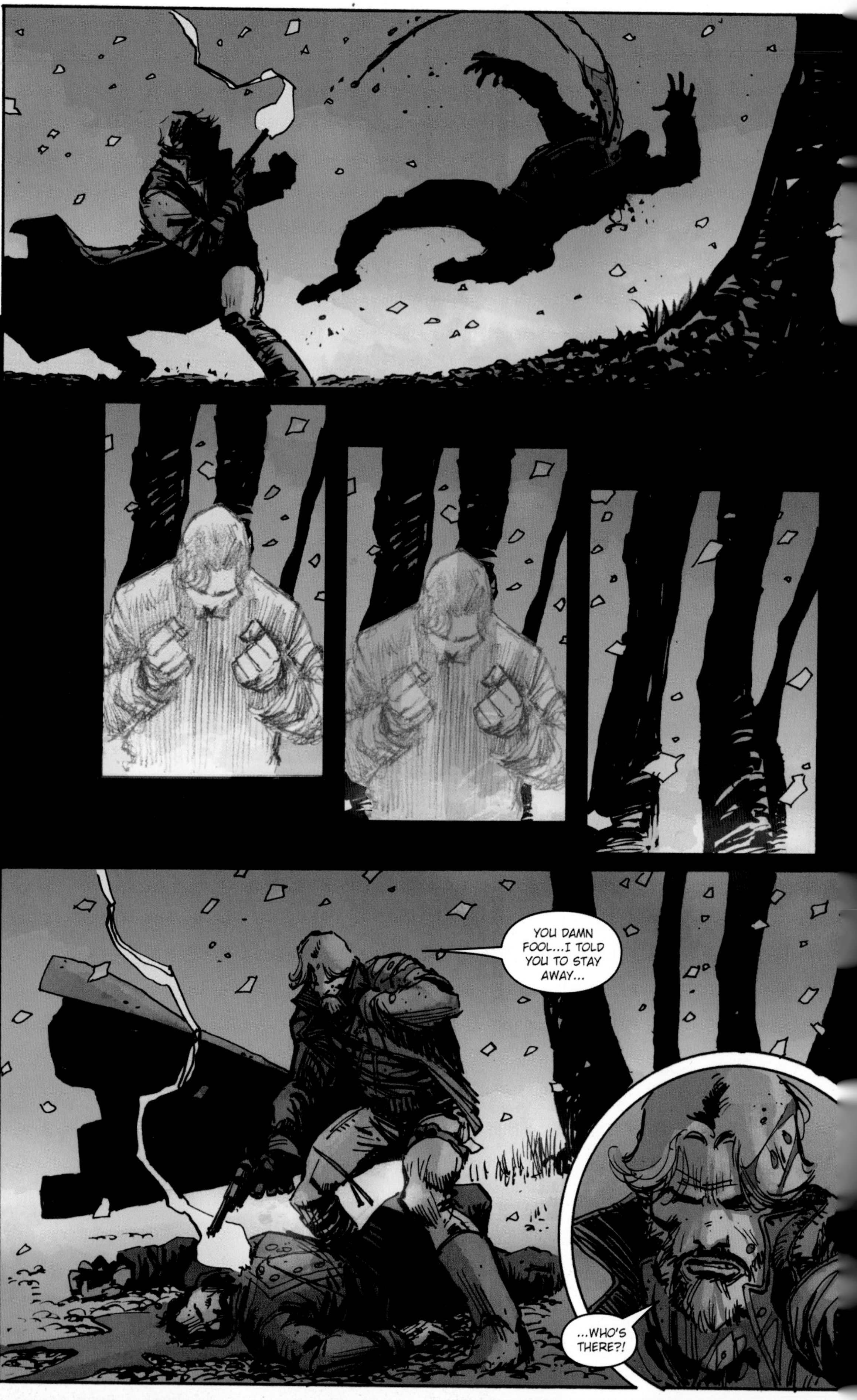
YOU DAMN FOOL...I TOLD YOU TO STAY AWAY...
...WHO'S THERE?!

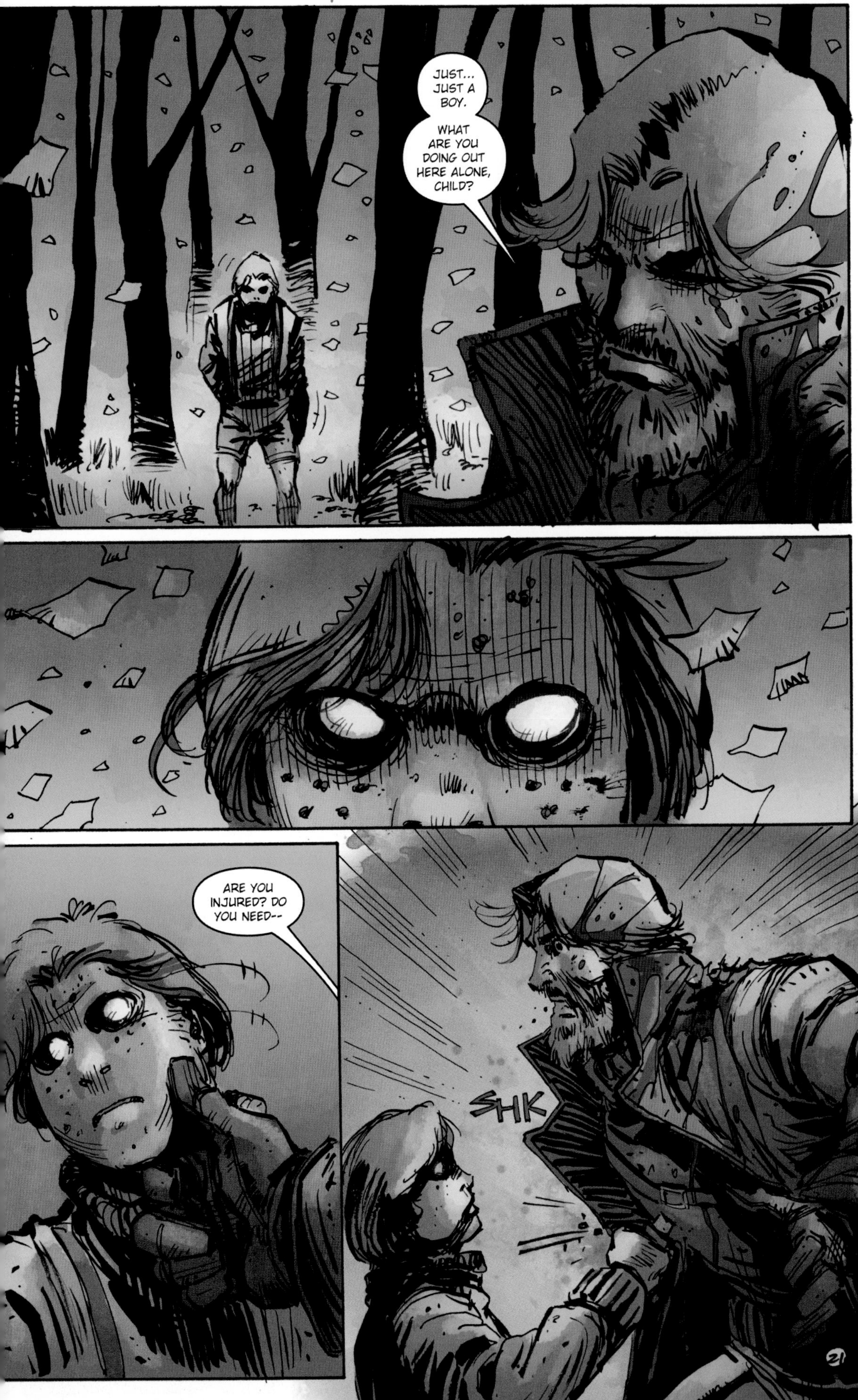
JUST... JUST A BOY.
WHAT ARE YOU DOING OUT HERE ALONE, CHILD?
ARE YOU INJURED? DO YOU NEED--
SHK

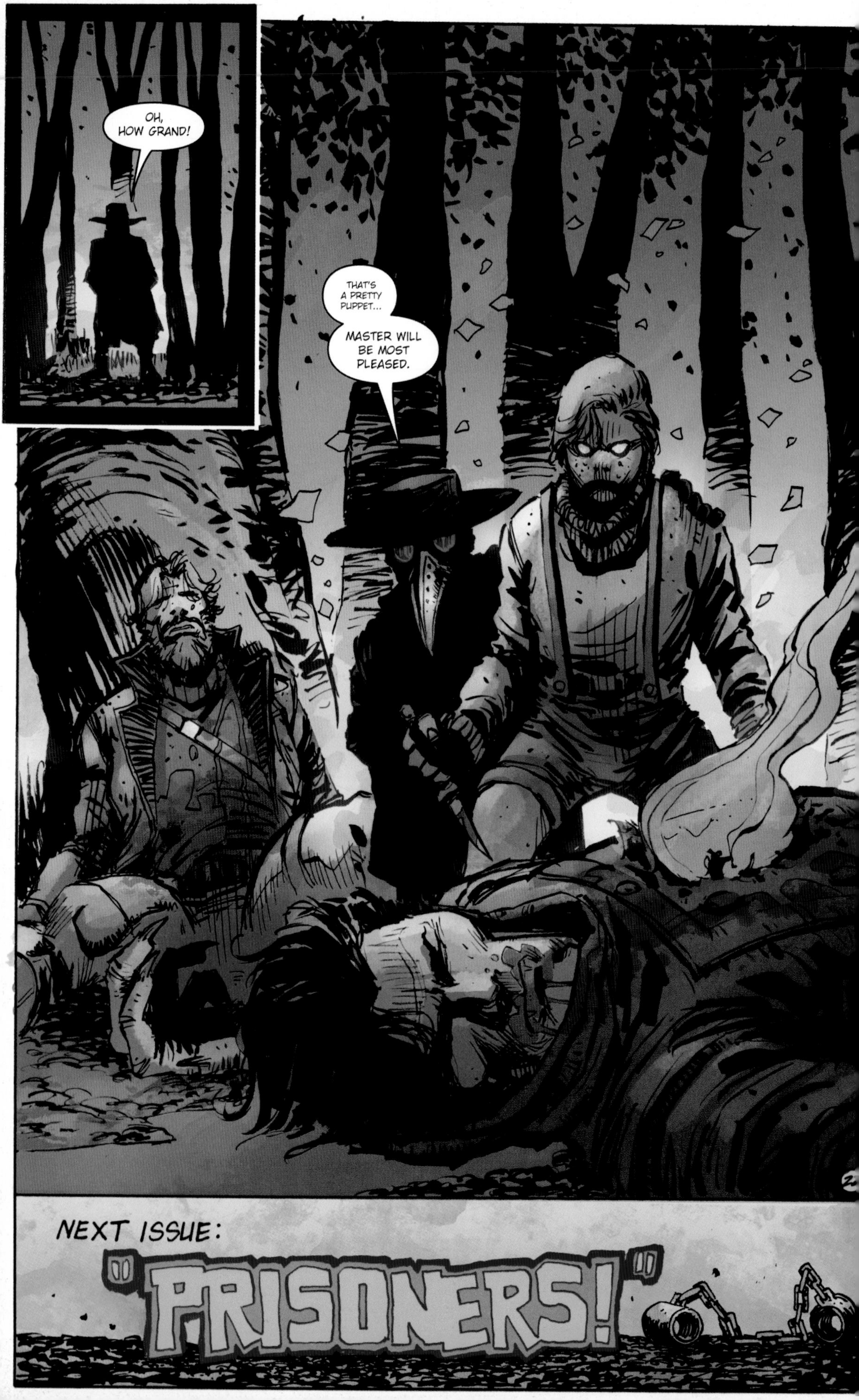
OH, HOW GRAND!
THAT'S A PRETTY PUPPET...
MASTER WILL BE MOST PLEASED.
NEXT ISSUE:
"PRISONERS!"

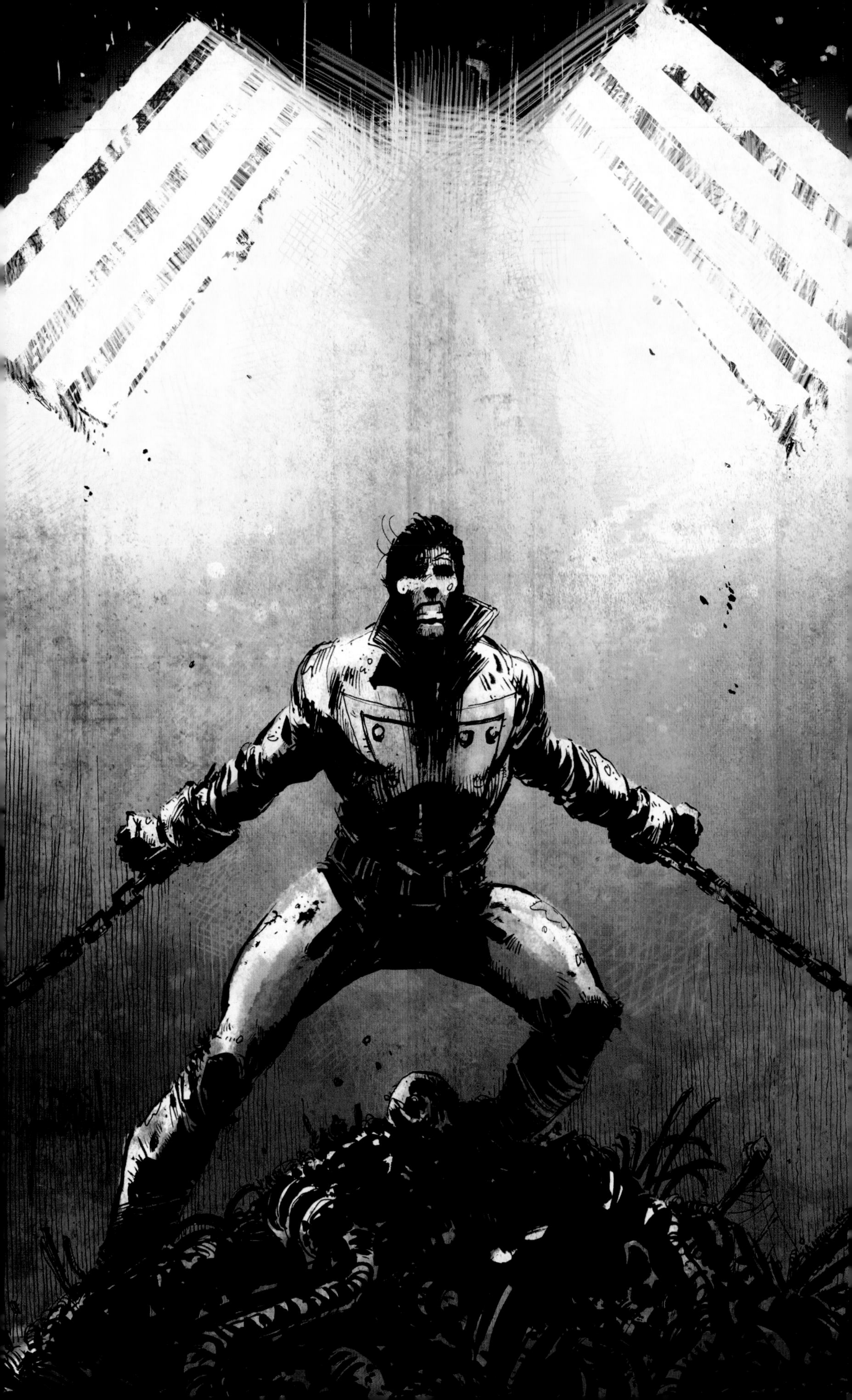

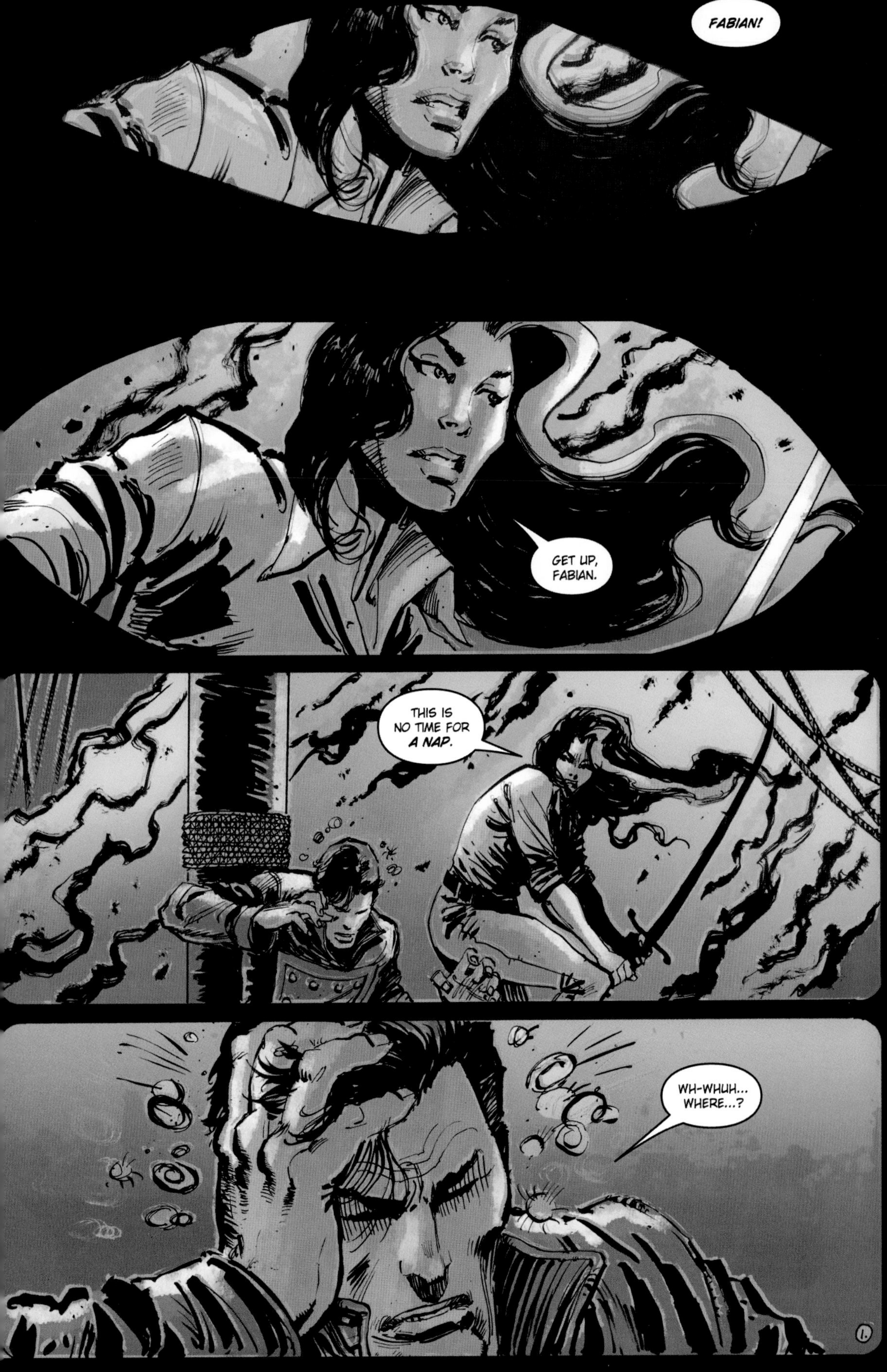
FABIAN!
GET UP, FABIAN.
THIS IS NO TIME FOR A NAP.
WH-WHUH... WHERE...?

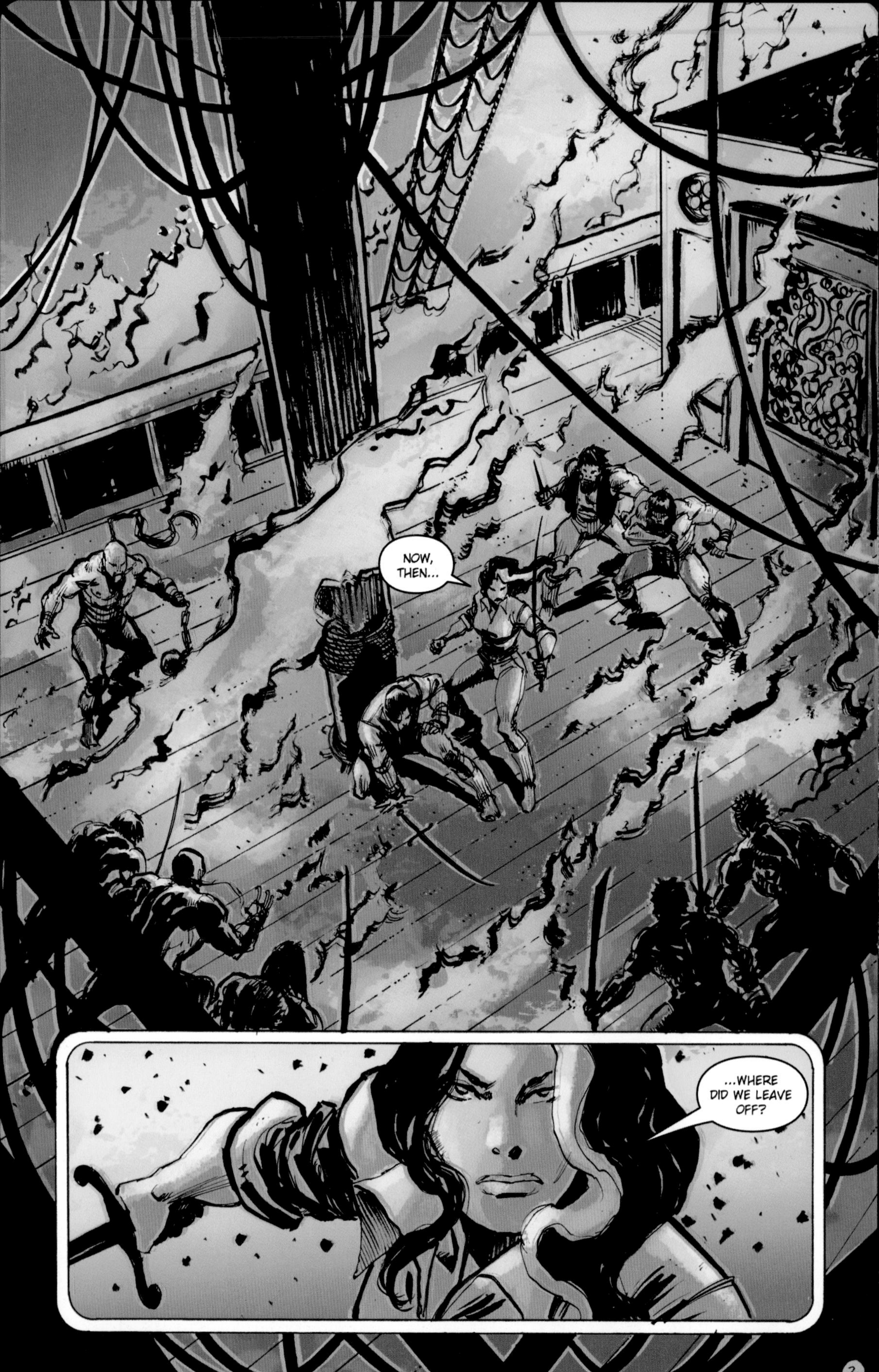
NOW, THEN...
...WHERE DID WE LEAVE OFF?

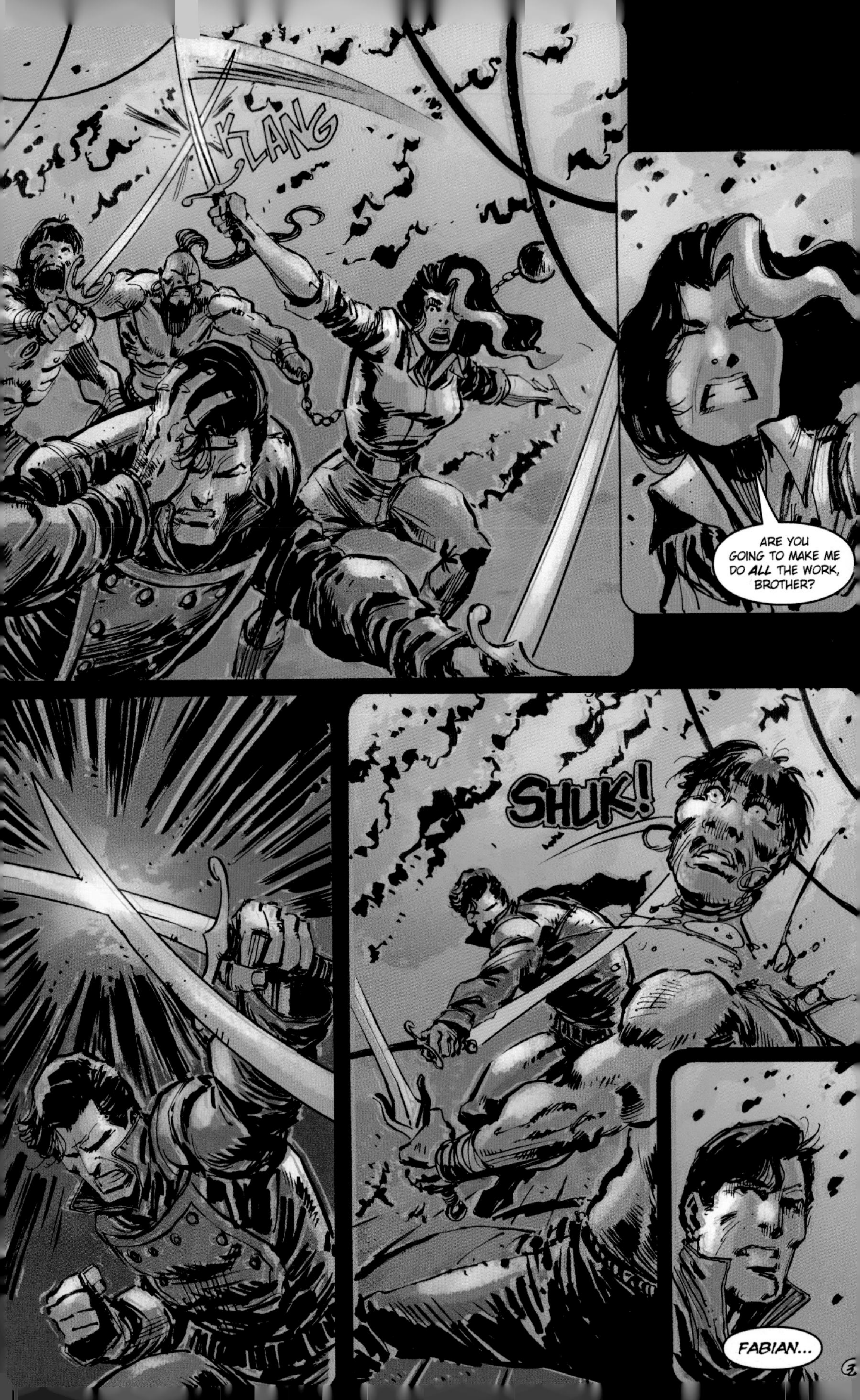
KLANG
ARE YOU GOING TO MAKE ME DO ALL THE WORK, BROTHER?
SHUK!
FABIAN...

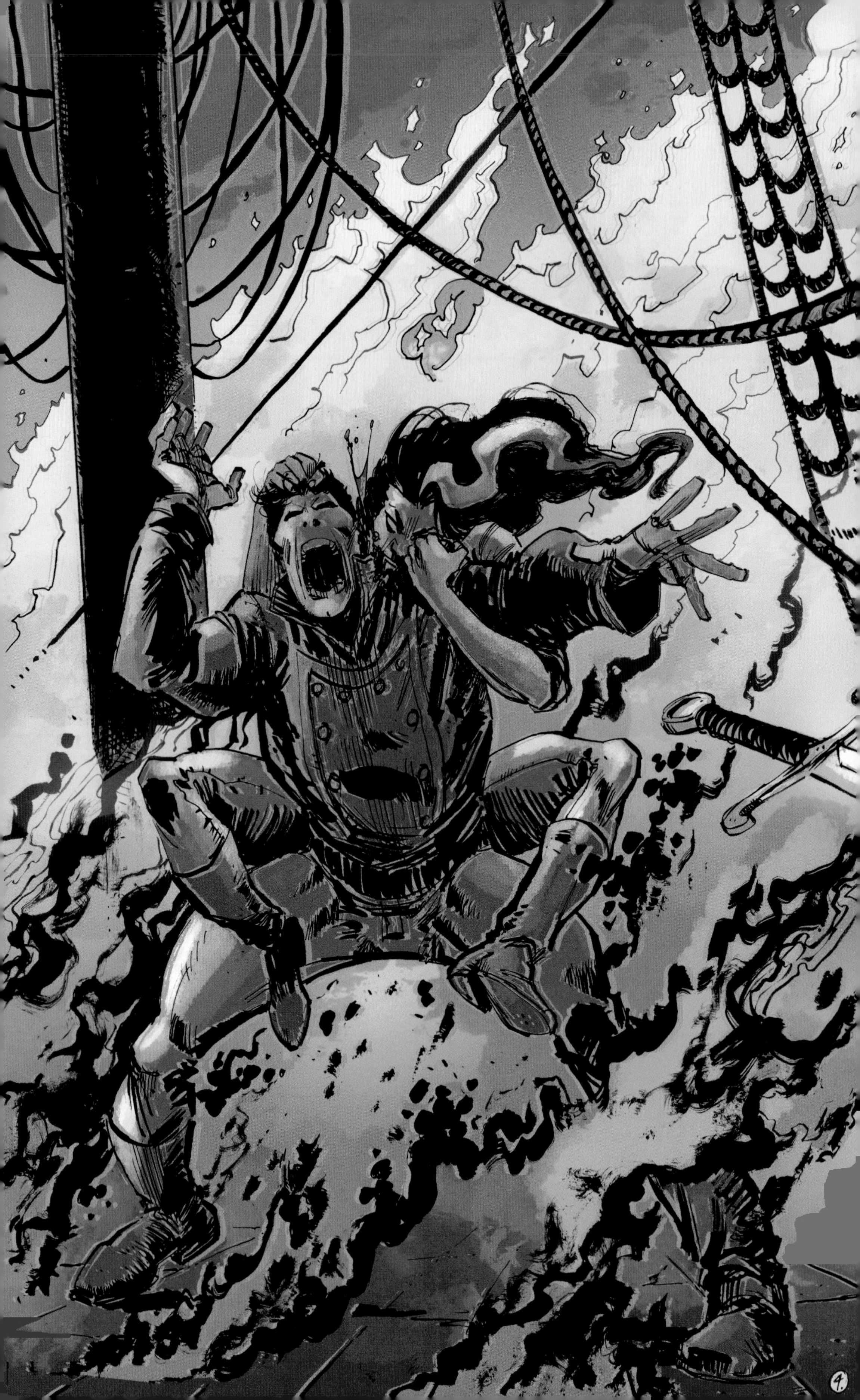

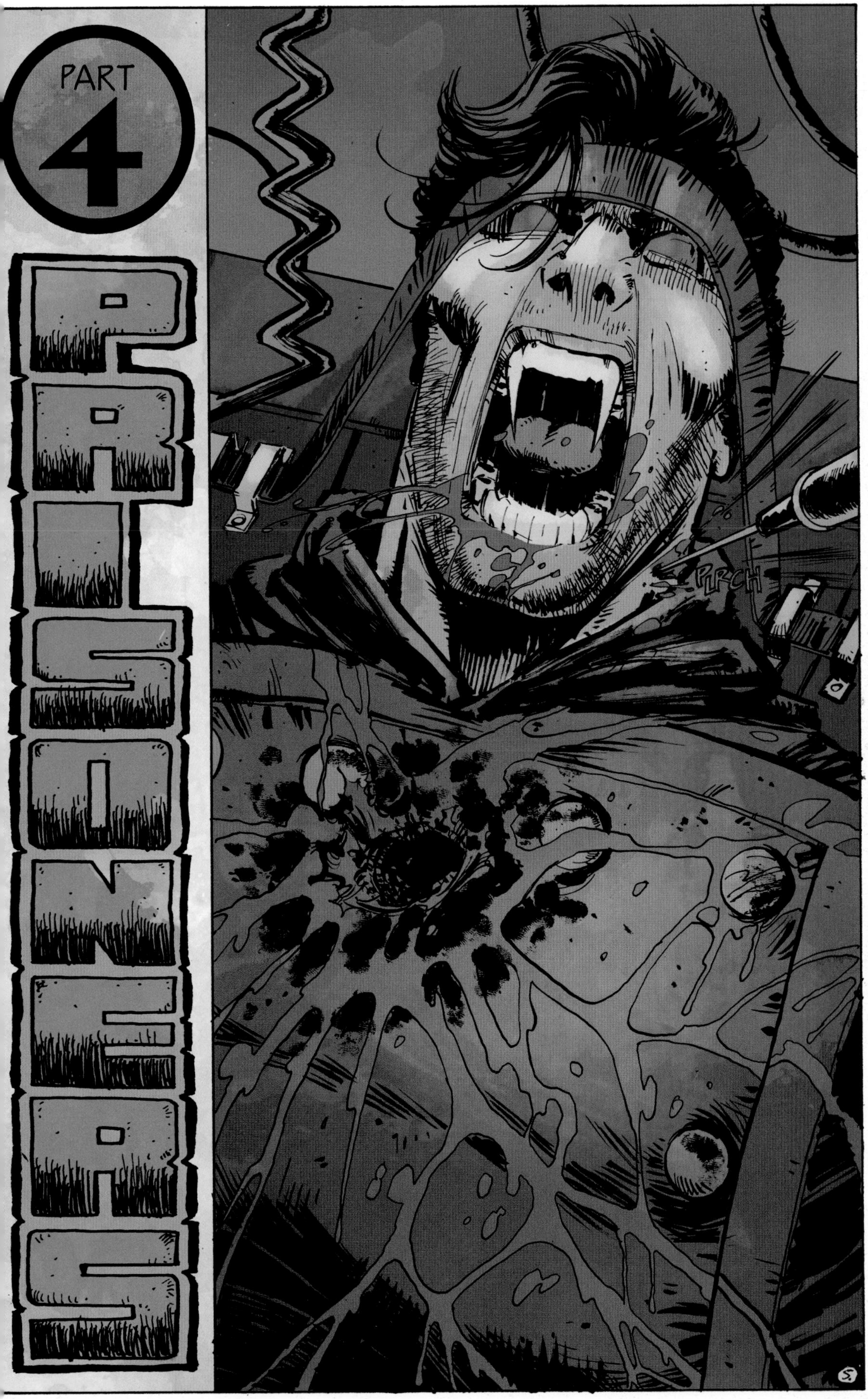
PART 4
PRISONER
PLRCH

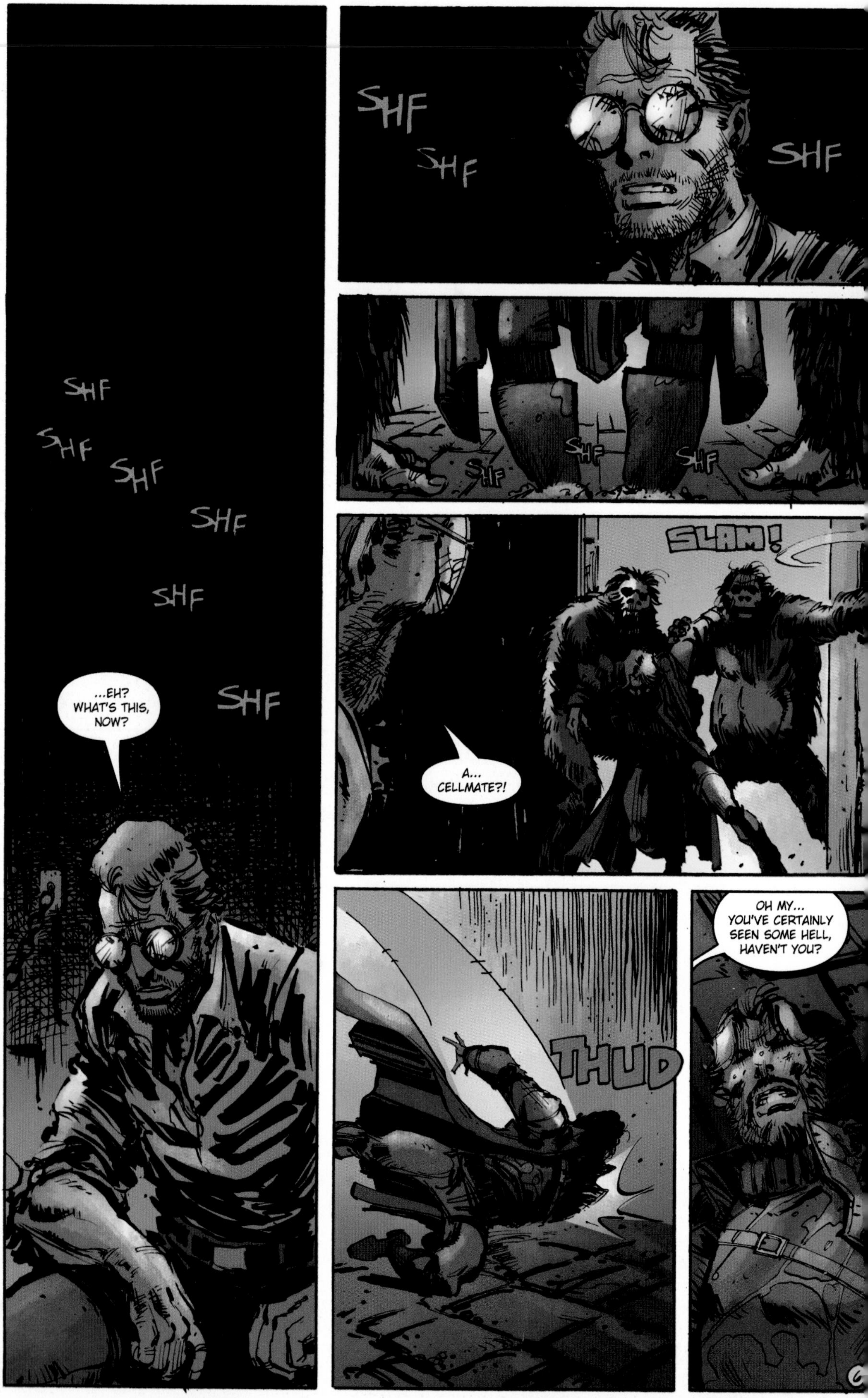
SHF
SHF
SHF
SHF
SHF
SHF
...EH? WHAT'S THIS, NOW?
SHF
SHF
SHF
SHF
SHF
SHF
SHF
SLAM!
A... CELLMATE?!
THUD
OH MY... YOU'VE CERTAINLY SEEN SOME HELL, HAVEN'T YOU?

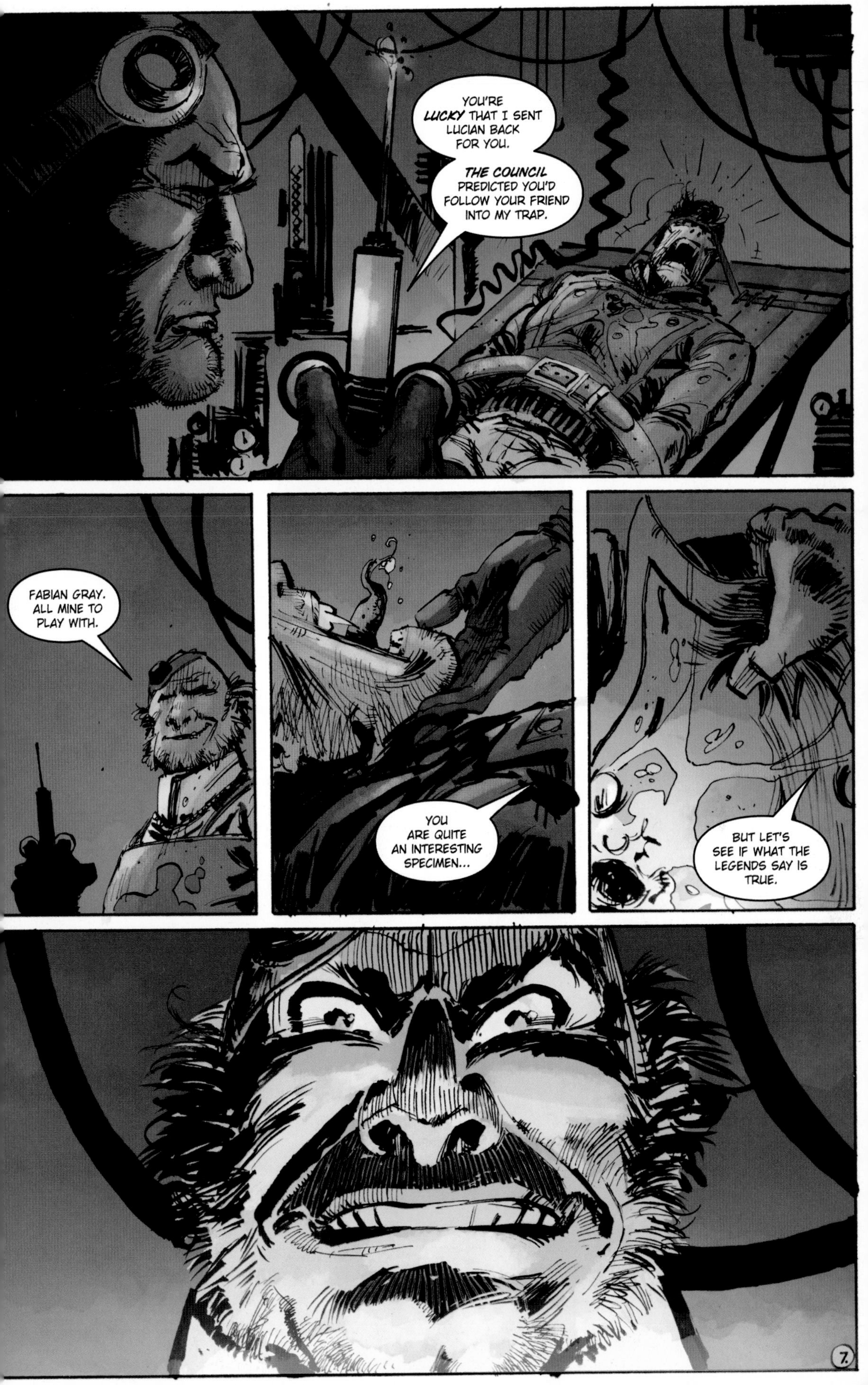
YOU'RE *LUCKY* THAT I SENT LUCIAN BACK FOR YOU.
THE COUNCIL PREDICTED YOU'D FOLLOW YOUR FRIEND INTO MY TRAP.
FABIAN GRAY. ALL MINE TO PLAY WITH.
YOU ARE QUITE AN INTERESTING SPECIMEN...
BUT LET'S SEE IF WHAT THE LEGENDS SAY IS TRUE.

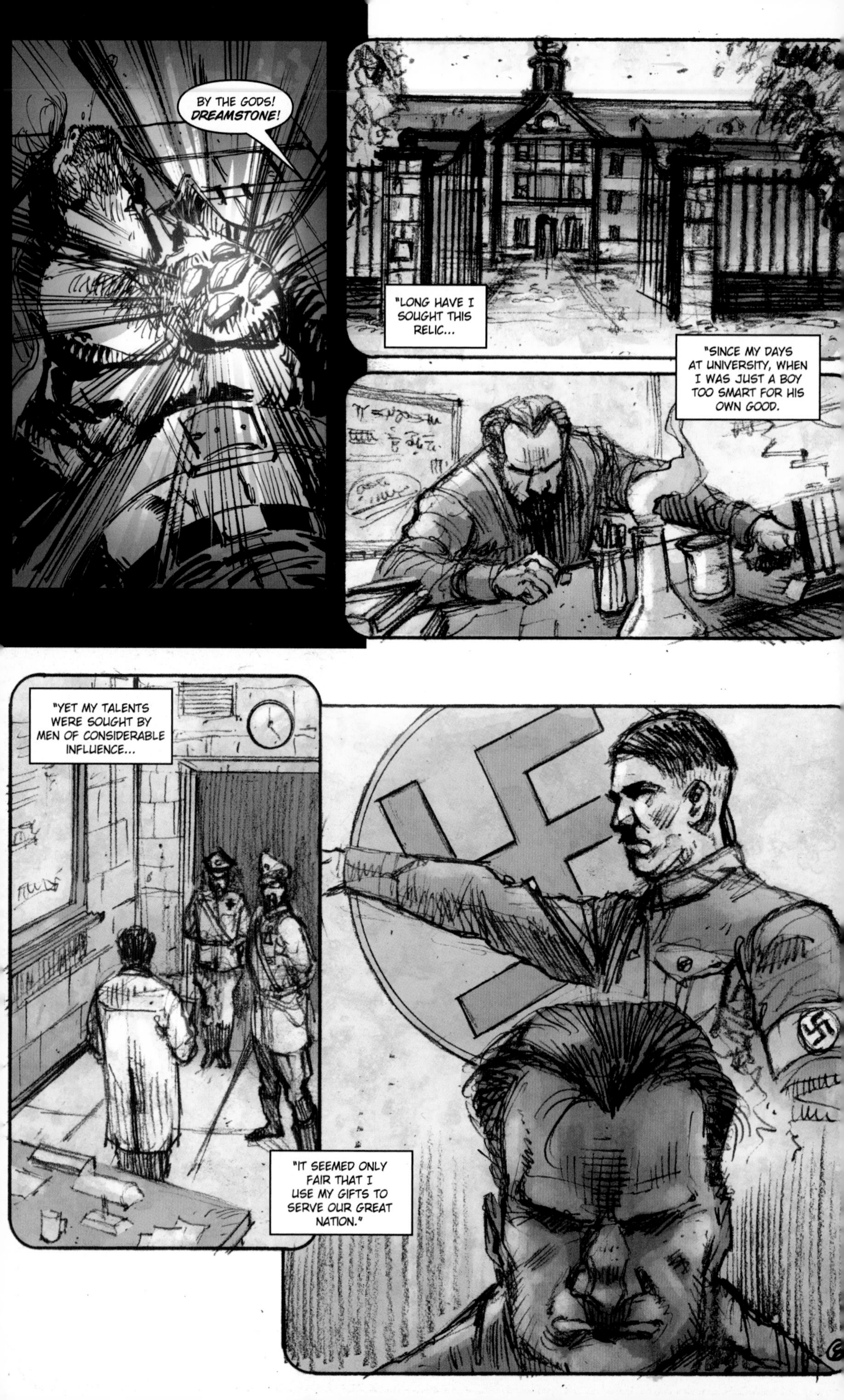

BY THE GODS! *DREAMSTONE!*
"LONG HAVE I SOUGHT THIS RELIC...
"SINCE MY DAYS AT UNIVERSITY, WHEN I WAS JUST A BOY TOO SMART FOR HIS OWN GOOD.
"YET MY TALENTS WERE SOUGHT BY MEN OF CONSIDERABLE INFLUENCE...
"IT SEEMED ONLY FAIR THAT I USE MY GIFTS TO SERVE OUR GREAT NATION."

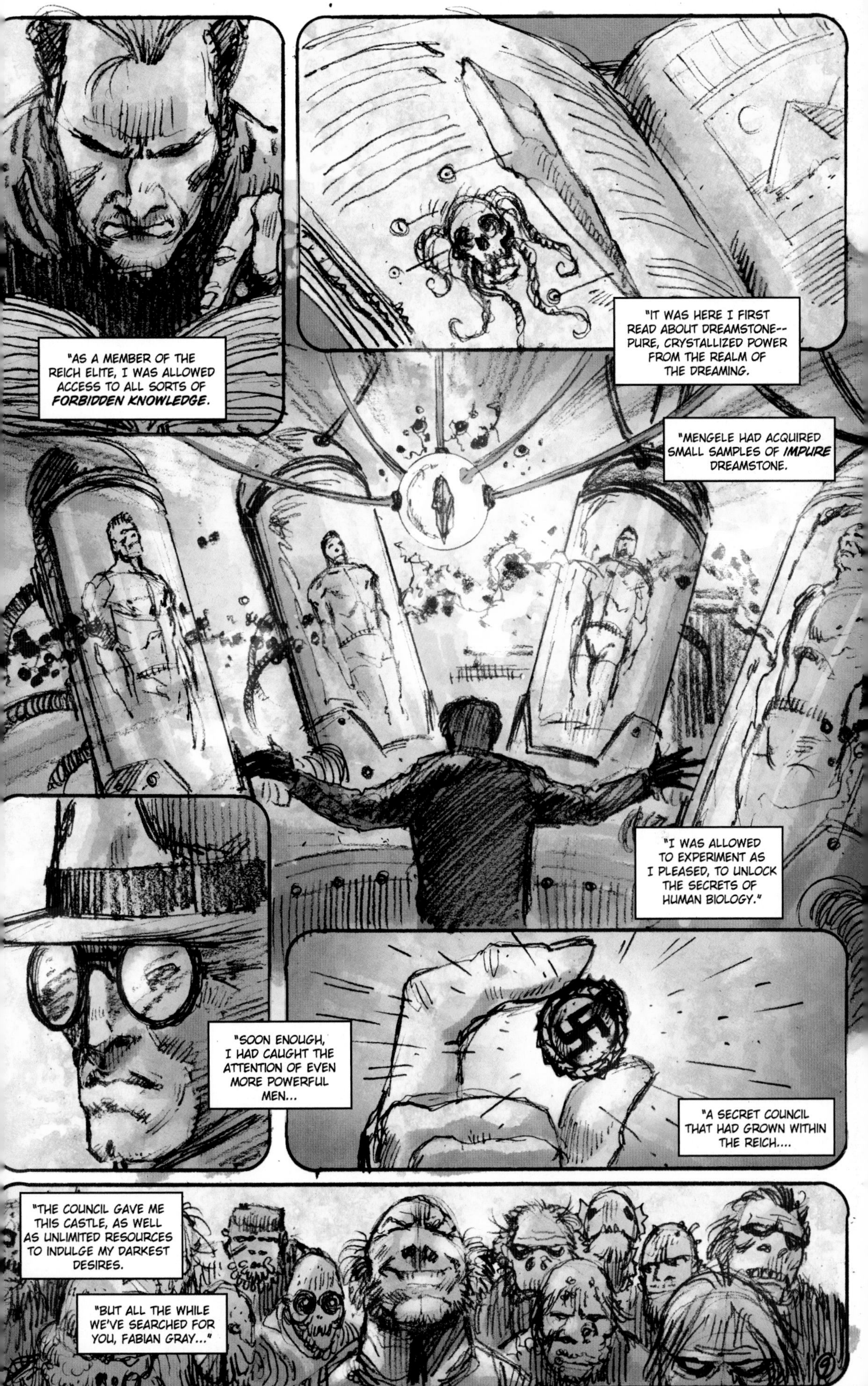

"AS A MEMBER OF THE REICH ELITE, I WAS ALLOWED ACCESS TO ALL SORTS OF FORBIDDEN KNOWLEDGE.
"IT WAS HERE I FIRST READ ABOUT DREAMSTONE-- PURE, CRYSTALLIZED POWER FROM THE REALM OF THE DREAMING.
"MENGELE HAD ACQUIRED SMALL SAMPLES OF IMPURE DREAMSTONE.
"I WAS ALLOWED TO EXPERIMENT AS I PLEASED, TO UNLOCK THE SECRETS OF HUMAN BIOLOGY."
"SOON ENOUGH, I HAD CAUGHT THE ATTENTION OF EVEN MORE POWERFUL MEN...
"A SECRET COUNCIL THAT HAD GROWN WITHIN THE REICH....
"THE COUNCIL GAVE ME THIS CASTLE, AS WELL AS UNLIMITED RESOURCES TO INDULGE MY DARKEST DESIRES.
"BUT ALL THE WHILE WE'VE SEARCHED FOR YOU, FABIAN GRAY..."

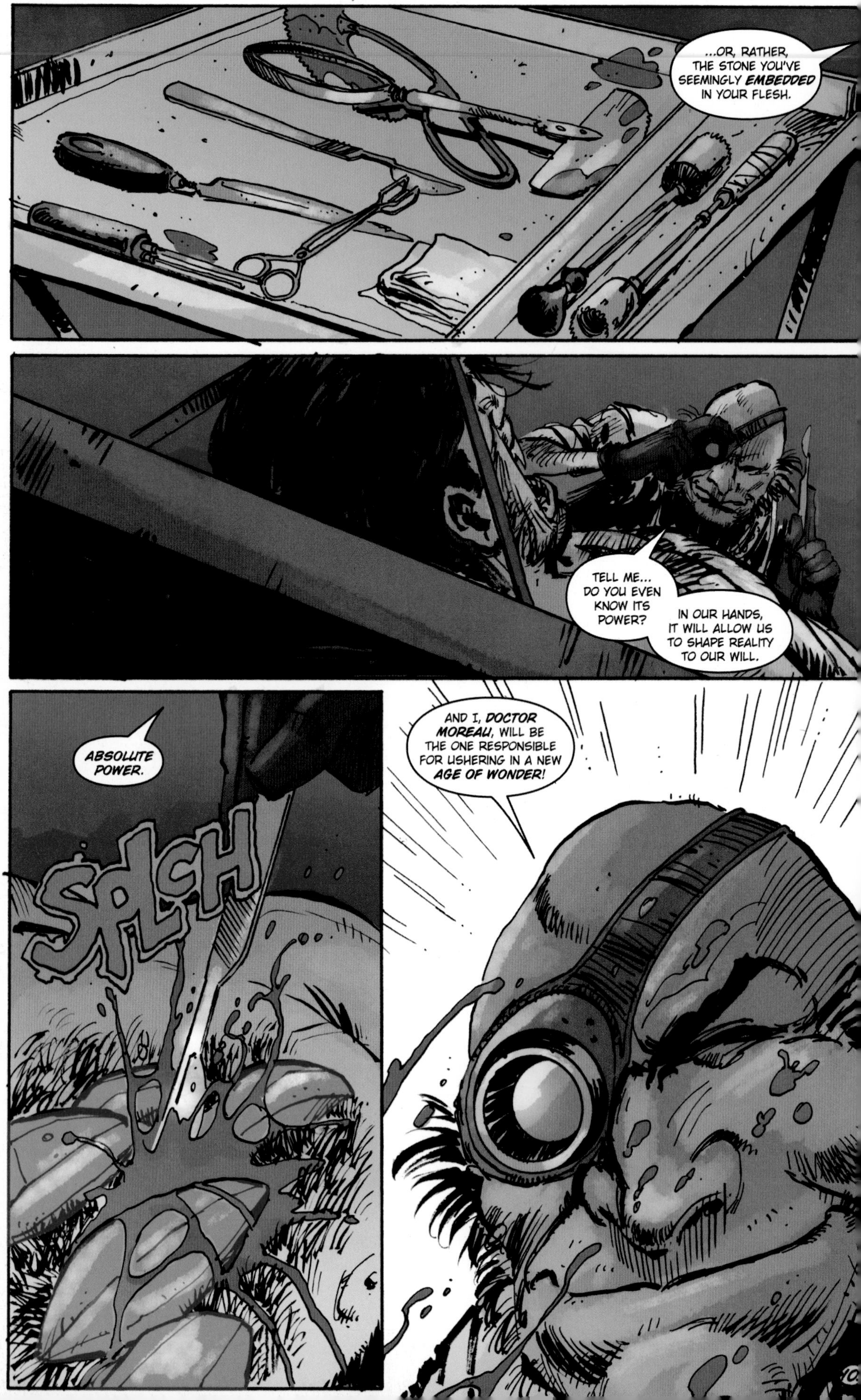
...OR, RATHER, THE STONE YOU'VE SEEMINGLY *EMBEDDED* IN YOUR FLESH.
TELL ME... DO YOU EVEN KNOW ITS POWER?
IN OUR HANDS, IT WILL ALLOW US TO SHAPE REALITY TO OUR WILL.
ABSOLUTE POWER.
SPLCH
AND I, *DOCTOR MOREAU*, WILL BE THE ONE RESPONSIBLE FOR USHERING IN A NEW *AGE OF WONDER!*

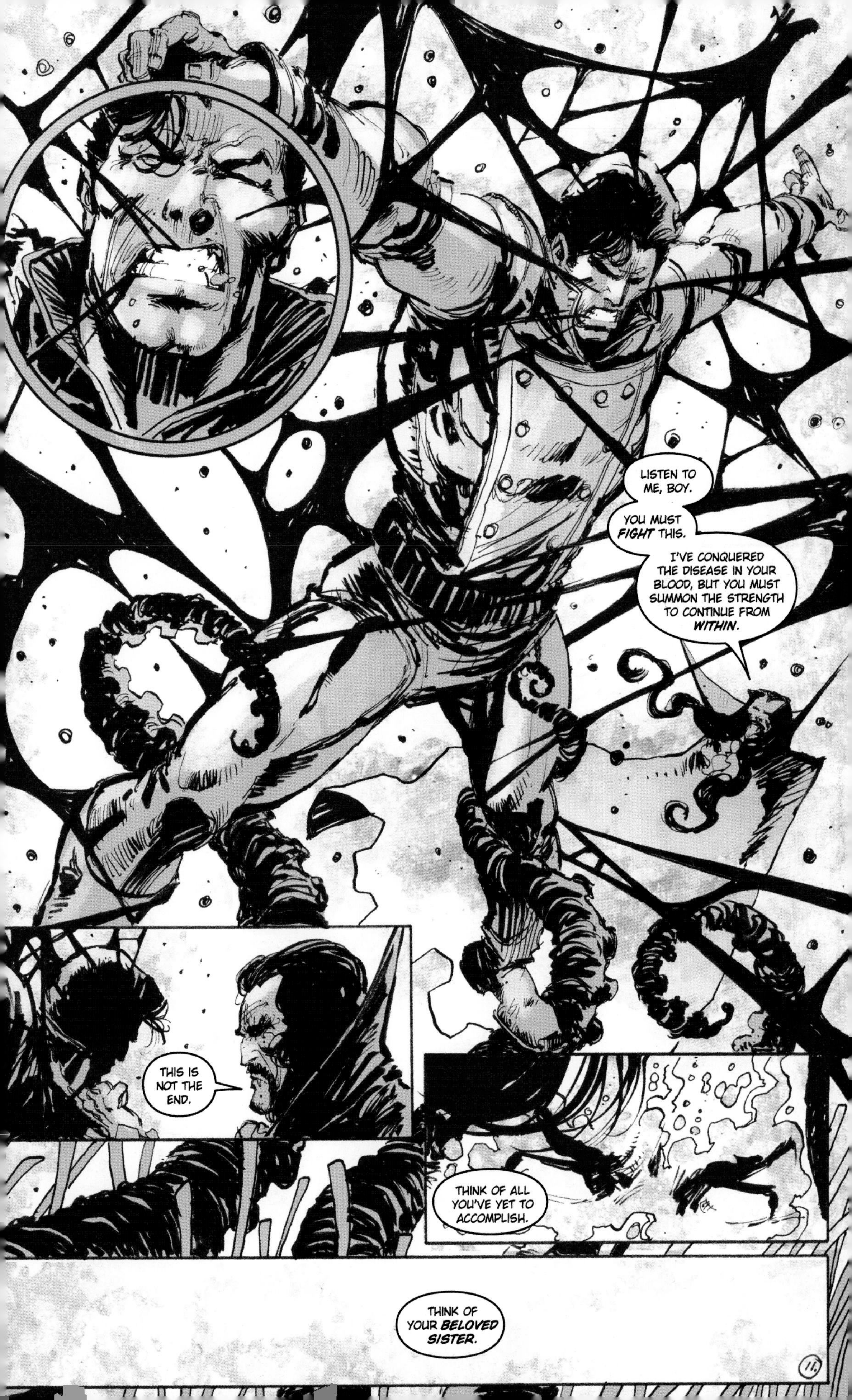
LISTEN TO ME, BOY.
YOU MUST *FIGHT* THIS.
I'VE CONQUERED THE DISEASE IN YOUR BLOOD, BUT YOU MUST SUMMON THE STRENGTH TO CONTINUE FROM *WITHIN*.
THIS IS NOT THE END.
THINK OF ALL YOU'VE YET TO ACCOMPLISH.
THINK OF YOUR *BELOVED SISTER*.

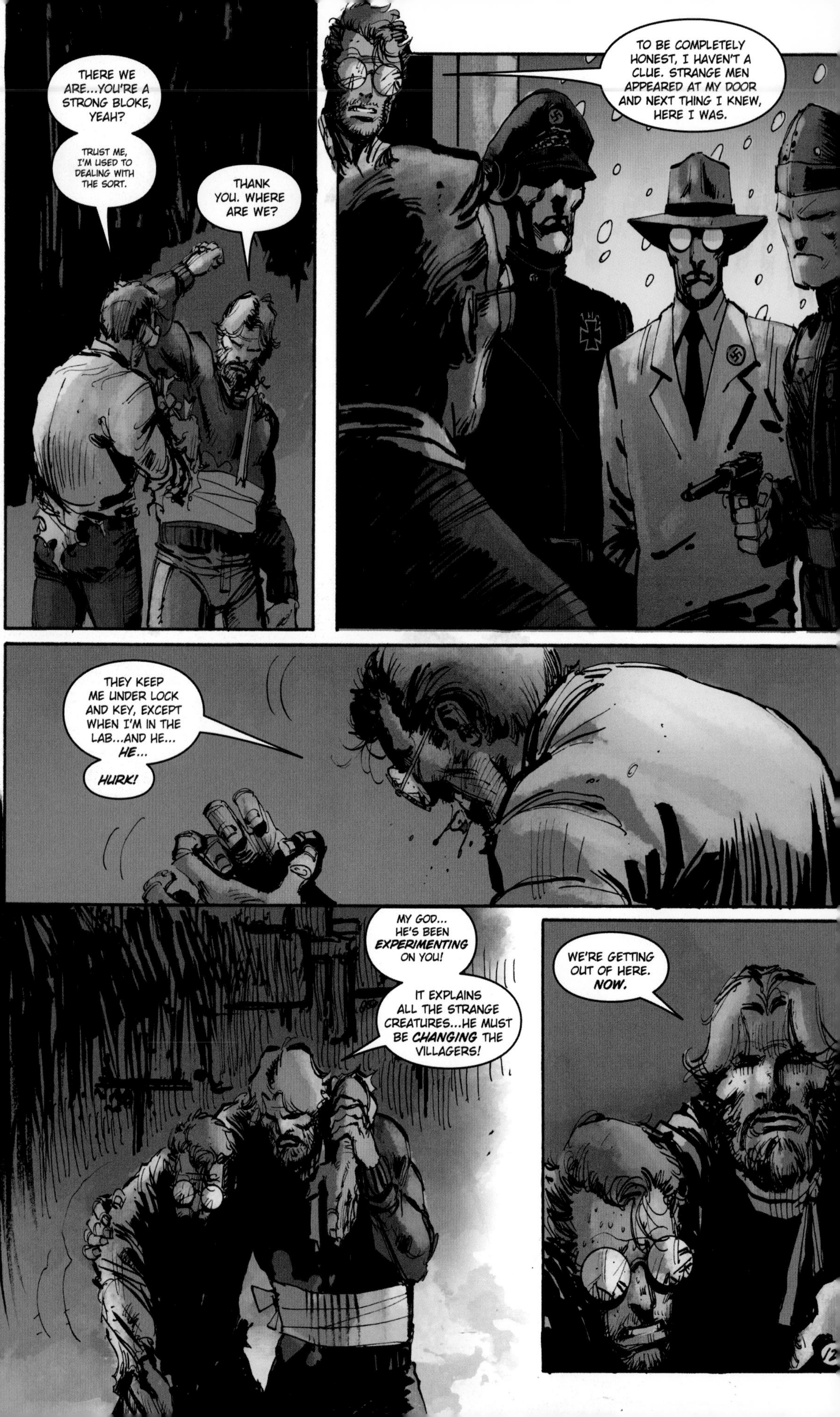

THERE WE ARE...YOU'RE A STRONG BLOKE, YEAH?
TRUST ME, I'M USED TO DEALING WITH THE SORT.
THANK YOU. WHERE ARE WE?
TO BE COMPLETELY HONEST, I HAVEN'T A CLUE. STRANGE MEN APPEARED AT MY DOOR AND NEXT THING I KNEW, HERE I WAS.
THEY KEEP ME UNDER LOCK AND KEY, EXCEPT WHEN I'M IN THE LAB...AND HE... HE...
HURK!
MY GOD... HE'S BEEN EXPERIMENTING ON YOU!
IT EXPLAINS ALL THE STRANGE CREATURES...HE MUST BE CHANGING THE VILLAGERS!
WE'RE GETTING OUT OF HERE. NOW.

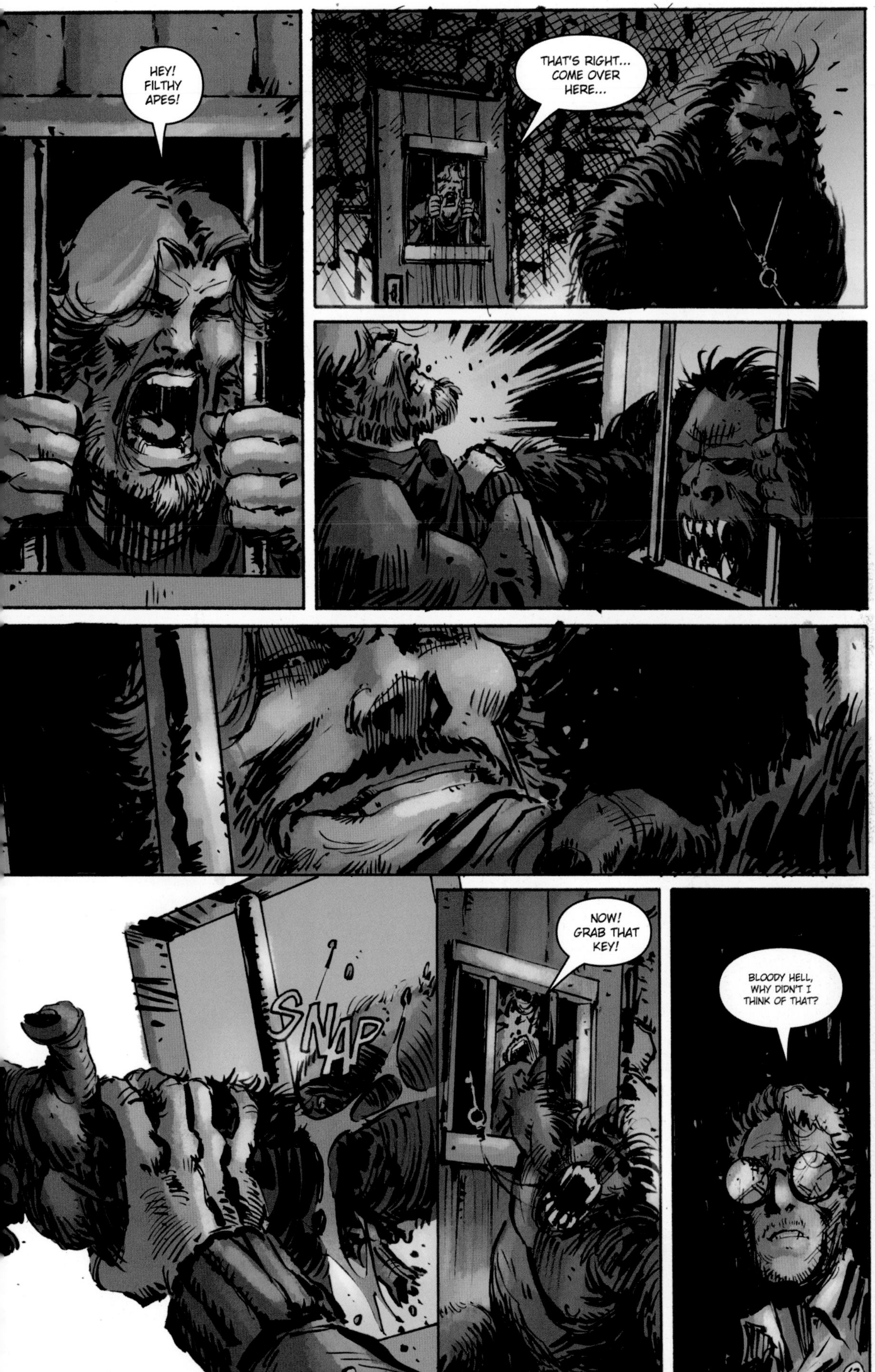
HEY! FILTHY APES!
THAT'S RIGHT... COME OVER HERE...
SNAP
NOW! GRAB THAT KEY!
BLOODY HELL, WHY DIDN'T I THINK OF THAT?
13.

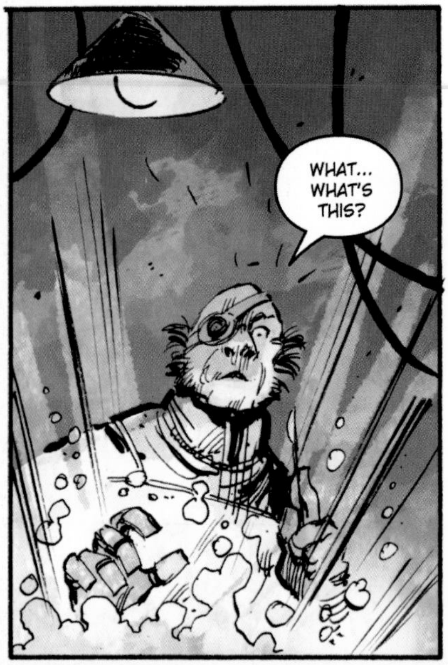
WHAT... WHAT'S THIS?

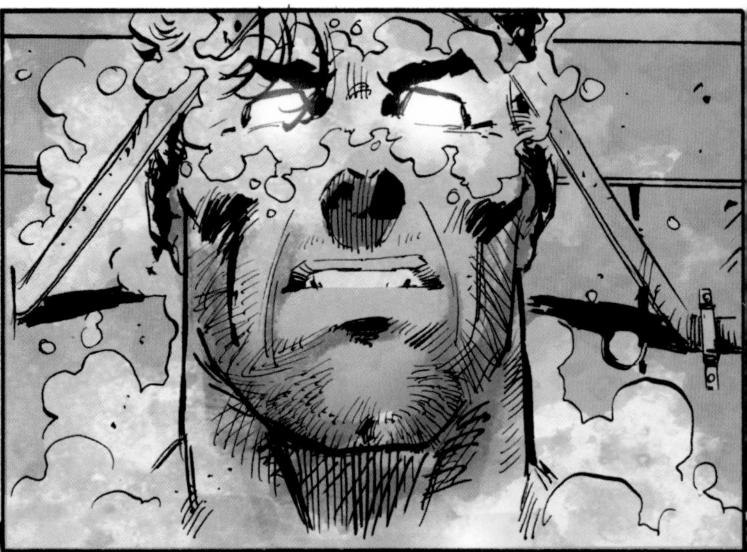

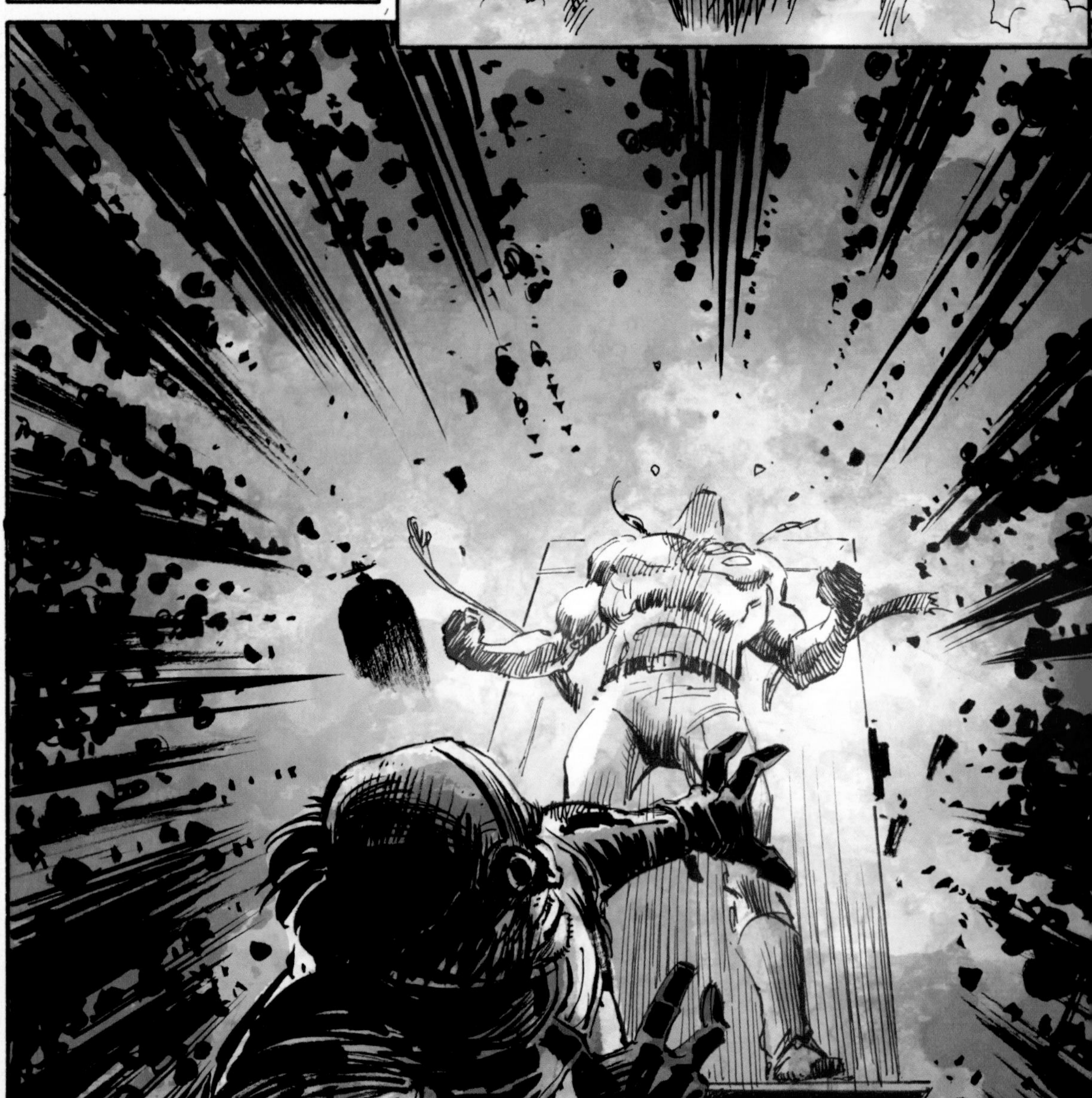

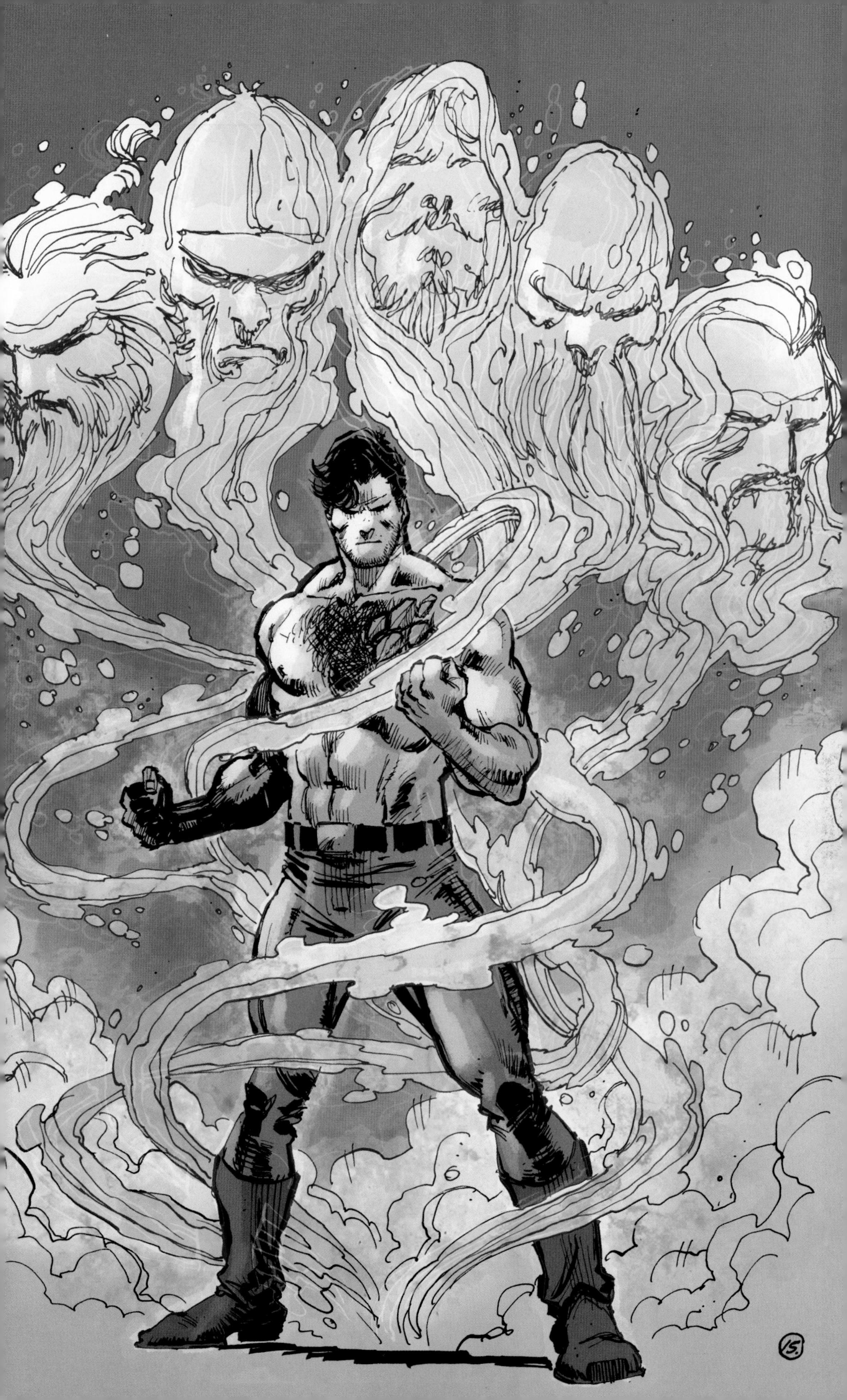

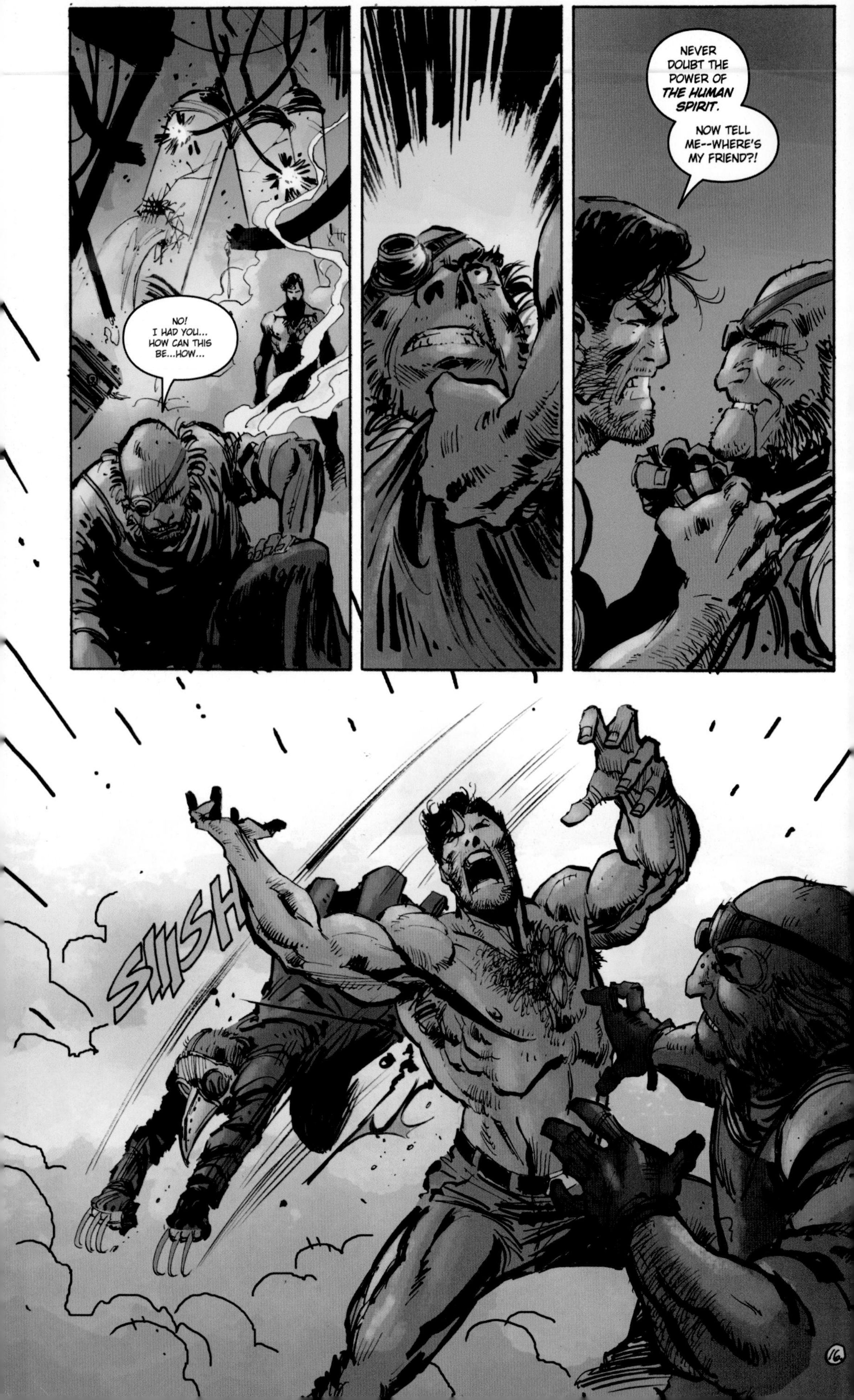
NO! I HAD YOU... HOW CAN THIS BE...HOW...
NEVER DOUBT THE POWER OF THE HUMAN SPIRIT.
NOW TELL ME--WHERE'S MY FRIEND?!
SHHSH
16

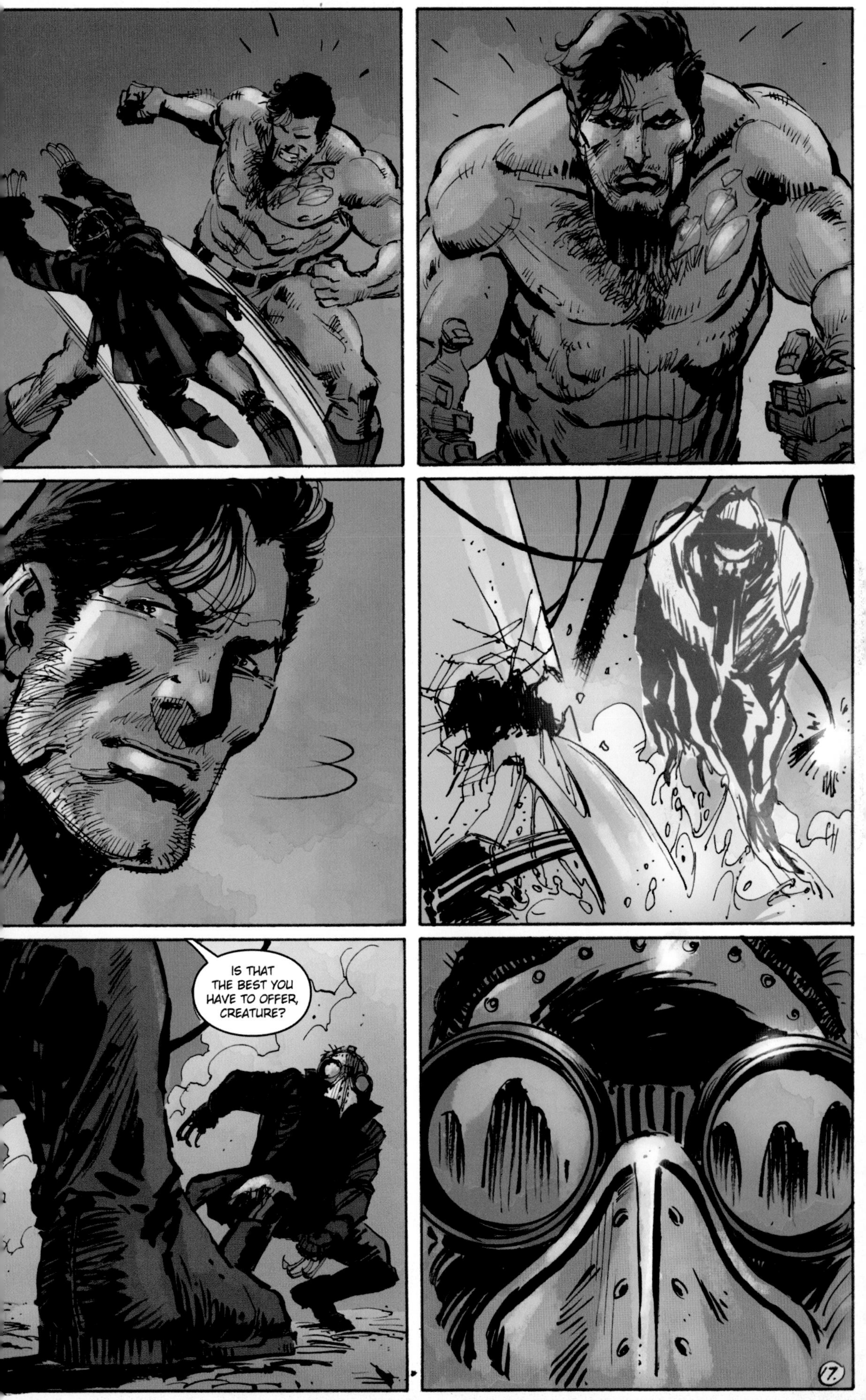
IS THAT THE BEST YOU HAVE TO OFFER, CREATURE?

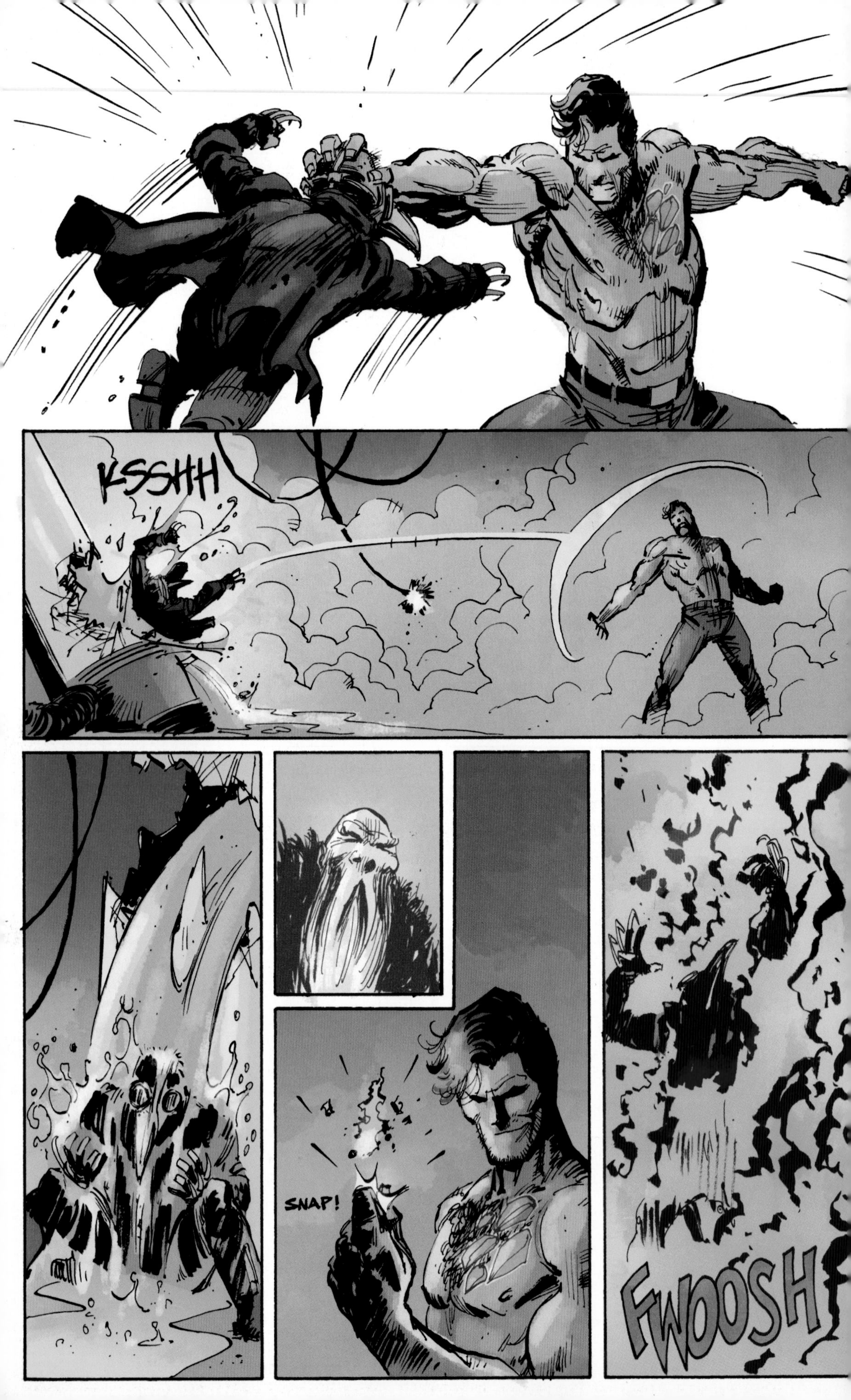
KSSHH
SNAP!
FWOOSH

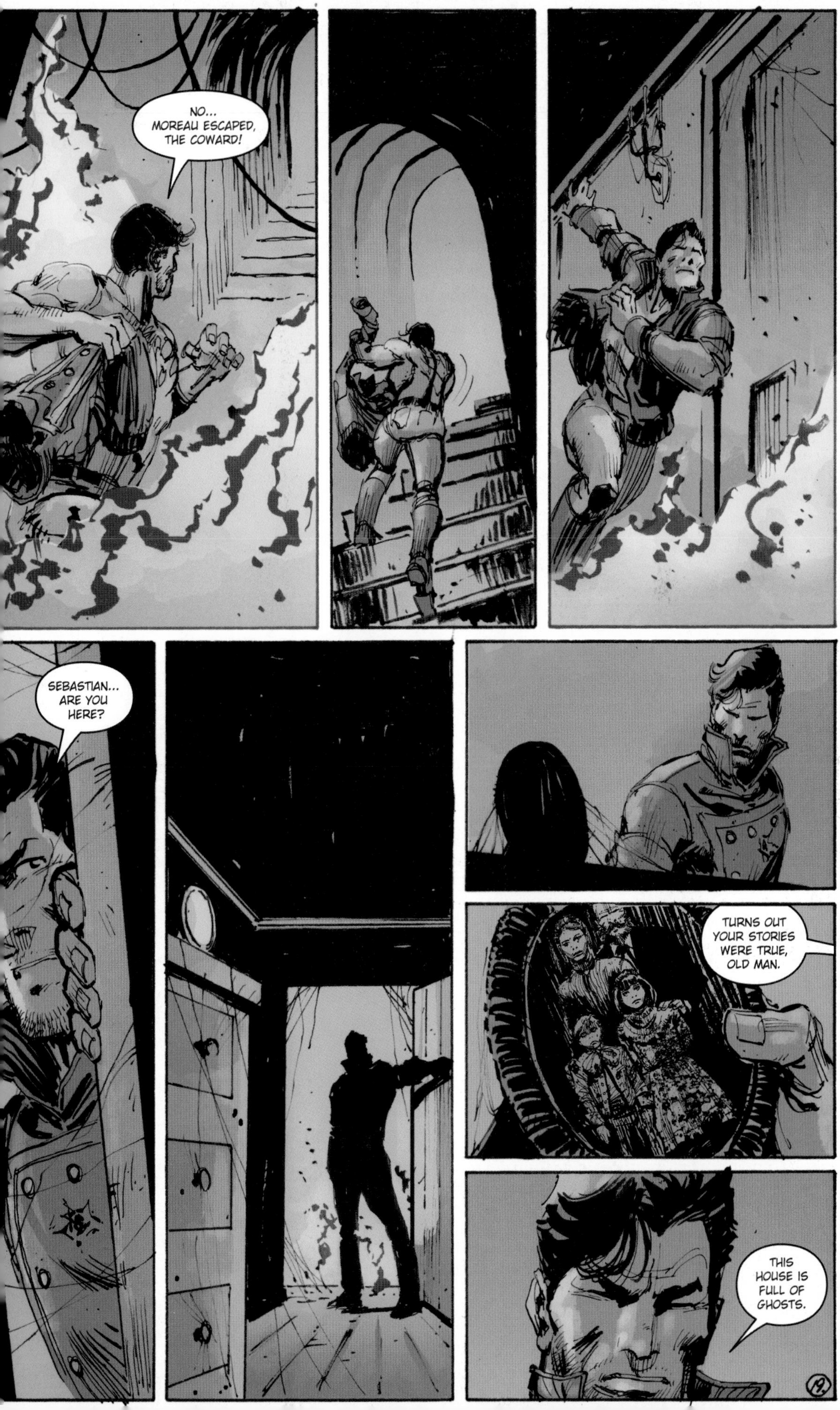
NO... MOREAU ESCAPED, THE COWARD!
SEBASTIAN... ARE YOU HERE?
TURNS OUT YOUR STORIES WERE TRUE, OLD MAN.
THIS HOUSE IS FULL OF GHOSTS.
19

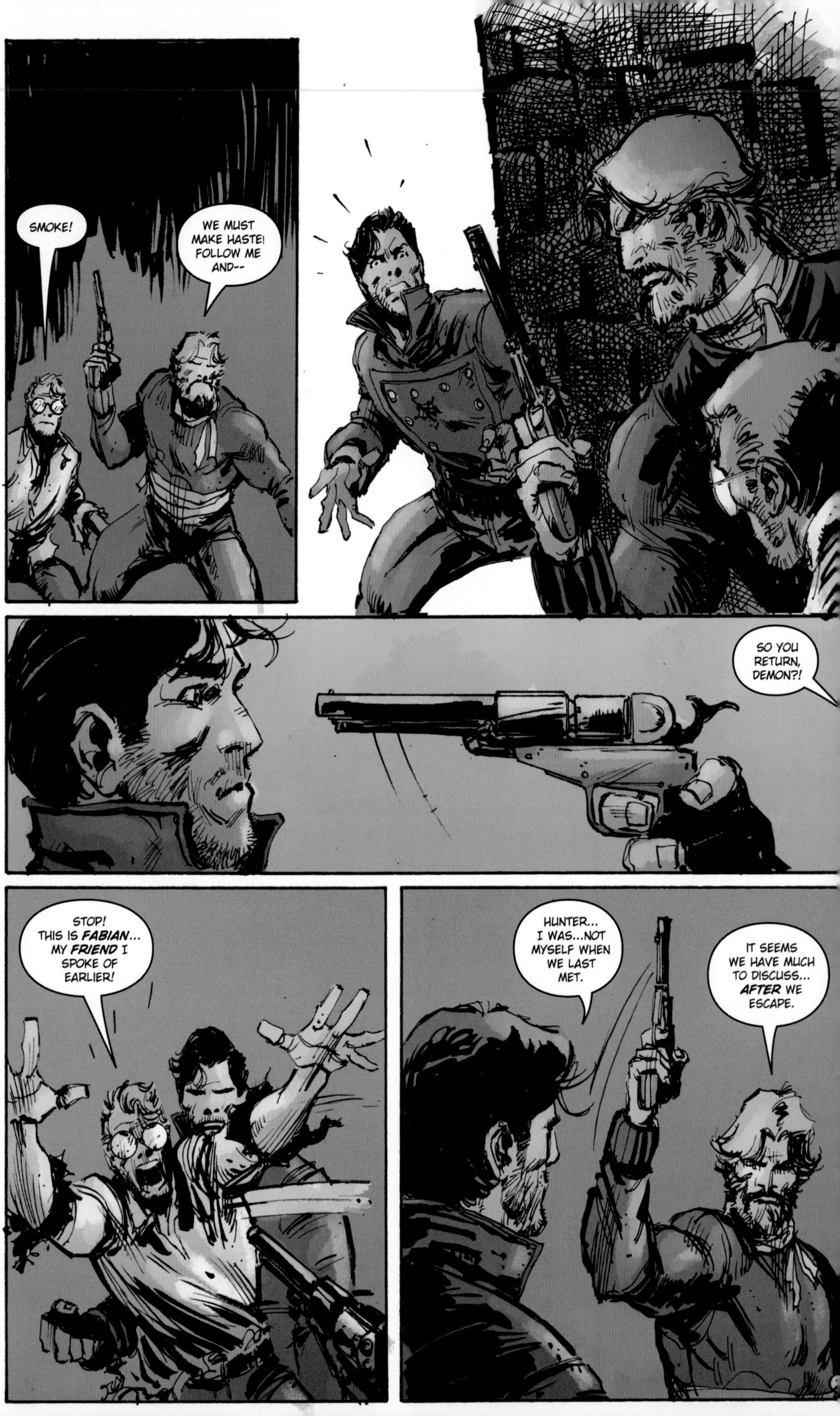
SMOKE!
WE MUST MAKE HASTE! FOLLOW ME AND--
SO YOU RETURN, DEMON?!
STOP! THIS IS *FABIAN*... MY *FRIEND* I SPOKE OF EARLIER!
HUNTER... I WAS...NOT MYSELF WHEN WE LAST MET.
IT SEEMS WE HAVE MUCH TO DISCUSS... ***AFTER*** WE ESCAPE.

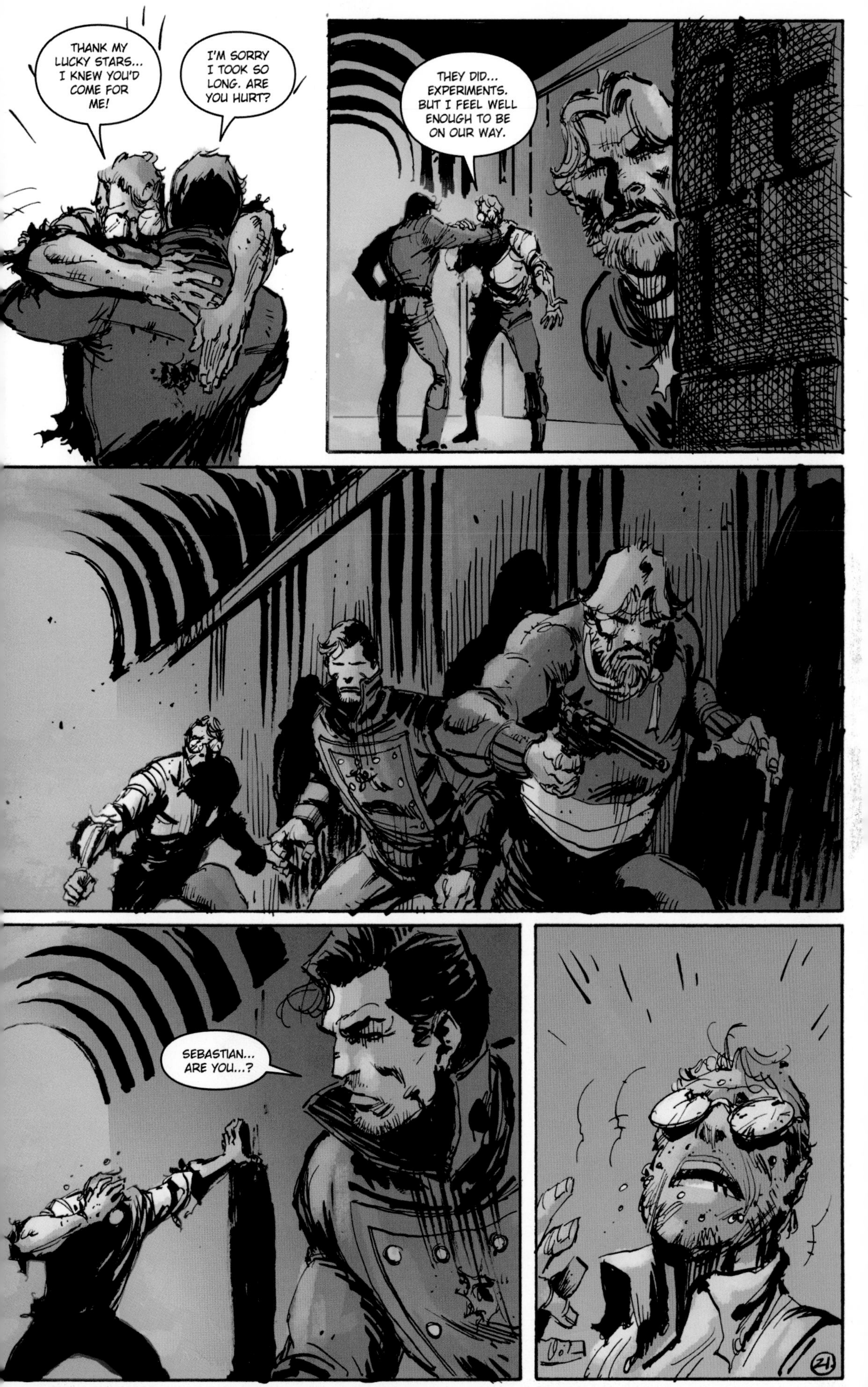
THANK MY LUCKY STARS... I KNEW YOU'D COME FOR ME!
I'M SORRY I TOOK SO LONG. ARE YOU HURT?
THEY DID... EXPERIMENTS. BUT I FEEL WELL ENOUGH TO BE ON OUR WAY.
SEBASTIAN... ARE YOU...?

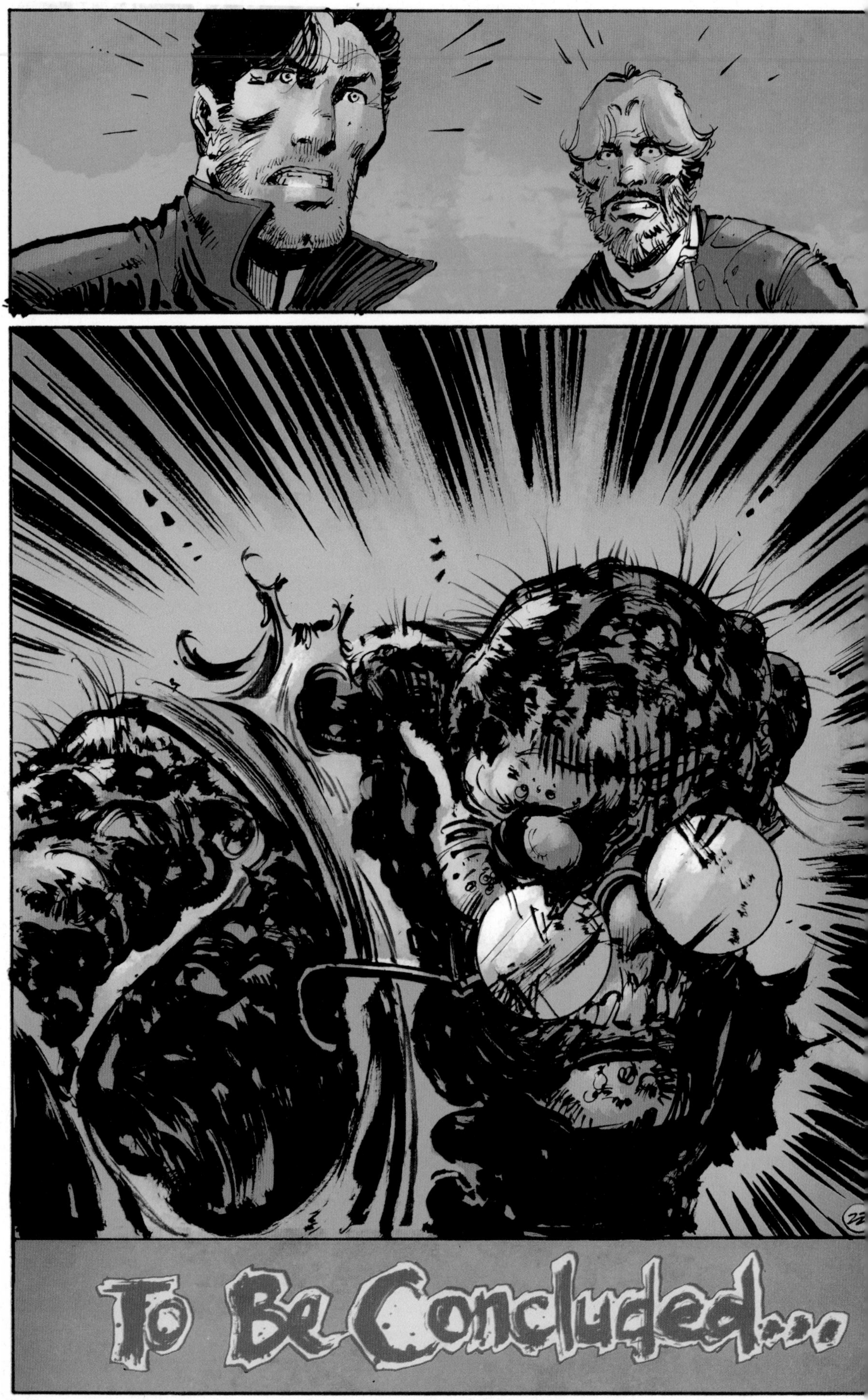
To Be Concluded...

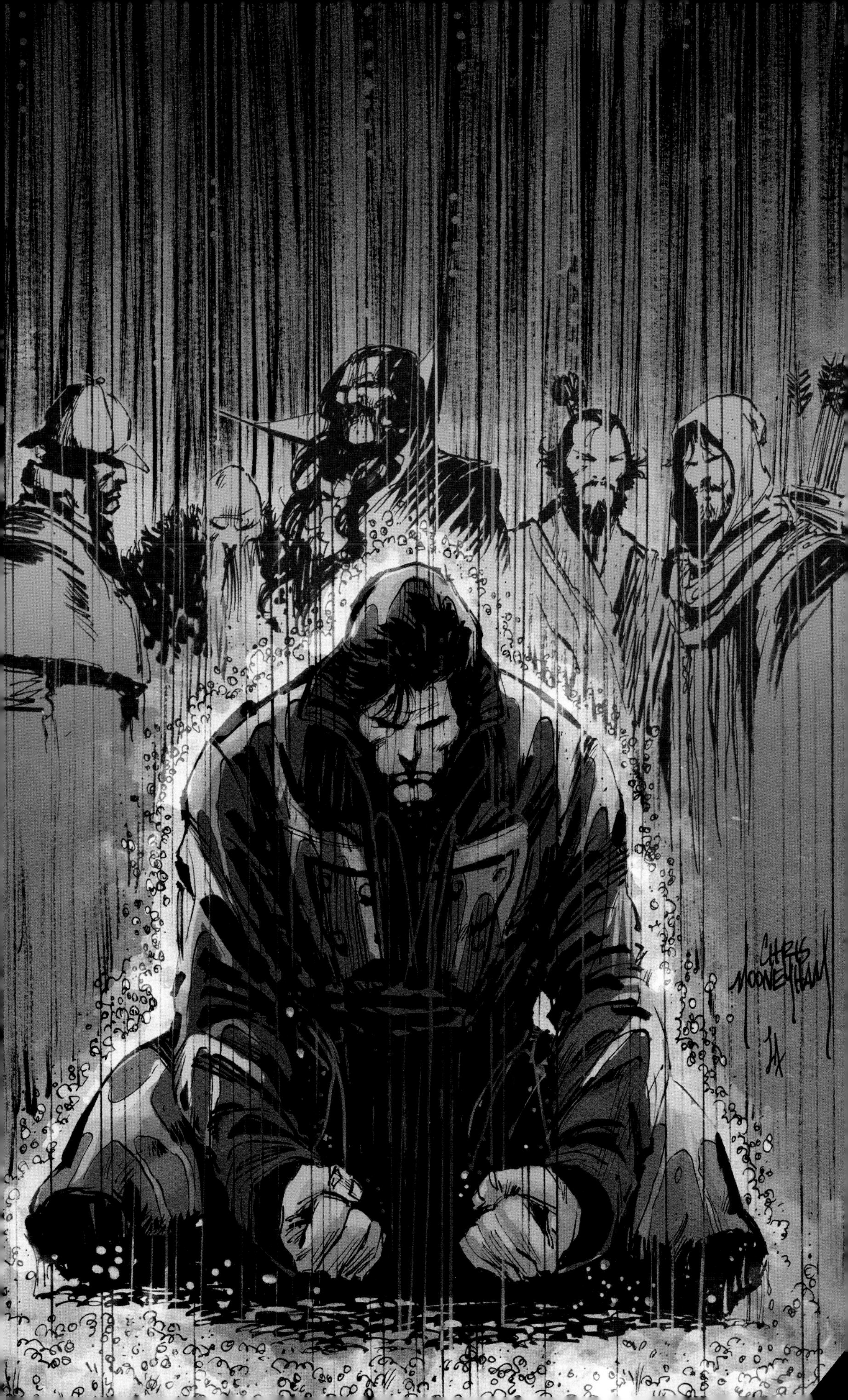
CHRIS MOONEYHAM

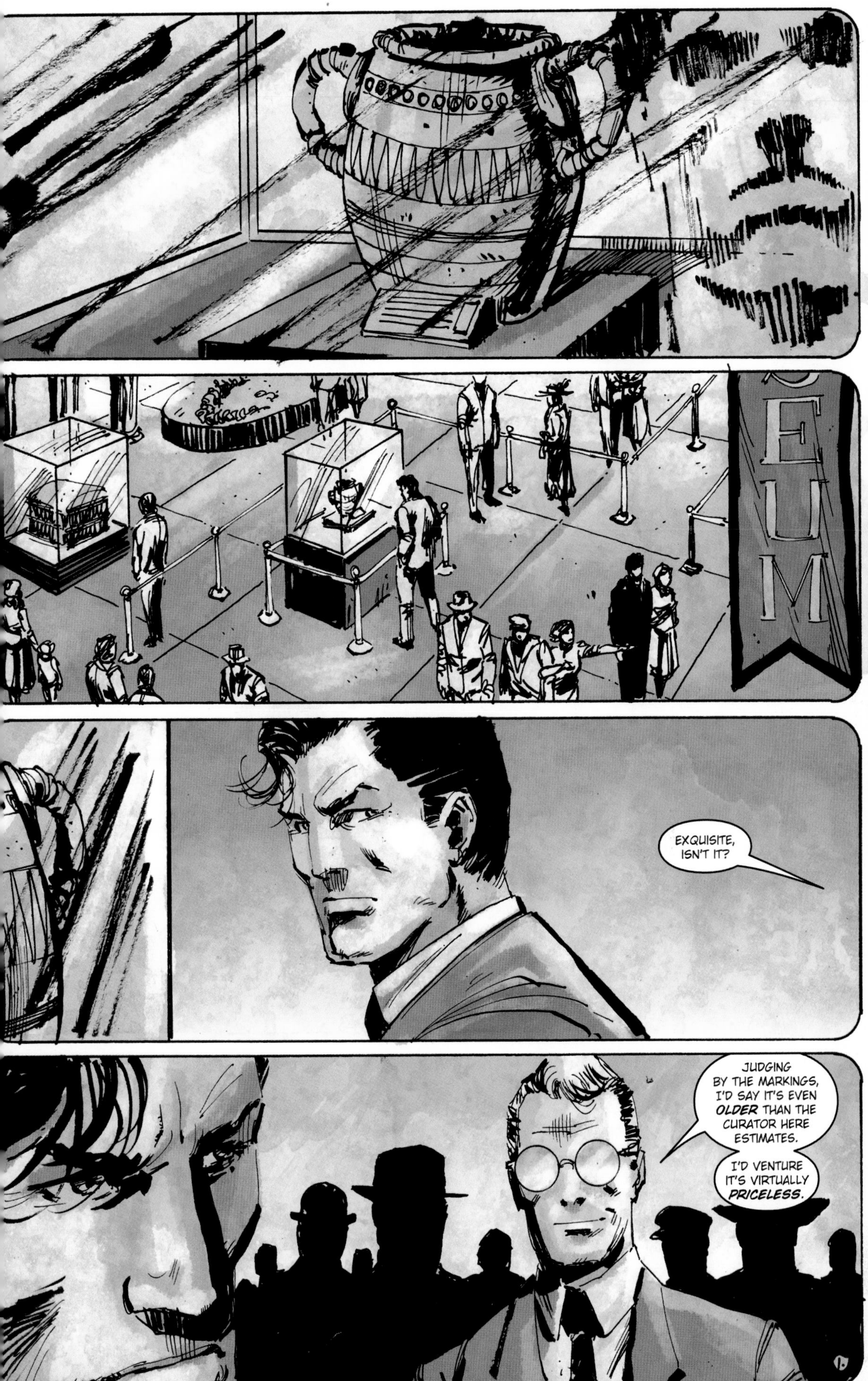
EXQUISITE, ISN'T IT?
JUDGING BY THE MARKINGS, I'D SAY IT'S EVEN OLDER THAN THE CURATOR HERE ESTIMATES.
I'D VENTURE IT'S VIRTUALLY PRICELESS.

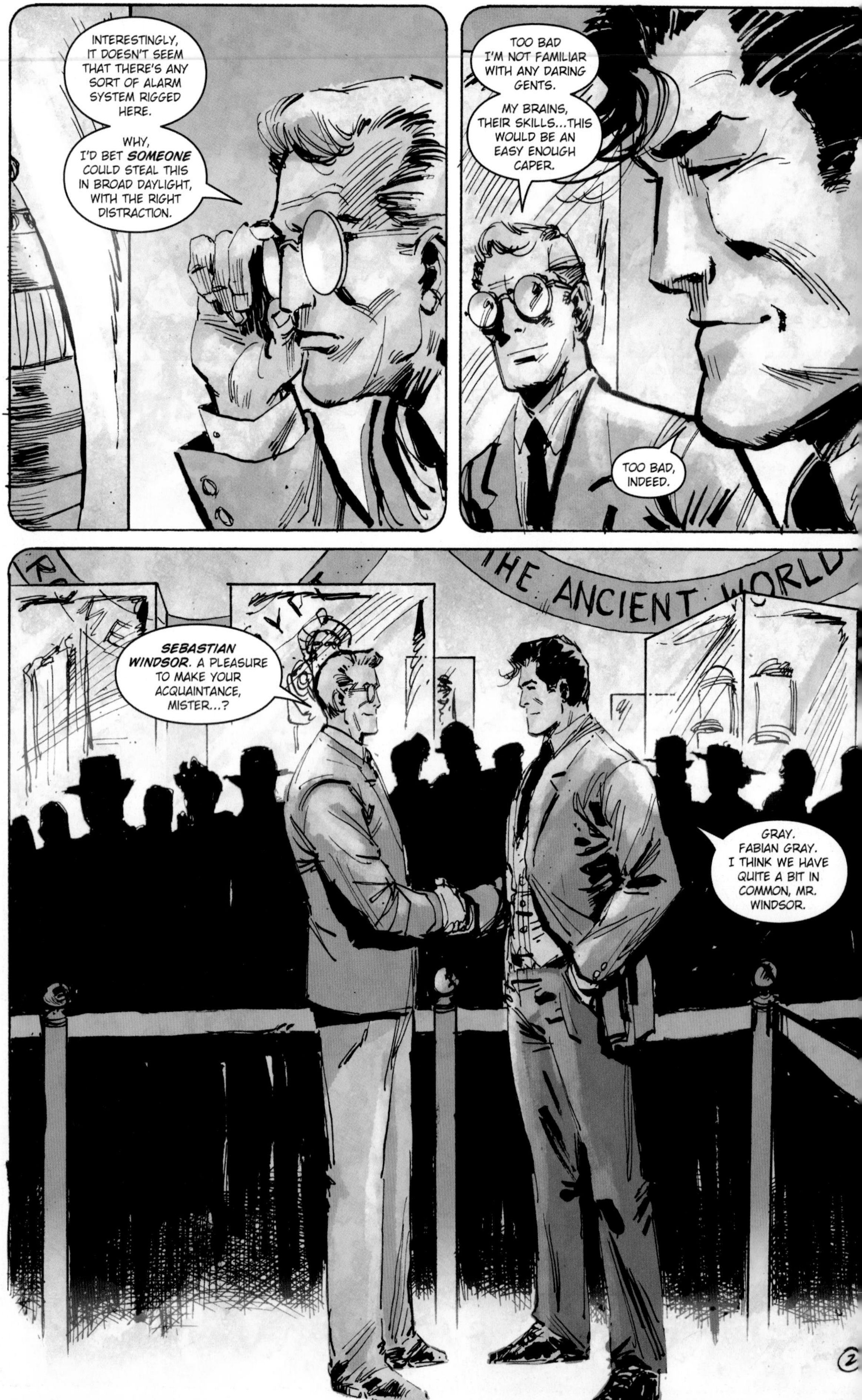
INTERESTINGLY, IT DOESN'T SEEM THAT THERE'S ANY SORT OF ALARM SYSTEM RIGGED HERE.
WHY, I'D BET **SOMEONE** COULD STEAL THIS IN BROAD DAYLIGHT, WITH THE RIGHT DISTRACTION.
TOO BAD I'M NOT FAMILIAR WITH ANY DARING GENTS.
MY BRAINS, THEIR SKILLS...THIS WOULD BE AN EASY ENOUGH CAPER.
TOO BAD, INDEED.
THE ANCIENT WORLD
SEBASTIAN WINDSOR. A PLEASURE TO MAKE YOUR ACQUAINTANCE, MISTER...?
GRAY. FABIAN GRAY. I THINK WE HAVE QUITE A BIT IN COMMON, MR. WINDSOR.
2

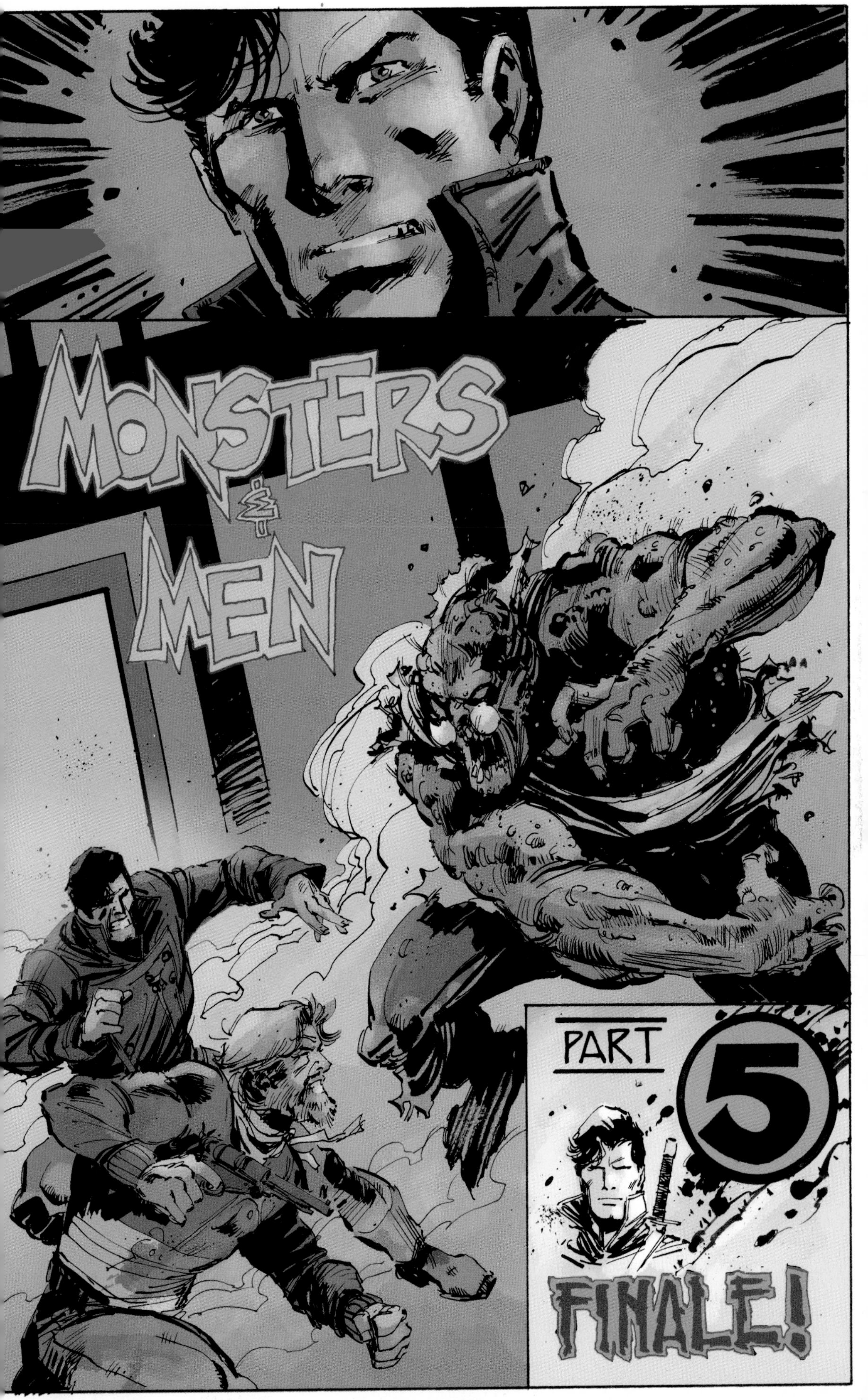
MONSTERS & MEN
PART 5
FINALE!

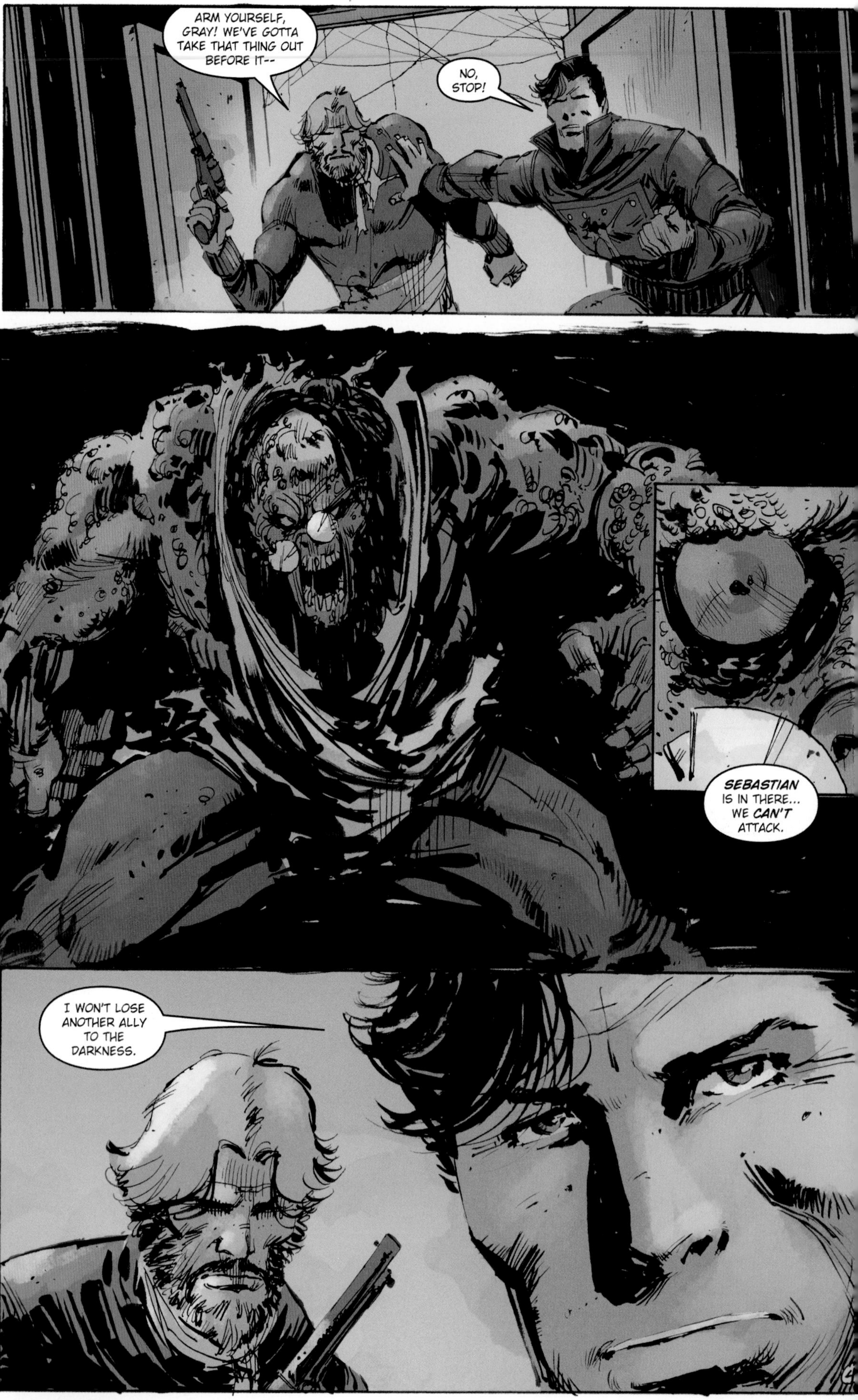
ARM YOURSELF, GRAY! WE'VE GOTTA TAKE THAT THING OUT BEFORE IT--
NO, STOP!
SEBASTIAN IS IN THERE... WE CAN'T ATTACK.
I WON'T LOSE ANOTHER ALLY TO THE DARKNESS.

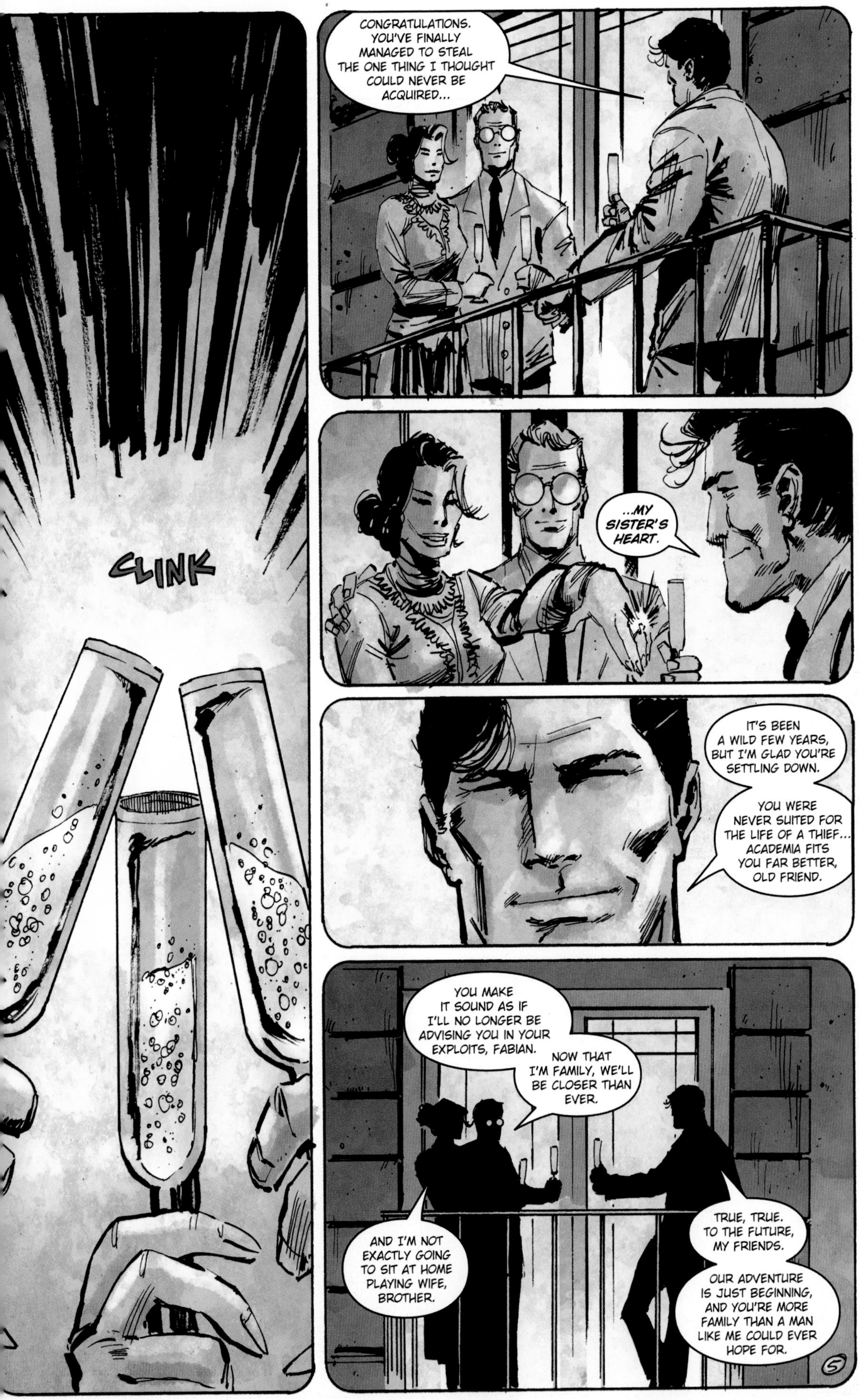
CLINK
CONGRATULATIONS. YOU'VE FINALLY MANAGED TO STEAL THE ONE THING I THOUGHT COULD NEVER BE ACQUIRED...
...MY SISTER'S HEART.
IT'S BEEN A WILD FEW YEARS, BUT I'M GLAD YOU'RE SETTLING DOWN.
YOU WERE NEVER SUITED FOR THE LIFE OF A THIEF... ACADEMIA FITS YOU FAR BETTER, OLD FRIEND.
YOU MAKE IT SOUND AS IF I'LL NO LONGER BE ADVISING YOU IN YOUR EXPLOITS, FABIAN.
NOW THAT I'M FAMILY, WE'LL BE CLOSER THAN EVER.
AND I'M NOT EXACTLY GOING TO SIT AT HOME PLAYING WIFE, BROTHER.
TRUE, TRUE. TO THE FUTURE, MY FRIENDS.
OUR ADVENTURE IS JUST BEGINNING, AND YOU'RE MORE FAMILY THAN A MAN LIKE ME COULD EVER HOPE FOR.
5

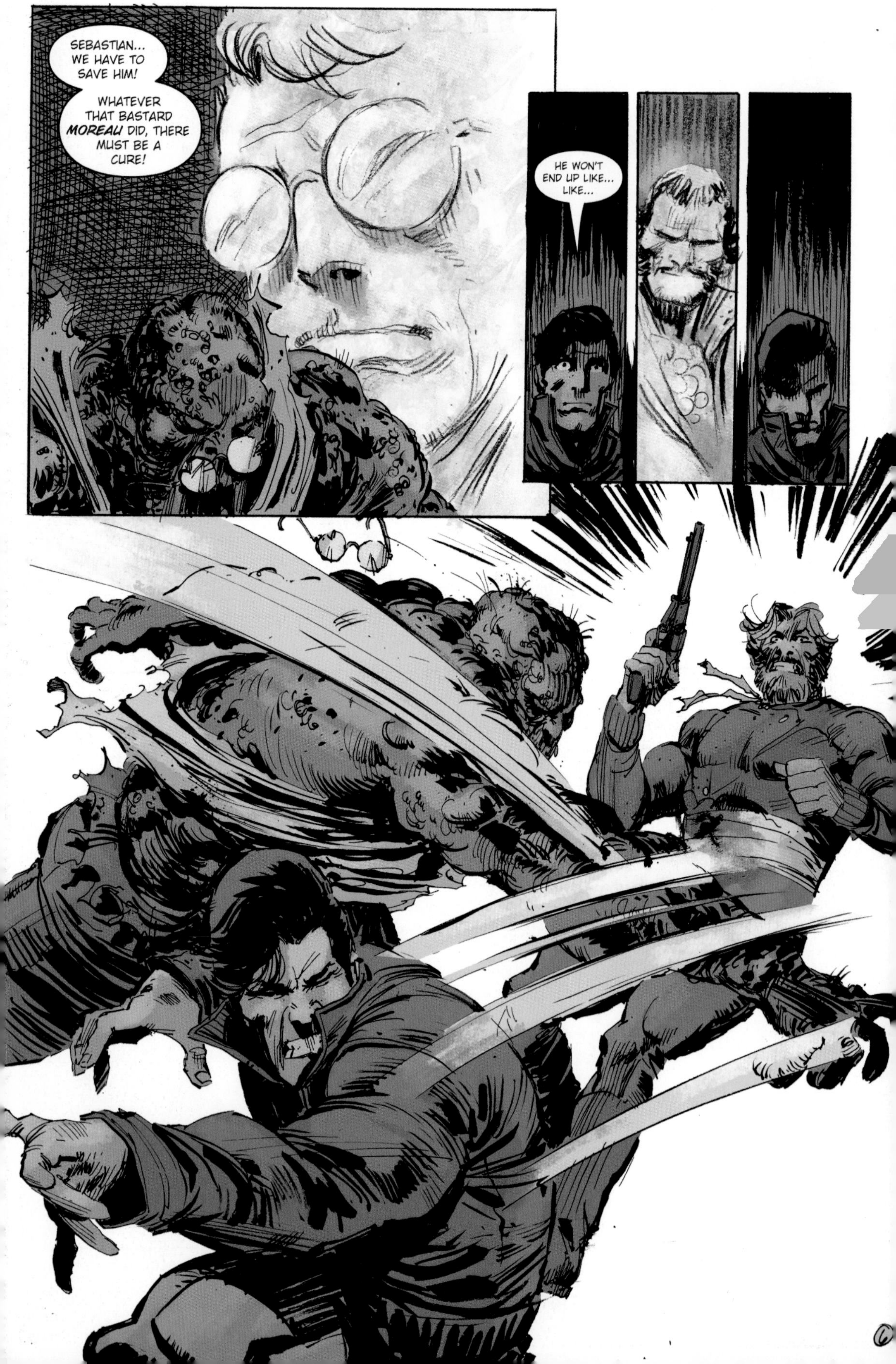

SEBASTIAN... WE HAVE TO SAVE HIM!
WHATEVER THAT BASTARD MOREAU DID, THERE MUST BE A CURE!
HE WON'T END UP LIKE... LIKE...

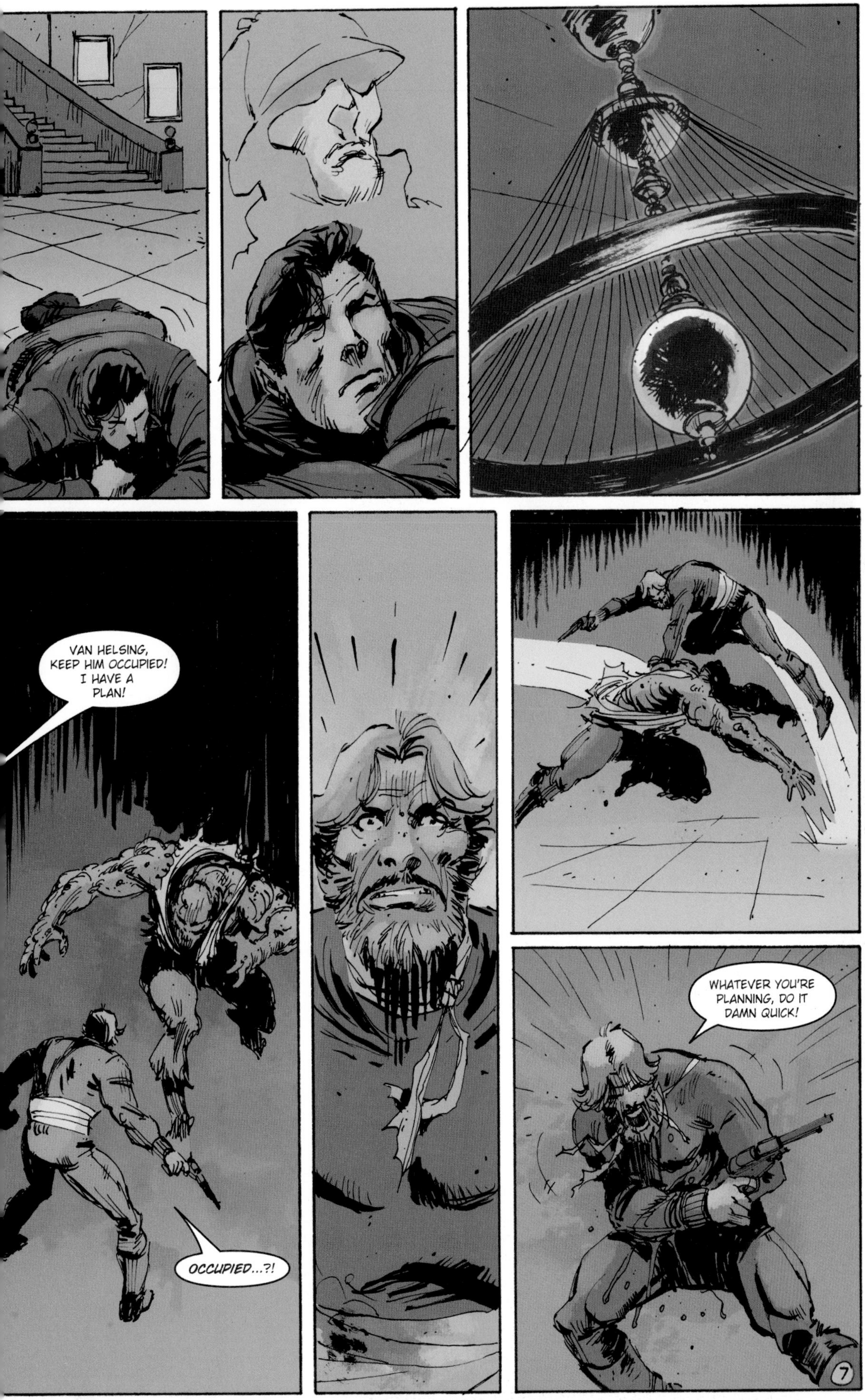
VAN HELSING, KEEP HIM OCCUPIED! I HAVE A PLAN!
OCCUPIED...?!
WHATEVER YOU'RE PLANNING, DO IT DAMN QUICK!
7

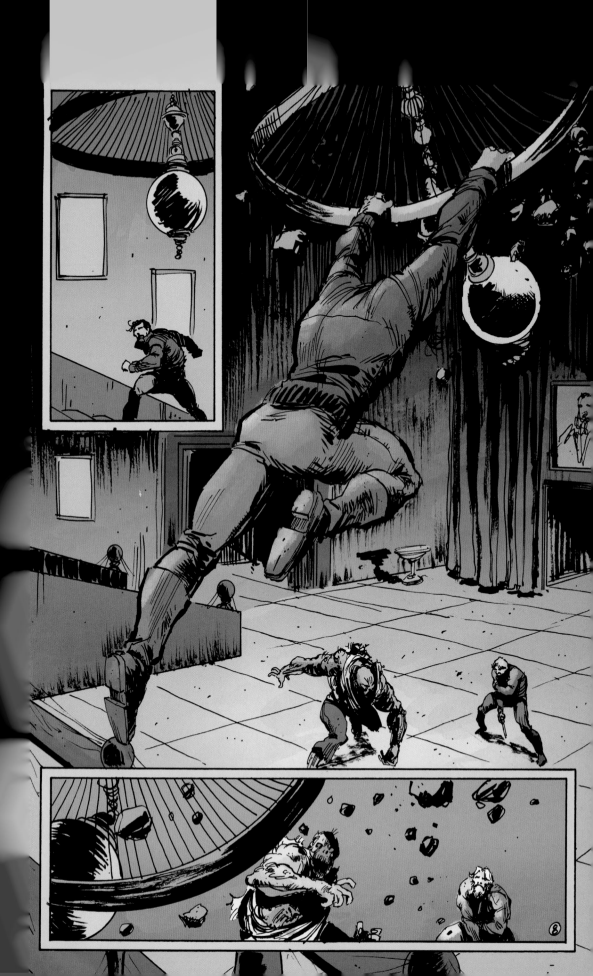

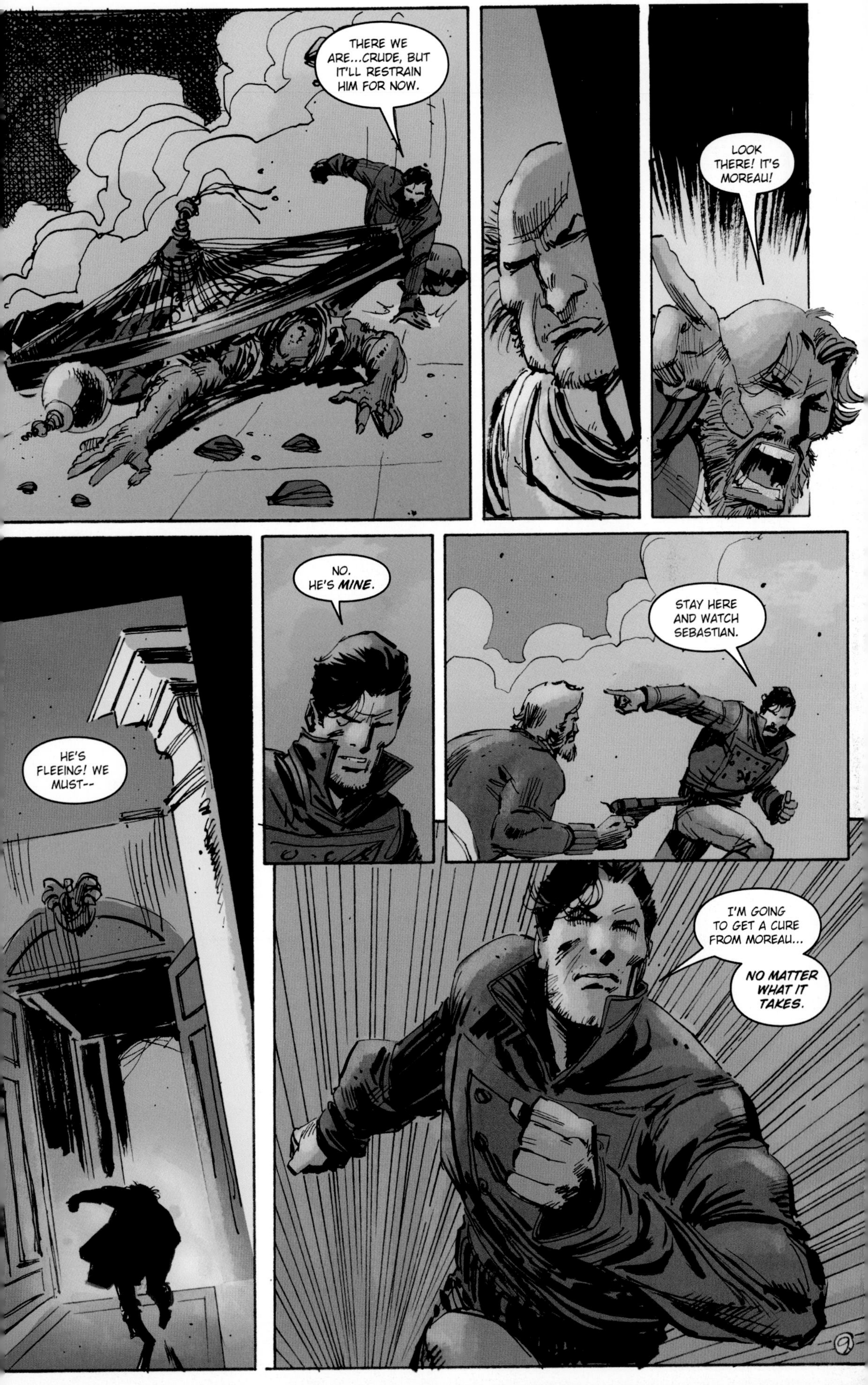
THERE WE ARE...CRUDE, BUT IT'LL RESTRAIN HIM FOR NOW.
LOOK THERE! IT'S MOREAU!
HE'S FLEEING! WE MUST--
NO. HE'S *MINE*.
STAY HERE AND WATCH SEBASTIAN.
I'M GOING TO GET A CURE FROM MOREAU...
NO MATTER WHAT IT TAKES.
9

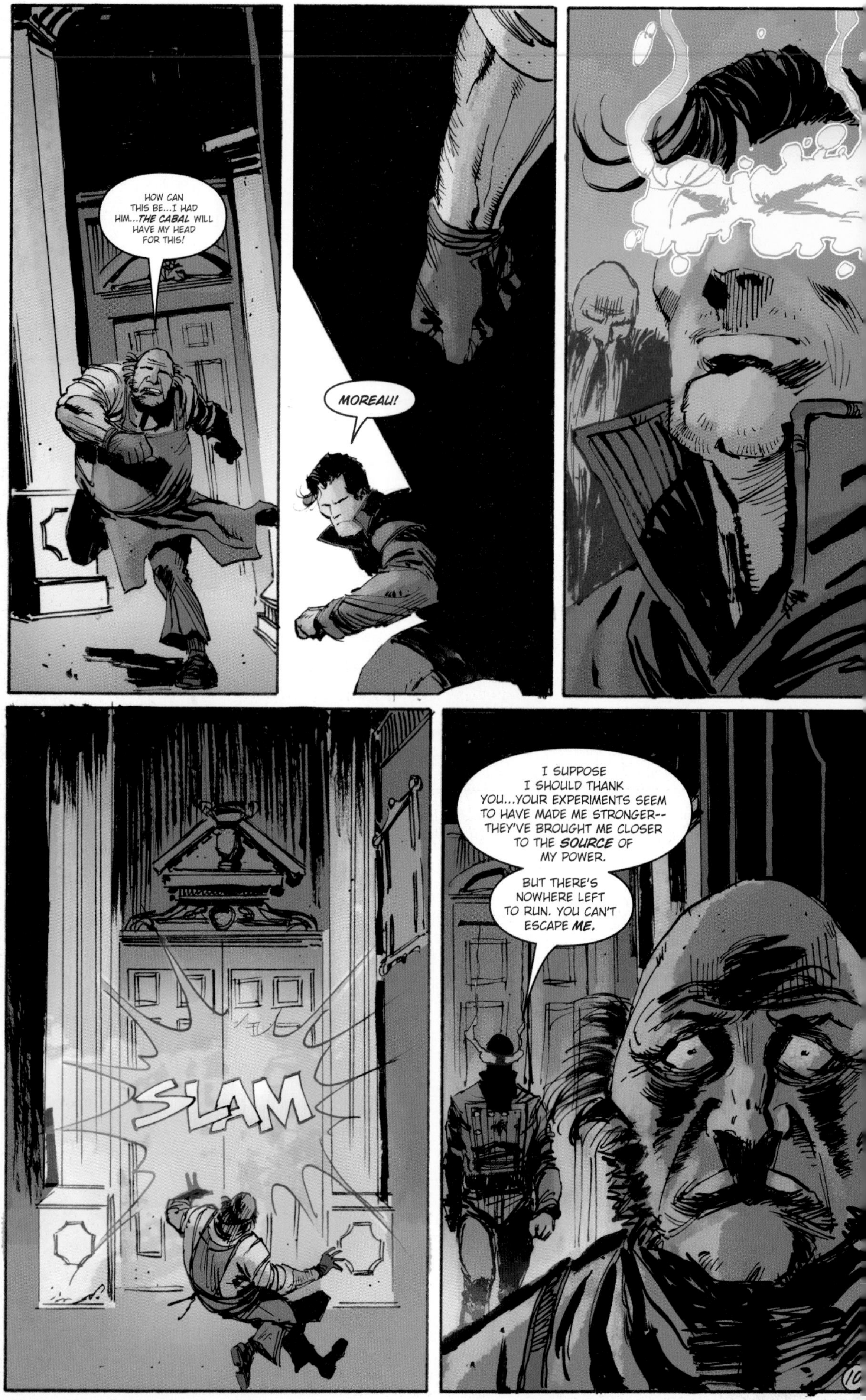
HOW CAN THIS BE...I HAD HIM...THE CABAL WILL HAVE MY HEAD FOR THIS!
MOREAU!
SLAM
I SUPPOSE I SHOULD THANK YOU...YOUR EXPERIMENTS SEEM TO HAVE MADE ME STRONGER--THEY'VE BROUGHT ME CLOSER TO THE SOURCE OF MY POWER.
BUT THERE'S NOWHERE LEFT TO RUN. YOU CAN'T ESCAPE ME.

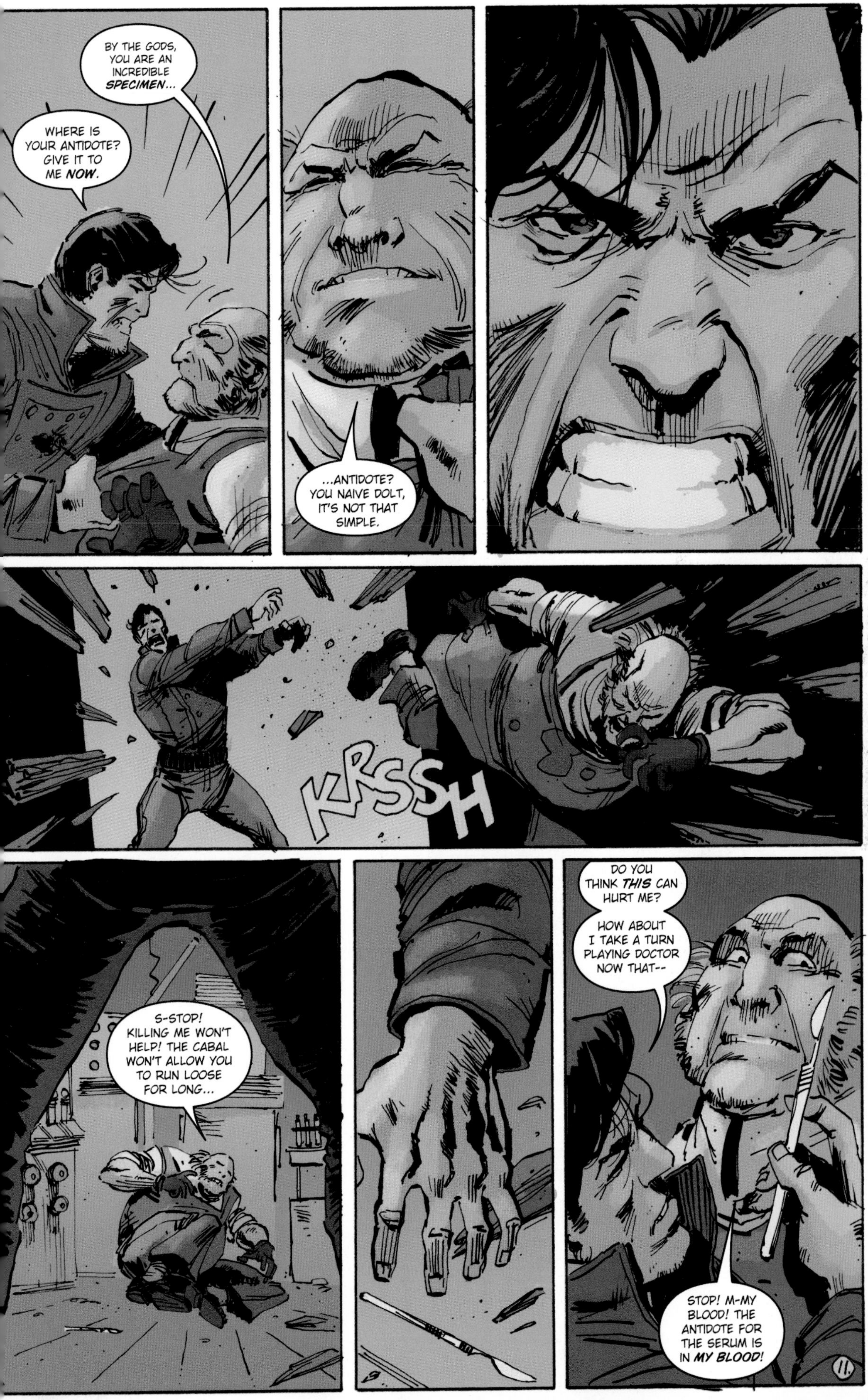

WHERE IS YOUR ANTIDOTE? GIVE IT TO ME NOW.
BY THE GODS, YOU ARE AN INCREDIBLE SPECIMEN...
...ANTIDOTE? YOU NAIVE DOLT, IT'S NOT THAT SIMPLE.
KRSSH
S-STOP! KILLING ME WON'T HELP! THE CABAL WON'T ALLOW YOU TO RUN LOOSE FOR LONG...
DO YOU THINK THIS CAN HURT ME?
HOW ABOUT I TAKE A TURN PLAYING DOCTOR NOW THAT--
STOP! M-MY BLOOD! THE ANTIDOTE FOR THE SERUM IS IN MY BLOOD!

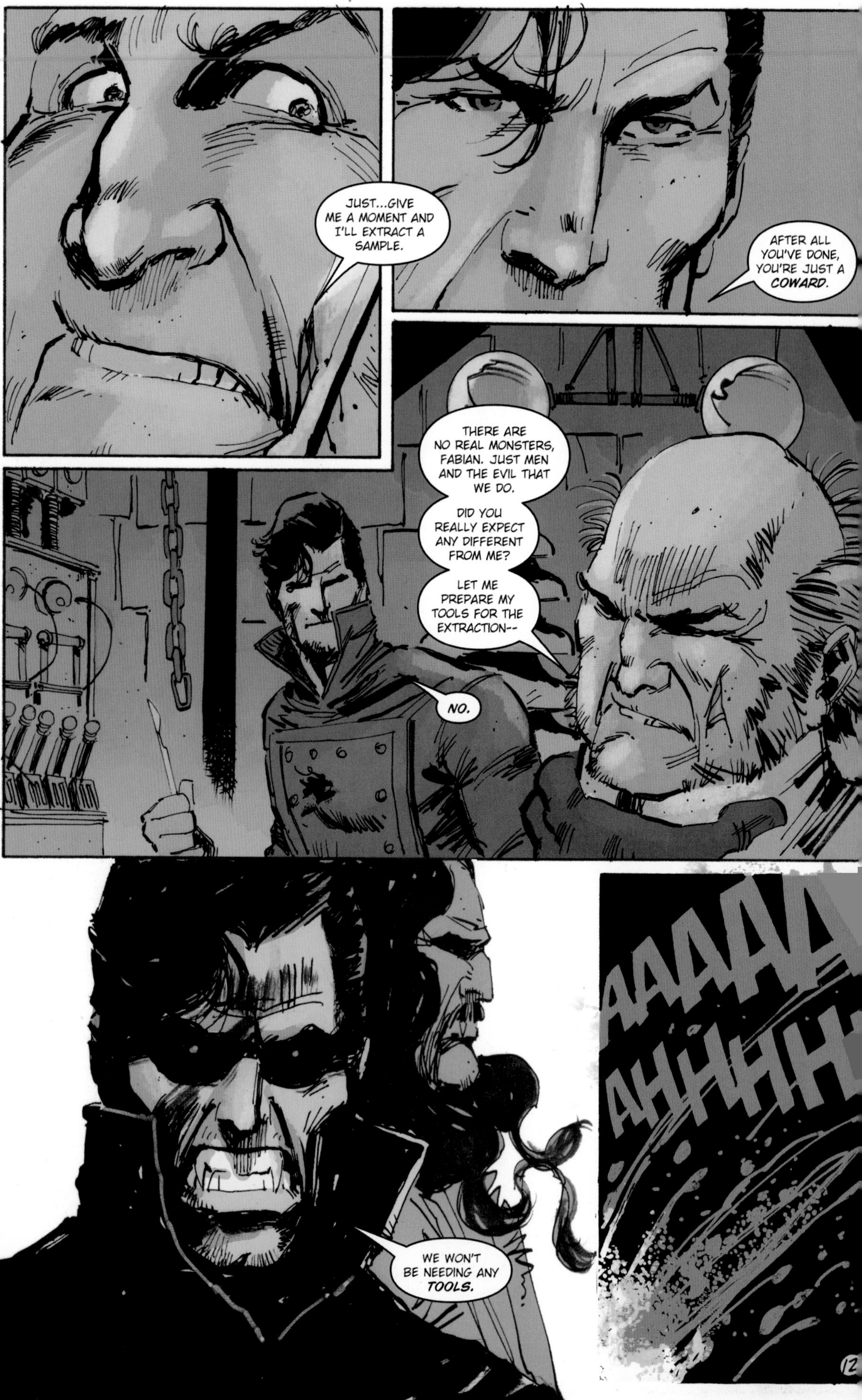
JUST...GIVE ME A MOMENT AND I'LL EXTRACT A SAMPLE.
AFTER ALL YOU'VE DONE, YOU'RE JUST A **COWARD**.
THERE ARE NO REAL MONSTERS, FABIAN. JUST MEN AND THE EVIL THAT WE DO.
DID YOU REALLY EXPECT ANY DIFFERENT FROM ME?
LET ME PREPARE MY TOOLS FOR THE EXTRACTION--
NO.
WE WON'T BE NEEDING ANY **TOOLS.**
AAAAA AHHHH

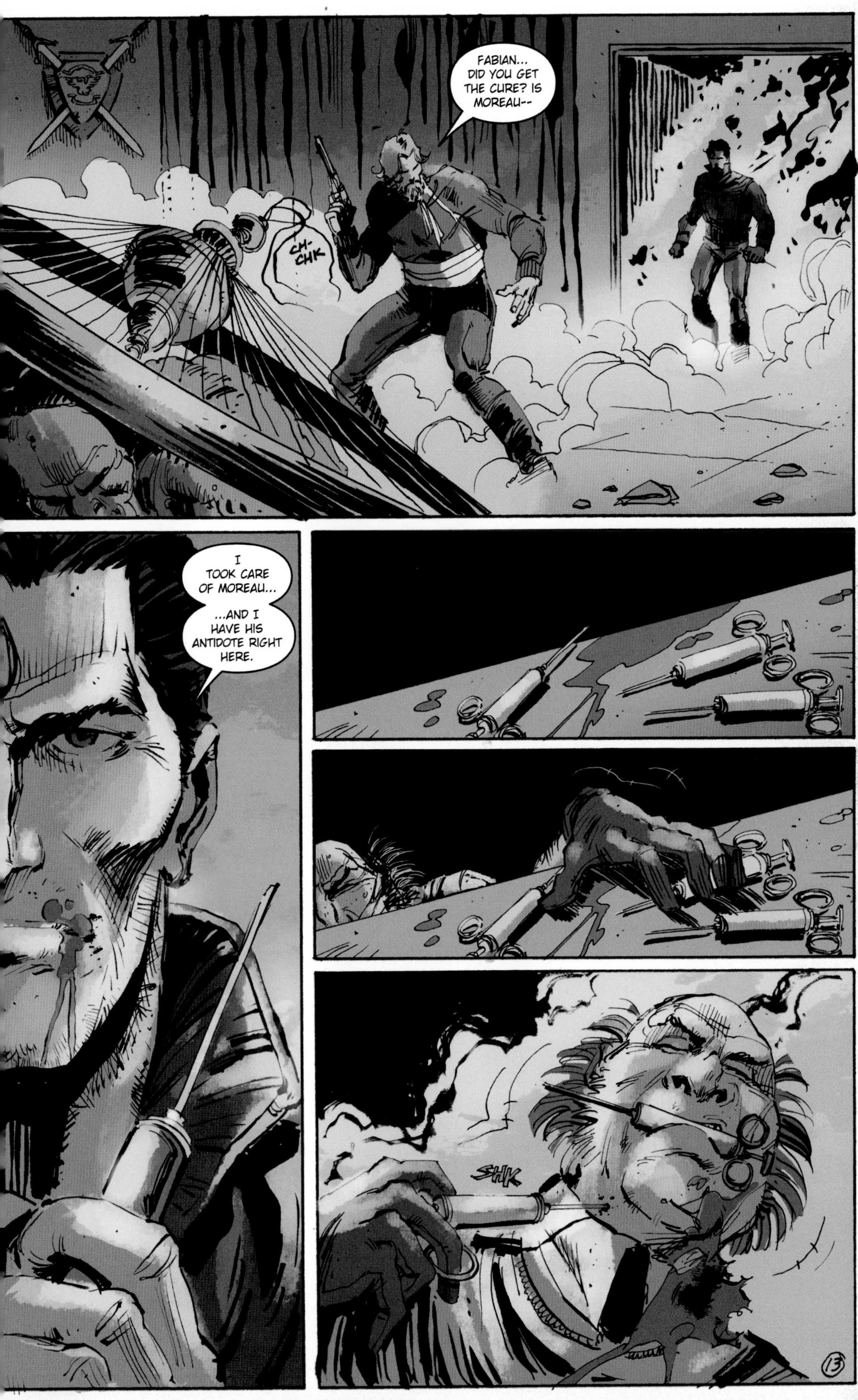
FABIAN... DID YOU GET THE CURE? IS MOREAU--
CH-CHK
I TOOK CARE OF MOREAU...
...AND I HAVE HIS ANTIDOTE RIGHT HERE.
SHK
13

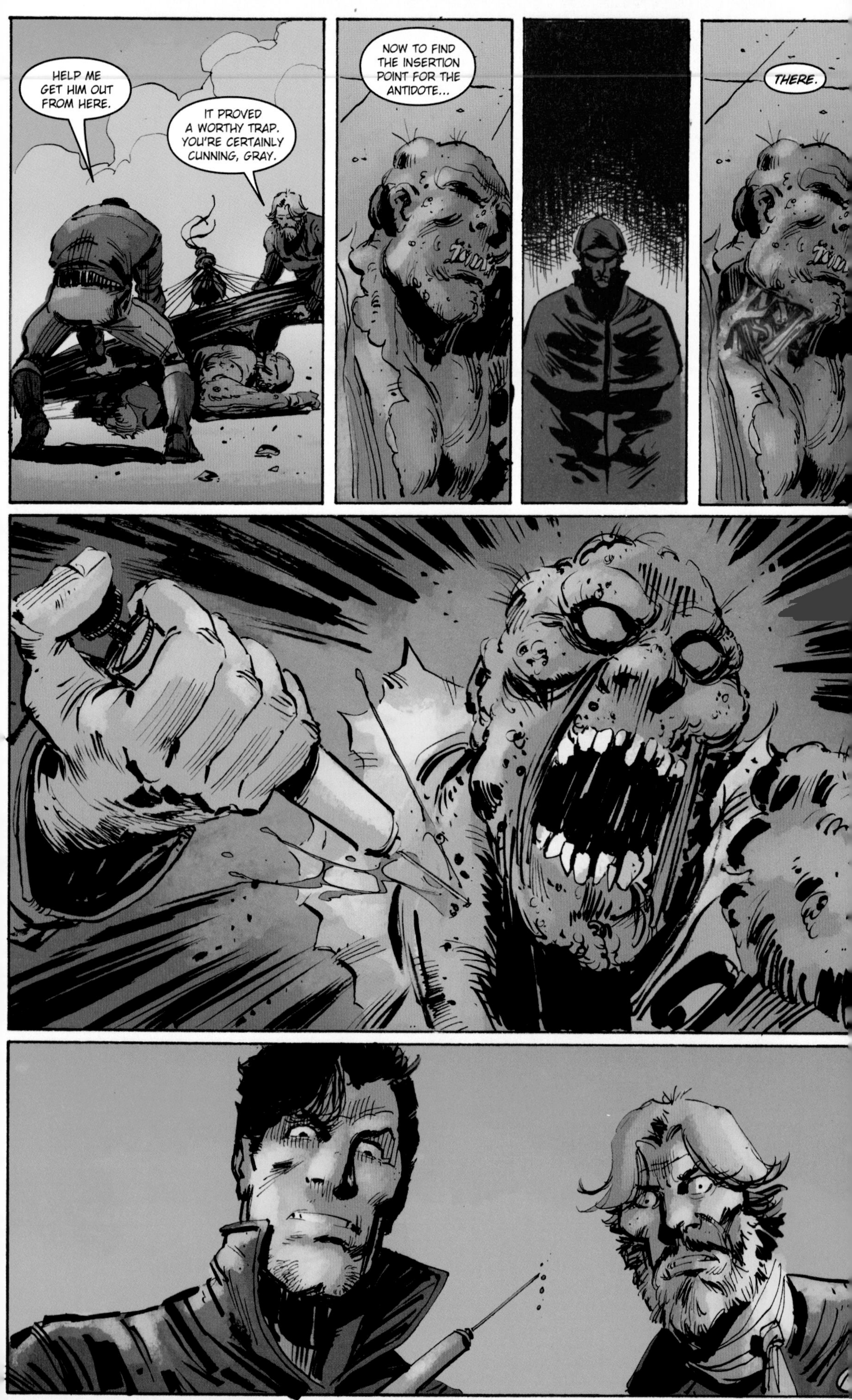
HELP ME GET HIM OUT FROM HERE.
IT PROVED A WORTHY TRAP. YOU'RE CERTAINLY CUNNING, GRAY.
NOW TO FIND THE INSERTION POINT FOR THE ANTIDOTE...
THERE.

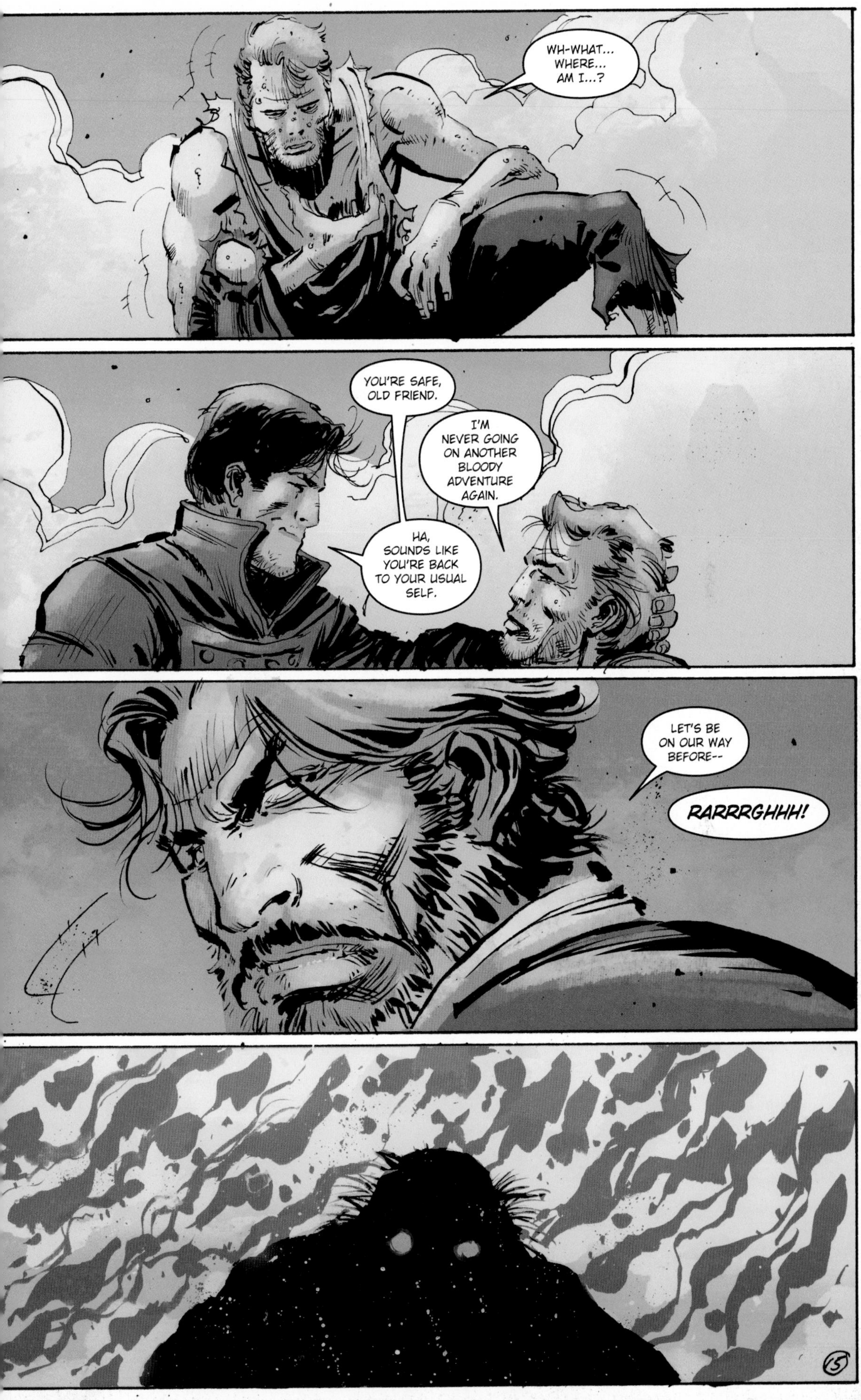
WH-WHAT... WHERE... AM I...?
YOU'RE SAFE, OLD FRIEND.
I'M NEVER GOING ON ANOTHER BLOODY ADVENTURE AGAIN.
HA, SOUNDS LIKE YOU'RE BACK TO YOUR USUAL SELF.
LET'S BE ON OUR WAY BEFORE--
RARRRGHHH!

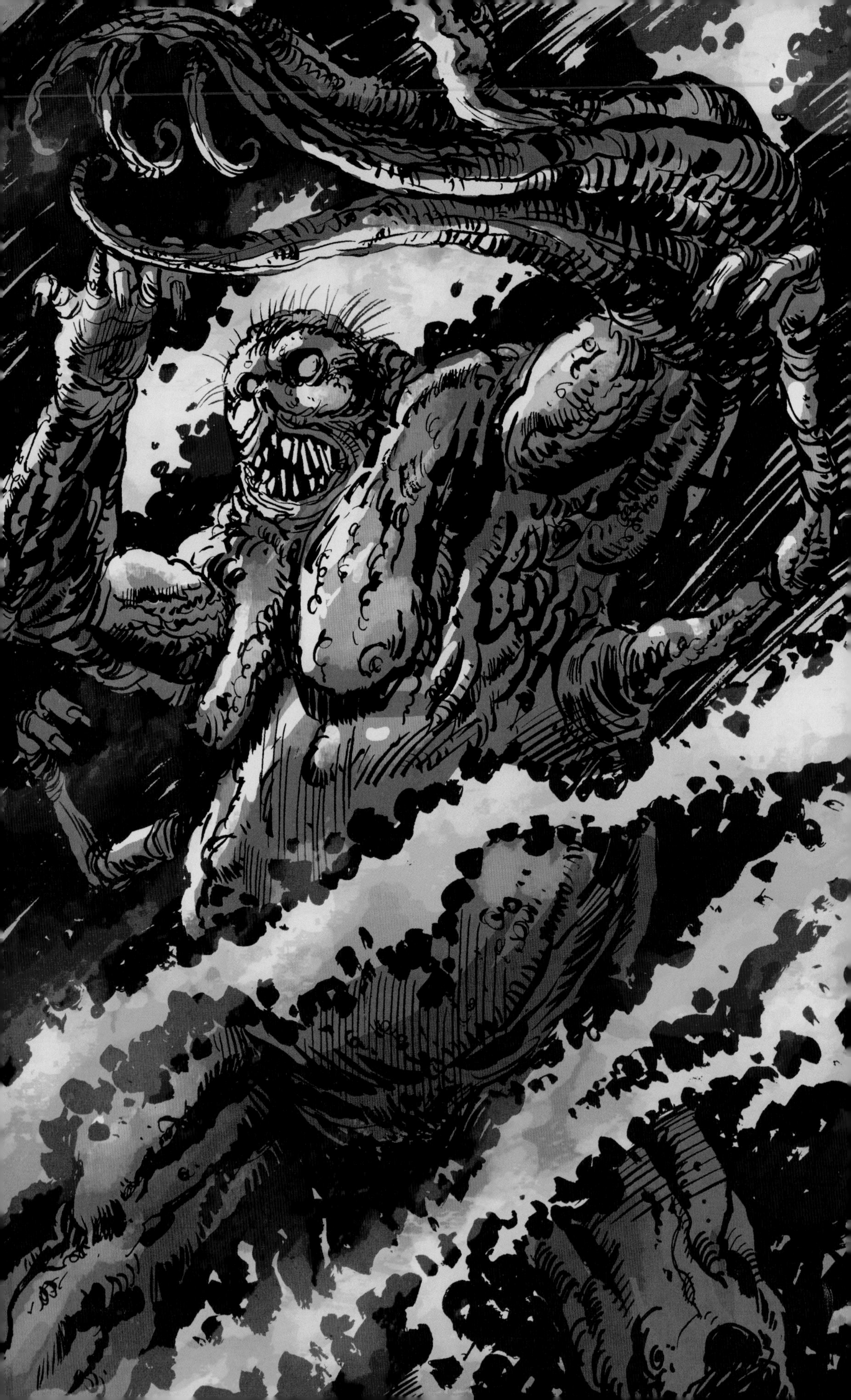

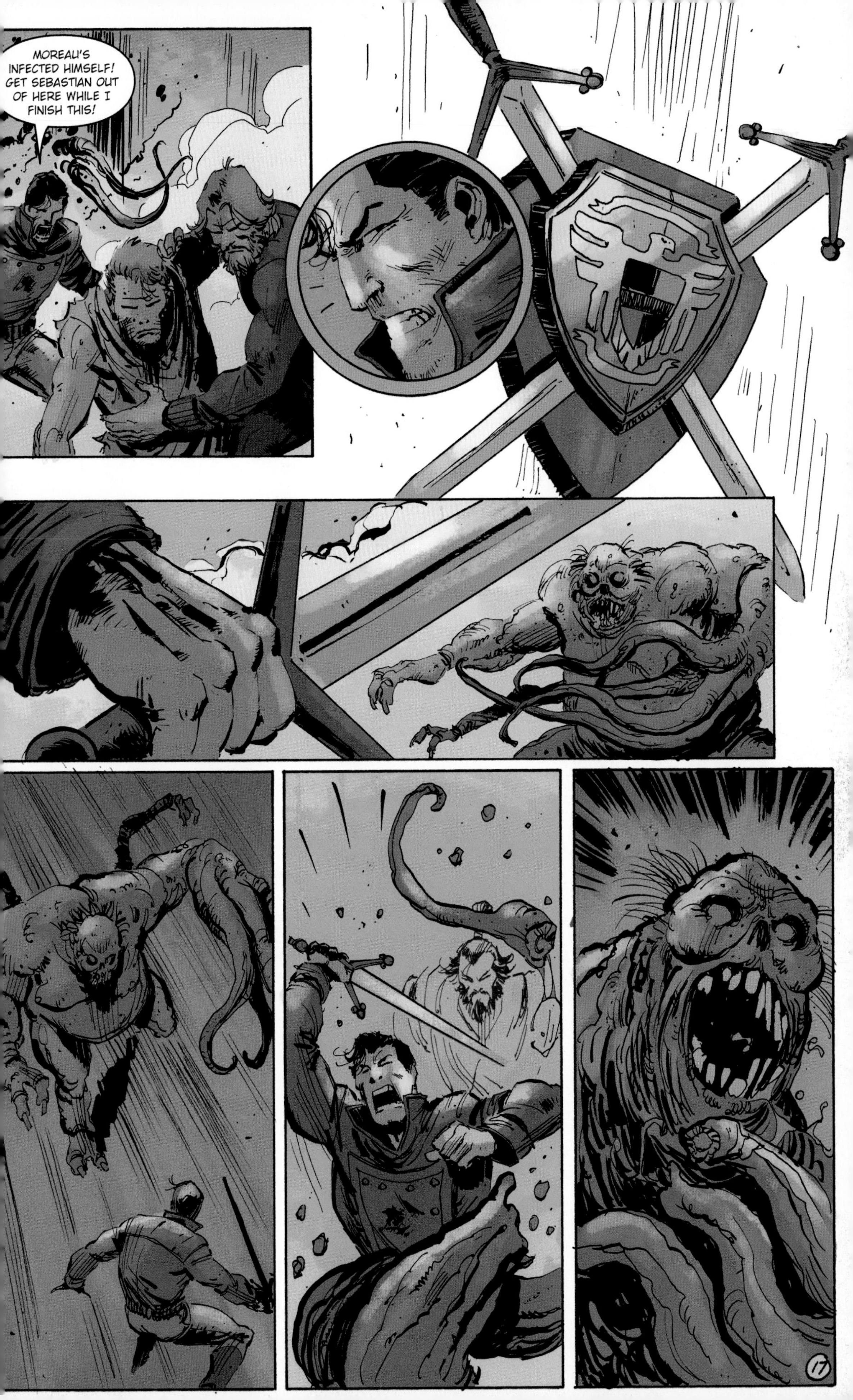
MOREAU'S INFECTED HIMSELF! GET SEBASTIAN OUT OF HERE WHILE I FINISH THIS!
17

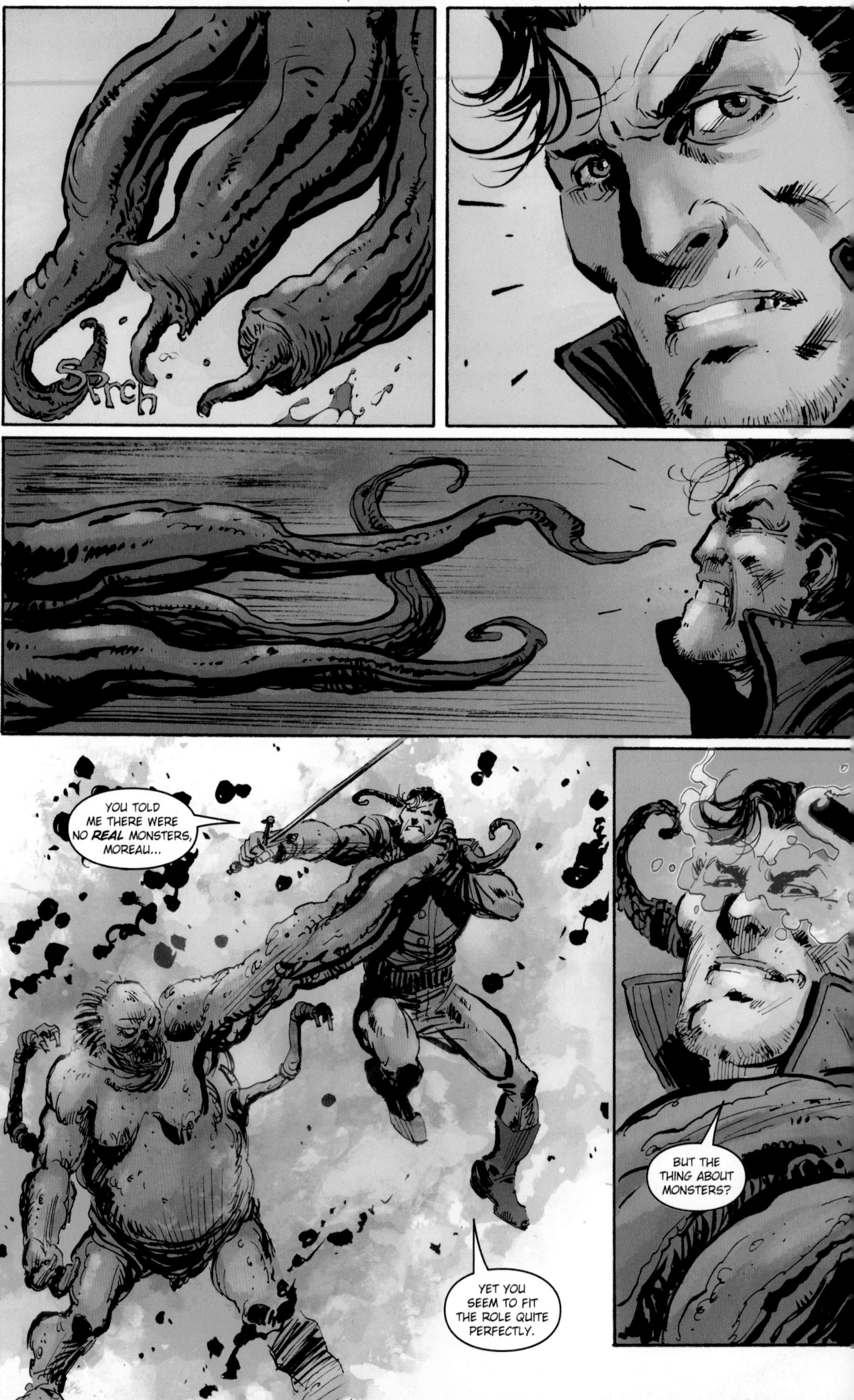

SPRCH
YOU TOLD ME THERE WERE NO REAL MONSTERS, MOREAU...
YET YOU SEEM TO FIT THE ROLE QUITE PERFECTLY.
BUT THE THING ABOUT MONSTERS?

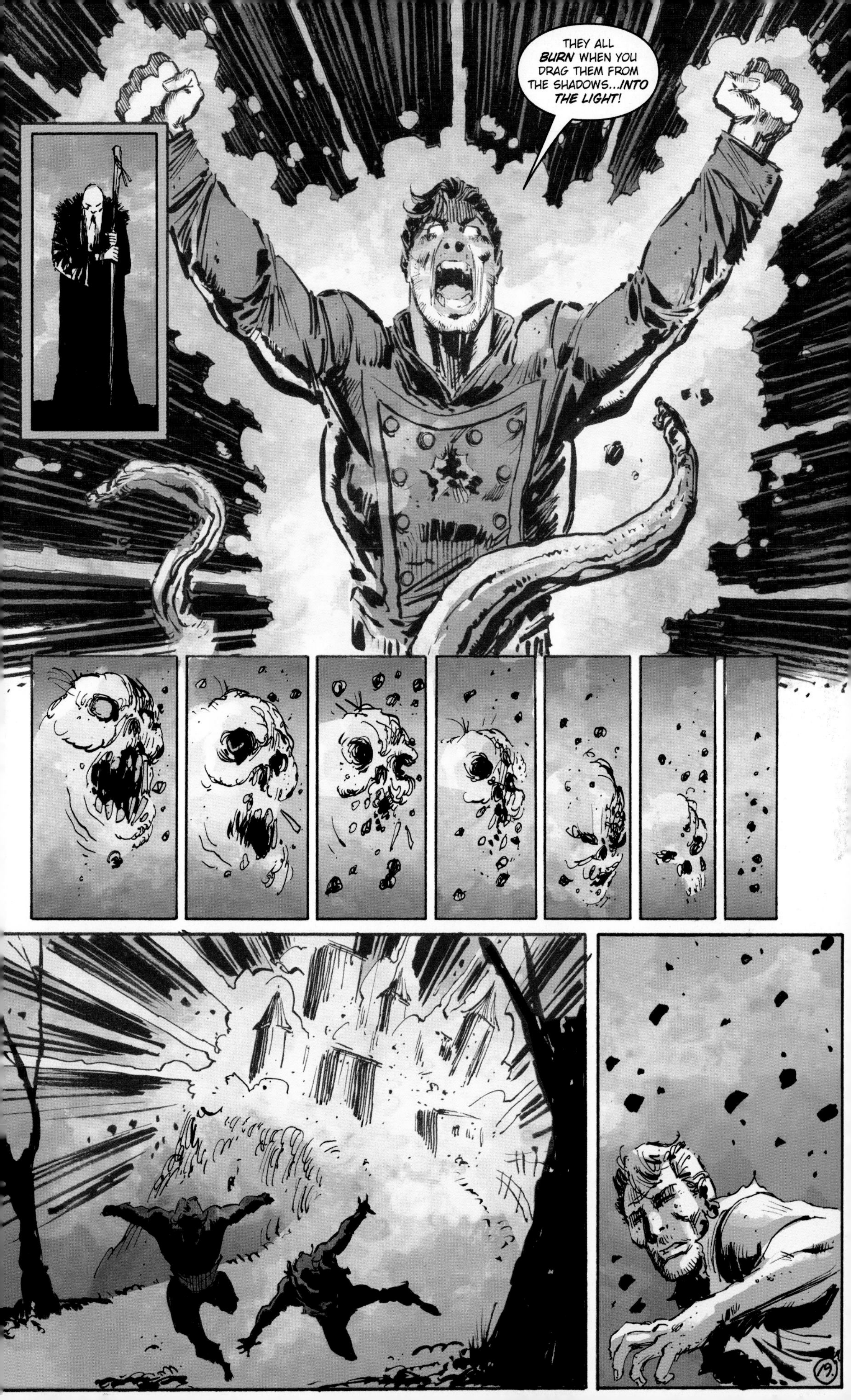
THEY ALL BURN WHEN YOU DRAG THEM FROM THE SHADOWS...INTO THE LIGHT!
19

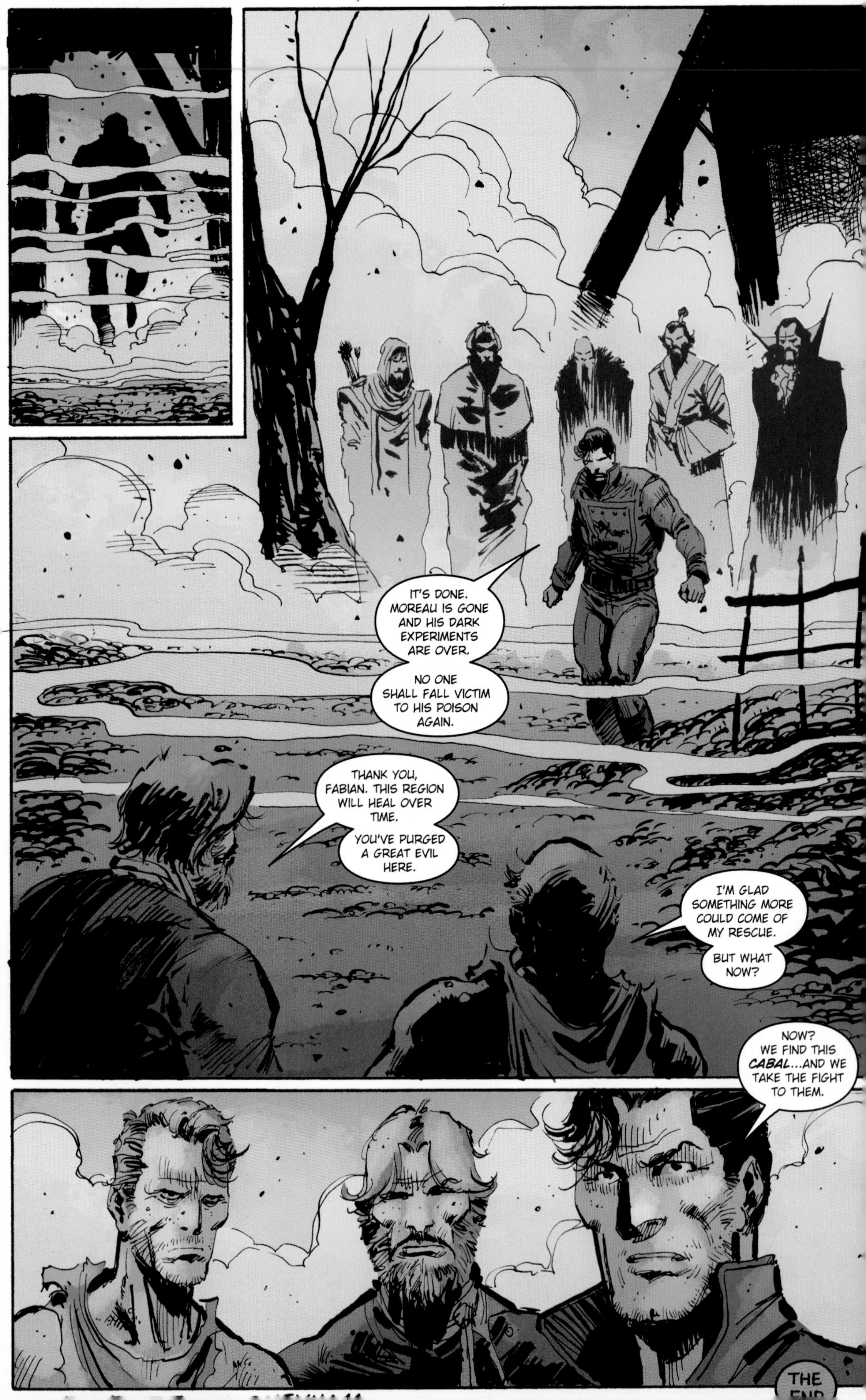
IT'S DONE. MOREAU IS GONE AND HIS DARK EXPERIMENTS ARE OVER.
NO ONE SHALL FALL VICTIM TO HIS POISON AGAIN.
THANK YOU, FABIAN. THIS REGION WILL HEAL OVER TIME.
YOU'VE PURGED A GREAT EVIL HERE.
I'M GLAD SOMETHING MORE COULD COME OF MY RESCUE.
BUT WHAT NOW?
NOW? WE FIND THIS CABAL...AND WE TAKE THE FIGHT TO THEM.
THE

epilogue

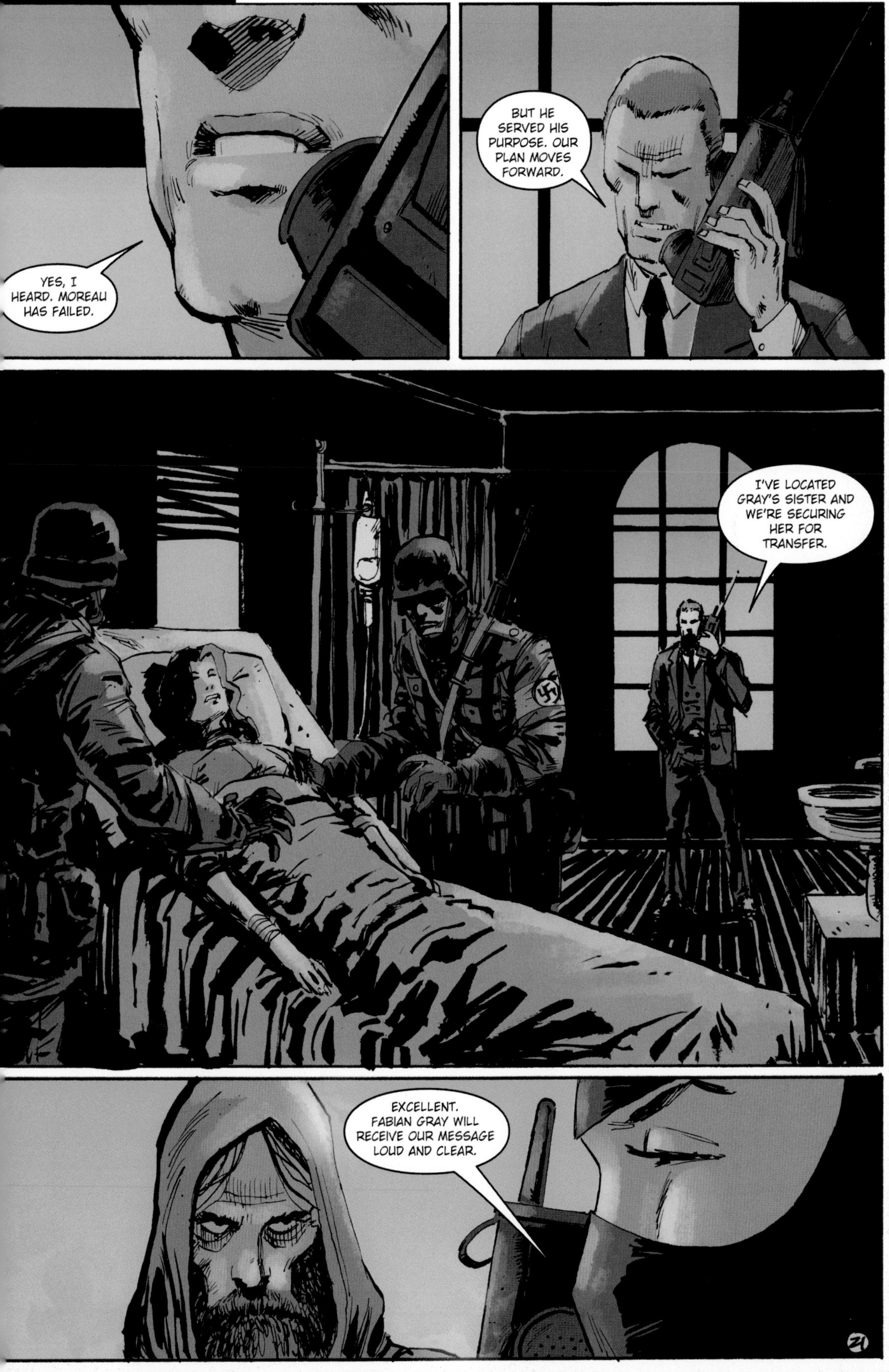
YES, I HEARD. MOREAU HAS FAILED.
BUT HE SERVED HIS PURPOSE. OUR PLAN MOVES FORWARD.
I'VE LOCATED GRAY'S SISTER AND WE'RE SECURING HER FOR TRANSFER.
EXCELLENT. FABIAN GRAY WILL RECEIVE OUR MESSAGE LOUD AND CLEAR.

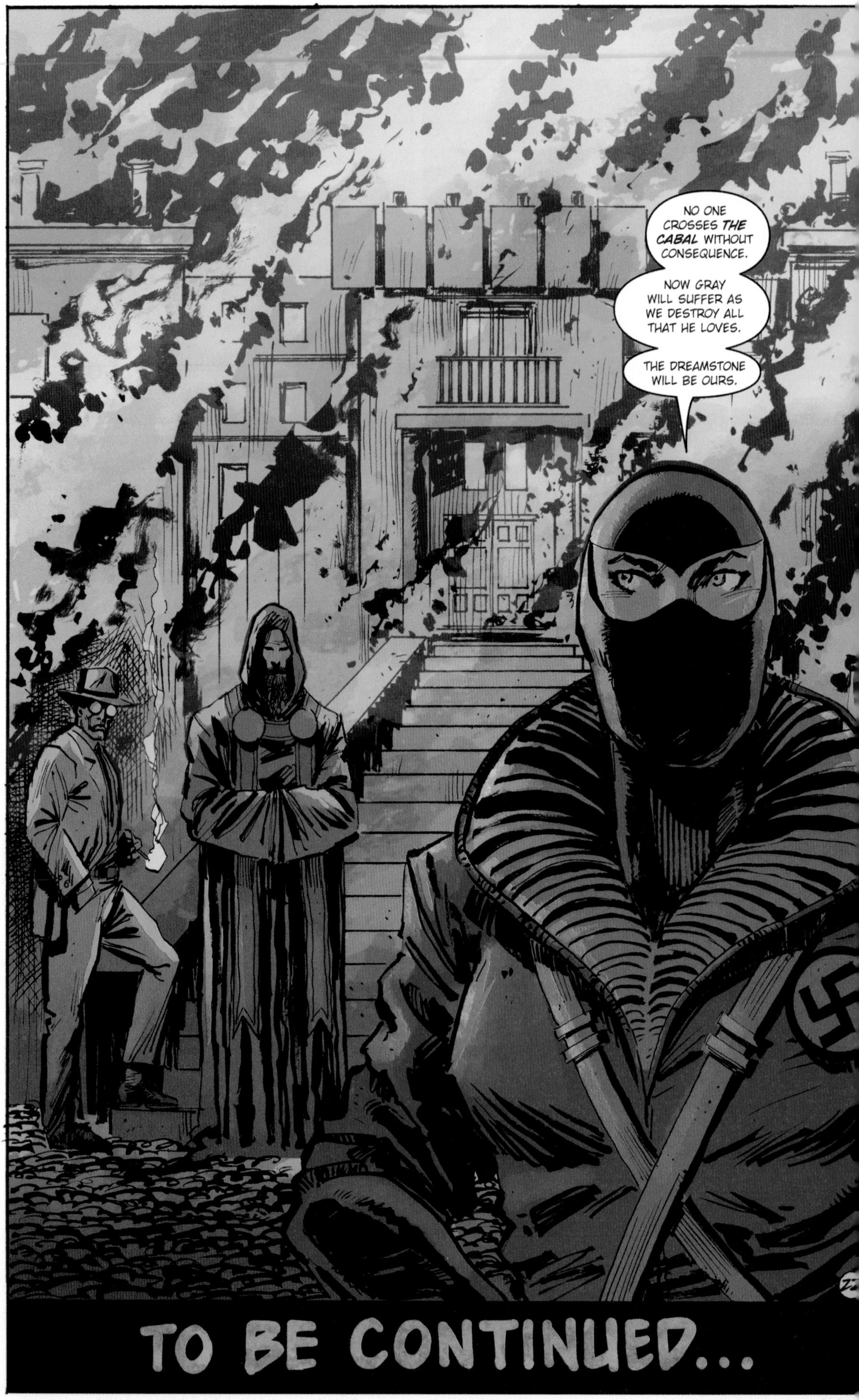
NO ONE CROSSES THE CABAL WITHOUT CONSEQUENCE.
NOW GRAY WILL SUFFER AS WE DESTROY ALL THAT HE LOVES.
THE DREAMSTONE WILL BE OURS.
TO BE CONTINUED...

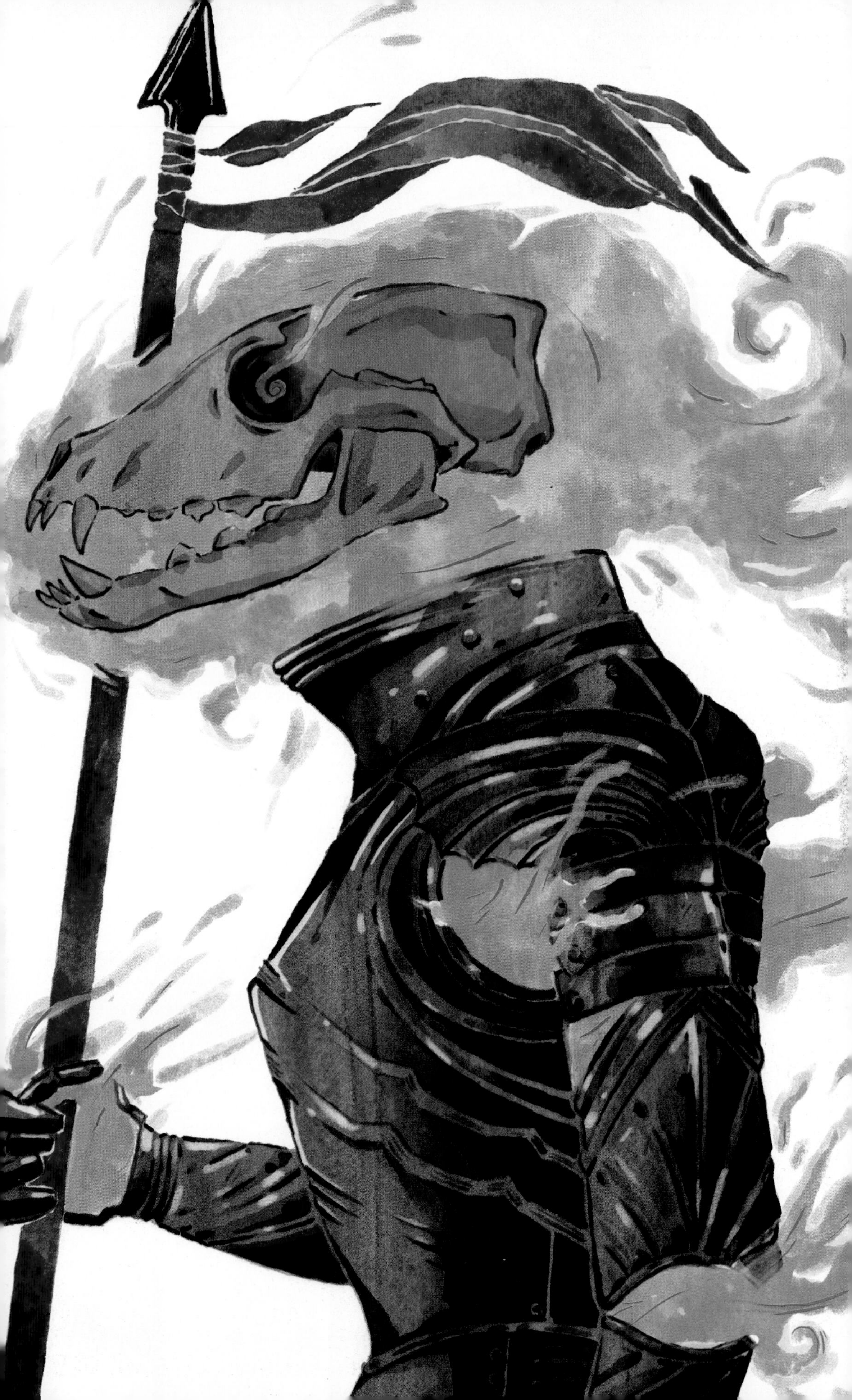

The Demon and the Dreamstone

A *FIVE GHOSTS* TALE
BY S.M. VIDAURRI

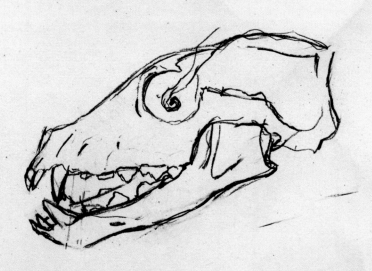

FIVE GHOSTS CREATED BY BARBIERE & MOONEYHAM

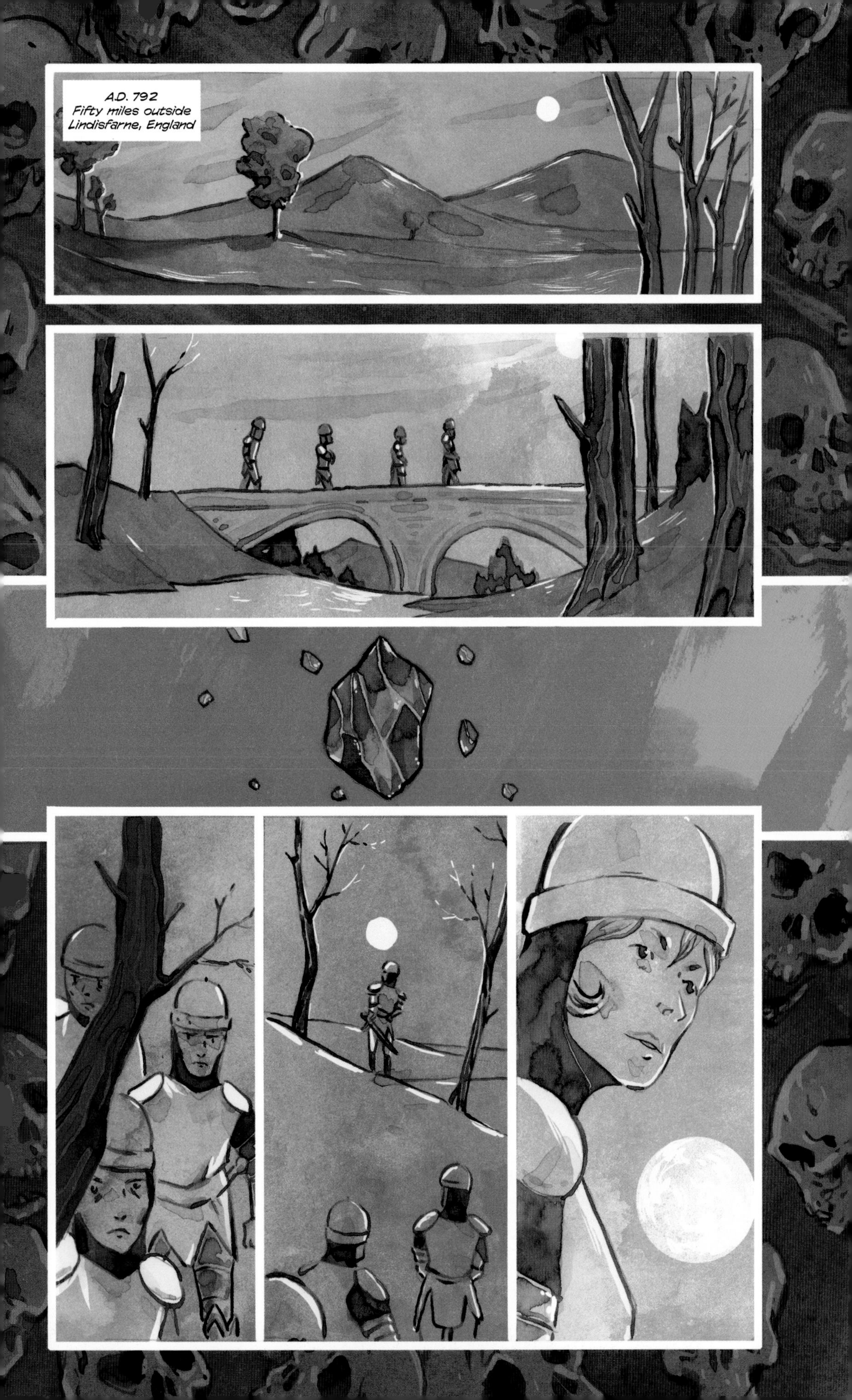
A.D. 792
Fifty miles outside
Lindisfarne, England

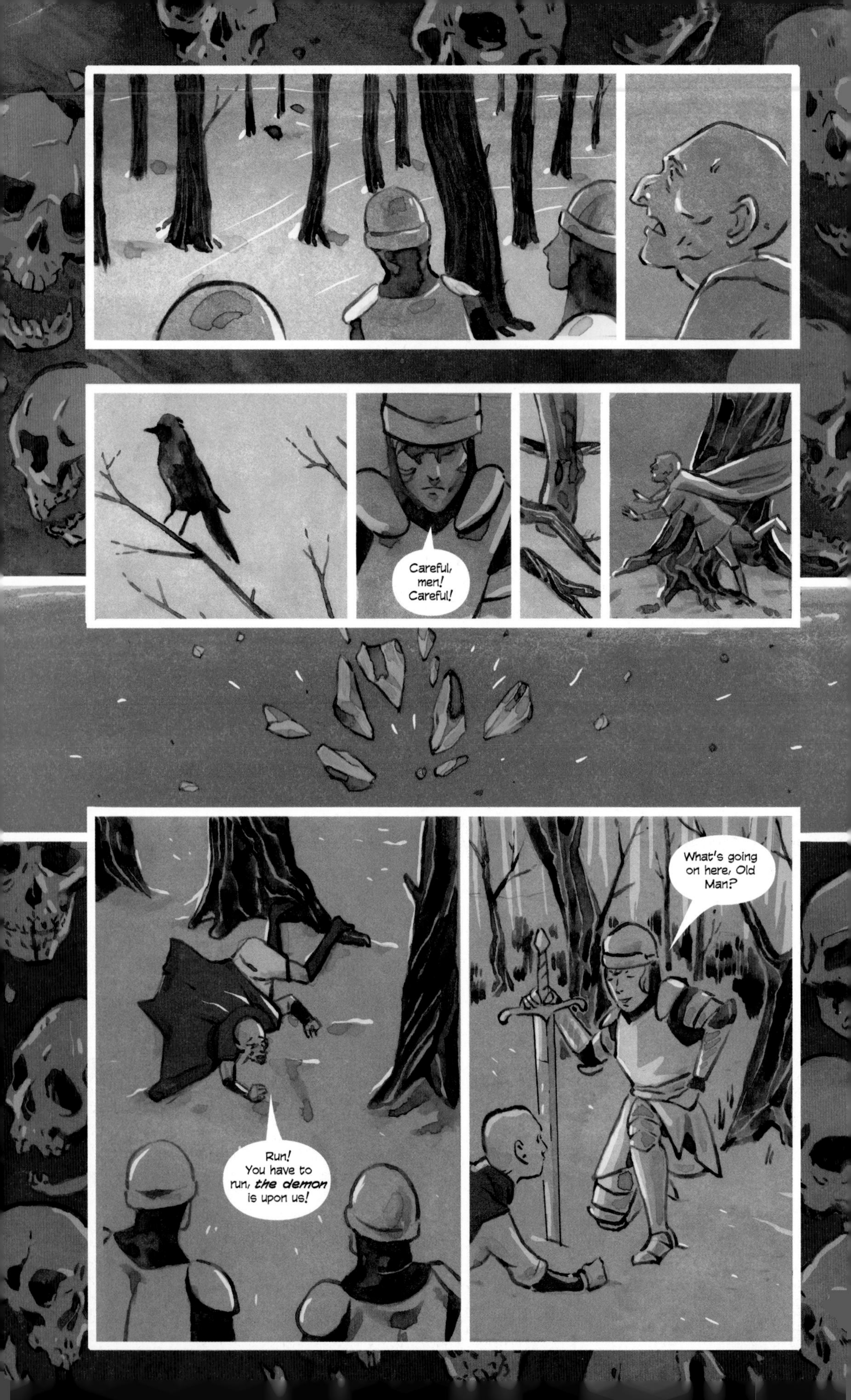
Careful, men! Careful!
Run! You have to run, *the demon* is upon us!
What's going on here, Old Man?

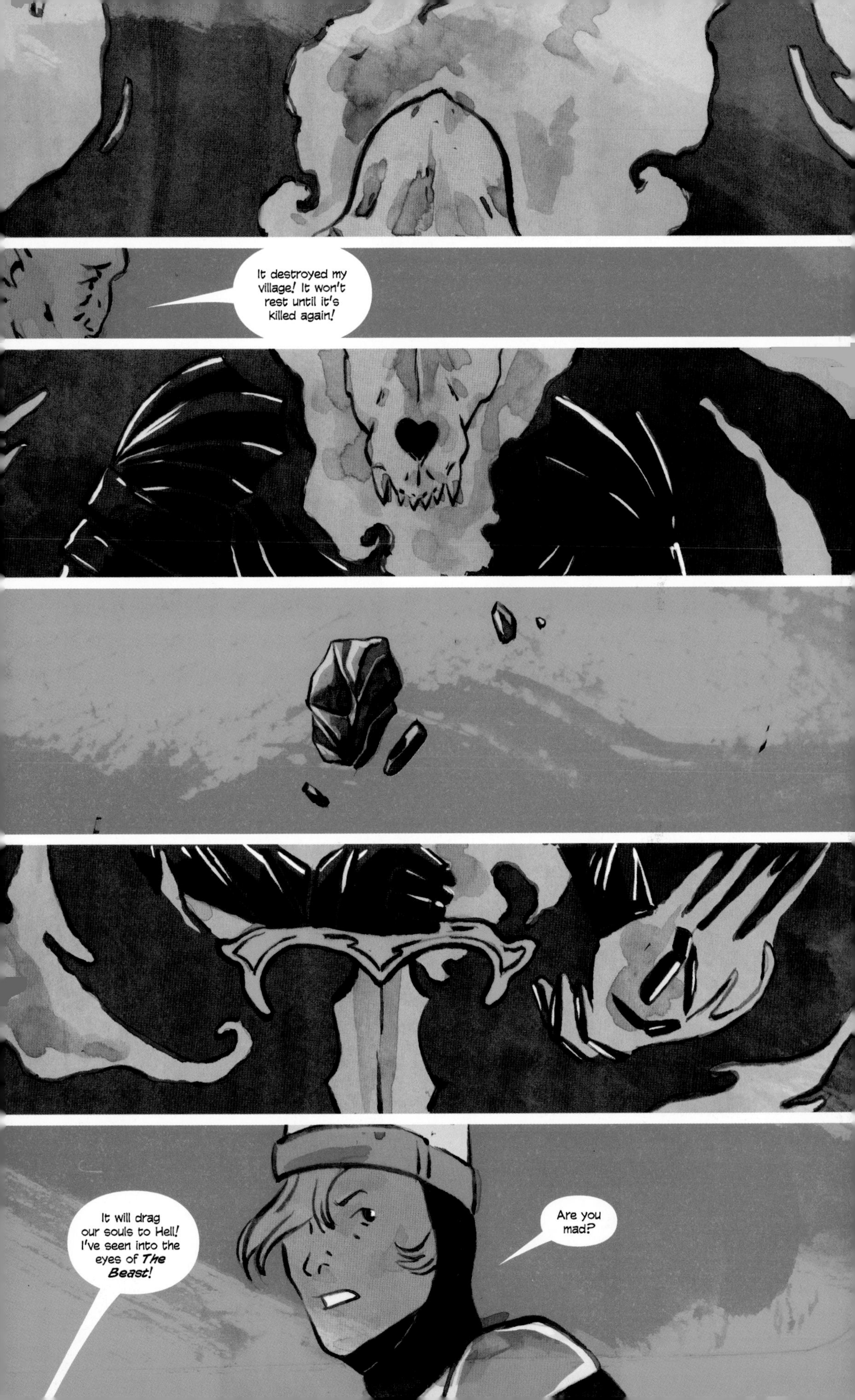

It destroyed my village! It won't rest until it's killed again!
It will drag our souls to Hell! I've seen into the eyes of *The Beast!*
Are you mad?

The Beast! The Devil himself! He walks upon cloven hooves with the head of a demon!

Surely this is the end for-- GAHHH!

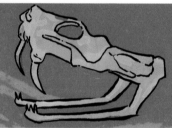

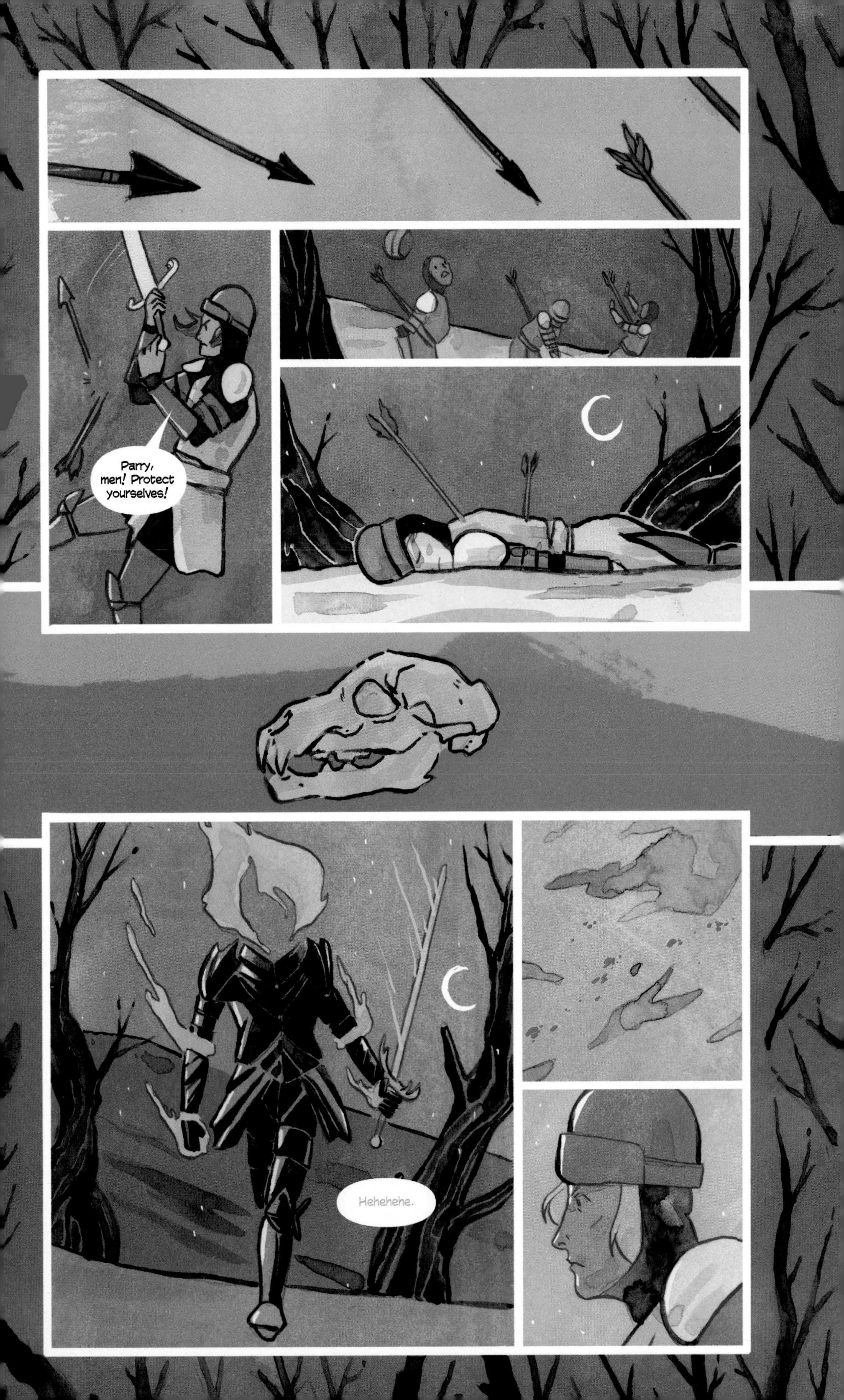
Parry, men! Protect yourselves!
Hehehehe.

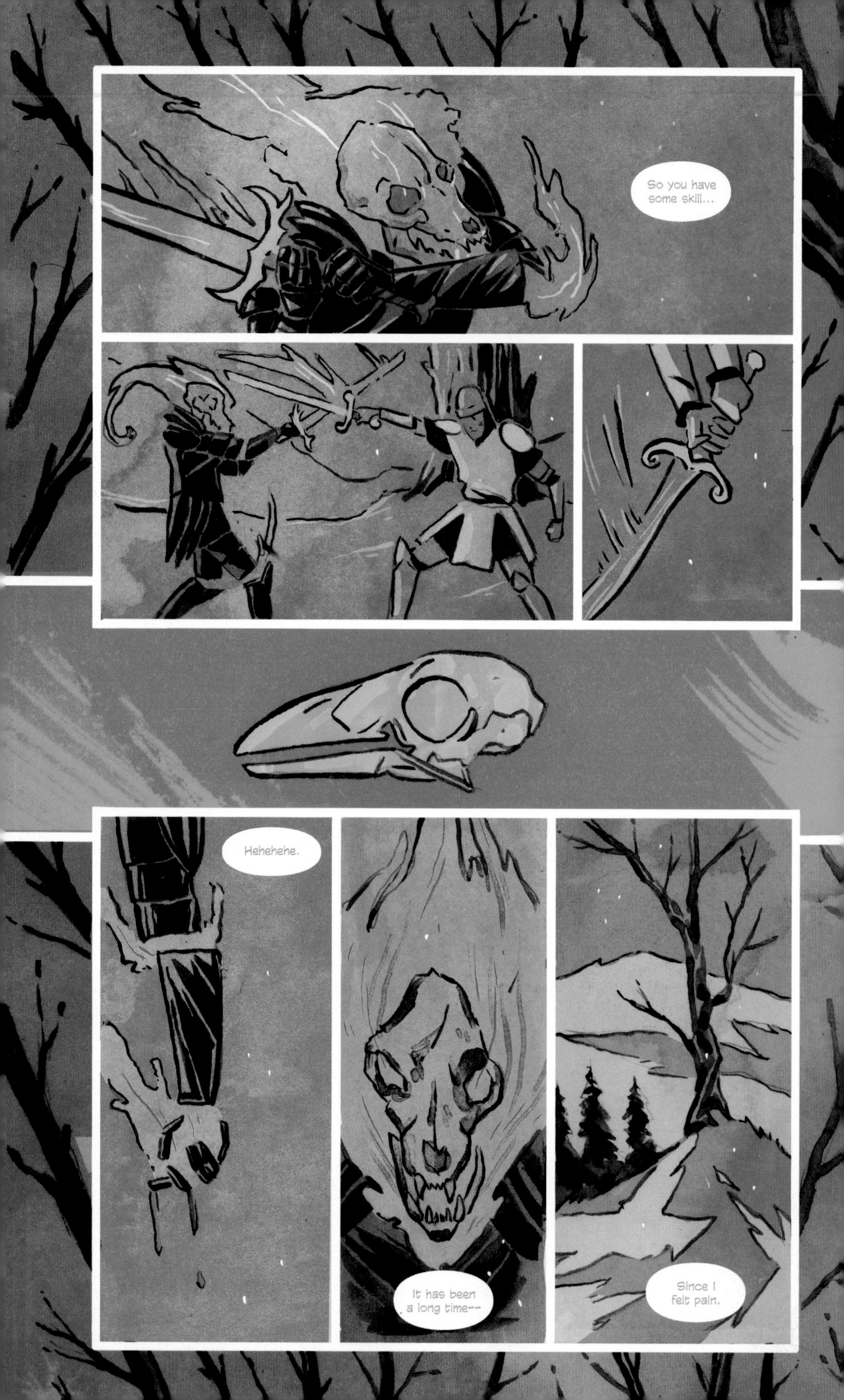
So you have some skill...
Hehehehe.
It has been a long time--
Since I felt pain.

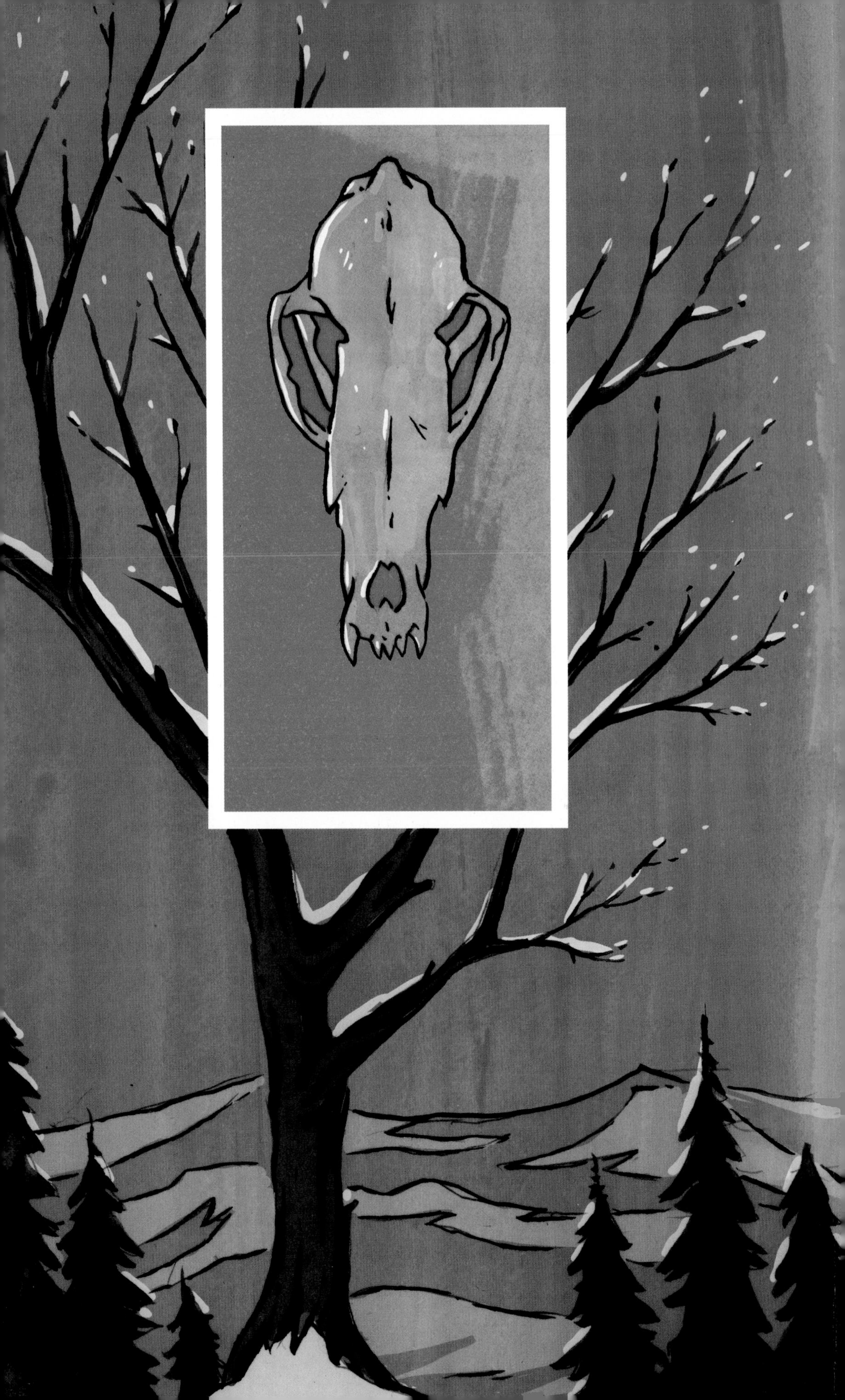

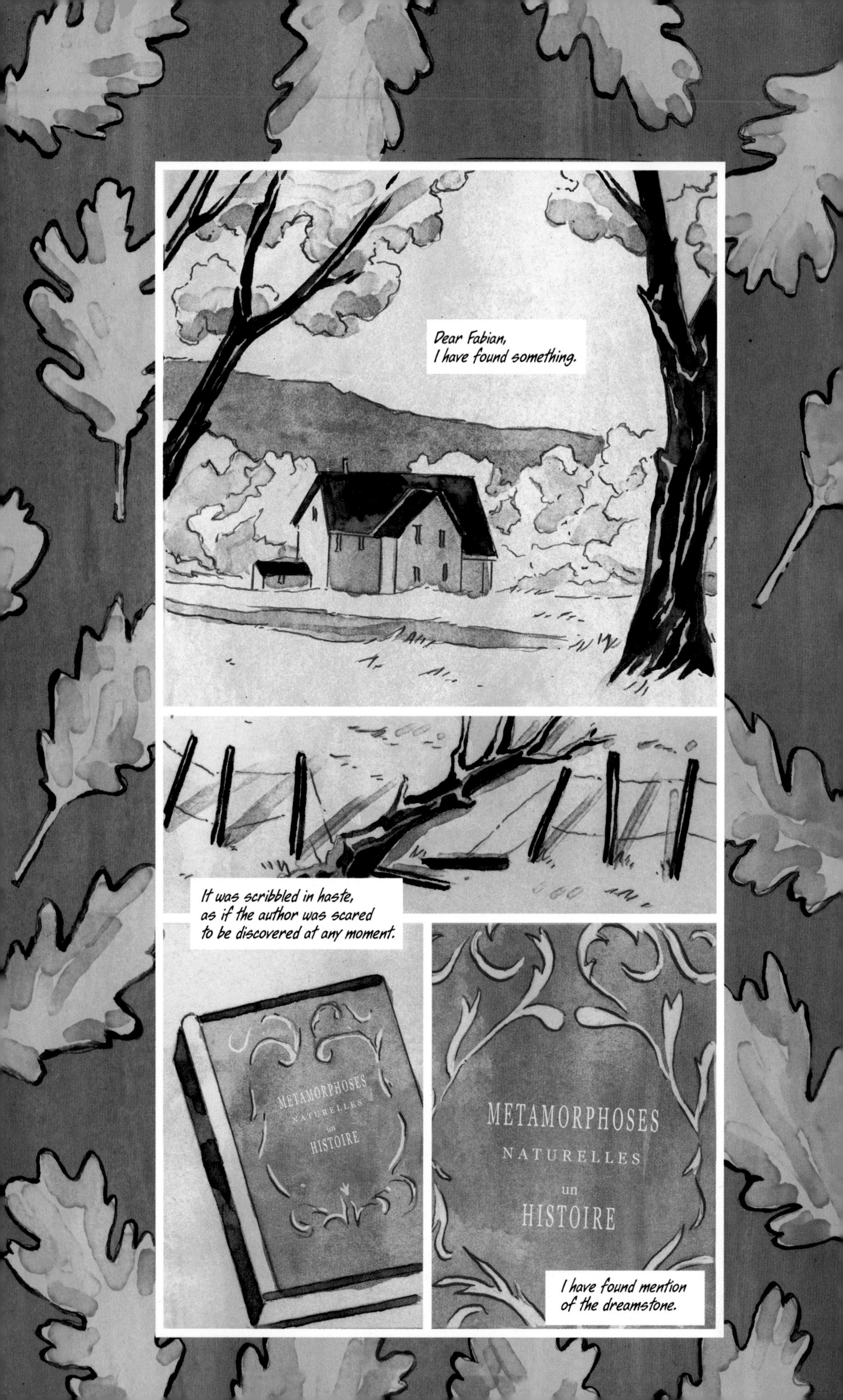
Dear Fabian,
I have found something.
It was scribbled in haste,
as if the author was scared
to be discovered at any moment.
METAMORPHOSES
NATURELLES
un
HISTOIRE
METAMORPHOSES
NATURELLES
un
HISTOIRE
I have found mention
of the dreamstone.

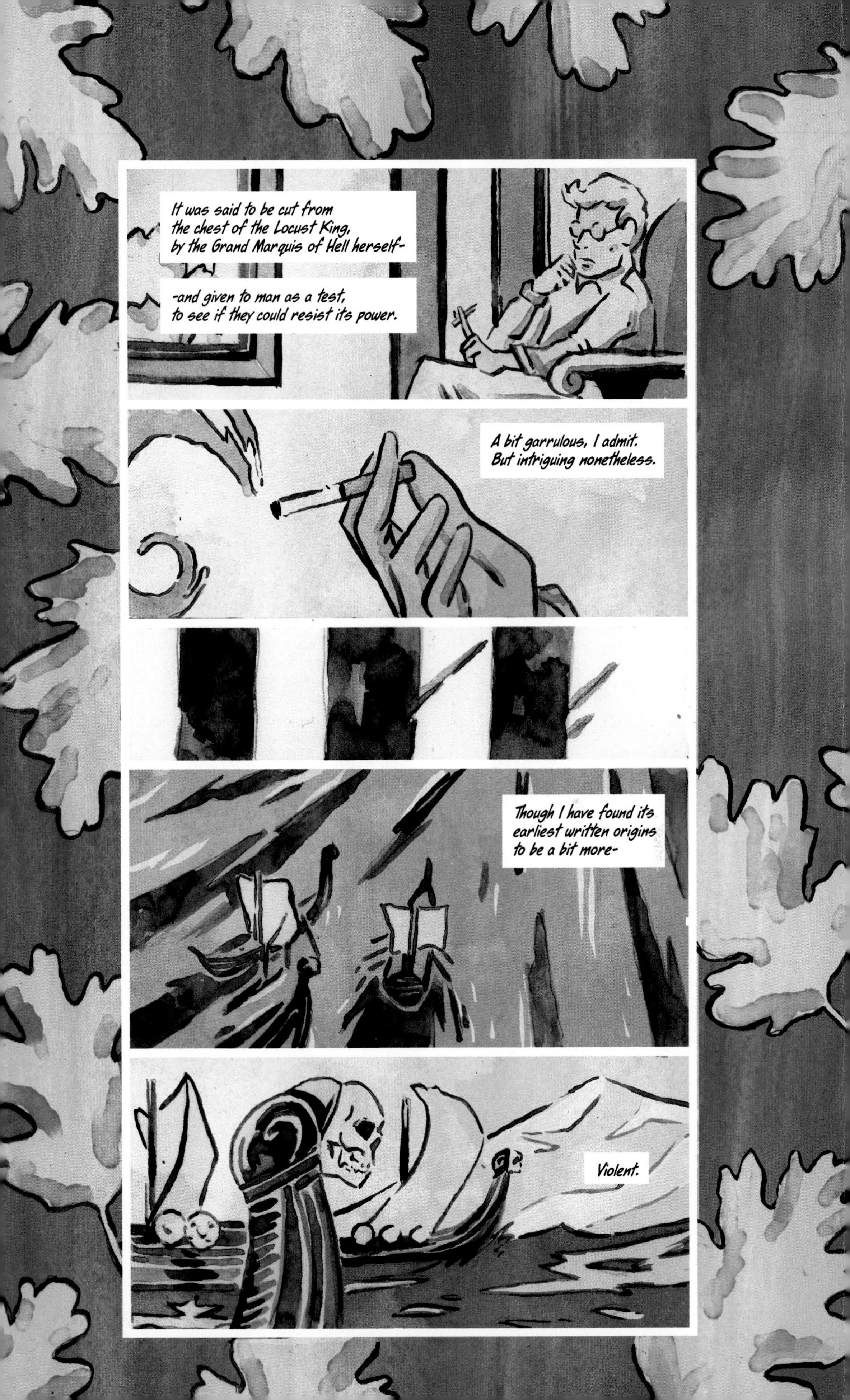
It was said to be cut from the chest of the Locust King, by the Grand Marquis of Hell herself-
-and given to man as a test, to see if they could resist its power.
A bit garrulous, I admit. But intriguing nonetheless.
Though I have found its earliest written origins to be a bit more-
Violent.

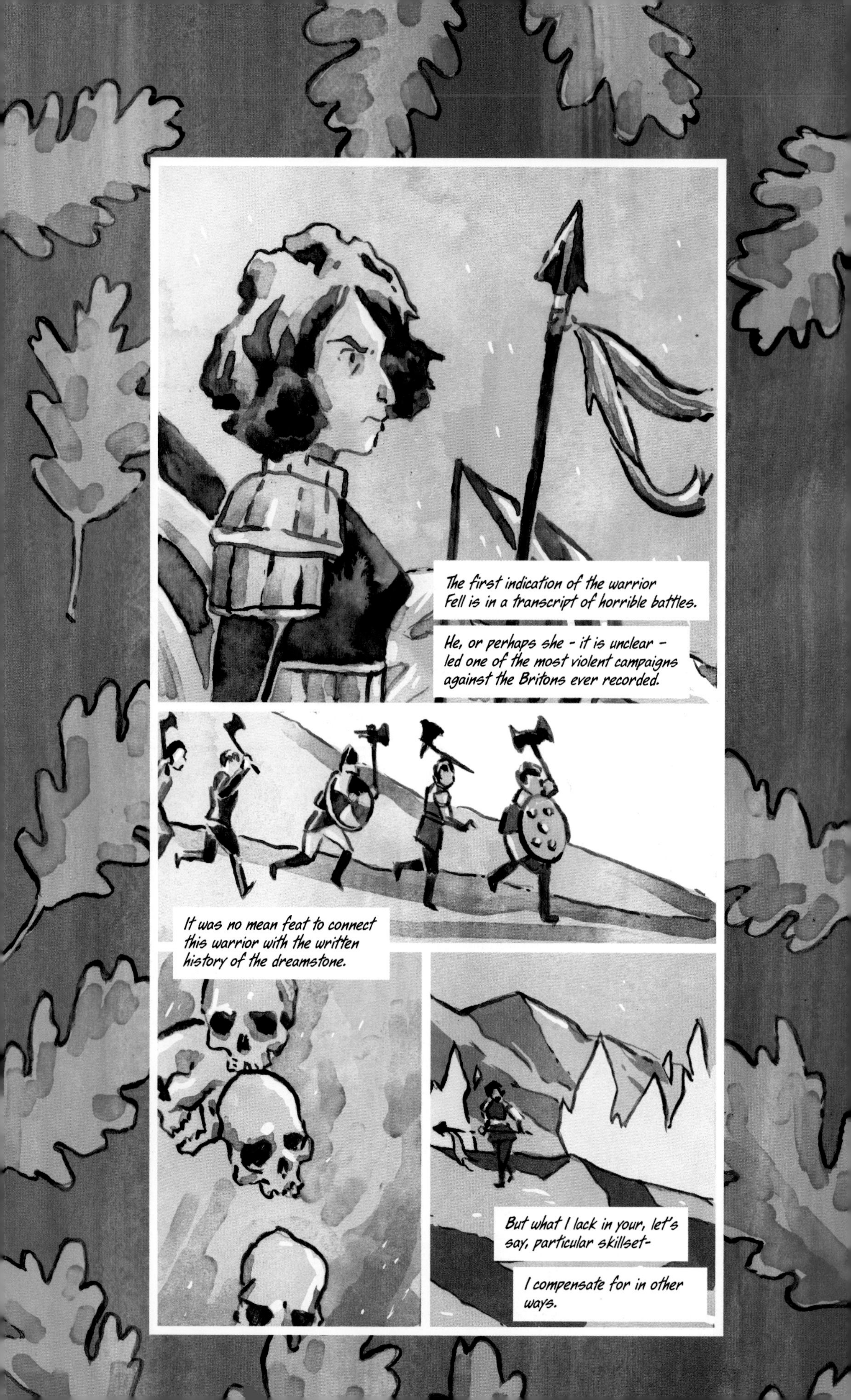
The first indication of the warrior Fell is in a transcript of horrible battles.
He, or perhaps she - it is unclear - led one of the most violent campaigns against the Britons ever recorded.
It was no mean feat to connect this warrior with the written history of the dreamstone.
But what I lack in your, let's say, particular skillset-
I compensate for in other ways.

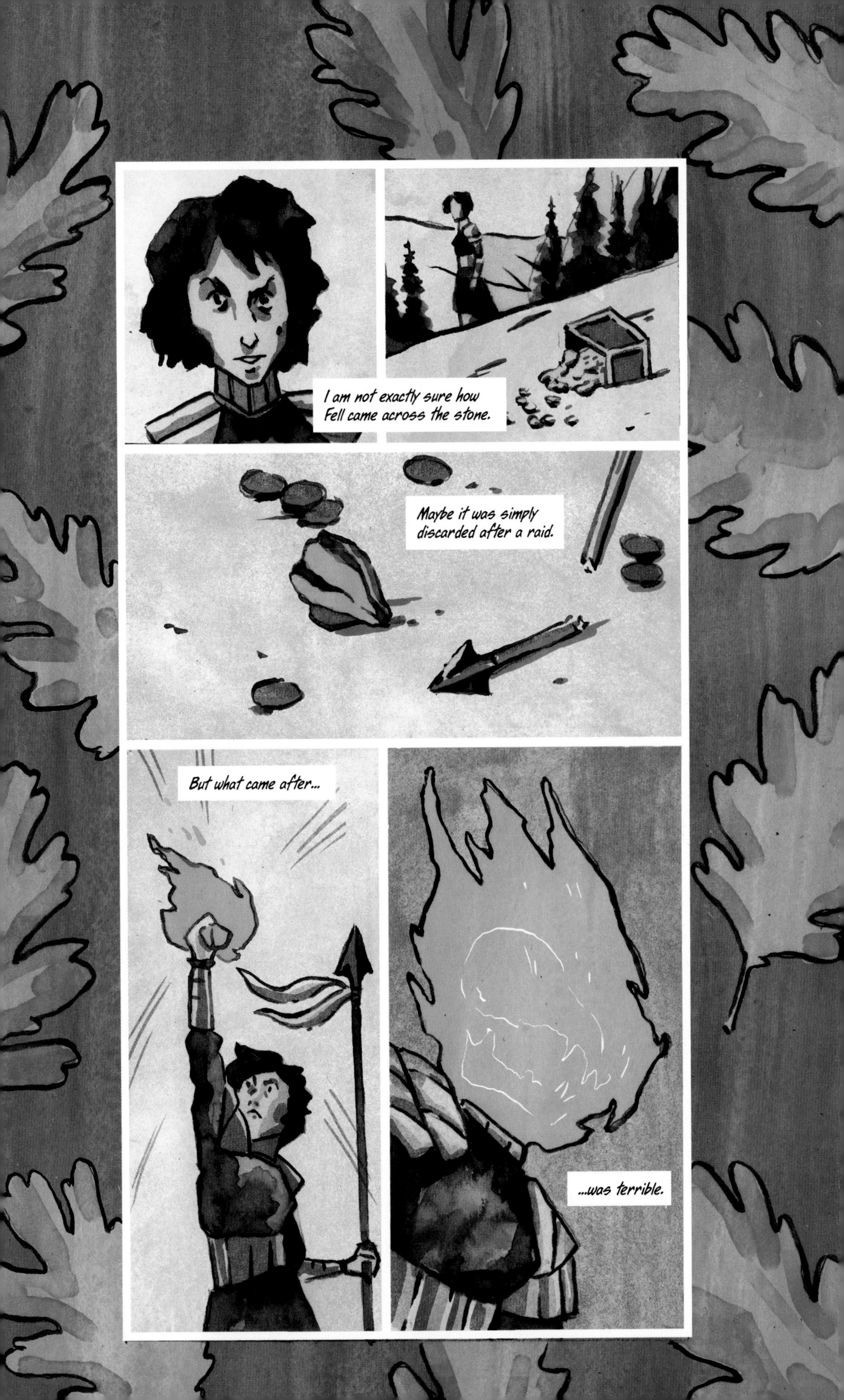
I am not exactly sure how Fell came across the stone.
Maybe it was simply discarded after a raid.
But what came after...
...was terrible.

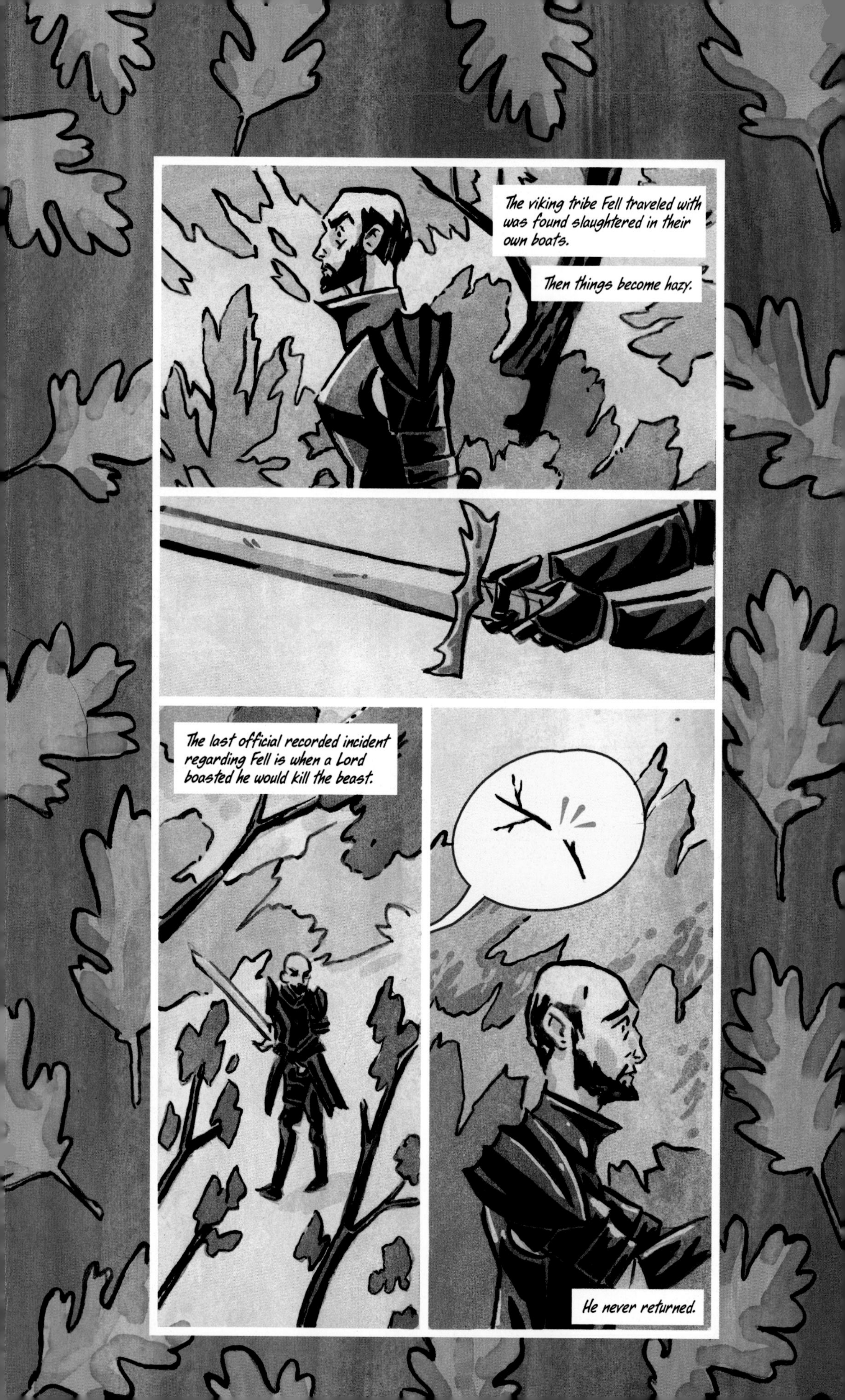
The viking tribe Fell traveled with was found slaughtered in their own boats.
Then things become hazy.
The last official recorded incident regarding Fell is when a Lord boasted he would kill the beast.
He never returned.

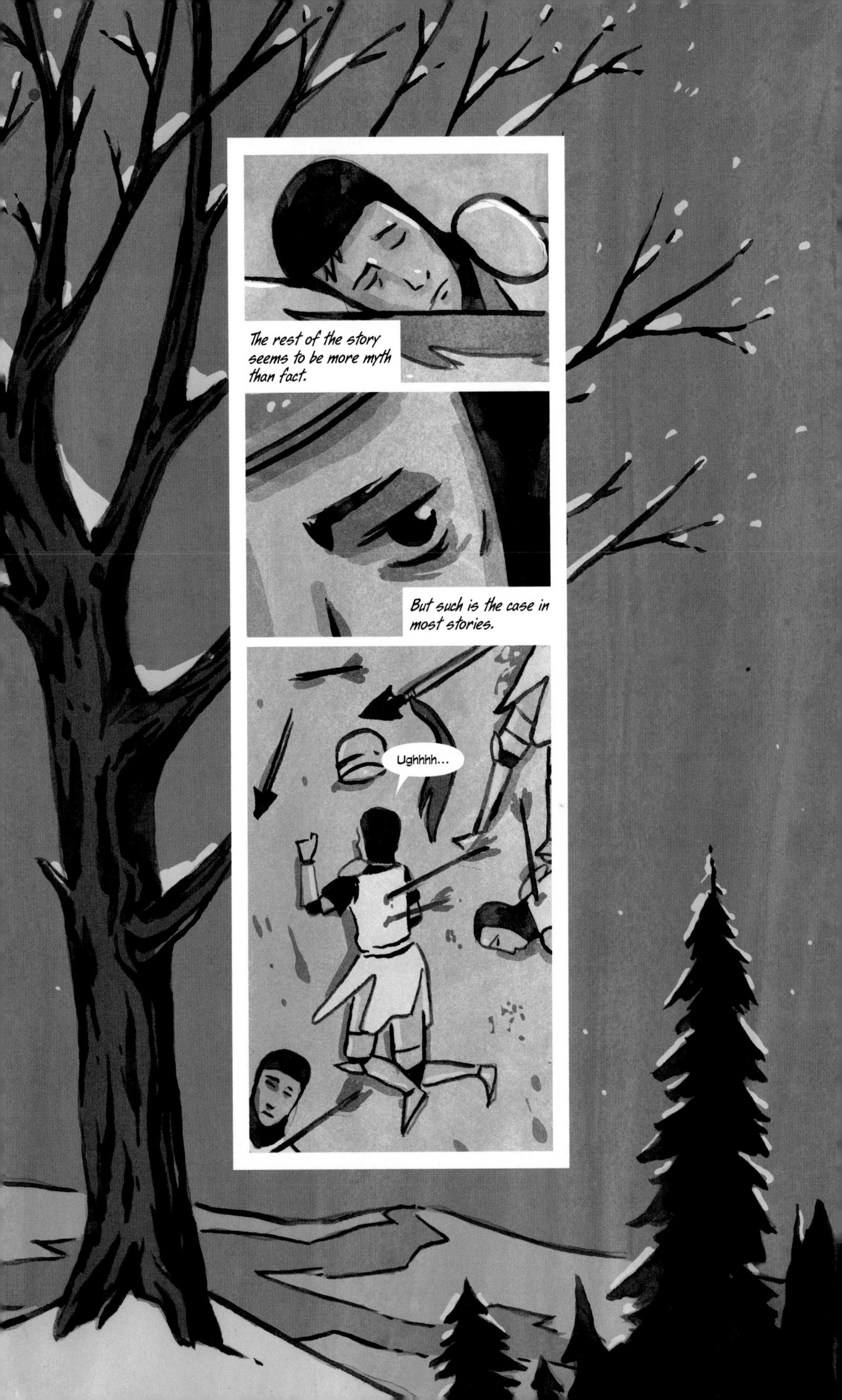
The rest of the story seems to be more myth than fact.
But such is the case in most stories.
Ughhhh...

As we know, the dreamstones hold immeasurable power.

Even with a heart as good as yours, you face troubling influence from your stone...

Imagine how it would affect one of pure evil?

Will you come now?

Have you prepared yourself?

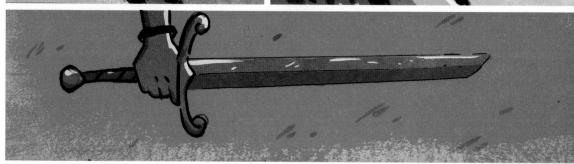

Very good.

Hehehehe.

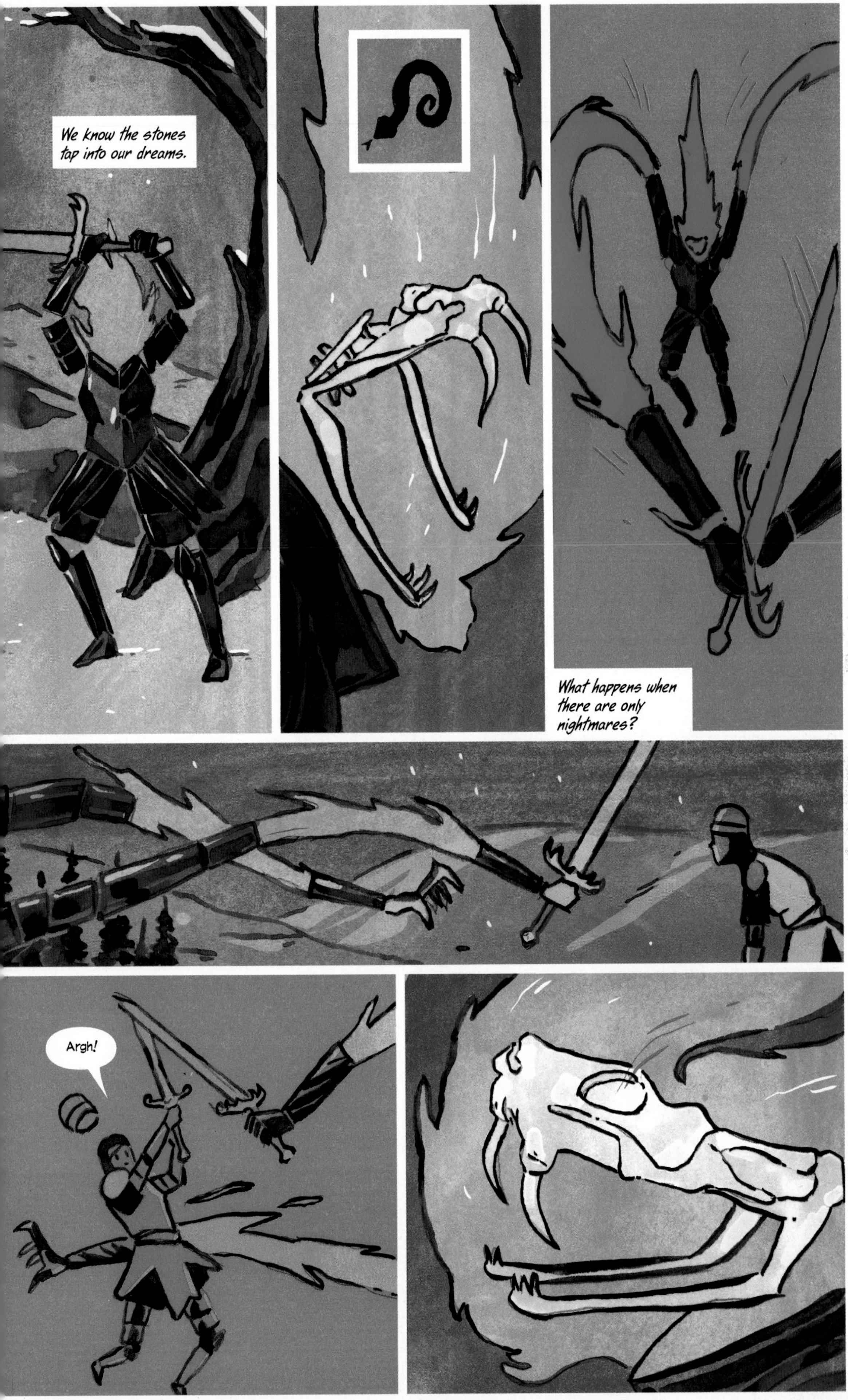
We know the stones tap into our dreams.
What happens when there are only nightmares?
Argh!

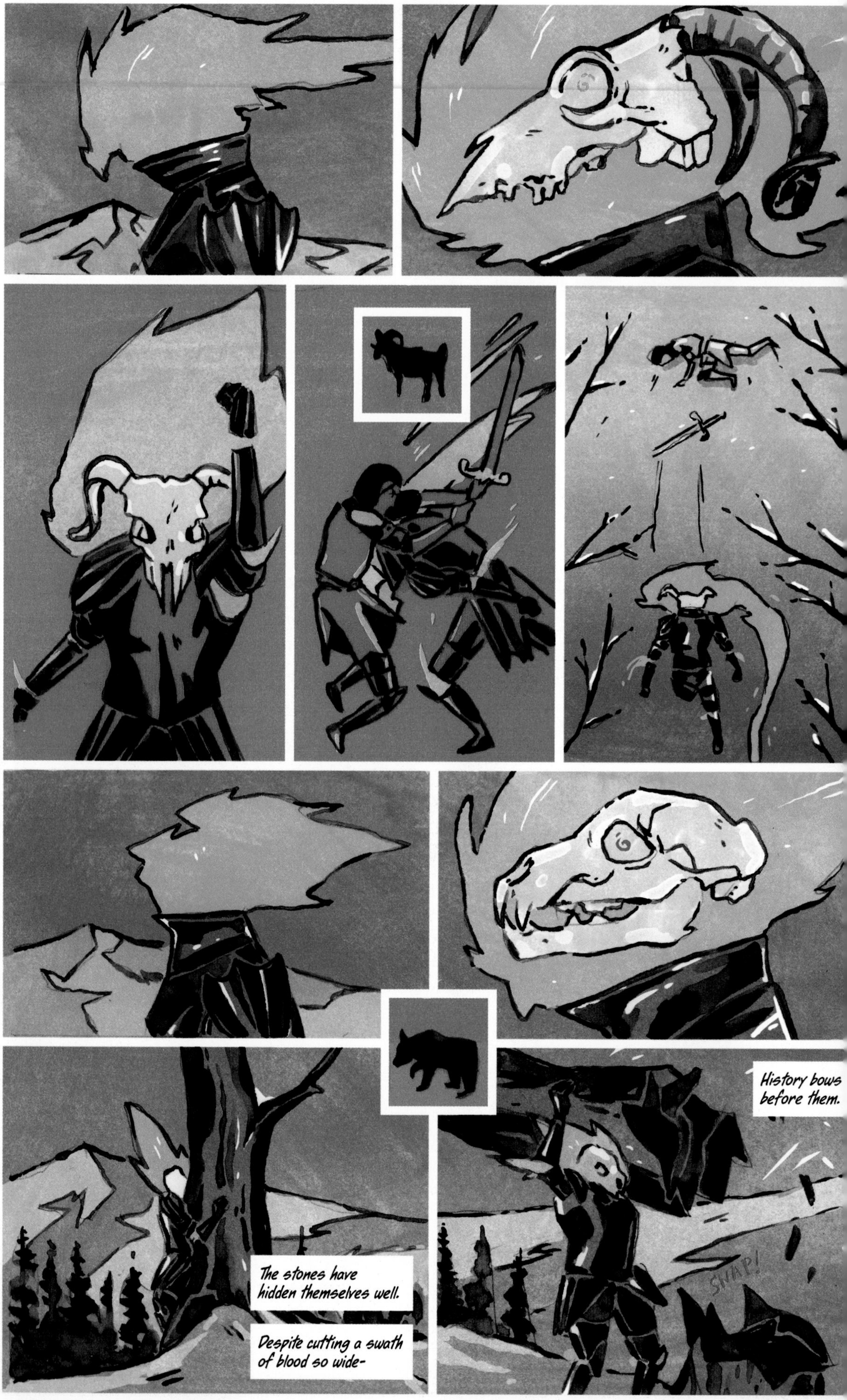
The stones have hidden themselves well.
Despite cutting a swath of blood so wide-
History bows before them.
SNAP!

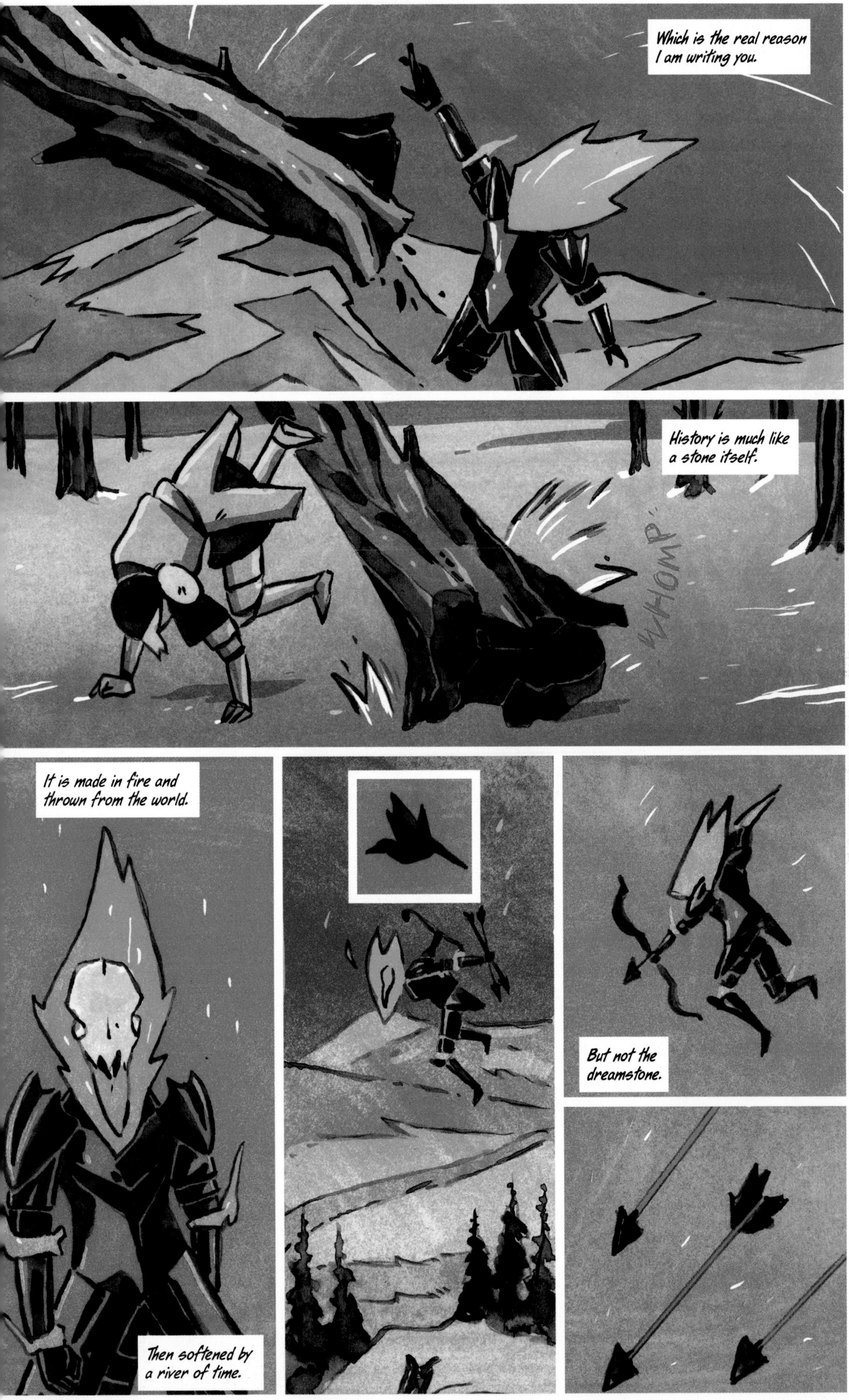

Which is the real reason I am writing you.
History is much like a stone itself.
WHOMP
It is made in fire and thrown from the world.
Then softened by a river of time.
But not the dreamstone.

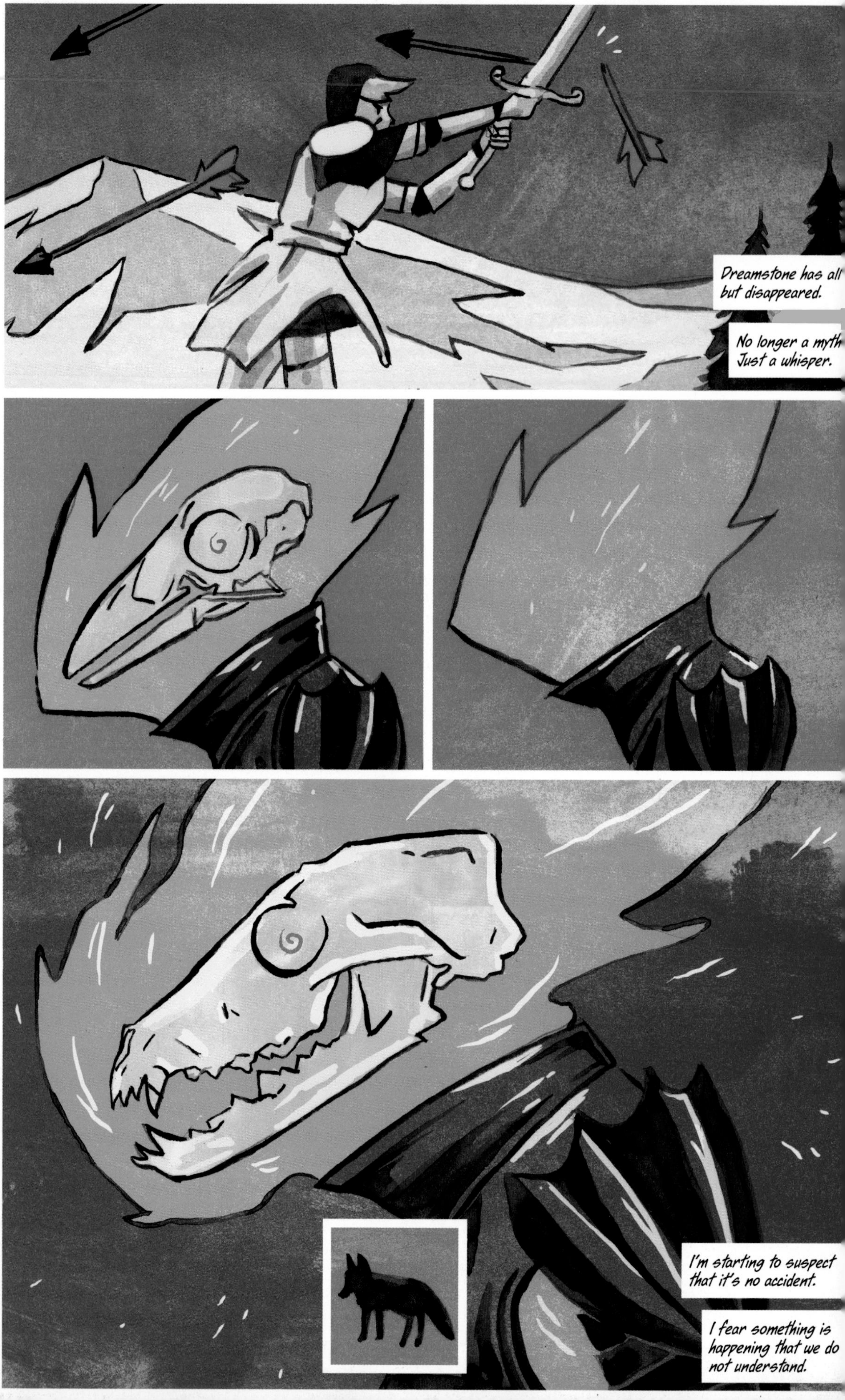
Dreamstone has all but disappeared.
No longer a myth Just a whisper.
I'm starting to suspect that it's no accident.
I fear something is happening that we do not understand.

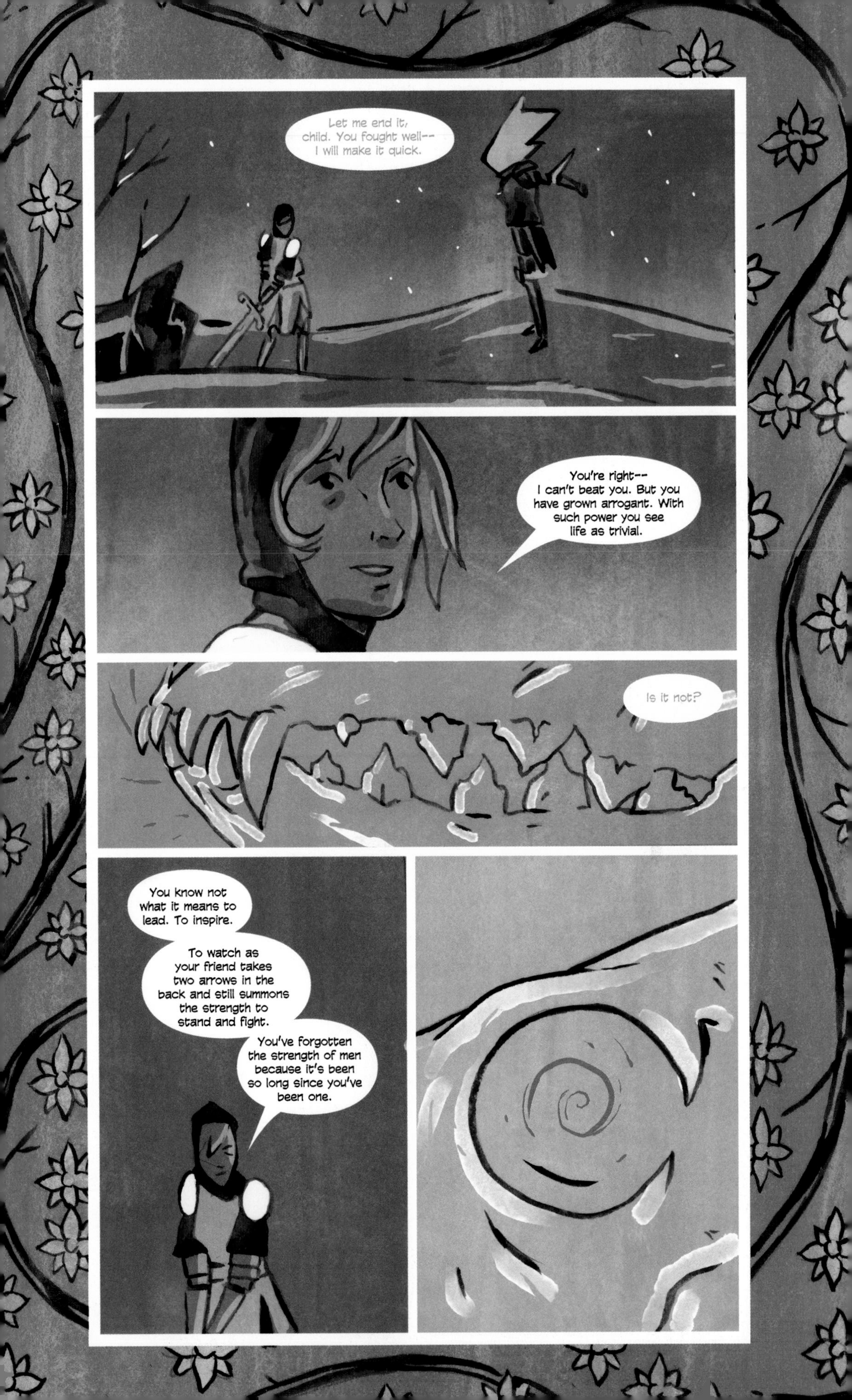
Let me end it, child. You fought well-- I will make it quick.
You're right-- I can't beat you. But you have grown arrogant. With such power you see life as trivial.
Is it not?
You know not what it means to lead. To inspire.
To watch as your friend takes two arrows in the back and still summons the strength to stand and fight.
You've forgotten the strength of men because it's been so long since you've been one.

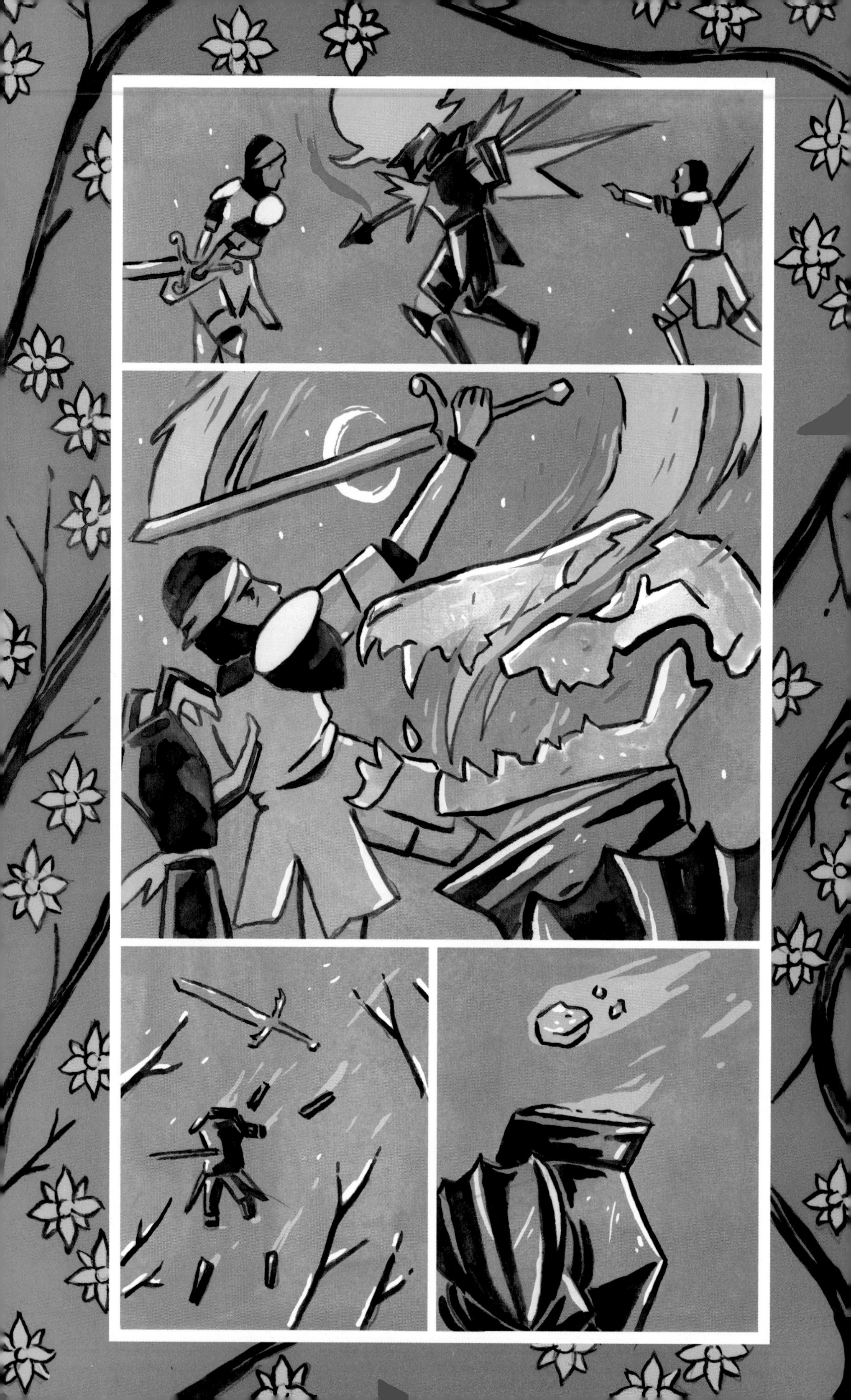

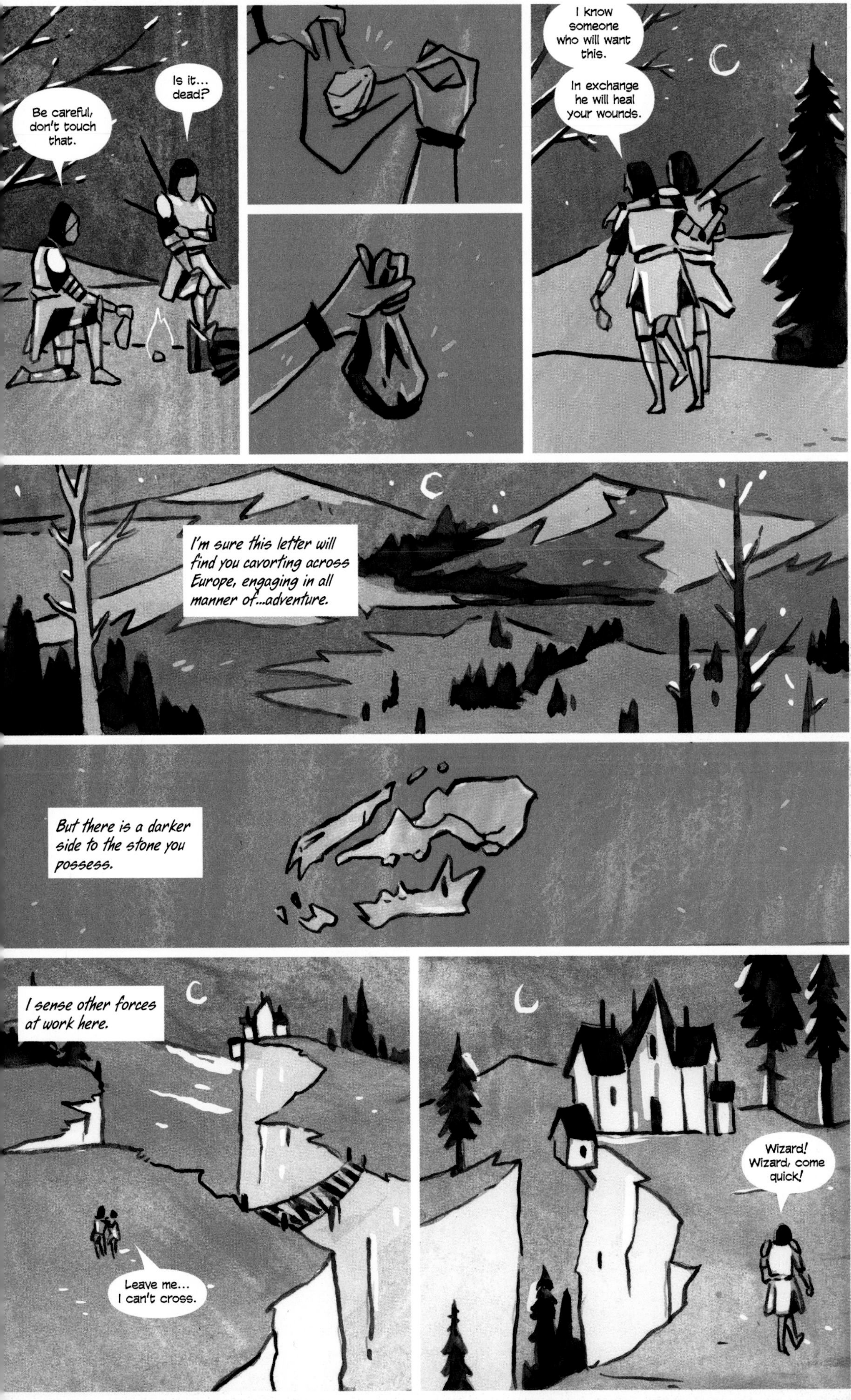
Is it... dead?
Be careful, don't touch that.
I know someone who will want this.
In exchange he will heal your wounds.
I'm sure this letter will find you cavorting across Europe, engaging in all manner of...adventure.
But there is a darker side to the stone you possess.
I sense other forces at work here.
Leave me... I can't cross.
Wizard! Wizard, come quick!

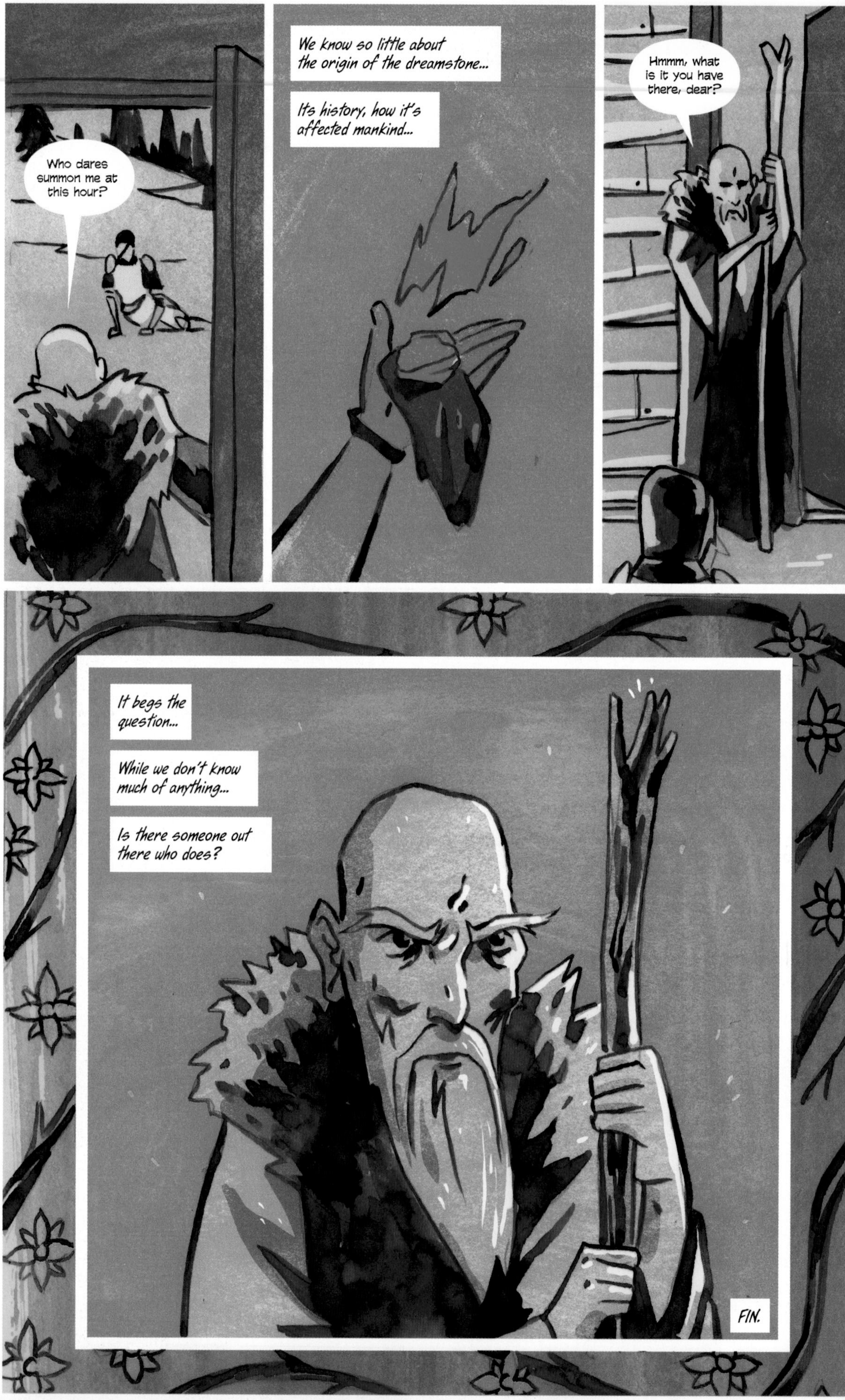
Who dares summon me at this hour?
We know so little about the origin of the dreamstone...
Its history, how it's affected mankind...
Hmmm, what is it you have there, dear?
It begs the question...
While we don't know much of anything...
Is there someone out there who does?
FIN.

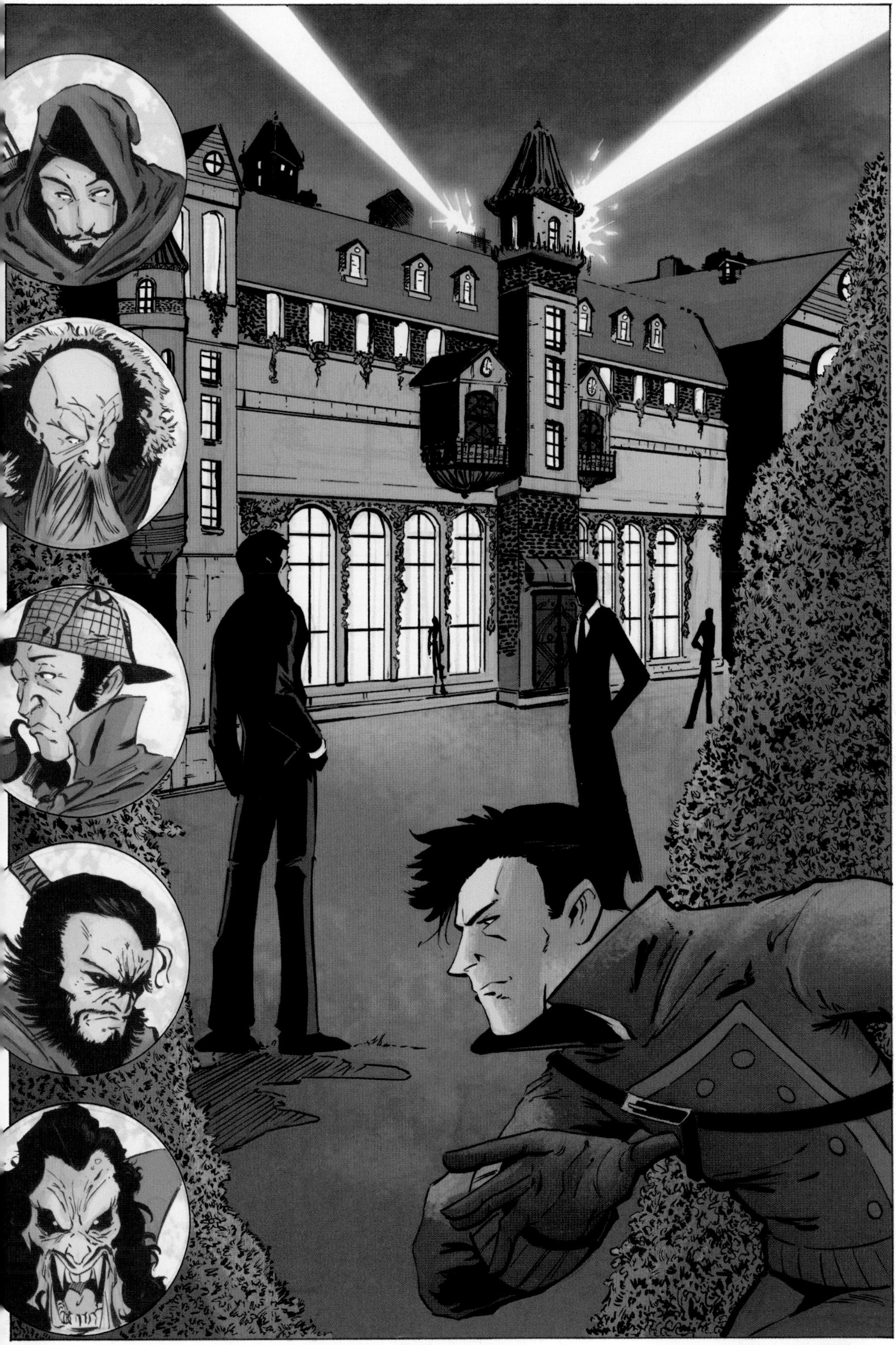

"BOATS AGAINST THE CURRENT"

WORDS: FRANK J. BARBIERE
ART: JAMIE JONES
COLORS: KELLY FITZPATRICK

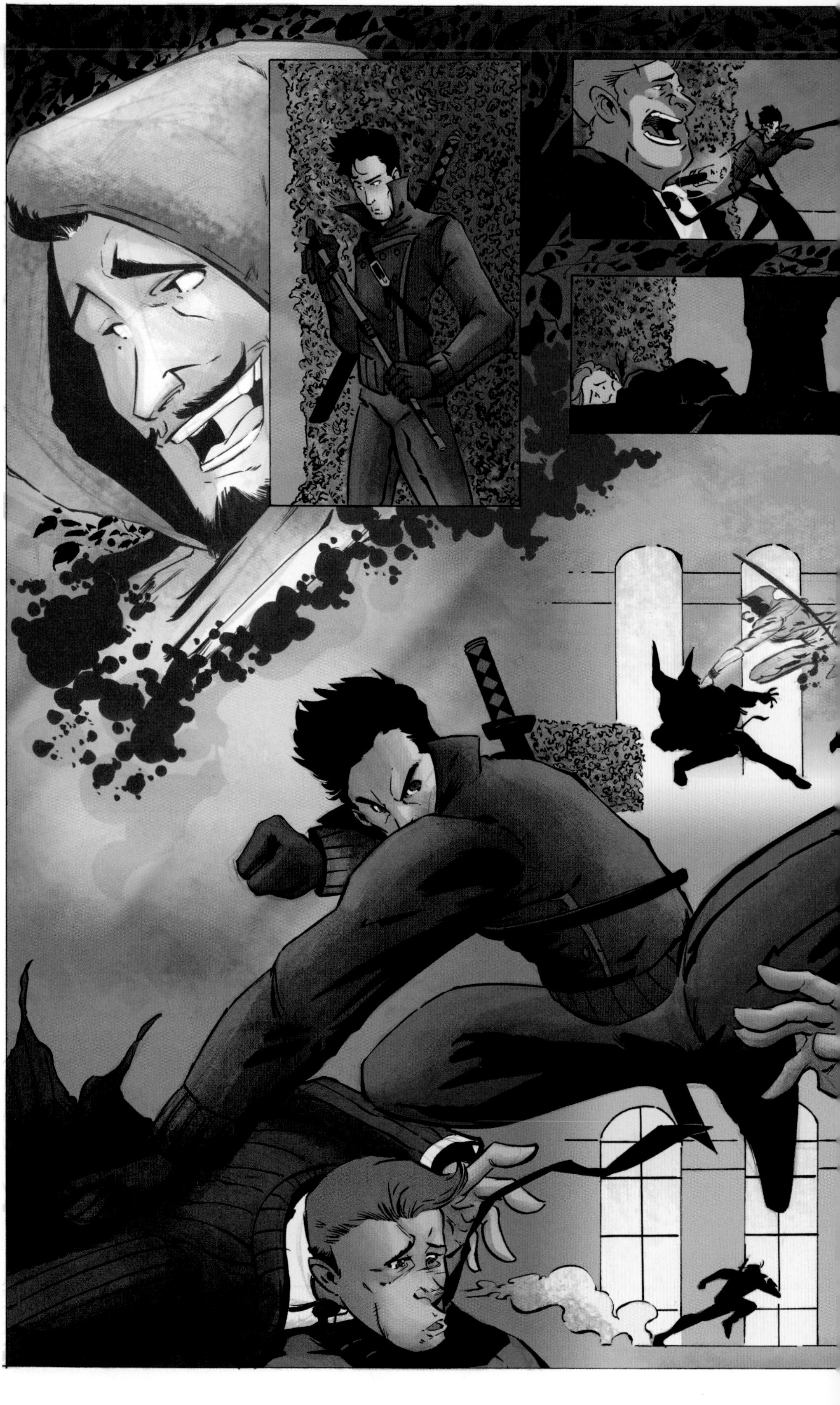

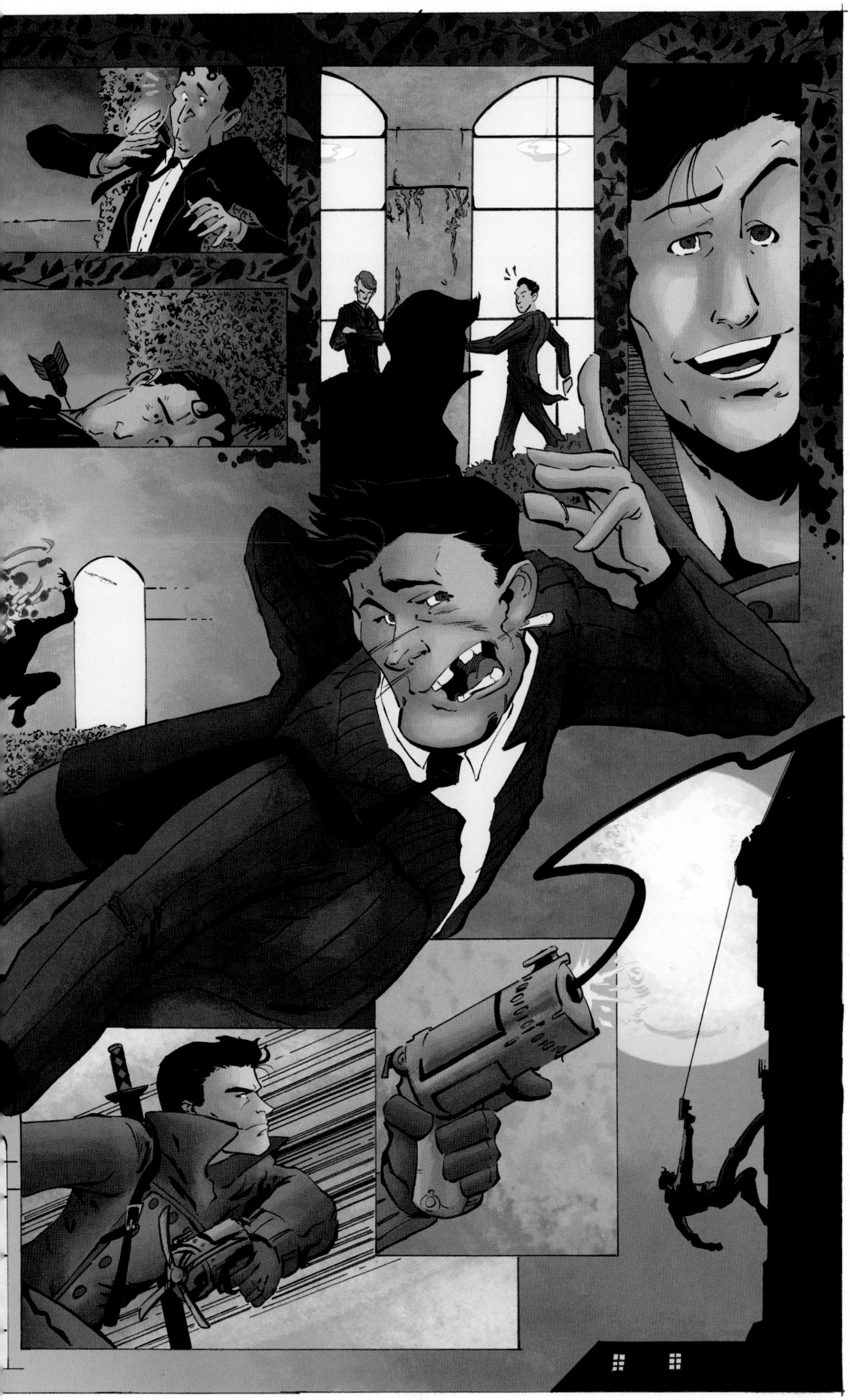

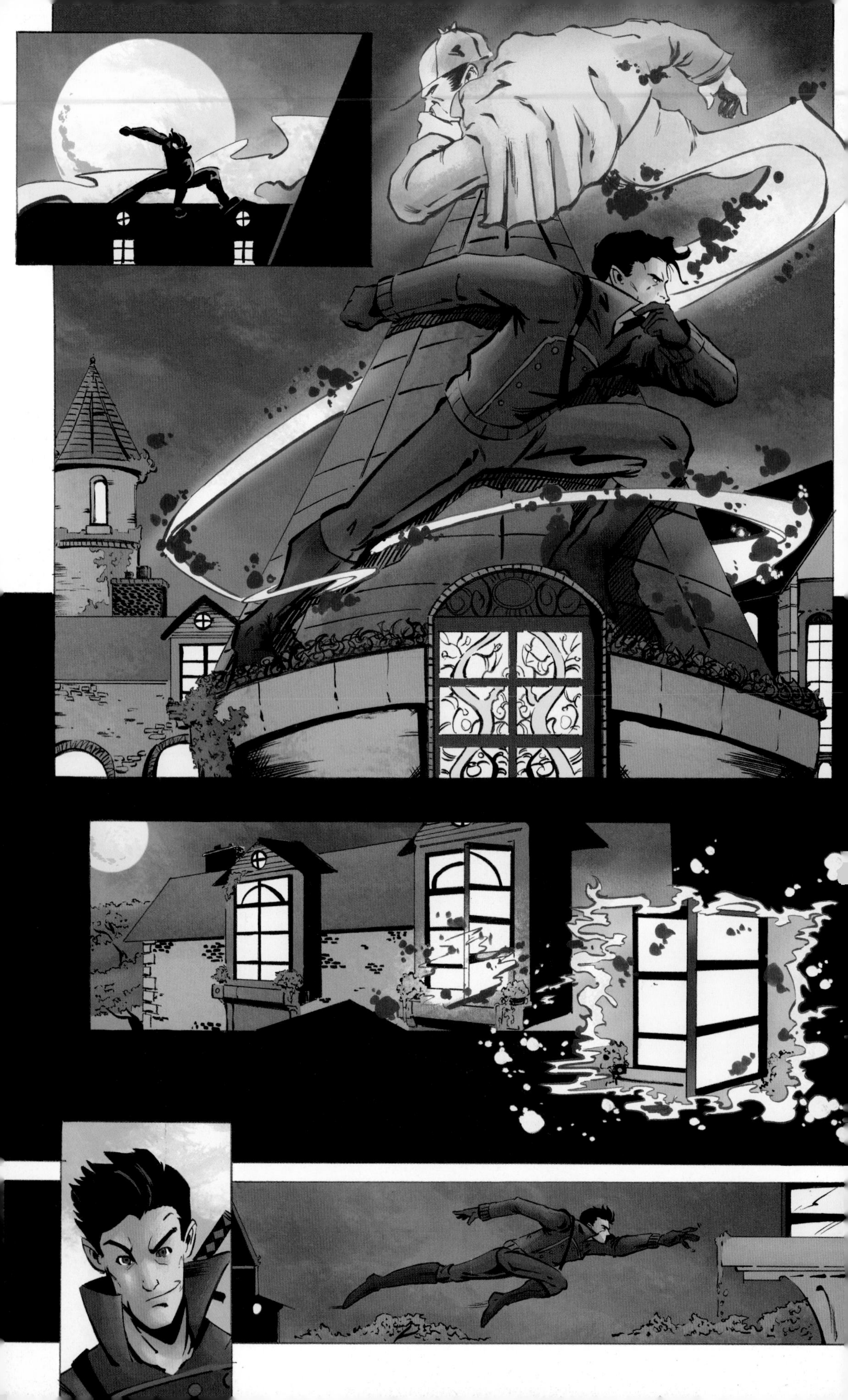

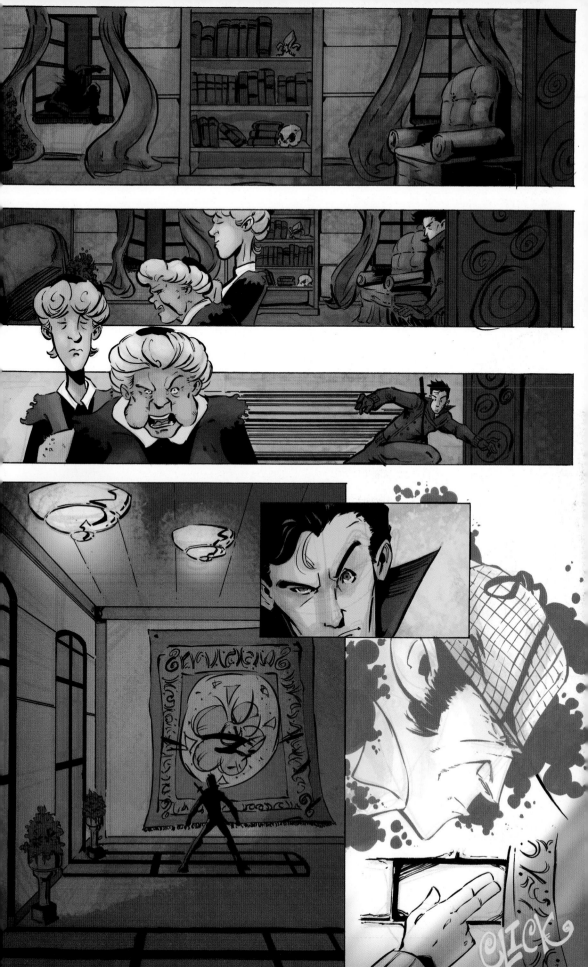

CLICK

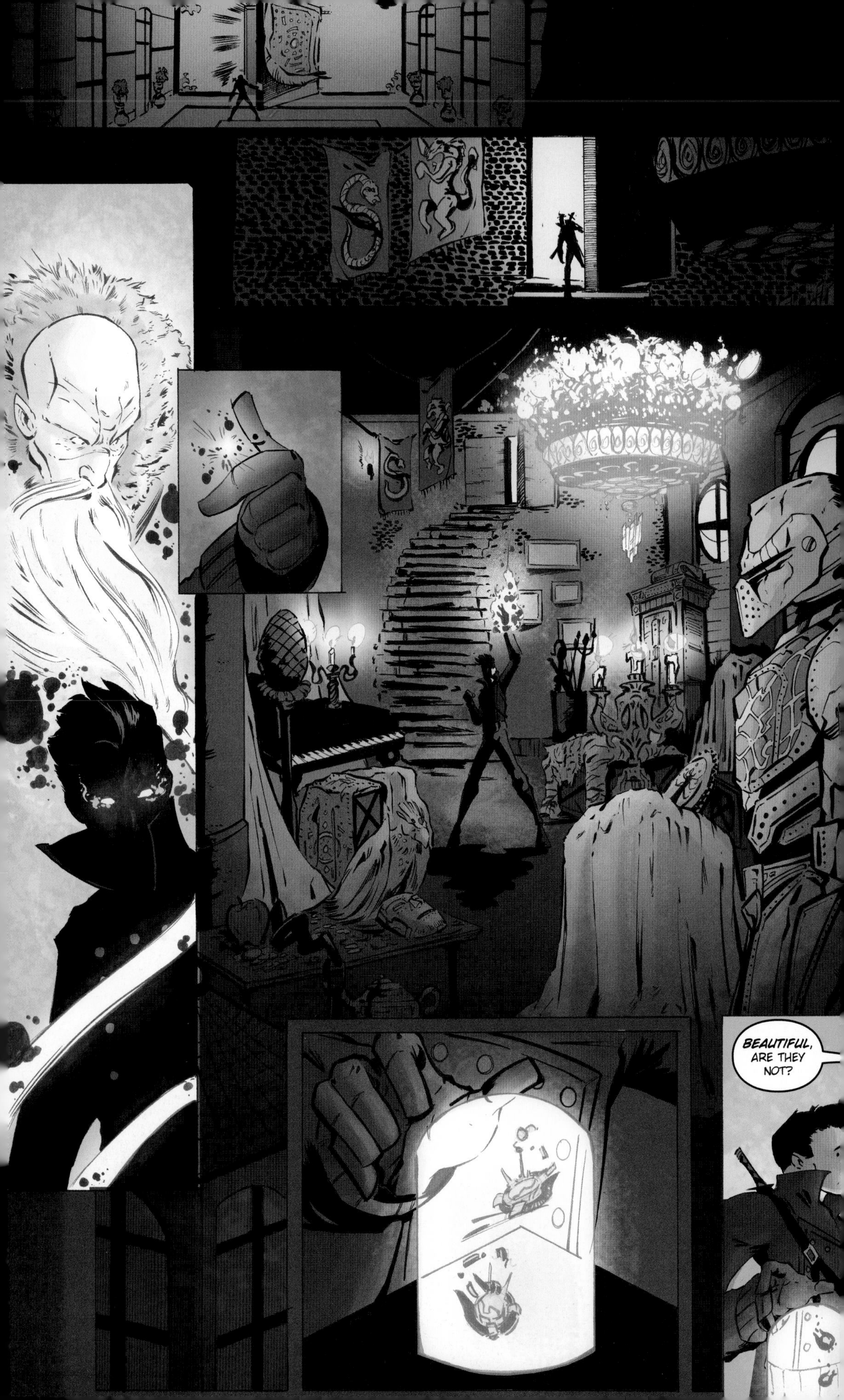
BEAUTIFUL, ARE THEY NOT?

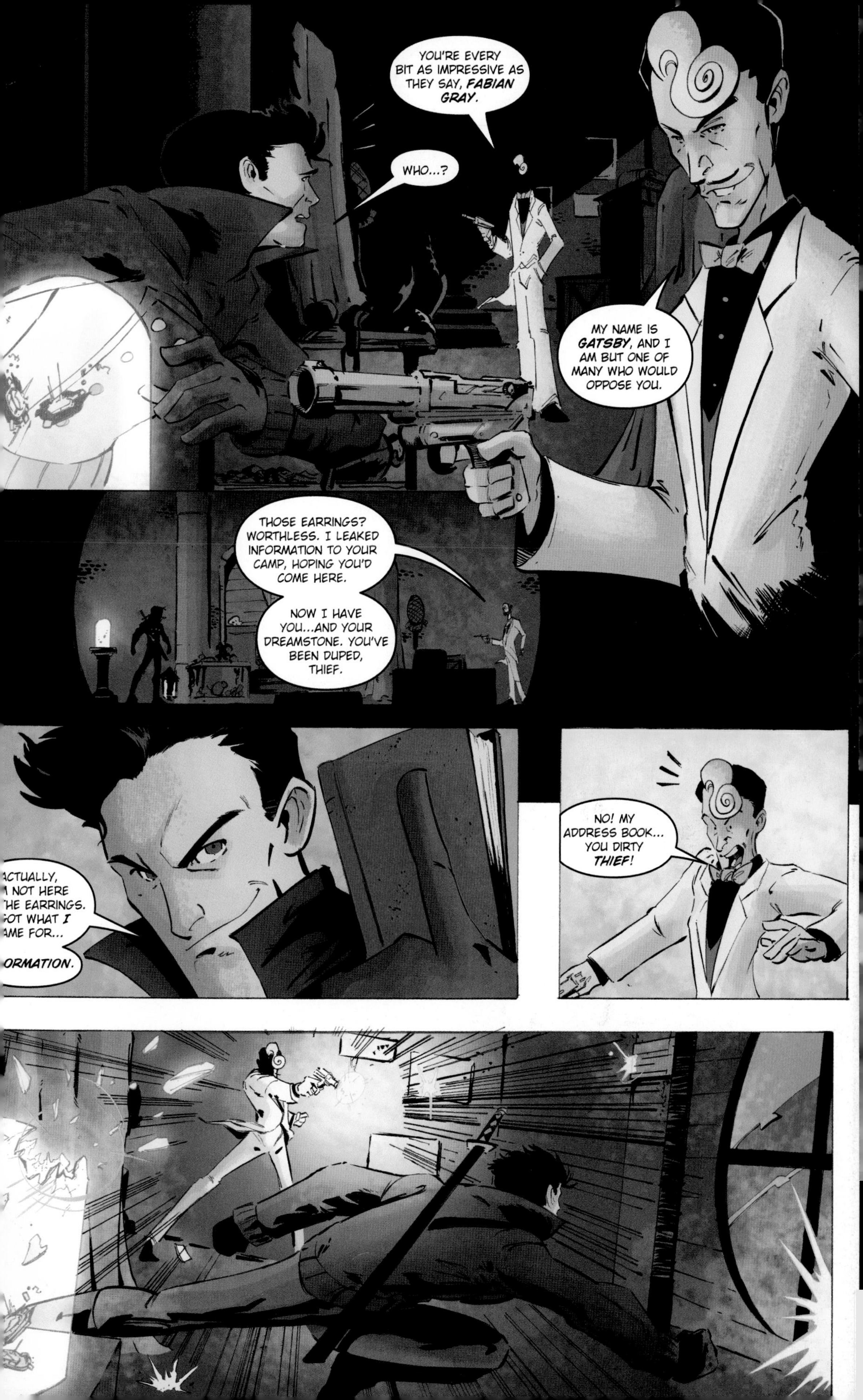
YOU'RE EVERY BIT AS IMPRESSIVE AS THEY SAY, **FABIAN GRAY**.
WHO...?
MY NAME IS **GATSBY**, AND I AM BUT ONE OF MANY WHO WOULD OPPOSE YOU.
THOSE EARRINGS? WORTHLESS. I LEAKED INFORMATION TO YOUR CAMP, HOPING YOU'D COME HERE.
NOW I HAVE YOU...AND YOUR DREAMSTONE. YOU'VE BEEN DUPED, THIEF.
CTUALLY, M NOT HERE THE EARRINGS. GOT WHAT *I* AME FOR...
ORMATION.
NO! MY ADDRESS BOOK... YOU DIRTY ***THIEF***!

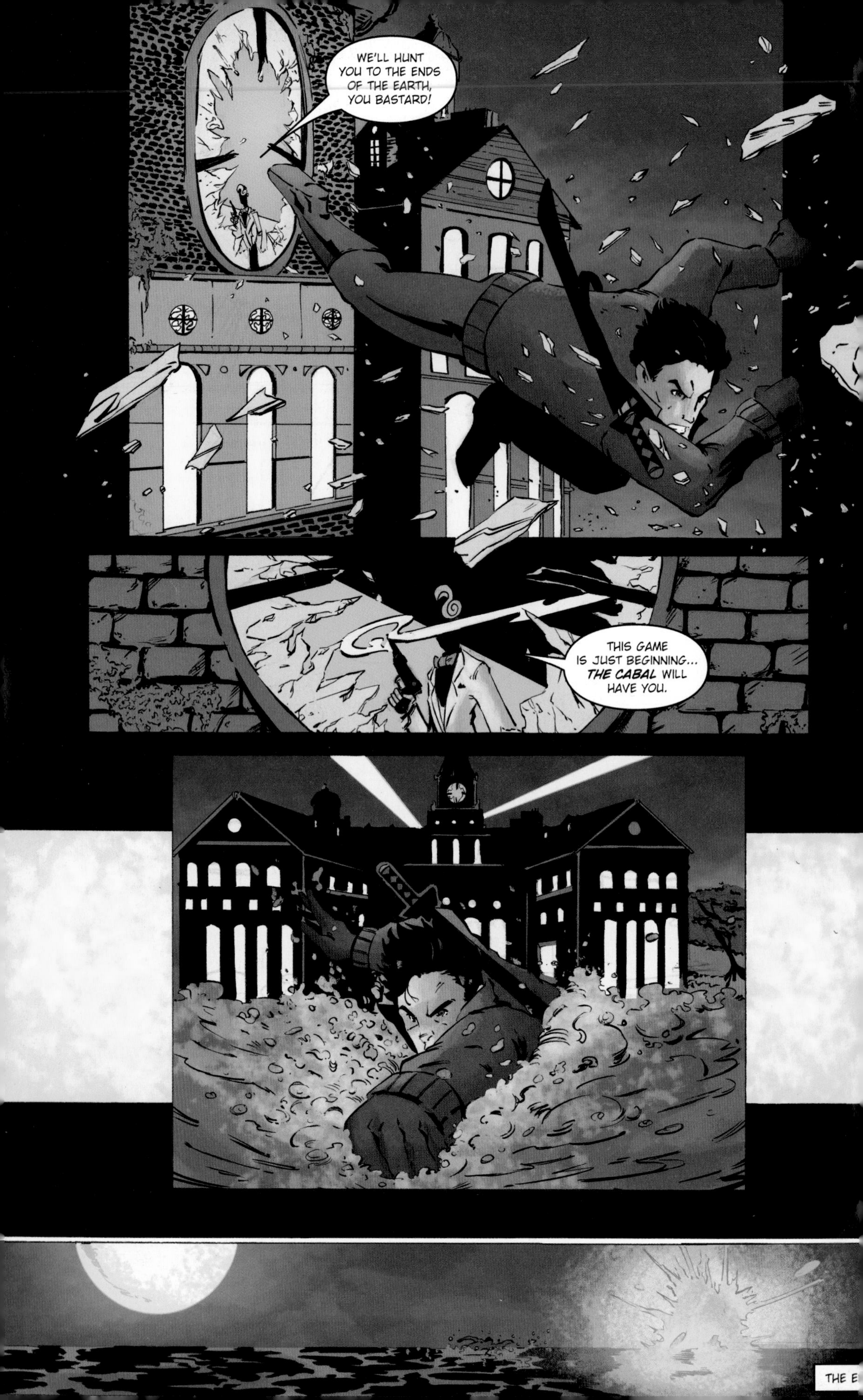
WE'LL HUNT YOU TO THE ENDS OF THE EARTH, YOU BASTARD!
THIS GAME IS JUST BEGINNING... THE CABAL WILL HAVE YOU.
THE E